VERMISST

Also by Jonathan Nicholas:

Hospital Beat
Kibbutz Virgin
The Tragic Romance of Africa
Oz – A Hitchhiker's Australian Anthology
Who'd Be a Copper?
Cherry Picking – Life Between the Sticks
Kittyhawk Down

VERMISST
MISSING IN RUSSIA

THE LENINGRAD FRONT, 1943, THROUGH THE EYES OF A GERMAN FIGHTER PILOT

Jonathan Nicholas

The Book Guild Ltd

First published in Great Britain in 2023 by
The Book Guild Ltd
Unit E2 Airfield Business Park,
Harrison Road, Market Harborough,
Leicestershire. LE16 7UL
Tel: 0116 2792299
www.bookguild.co.uk
Email: info@bookguild.co.uk
Twitter: @bookguild

Copyright © 2023 Jonathan Nicholas

The right of Jonathan Nicholas to be identified as the author of this
work has been asserted by them in accordance with the
Copyright, Design and Patents Act 1988.

All rights reserved. No part of this publication may be
reproduced, transmitted, or stored in a retrieval system, in any form or by any means,
without permission in writing from the publisher, nor be otherwise circulated in
any form of binding or cover other than that in which it is published and without
a similar condition being imposed on the subsequent purchaser.

Whilst based on real events, this work is entirely fictitious and bears no resemblance
to any persons living or dead.

Typeset in 12pt Adobe Jenson Pro

Printed and bound in the UK by TJ Books LTD, Padstow, Cornwall

ISBN 978 1915603 661

British Library Cataloguing in Publication Data.
A catalogue record for this book is available from the British Library.

To aviators everywhere

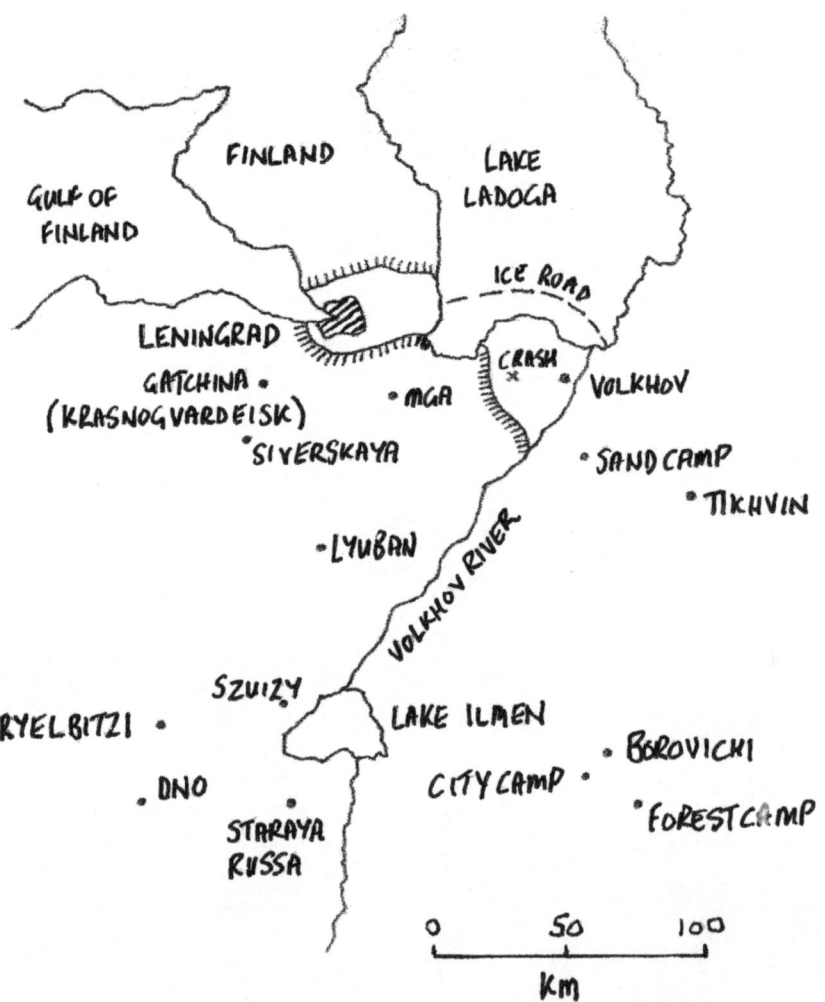

The Leningrad Front

Russia
26th *January 1943*

SHUFFLING INTO THE GLOOM, OUR BREATH BILLOWING around us like grey cumulus, we huddled over a single bunker stove struggling to make any impact in the wooden building. The last man in, encouraged to shut the door, did so with an exaggerated bang, causing long stilettos of ice to fall. The CO and adjutant, standing nearest the stove, were warm enough to remove their gloves and unbutton their jackets; the CO's Knight's Cross of the Iron Cross glinted in the rising steam from his uniform.

Where would we be flying today? As far south as Lake Ilmen or perhaps much closer? Leningrad itself? These days it could be anywhere. We should have known what was coming when we saw the latest map pinned to the wall: Lake Ladoga. A black dotted line arced across the southern end from east to west with the words 'ICE ROAD' in red.

"Ivan has been bragging that he's breaking the siege," the CO said calmly, tapping the map before turning to us, our glowing faces partially obscured by turned-up collars. "So it's up to us to put a stop to it," he said, a wry smile spreading across his face like a tiny wave curling up on a beach. There was nodding approval before the specifics: where we would assemble, direction of approach, minimum height, and order of play.

Today we were ground strafing, not in pairs on a free hunt but all together. The target was a column of mixed transport vehicles loaded with food and ammunition, possibly tanks, armoured cars, and other military equipment such as anti-aircraft guns.

"Use everything you have to destroy the target quickly, gentlemen," the CO told us, "and return here directly, with no deviations."

It all seemed routine, and a few minutes later we stepped outside, heading for the canteen. We ate captured American meat for breakfast, dark bread, fig substitute coffee, and a nip of target schnapps. I wasn't to know that in less than an hour I would very nearly bring back up the whole lot in my cockpit.

In the murky dawn light the engines of our Messerschmitt 109 Gs were pre-heated in turn; they simply wouldn't start otherwise. As for us, we counted ourselves lucky at Siverskaya, living in a brick-built barrack with two enormous stoves burning a plentiful supply of wood. Minus forty-five is the kind of cold that bites deep into the skin, and as soon as you stop, you freeze. Getting anything mechanical or biological to work proved miraculous, but we had to keep going because the enemy never stopped.

We all took a quick trip to the latrine, the last act before flying. Nobody lingered in the unheated sheds near the woods. The deep pits dug in the summer were almost full, but thankfully, unlike then, they produced less odour and no flies. Finally, after checking my map and my loaded P08, I was ready for the parachute.

My 109 already running, with careful steps I crossed the ice to climb aboard. Karl strapped me in as usual, though I could barely recognise him, with his collar turned up and face obscured by the black scarf his mother had sent him.

We had a calm day, clear and cloudless, with excellent visibility, the first time in more than a week. Heavy snow had fallen non-stop for so long everyone available had been drafted in to clear it away.

We gathered a full squadron of twelve, flying in the usual groups of four. This rarely happened nowadays, so we were lucky. Karl shut the canopy and dropped off the wing. My engine generated welcome heat and I scanned the instruments. Temperatures and pressures within limits but still very low, so we idled for a moment longer before taking off across the ice in fours, line abreast.

The lake appeared as a vast expanse of flat virgin snow, so we dropped down to a hundred metres, constantly looking out for Ivan now we were over his territory.

Our target was a meandering grey snake stretching far across the ice, like the dotted line on the map: a motorised column, perhaps, hundreds of miscellaneous vehicles trundling along in the bright winter morning.

Attacking in line astern, I was third in, down to fifty metres, perhaps even less, fixing my gunsight on the centre of the column. Holding steady, I fired everything, the vibration shaking my airframe with the heady smell of cordite joining oil and leather.

I tugged at the bomb release and dozens of white-painted SD-2 'Butterfly' bombs disappeared amongst the enemy.

Ready to climb in an instant to avoid flying debris, we waited for the usual explosions from vehicle fuel tanks, but nothing. They clearly had no flak guns either, because the air was quiet, save for our guns. I heard brief R/T chatter, excited shouts confirming there was nothing coming up other than small arms fire.

The others flew in, raking the column in turn, waiting several minutes before I lined up for my second. This time I decided to take a closer look. At twenty metres the results of our actions became clear: no vehicles, merely a solid line, several kilometres long, of men, trudging across the ice, five or six abreast in a miserable sub-zero march.

Why didn't they run? They could disperse across the frozen lake and escape, but they remained together as an easy target.

Then I saw the reason; they were trapped inside a deep gully cut through the snow which had frozen solid, thick impenetrable walls of ice either side, three metres high, impossible to climb.

Scrambling up the sides, only to slide inexorably back down again, they remained in the path of our bullets and cannon shells, stepping on our invisible butterfly bombs, as some hacked at the walls with rifle butts, trampling one another.

My breakfast rose in my throat like hot magma. Pressing my oxygen mask onto my face, I turned on the full flow. Then I dropped down over the centre, pressing my gun button again, staring ahead. I knew what I was doing: a two-second burst, then a pause, then another two seconds, and then the cannons, the recoil thudding through my feet into my legs.

Up and down the column we flew, killing everything, until twenty minutes later all twelve of us had finished, the shuffling snake dead. Soon it would all freeze, probably even before we'd gone, leaving a vivid scarlet line, like a major road on a map.

No-one spoke over the R/T, no excited comments or shouts of victory. I can only guess how many we'd killed, at least several hundred, probably thousands. We didn't discuss it afterwards; those involved who survived the war never spoke of it.

We flew aeroplanes. It was our job, what I'd always wanted to do, ever since I could remember. They gave us the aeroplanes for free, starting with a wood and fabric glider, finishing with a Focke-Wulf 190-A5, a superb machine, with so many others in between.

They taught us how to fly each one. We could even write our names on the side, decorate them with badges, and treat them as our own. In return they told us where to fly, and what to shoot at.

That was the deal.

Part 1

1

Germany
January 1939

I'D ALWAYS LOVED AEROPLANES; FROM MY MID-TEENS Uetersen airfield, six kilometres south of my hometown, Elmshorn, was busy with Ju52s, Heinkel 111s, and even Messerschmitt 109s. The pilots would show off whenever they saw us, particularly those in the 109s, dipping their wings and flying so low we could see their faces.

Like most men his age my father had spent months of his youth in the Flanders mud during the 1914–18 war, so he told me I must never join the infantry. I decided to enrol as ground crew in the air force and take it from there. With no flying experience I didn't feel confident enough to become a pilot.

At eighteen, I was disappointed to find six months in the Labour Service awaited first. It seemed everyone had to do it, without exception. It meant hard physical work for a skinny boy, unlike my friend Wolfram with muscles in his arms as big as any adult. He had an older, super-fit brother with whom he did press-ups, and Wolfram also chopped wood.

Elmshorn is ten kilometres north-west of Hamburg, with the River Elbe a few kilometres to the west and Denmark eighty kilometres north. At least I would be local, based in barracks at Pinneberg, a few kilometres nearer the city.

The Labour Service was as bad as I'd suspected and the uniform drab, but I found good points, such as new work shorts, shirts, trousers, boots, and of course, a new spade. But the best part was the bicycle, a brand-new Herrenrad, olive green with brown leather seat and shiny black handle grips. I'd never had anything like it before, so I was really pleased.

The first few exhausting weeks we spent clearing snow from roads and important buildings, issued thick great-coats with the Labour Service badge of the upwards pointing spade; these together with the non-stop hard work kept us warm.

Working twelve-hour days in the week and ten hours on Saturdays, we had Sundays to rest, which we desperately needed. Thankfully we enjoyed plentiful food, all having great appetites.

"For the next few weeks you will be digging drainage ditches," our group leader announced early one morning in the first lengthening days of spring.

Without him telling us where, we marched north from Pinneberg, spades on our shoulders, singing. As we passed through the main gate at Uetersen airfield a Ju88 thundered overhead. Could this be where we'd be working?

A hundred of us assembled at the edge of the field where air force engineers and our group leaders scanned a map, nodding and pointing. Divided into teams we began digging. After three hours we stopped for coffee and at lunchtime we ate in an air force canteen. Fantastic; the best part, of course, was the constant roar of aeroplanes.

The pilots stepped from their machines like gods, and occasionally they'd allow us a look inside. Such was their status they even signed autographs, shaking hands with us before climbing in and disappearing into the clouds.

After the smart uniforms and authority of the Hitler Youth I found it demeaning to be a manual labourer, but the patriotic singing and marching kept us going. As the weather improved we were split into smaller groups, riding ever longer distances on our bikes to help farmers with preparing the fields and crop planting, or looking after livestock, mainly pigs. Food production was vital for the country and encouraged everywhere. My father even started growing vegetables in our back garden, as did most of our neighbours.

For a brief period after the Labour Service I found myself between jobs, a nonentity, wearing plain clothes. The only time in my life since the age of ten I didn't possess a uniform. I felt totally lost, and it made me nervous. Embarrassed and ashamed to be seen in public, I couldn't wait to be part of it all again, so when my call-up papers for the air force arrived, relief flooded through me.

2

10th June 1939

As I stepped down from the bus at Quakenbruck Aviation School, four 109s roared past, barely clearing the trees. A young soldier standing at a red and white-striped sentry box glanced in my direction, hunching his rifle in his right arm, the 109s breaking his daydream. A pedal cycle, like the ones we had in the Labour Service, straddled the pavement opposite, obviously his.

"Papers!" he demanded, with a practised blank stare. Everyone in authority shouts, as though we've all become deaf.

Placing my suitcase on the warm tarmac, I reached inside my jacket, the fingertips of my left hand touching the wetness in the right armpit of my shirt.

He snatched my papers and began scrutinising every word.

A huge angry-looking stone eagle gazed down at us in relief from the wall behind our heads, with the words 'Erected in 1935 under the government of Adolf Hitler' written underneath.

Finally he folded my papers and reached behind.

"Go to the left; here's a map," he ordered, handing me several sheets of paper. "Your quarters are marked here, new cadets, see?" adding in a more conciliatory tone, as he handed everything back, "There's a briefing at 1800 hours, so don't miss it."

He'd obviously finished because his gaze then fixed elsewhere, probably on his pedal cycle. I wanted to ask more questions, and I got the impression he wanted to engage with me, but the formal nature of our encounter prevented it.

After finding a bed in a smart barrack, I shook hands with some of my new comrades: Karl from the Rhineland, Sepp from north Germany, and Heinz from the south. Everyone was a similar age, or so it seemed, with aeroplanes the main topic of conversation, in an atmosphere of nervous excitement. As one of the later arrivals, I unpacked and we all made our way to the main hall.

Sitting in neat rows of steel and canvas chairs, we chatted noisily until an air force officer with a bright-red face and a uniform glittering with decorations entered. We stopped immediately and stood to attention.

A general at the very least, so I thought, he was actually an air force colonel, with two pips on his shoulders, the man in charge. He smiled broadly as his decorations glinted, catching the evening sunlight from the windows, particularly the Knight's Cross around his neck. It meant he'd shot down a lot of enemy aeroplanes, so I wanted one too, as did everyone else in the packed hall.

He straightened his cap before gripping the lectern with both hands so tightly his knuckles whitened, as though at the controls of an aeroplane in combat.

Fixing his eyes around the room, within a few seconds he'd secured absolute silence.

"Welcome gentlemen," he began quietly, with total command. "Your journey begins here. Who knows where it will take you, but remember this, there is no limit, and so this is up to you. Be in no doubt you are members of the greatest air force in the world and part of the most powerful war machine in history."

He spoke with great conviction and in return everyone listened, transfixed.

"You will secure the skies above Germany and beyond. Germany's enemies are watching closely because they despise us, gentlemen, and they fear us. But do you know something? They envy us. They envy our leader, the way he has made Germany strong, and because of this, they will try to stop us, but you will help to see off with great pride and bravery anyone who dares to attack us. Germany's glorious future is in your hands. Listen to everything you are told, work hard, and you will all succeed."

He smiled and adjusted his cap, releasing his grip on the lectern.

"But gentlemen…" he hesitated before glancing to his left at the other officers, obviously close comrades, "you will be working on the best aeroplanes in the world, and you will enjoy every minute of your time, secure in the knowledge that the whole of Germany will be cheering you on. Good luck to you all!"

I didn't know whether to clap or cheer, or both. Before he stepped away, his red face glowing even brighter, his mouth opened wide, exposing teeth like a snarling wolf.

"Heil Hitler!" he shouted, to which the whole room saluted, responding in unison with, "Heil Hitler!"

*

Why does crawling through mud in uniform with full combat equipment, wearing a gas mask, make us good aeroplane mechanics? Or wading through a filthy foul-smelling stagnant pond, carrying a rifle above our heads? This was nothing to do with aeroplanes and for a while I thought I was back in the Labour Service.

We were shouted at constantly by an ugly, overbearing sergeant, taking great pleasure in seeing others suffer. This man became our hate figure and very soon – within minutes – we all wanted to kill him. From the start we were taught infantry methods of crossing open ground and approaching buildings, in between squatting exercises with our rifles and yet more crawling through mud. Luckily it was summer and so this wasn't too bad, but I can only imagine what it would be like in winter, and how cold the pond would be.

My first full day at Quakenbruck, and I felt disappointment at our formal induction into the adult military. We marched everywhere, and two hours after rolling around in the mud we were expected to stand to attention by our beds for kit inspection. Everyone ran around, frantically scrubbing boots and cleaning rifles, the atmosphere charged with nervous excitement and fear, all to the heady mix of tobacco smoke and boot polish.

Even though smoking was officially frowned upon, we were issued a cigarette ration; our government claimed to have found links to smoking and cancer, and it was certainly discouraged, particularly among women, but most men smoked. I hadn't yet started, so I bartered my Reemtsma R6 cigarettes for extra schnapps and postage stamps, also issued on ration.

We didn't have to pay for anything: accommodation, food, drink, even washing equipment and razor blades, though I still didn't need to shave every day. We had thirty marks, a month's pay in advance, for which we queued up at the paymaster's office to receive our cheques. I thought it a reasonable sum, but we had nothing to spend it on.

Issued with far too many uniforms, if one wouldn't come clean in time for inspection, we'd change into another in a kind of frantic rotation. Even a speck of dirt would put us on punishment drill.

3

First such punishment for me was an entire night shift on guard duty, standing at the main gate in full kit, including steel helmet and Mauser rifle, for a mere speck of mud on my boots.

After being taught to use every firearm the army had at the time, including the MP38 machine pistol, I could shoot well with a rifle but not with a P08 pistol. The MG15 machine gun was a lot of fun: mounted on a tall wooden post, with targets launched through the air from left to right in front of us. I missed every time at first, as most people did, much to the instructor's amusement.

"Anticipate where the target will be, not where it actually is, aim ahead," he told us.

This seemed unnatural, shooting into empty space, but the results were spectacular. What a revelation, and surely one of shooting's greatest secrets. I soon realised how this principle could apply when flying a fighter or in a flak battery.

Our comradeship developed into a deep sense of pride and loyalty to the air force: singing while marching drowned out the stamping of our hobnail boots. Did the daily routine of drill, shooting, sport, manoeuvres, and inspections all become easier or were we just getting used to it? Despite always having a huge appetite, I became leaner and fitter than ever before.

We made good use of the cinema, which played all the latest newsreels in between the main feature, usually an exciting patriotic film, always German, of course, never anything from Hollywood or England.

Aeroplanes, the air force, and girls were always our main topics of conversation. With Sundays off, on fine days I sat with friends at the perimeter of the airfield, practising aircraft recognition, with constant arguments about the different types.

In August 1939 our evenings in the cinema took on a new seriousness, provoking huge anger. Newsreel footage showed ethnic Germans fleeing persecution in Poland, with reports of thousands being slaughtered. Why were the Poles being so terrible? Why would the rest of the world simply stand by, doing nothing?

"I was raped countless times and all my children murdered, simply for being German," said one frightened woman into the camera.

We shouted at the screen, shaking our fists with rage. The next newsreel told us the Polish army constantly fired at German soldiers along the border, killing some, while our brave comrades reluctantly fired back.

How much longer could Germany tolerate this provocation? It seemed far worse than the suffering inflicted on Germans in Czechoslovakia the year before. This was stopped when our troops saved them, so perhaps the same would have to be done in Poland? We crowded into the cinema every night, and listened to the radio constantly.

At the time we believed everything without question, because we had no other source of information. We had absolute trust in the government; why would they lie about something so important? We saw the newsreels with our own eyes, and so it had to be true.

At noon on 1st September ecstatic cheering came from the dining hall. I ran inside to find everyone shouting, shaking their fists and smiling. Our troops had finally crossed the border into Poland.

From that moment the conflict became the major topic of conversation, and we followed its progress at every opportunity. The Poles were thought to have a huge army and a decent enough air force, and so we waited for news with great interest.

How shocking! France and Britain supported Poland! What had it got to do with them? Hadn't they seen the newsreels? Even more shock came when British bombers raided our northern ports, destroying houses and killing civilians in a totally unprovoked attack. Why? How dare they attack us? Most of their aeroplanes were shot down, but this was infuriating. I didn't think the British were such a barbarous and aggressive nation.

Our induction into the military took on a greater urgency, making us keen to get started. Within a few weeks our forces had crushed the Poles in a new lightning warfare, and linked up with our friends the Russians. It was all over so quickly.

The only issues remaining were the British and French; perhaps the way to subdue them was to invade, as we had done with the troublesome Poles.

When our time at Quakenbruck was over in December, we were so fired up with enthusiasm we would have happily swum across the Channel if necessary, to teach the British a lesson.

4

Given leave, I spent three days at home, which, if I'm honest, I found a waste of time. With none of my friends around, and awful weather, I spent most of it reading and listening to the radio. Although lovely to be home, of course, on my first night I unwittingly created a problem at the dinner table that I regretted for months.

I had no idea that asking for more food would upset my mother so much or cause such embarrassment; she simply didn't have any. I'd heard that rationing had started in August, but in the air force we'd become immune, and she never mentioned it in her letters, so when they showed me their *Essenmarken* ration books I gasped. Everything was rationed: milk, butter, cheese, eggs, even clothes, each person only allowed 550 grams of meat a week, and I'd probably eaten that in one meal.

My mother started crying so I put an arm around her as my father stood up to throw another log on the fire.

"We are alright," he murmured, "but she's been saving all she could for your visit, and now it's gone."

This made me very angry, not with my parents but with myself. I also remembered what the officer had said at Quakenbruck, about the world hating Germany.

"The British blockaded our ports and starved us half to death in 1917," my father said, "and it seems history is repeating."

In the morning I rose early and marched briskly to the local butcher before the shop opened. I used to run errands for him as a boy so, knowing he would be there, I banged on the back door, shouting, "Open up!"

Wearing my full uniform I startled him; he didn't recognise me at first.

"What's wrong? What's going on?" he protested, unlocking the door in a panic.

"Hello, Mr Dressler."

"Oh, it's you, Paul," he groaned, shaking his head and wiping his hands. "Do you know what time it is? What can I do for you?"

"Do you have any sausage?"

He smiled as though relieved, ushering me inside. After a mix of friendly persuasion, mild abuse of authority, and an extortionate five marks, Mr Dressler handed over a kilo of sausages and a loaf of bread.

From then on my letters home would always mention food, making sure I asked if they had enough. The next day I almost felt relief to be leaving, because they'd have one less mouth to feed.

With Christmas only a few days away, I wondered why my leave hadn't coincided with it, but the answer came when I returned to Quakenbruck: the postings list had arrived. We found we were all being sent to different locations around the country, without delay.

The next morning I climbed aboard a very cold and uncomfortable army lorry with ten others for a two-hour drive south to Gutersloh, an airfield town near Bielefeld, between Dortmund and Hanover.

The dining hall proudly displayed a huge, freshly cut spruce, filling the entire room with a wonderful pine smell, challenging the cooking odours and tobacco smoke. '*Tannenbaum*', 'Silent Night', and other carols were broadcast on the PA system.

On Christmas Eve a tall, red-faced pastor with thick grey hair led a carol service as we gathered around the tree. Once the festivities were over, my first few weeks were spent mainly in the classroom, learning about aero engines and the principles of flight relating to airframes and engines, which I found very interesting.

The weather turned particularly cold the first week of January 1940, when I spent a lot more time on guard duty, not as punishment but on a strict rota. We didn't anticipate anything coming our way from the British or French, with their aircraft and pilots being so poor, but we still had to maintain readiness.

Ten of us went to Ludwigsfelde aero engine plant, a few miles south-west of Berlin. This time I knew my colleagues and we stayed in wonderful accommodation provided by Daimler-Benz.

Girls worked in the factory offices, and sometimes they walked near us in pairs, laughing and teasing, before scurrying away back up the wooden staircase. In return we would show off, whistling and shouting, never making any serious conversation. This continued for several days until they did something fantastic; they stopped to talk. Nobody had yet been serious with a girl, including me, because we'd all been so very busy with the Hitler Youth. Our contact therefore remained innocent but still wonderful.

One girl, her shoulder-length hair as red as a summer sunset, caught my eye, so I made sure I always stood close when they came near. After several failed attempts at conversation, I discovered she was a typist. Thrilled when she moved closer, for a few moments, the factory disappeared; we were the only people in the world, standing in a vast empty space.

The Daimler-Benz mechanics showed us with great enthusiasm how their engines were assembled, and I found the whole process fascinating. Eventually we learned to disassemble and reassemble a DB600 engine and in teams of six we raced one another against the clock. The girls from the offices would cheer as we showed off.

On the last morning at Ludwigsfelde, some of the girls gathered around to say goodbye, but red hair was nowhere to be seen. The lorry started and some of my comrades exchanged names and addresses with girls standing at the back of the open vehicle. As I shuffled further along the bench seats, a mop of red appeared.

"What's your name?" she demanded.

"Paul, Paul Goetz," I replied, wanting to jump out. "What's yours?"

"Inge Forbig. Write to me, here, at the factory," she said; as the lorry moved off, the girls stood in a group, waving together as though on a station platform.

*

The Genshagen plant emerged from the forest, south of Berlin. The approach road gave no indication a huge factory would be at the end, surrounded by pine trees, as though specifically created for year-round concealment. Here we shared wonderful log cabins and worked on the DB601 engine with the 20mm cannon running through it.

I wrote a letter to Inge, addressed to the Daimler-Benz plant at Ludwigsfelde, thirty kilometres away, mainly to see if it would reach her. To my surprise within a week she replied. In three pages of beautiful handwriting, she told me she lived with her parents, close to the factory, and her older brother was in the army. I wrote back that same evening.

We worked long hours at Genshagen during the week and on three Sundays I took a bus to Ludwigsfelde to see Inge. On each of my visits we strolled around a park near the plant for several hours like a middle-aged, married couple, wondering what we might do after the war. On the last occasion we even held hands.

After two months we gathered at the main entrance with all our kit, for another move. A small group of us travelled in a lorry to Berlin's Tempelhof airfield, delighted to board a waiting Ju52 trimotor, the first time I'd been in an aeroplane that would actually take off. We sat on bench seats opposite one another, chatting excitedly like schoolboys, as the engines started.

We soon became airborne, in a very slow and smooth take-off. The world is an entirely different place from above, and I couldn't tear myself away from the window. I felt an odd familiarity with flying, as though I'd done it before, and I found myself nodding at every turn and change in engine pitch.

My comrades chatted to one another loudly above the noise, and Ernst and Friedrich, who had also never flown before, joined me at my window.

We turned south as the late winter sun dipped towards the horizon on our right.

After twenty minutes one of the crew, a young pilot officer, emerged from the cockpit.

"We are flying to Sindelfingen, near Stuttgart; we'll be there in about two hours. There's a toilet at the back if you need it."

I envied him, as I suspect we all did, even though, if offered, most of us would prefer to fly fighters.

We landed at Sindelfingen, a huge Mercedes-Benz plant, in the dark. I noticed many types of aeroplanes around the airfield, all brightly lit with no apparent fear of the RAF.

At the edge of the airfield we marched to huts where, after soup and bread, we spent our first night. In the morning, following a superb breakfast, we found more engines, learning how these interacted directly with the cockpit, the electrics, hydraulics, and also the propellers. After a mug of coffee from the works canteen we marched to another part of the plant, closer to the airstrip.

We rounded the corner to find, sitting at the open doors of a huge hangar, a combat-ready Messerschmitt 109 E, fierce and wonderful, with all its camouflage markings, insignia, and oil streaks as though it had just come from a battle. We could hardly contain our excitement as the mechanics told us it had indeed been in action only the week before and had just been overhauled after lengthy combat operations. The pilot had apparently shot down five Hurricanes and a Spitfire in this very aeroplane, but now it would need a final check, test, and thorough clean before returning to the front line.

On their instruction we scrambled onto it like giddy children, chattering loudly and running our hands over it as though a priceless artefact, which to us, of course, it was.

"How exciting!" I exclaimed when we were told we would each take a turn at sitting in the cockpit.

By pure chance I went first. An air force corporal in black overalls and a Mercedes-Benz mechanic stood on the wings either side of the cockpit as I lowered myself in. It seemed too small, but as soon as my bottom settled into the seat it fitted as though tailor-made. Even allowing for the fact I had no parachute it all felt right. My feet automatically resting on the rudder pedals, I could reach everything else with ease. I knew enough about the engine to quickly run through the starting procedure in my head, moving my left hand around the cockpit.

"My name is Otto," the corporal said, addressing me first and then the others gathered around. "When you are in the field you will be expected to start the aeroplanes as well as repair and maintain them. You will now each be allowed to do this." He turned to me. "Would you like to start her up?"

I smiled, wanting to shout 'yes!' as loudly as I could, but I nodded, grinning like an idiot.

5

"Stand clear," Otto shouted as another man in black overalls jumped onto the right wing with a crank handle. The starting procedure was the same as at an operational airfield, and I imagined we were there, just for a moment. The mechanic leaned in, and we went through it together: brakes on, circuit breakers pushed in, radiator flap open, propeller set to manual, throttle set, both magnetos on, and ready with the starter switch.

Most of it was familiar: a matter of translating it into the cockpit. The man turned the crank and I heard the inertia wheel whirring slowly, gathering momentum. The fuel pressure gauge twitched and I primed the engine. After fifteen turns he withdrew the crank. I held out the starting handle until, a few seconds later, the aeroplane thundered into life.

The DB600, a liquid-cooled inverted V12, sent hot grey smoke from the exhausts over the wing. The instrument panel vibrated more than I imagined and I noticed the temperatures and pressures straight away. For me this was the first time everything fitted into place.

After the quickest five minutes of my life I shut it down and climbed out like a child on his birthday, viewed with envious disdain by the others. That night I wrote an excited letter home saying how I had become 'very familiar with the 109, just like a pilot' and all subsequent letters from home burst with pride.

We had four amazing days with that aeroplane, checking, cleaning, and shamelessly abusing it – with the greatest respect – before the pilot appeared unannounced one morning: tall, blond-haired in a shiny leather flying jacket and conspicuous Knight's Cross around his neck.

He jumped up, throwing a small bag inside before climbing in. He must have known we were watching enviously as Otto chatted to him like an old friend while strapping him in.

A mechanic then took hold of the crank, and a few seconds later, as the whirring increased, he jumped down and joined the rest of us. The pilot closed the canopy and released the brakes, then taxied across the apron towards the runway, his engine revving occasionally and controls moving around. Quite unconsciously we all stood in a line, watching, as the 109 roared along the concrete and lifted off. Instead of disappearing immediately, it banked left before turning towards us, fast and low as though strafing the airfield. At an incredible speed the 109 then climbed away and disappeared, heading south-west. We all cheered.

Two weeks later we headed off yet again, this time by road in the back of another draughty lorry, heading north-east on the autobahn. I'd never seen so many flags as we passed through Nuremburg, and it looked fantastic.

This six-hour trip to Leipzig was particularly cold and uncomfortable. I found airframes the least exciting. The only thing I took from it was advice to keep a piece of chalk handy to write on the aeroplane. These ten days went very slowly.

Before we left Leipzig we met the V12 Jumo 211 engine at the nearby Junkers plant. A new pressurised cooling system had just been added and they ensured we understood this thoroughly, while assembling and disassembling the engine.

In February 1940 we heard in the newsreels that a German vessel, the *Altmark*, was stopped and seized by the British in neutral Norwegian waters in a blatant act of piracy. Some of the crew were killed.

"How outrageous!" we all cried.

Clearly the Norwegians were helping the British in blockading Germany, just as we thought, and so in April our forces had no choice but to enter Norway through Denmark to put a stop to it.

The newsreels showed our troops greeted by smiling Danes with flowers and gifts, in more of a natural annexation than an occupation, just like Austria.

The British continued causing trouble in Norway, particularly around the town of Narvik in the north, but they were easily crushed and sent fleeing back across the North Sea. In revenge they dropped thousands of fire tablets over Germany, nasty little incendiary devices the size of a hand, that would set fire to houses, barns, and fields. What a cowardly thing to do and, as the newsreels said, clearly intended to terrorise civilians.

In early May 1940 the French began massing huge numbers of troops on their northern border, with the obvious intention of pushing through Belgium to attack Germany. Many units of the British army and RAF were involved in what was clearly a planned invasion. We had to stop it before it began. French and British aeroplanes, with the help of the Dutch and the Belgians, fired at German civilians in the streets and so, yet again, Germany had to act.

On 10th May our forces crossed into Belgium and Holland to huge shouts of approval. Any sense of foreboding immediately vanished when we heard how quickly the army was progressing, with air force help, in what became known as a lightning war, a *Blitzkrieg*, in a similar fashion to the advance across Poland. Everyone sang and cheered at dinner, all in high spirits, at such wonderful news.

Yet again Germany had been successful in defending herself.

A few days later we were passengers again in the back of an army lorry, but thankfully only fifty kilometres to the huge BMW plant at Oschersleben, west of Magdeburg. This was entirely different in every respect to what we'd seen before. The first-class, newly built accommodation and, in fact, the whole place, had a bustling and exciting atmosphere, perhaps thanks to all the latest news.

BMW were working on all sorts of new ideas in support of the war, a lot of which they wouldn't tell us about or let us see. The main reason for our presence was to get a thorough working knowledge of their 801 air-cooled radial engine.

"What an impressive design, absolutely nothing like the DB 600 in the 109, but easier to get at and remove from the airframe," I remarked, thinking out loud.

It had already seen success in the Ju88 and Dornier Do217 and was the power plant for an exciting new single-engined fighter made by Focke-Wulf.

In June 1940, I qualified as an air force mechanic, and was formally presented with my black overalls, the official ground crew uniform. I had become one of the 'black men', as we were called, soon to find out where I would be sent for my first operational posting. It could be anywhere inside Germany or perhaps the front line, wherever that might be.

The British had fled across the Channel from Dunkirk,

leaving all their weapons strewn across the beaches, and on 14th June Paris was ours.

Inge and I still exchanged letters, and in my latest from home, my father mentioned the war for the first time. He stated he couldn't believe what Germany had achieved.

6

Holland

June 1940

To my surprise they allowed me a few days' leave before my posting. It seemed the entire country was buzzing. My mother fussed over me far too much as usual, and her face lit up when I gave her some dried meat wrapped in newspaper, thanks to a very friendly lady in the Oschersleben canteen.

My father constantly fired questions at me, mainly about the war, such as, "Are we really in Paris?"

He kept repeating the sad fact that he had spent many months of his youth stuck in Flanders.

"So how can the German army now be in France? So much for Versailles," and he laughed, shaking his head.

"It's all true," I said, with a smile. "I've spoken to comrades who've been there. Isn't it fantastic?"

I took some French cigarettes from my pocket. "Here, I have something for you," handing them over.

These were in addition to the usual Reemtsma ration cigarettes, which he didn't particularly like but still accepted.

He offered me one of his favourite Trommler cigarettes, and was surprised when I told him I didn't smoke.

"If you'd joined the army and spent all your time in a muddy trench you'd be smoking by now," he groaned with friendly disdain.

No doubt a huge part of the excitement in Germany was due to the fact that the old foe, France, had been vanquished so swiftly and the injustices of the Versailles Treaty corrected. The whole country celebrated, with cheerful music on the radio and passionate speeches by our government leaders. Everything seemed quite surreal, as though we were all living a fantastic dream.

On my return to Quakenbruck on 26th June 1940 I'd find out where I would be posted. The list stated my next destination would be a brand-new fighter squadron, JG54, currently based at an airfield in Holland called Schiphol.

I'd never been to Holland, and since it was one of our new territories, it didn't seem as though I'd be travelling to a different country, just another part of Greater Germany.

Dreading another long, uncomfortable ride in the back of a lorry, I joined four others heading for Altenburg airfield. We hitched a lift in a BMW factory lorry, arriving mid-morning at the busiest airfield I'd ever seen, with Dornier Do17s, Heinkel 111s, Ju88s, and Me110s all buzzing around like flies at a summer picnic.

A Ju52 would be leaving for Schiphol in the afternoon so we had to sit and wait. We found a food service canteen where we drank coffee and read numerous copies of *The Eagle*, the air force magazine, while watching the aeroplanes.

As I finished my second cup, four noisy bomber crewmen in full flying gear joined us. They were a pilot officer and three

NCOs, probably from the same aeroplane, judging by the way they spoke to one another, using the informal pronoun 'du' instead of 'sie' with first names. They carried small luggage bags along with the usual flight bags and the officer ordered coffee for them all. I wanted to ask which aeroplane they flew, and whether they had seen any combat, but didn't; I merely watched and listened.

Catching the pilot's attention, I nudged a few chairs at the next table and they sat down, barely acknowledging us, perhaps because we wore black overalls, rather than flying suits.

However, the officer spoke to us directly after his first sip of coffee. "You're waiting for a flight?"

"Yes, sir," I replied, without hesitation. "We've been posted to Schiphol."

"Ah, JG54, their new home, if I'm not mistaken, 109s, Emils, I think." He paused, looking out the window briefly and then back at us. "It's a pity I didn't know before; you could have taken a gift to a friend of mine there."

I nodded and smiled.

Looking at our new overalls, he made the appropriate assumption. "Is it your first posting?"

"Yes, sir." I stood up, unsure as to whether I should address him by his rank.

"When is your flight?" he asked, indicating for me to sit down.

"Sometime this afternoon, a Ju52." I sat and turned to the sky, as if to check its arrival.

The officer laughed, almost choking on his coffee, not just a chuckle but a great belly laugh. "In an old tin trimotor? It would be quicker to walk!" He shook his head before a brief seriousness spread across his face. "Wait a moment," he said, leaning towards his comrades, whispering, to which one of them shrugged and nodded, glancing across at me, briefly making eye contact.

The other two looked indifferent, or didn't hear. Whatever, they agreed.

"I'm sure you and your friends know everything about my aeroplane's engines, so it's only fair that I offer you a trip with us, in a fast bomber, not a tin can, is it not?" He smiled, probably expecting a reply, so I nodded.

I wanted to know what aeroplane he meant, though I had my suspicions. At the time I only knew of one aeroplane that had the nickname 'the fast bomber'.

"We can only take two of you, sadly, but we are ready as soon as we've finished our coffee."

Werner must have been listening, because to my astonishment he had already stood up, his bag on his shoulder. Werner was like that, very perceptive. Over two metres tall, well-built and super-fit, with thick, blond hair and deep blue eyes, perfect material for the SS, should he have been interested, which he wasn't. Quietly spoken, he just wanted to be around aeroplanes.

Oddly enough I felt protective of him, despite his size, because he was a month younger than me. Anyway, everybody nodded, the matter settled.

Coffees finished, we parted from our other comrades, Gunter and Karl, with a mix of surprise and disappointment on their faces, following the aircrew outside. We didn't have far to walk.

The crew boarded a Ju88 bearing an Edelweiss crest on the right side of the fuselage. We each received a parachute, clearly reserves and, frankly, not looking like they'd work, and strapped them on before climbing in, bags first.

Werner smiled, saying one word to me as we boarded: 'Jumos', to which I nodded.

The engines were obviously familiar. At a guess this looked like an A1, belonging to KG51, and I was right, the result of hours spent aeroplane spotting.

"We are on our way to an airfield near Lille, but we will stop at Schiphol, and you'll be there in no time, so welcome aboard."

As we wedged ourselves into the lower part of the cabin, the rear gunner didn't seem too impressed at having an audience. There wasn't much space with MG15 machine-gun magazines stacked all around, other bags, probably mail and personal effects, and a beautifully crisp officer's uniform hanging from a canopy lever.

Within a few minutes both engines were running up, magnetos tested, along with idle speed, pressures and temperatures, and I heard every nuance in engine tone like a piano tuner at the keyboard.

Brakes off, we taxied to the runway, the controls moving around and flaps lowered ten degrees. We didn't stop or even pause. At barely ten metres the undercarriage was stowed along with the flaps, and we sped over the ground, gaining speed incredibly quickly before turning away in a gentle fifteen degree climbing turn, westward.

As we levelled off, Werner swapped places with the rear gunner and I crouched behind the pilot's seat as best I could, sitting on a box, enjoying every moment, despite the cramped conditions. The view was amazing, powering along at one thousand metres, the aeroplane settling at an impressive 360kph. I fell in love with the Ju88 and thoughts of piloting one filled my head.

The atmosphere in the cockpit was light-hearted, almost jovial, with little concern we might be attacked. The crew communicated with one another using monosyllabic words, nods, and hand gestures, the way good friends do. The smell of new rubber, aviation fuel, and stale sweat, testament to the many hours they'd spent together.

The radio operator asked where I grew up, stating he originally lived in Salzburg, proudly adding that I'd find many Austrians in JG54. I didn't think to ask why.

An odd droning noise began which, at first, I couldn't place. Not a rough-running engine, too intermittent, for I knew every permutation possible and the pitch varied too wildly. No smoke anywhere either, so it couldn't be an engine problem, and yet this odd sound persisted, growing ever louder. I couldn't understand it and felt huge disappointment at not working it out.

As the pilot turned around to speak to me, it stopped. His face was impossibly lined beyond his years, now only a few centimetres from mine, with tobacco and schnapps on his breath. Probably in his late thirties, therefore much older than me, he too asked where I lived.

"Elmshorn, near Hamburg," I said.

As he faced forward again, the noise resumed.

The radio operator smiled, nodding at the pilot, and I realised the odd droning noise and occasional high-pitch whirring came from our pilot singing, though I had no idea of the song. You might find it surprising that the pilot of a Ju88 fighter-bomber would behave like this, and I did at first, but then he captured the mood of us all, a blend of high confidence and supreme optimism.

After a while I had cramp in my legs, so I clambered further back into the fuselage, exchanging places with Werner again, and sat suspended in a canvas seat in the upper rear gunner's position. The weather looked superb as we passed over the fields at lightning speed.

Taking hold of the MG15, I imagined we were being pursued by a British Hurricane or French Morane-Saulnier. I was stupid enough at the time to wish that we were.

As I was deep in thought, the gunner tapped me on the back to resume his position. It seemed we were approaching our destination. I felt as though I'd been with this crew for days, or even years, everything seemed so oddly familiar. I couldn't believe an hour and a half had passed, and we'd almost covered the six hundred kilometres to Schiphol.

After a superb landing, Werner and I disembarked while the engines remained running. We shook hands with the crew and the pilot handed me a very expensive bottle of brandy with a name on a handwritten label attached.

"We can't stop," he shouted over the engine noise, "but can you do this favour for me, young man? Give this to Lieutenant Hans von Schmoller-Haldy, with my compliments?" he said before slamming the hatch shut.

I gripped the bottle as the aeroplane turned around neatly and took off. I stood watching as it faded to a speck, disappearing into the afternoon heat haze.

This was obviously the main reason we had landed at Schiphol: a very expensive brandy delivery service.

The memory of my brief time in that Ju88 remained with me for many years, and I often wondered what became of the crew.

7

"Just arrived?" someone shouted. A sergeant major approached, marching at double time.

"Yes, sir," I replied.

"Then come with me," indicating for us to follow.

We struggled to keep up with all our kit while trying to march in time. I didn't even see him appear, with so many people and vehicles moving around.

"Where are the other two?"

"They will be here later, sir," Werner said. "We were lucky, we caught an earlier flight." He winked at me.

"Never mind," the sergeant major replied, stopping to face us. "Take your things to Hut B and report back to me at the adjutant's office, there, in fifteen minutes. You can't miss it; it's the building with *Plaatskaartenbureau* written above the door." He laughed, pointing at the former Dutch ticket office.

We found our accommodation with a brief hello to those inside and marched in perfect time to the office, where we knocked on a shabby brown door.

"What are your names?" the same sergeant major asked, holding the door open.

"Privates Hoffman and Goetz, sir," I replied, both of us standing rigidly to attention.

"Come on in and relax; you're not in the Labour Service now. This is the air force. The adjutant is still flying, so you'll have to wait until he returns."

"I have something for Lieutenant Schmoller-Haldy," I said, tapping the bulge in my pocket.

"Oh, really?"

"I was asked to deliver it personally," I said, revealing the bottle.

"Right," the sergeant major said with a grin. "Then I'll have to take you both to the CO and you can make your delivery, can't you, Goetz? He can fill you in while you're there, and I don't expect him or the adjutant to do it again when the others arrive, do you understand?"

We both nodded. He looked as old as my father, though probably not.

"Follow me," he said.

Ten metres down the corridor we found the door in a similar state and not very grand for a major, the CO of No. 1 Group, JG54.

He knocked briefly before stepping inside. "These are the first two of today's lot, sir, Hoffman and Goetz."

The door remained open as the major glanced at us from behind a desk. He put down his pen and stood up.

We strode in, throwing up our smartest Hitler salute, right arms raised at the appropriate angle, with loud synchronised heel clicks.

He smiled but didn't reciprocate in any way. "Thank you, gentlemen," he said, moving over to shake our hands in turn. "Please take a seat," pointing at two very smart dining chairs in front of his desk.

"They've just moved us here from France, more's the pity. The wine's terrible, the locals are miserable, and the roads are shocking, but I suppose the beer is alright." He sat down. "I'm hoping they'll send us back soon, but for now we're scattered all over, mainly on the coast, as you'll find out. Either of you could be anywhere this time tomorrow."

He picked up his pen, pulled off the lid a couple of times and tossed it back onto his desk. "I don't usually do the meet-and-greet for everyone, except for new pilots, but I need to ask you something; besides, there's a lot you should know, so listen up. Feel free to fire a question at me as I'm rambling on, and I might even give you an answer; you never know."

As he leaned back in his chair the faded leather creaked in protest. "Fighter Wing Jadgeschwader 54 is divided into half a dozen groups, all operating autonomously, but together, if you know what I mean."

He glanced at a map on the wall to his right, and we dutifully followed his gaze. "We are No. 1 Group, and closest to us, No. 2 Group is now on some windswept island in the North Sea, Walcheren or Welcheren, I think it's called, God help them, and some are near Rotterdam. No. 3 Group is camped in a damp field near Amsterdam and up at Bergen right on the coast, almost in the bloody sea. I think High Command is worried about the British coming in over the Dutch coast, and they are right. But they are not a problem; Kinzinger and Strohauer each bagged a Blenheim yesterday only two days after we got here."

He paused, smiling a little, scrutinising us like a tailor assessing new clients. "My apologies, gentlemen, I've been rude. My name is Mettig, and I'm your commanding officer. How much flying experience do you have?"

The question took us both by surprise and for a moment we looked blankly at one another before shaking our heads. Did he think we were pilots?

"None, sir," Werner said, on behalf of us both.

He rubbed his forehead and then the afternoon stubble on his chin, clearly disappointed.

Martin Mettig was in his late thirties, appearing older perhaps because of his calm, mature demeanour, a lot like my father. I liked him immediately.

"I'm asking everyone at the moment, it's the main reason I wanted to see you. I hoped you'd have at least some flying time under your belts. Never mind, just remember we are always looking for pilots. Please give it some serious thought. The British are proving a little tougher than the Poles and their aeroplanes are better, not much, but they are, though it's obviously nothing we can't handle. Anyway…"

He stopped as he saw the neck of the bottle protruding from my pocket. "Is that for me? How very kind," he said, standing up and reaching around the desk to take it.

"It's for Lieutenant von Schmoller-Haldy, sir, sorry. It's from the Ju88 pilot. I didn't get his name."

He looked at the label with a grin as he sat down before opening a drawer and placing it gently inside. "Hans is in hospital. He was shot down by a Blenheim, would you believe, this morning. I've docked him a month's pay to add to his humiliation."

He laughed so loudly I thought he'd fall off his chair. "I'll see he gets it when he returns," he said, "though if I get time I might take it to him personally, to cheer him up."

He was obviously a friend, but his misfortune was not discussed any further.

"Anyway, the important thing for you is that we currently have mostly Emils, 109 E3s and E4s, with the DB600 engines, being replaced by Friedrichs as soon as we can get them. All very familiar, I'm sure."

I nodded, listening intently.

Lighting a cigarette, he glanced at the map loosely pinned to the wall. "Our air force has a huge area to cover, gentlemen, all of Western Europe, in fact, apart from Britain, of course, though this will obviously change soon. Once we have sorted out the British the war will be over and we can all go home, can't we?" He laughed.

In my naivety I thought he meant it. I believed everything anyone in authority told me, as we all did in those days.

"There are some fantastic plans ahead and you are crucial to our success, so welcome aboard."

Aeroplanes roared overhead and he stood up abruptly, shaking our hands again, indicating the meeting had finished. Although disappointed we'd let him down about the flying, the first seeds of an idea began forming in my head.

Gunter and Karl arrived in the Ju52 at 1800 hours and we ate together in the mess like fresh-faced boys at a new school.

Later, at dusk, while playing cards in our barrack, an angry sergeant stomped in, barking orders at everyone, sending me to a hangar five hundred metres away.

With two others I spent that entire first night replacing the engine of a 109, sustained by litres of sweet coffee until 0600 hours. The hangar doors had been closed without me being aware of the sun coming up. When eventually released, I slept until 0900 hours.

Then to my astonishment, straight after breakfast, I returned to the same hangar, fixing the flak-damaged fuselage of another 109 until 1900 hours, with only a half-hour break for a meal. Shattered, I collapsed on my bed only to spend all the next night working on a 109 engine that was rough running and no-one knew why. Eventually we had to disassemble most of it and reassemble it, and then it was okay.

The next day I worked on a Ju88, patching up hundreds of small bullet holes, and after a few hours' sleep, I worked all night on a 109.

This would be the pattern of our lives as air force ground crew, or 'black men'. The rotation of damaged aeroplanes and work was relentless. I soon became too exhausted to function properly, yet my comrades worked hard with the same amount of sleep, so I must have been weak, and I forced myself to carry on.

Though happy to be in the air force, I thought more about what the CO had told us. Pilots led exciting lives and many spoke of their flying in great detail. We heard amazing tales of air combat and miraculous escapes, triggering my imagination.

A few days after my arrival, on 27th June, one of our pilots returned from an op with a customary low pass over the airfield, waggling his wings as we all cheered wildly. He landed in a jubilant mood, telling us he had shot down two Blenheims over the North Sea, confirmed by other pilots. His 109 hadn't sustained a single hit on the airframe. Such events became increasingly common, and we expected nothing less.

In the first week of July Werner and I were flown to No. 2 Group at Bergen, on the north coast of Holland, in a Fieseler 156 Storch, belonging to the squadron. I thoroughly enjoyed the flight over the canals, the still water shimmering like strips of glass in the early morning sun, and tried hard to follow the pilot's navigation, the tiny Argus V8 chugging us along at scarcely more than 100kph.

After a perfect, gentle landing in a field by the sea, with no formal introductions we were immediately put to work fixing the engine of a 109. The beach only a few metres beyond the dunes, I looked up to see locals wandering idly past on the warm sand. Children were laughing and playing and occasionally when some of them caught sight of us they'd wave enthusiastically, to which we happily reciprocated.

Their parents, perhaps less keen, ushered them away, but any teenage girls walking close by would stop, shouting 'hello' and 'how are you' in German, giggling before waving and running away along the beach.

A freckle-faced mechanic on the other side of the engine waved back. "You're new, aren't you?" he asked me.

I nodded.

"The locals really love us," he said, "especially the girls." He winked, smiling. "I've had three already. You'll have a great time here."

8

As the afternoon sun lost strength I volunteered to sit in the 109 and test the engine. I didn't give anyone else a chance as I shouted for someone to jump up onto the wing with the crank. Making sure the brakes were on, I primed it twice, and soon after, it started perfectly.

The prop draught blew sand over the dunes and across the beach, lifting the skirts of two middle-aged women walking a tiny white dog, so they hurried away, closer to the sea.

Listening out for any rough running in the engine, other colleagues stared intently as I took it up to 1800rpm. Temperatures and pressures fine, when I saw the thumbs-up, I shut it down and closed the cowlings, job complete.

Still cleaning the last of the grease from my hands, I followed my new sergeant to an army camp bed amongst a row of others in a draughty wooden building like a large beach hut.

"You'll sleep here while you're working," he told us. "Most of the regular personnel are based in the town, two kilometres away, but you'll have to make do with this, for now."

He left us, and with a few nods of acknowledgement to others in the hut, we settled in. After a decent meal I slept soundly all night.

Early in the morning I returned to work on another 109 engine, continuing all day and into the evening until the light failed. We'd eaten a meal at around 1800 hours but when darkness fell, instead of sleep, I had to go to a hangar where another engine awaited. The six huge buildings at Bergen at first glance looked nothing like hangars, due to the false gabled roofs and shrubs around the paths, all designed to fool the enemy.

At midnight I wondered when I might get some sleep, and finally heard the good news that I could stand down at 0300 hours.

For the next few days we slept and ate when we could, working around the clock. On 15th July the war paid us a personal visit. Whether I was arrogant or naïve enough to think no-one would dare attack us, or more specifically me, I'm not sure.

When the alarm sounded I woke from a windswept, seafaring nightmare with my ship sinking in a gale; the reality, a shrill klaxon with multiple shouts of 'Alarm!' and someone running around our hut in a wild panic with an MP40 machine pistol in his hands.

Sitting on my bed in a daze, I sensed a rapid burrowing vibration underneath my feet, followed immediately by another, and then a blast I thought would flatten our trembling wooden hut as the bangs followed. The walls and furniture shook and the thin glass in the windows blew in against the thick curtains, which probably saved us all from serious injury.

Everyone around me fell to the floor so I instinctively joined them, my hands covering my head. Oddly enough I thought about my father, trying to accurately describe what it felt like to be shelled in the trenches. Now I truly understood.

I ran outside to find a trench when the next hut erupted in a mass of flame and debris in a direct hit, hurling me through the air like a football, landing in a stunned heap ten metres away. I had surely been blown to pieces and lost limbs, but miraculously, on quick inspection, I seemed unhurt, though my hearing had gone.

With several others, I grabbed a bucket and hurled water at the burning building, which could so easily have been ours. Amongst the debris I couldn't move far without stepping on spongy lumps wrapped in torn pieces of cloth. I had no idea what these were until I picked one up to examine it and wished I hadn't. I dropped it and immediately felt shame at handling a comrade in such a manner.

NCOs shouted orders in the darkness. Angry faces glowed orange by the flames as two figures emerged from the inferno, their clothing ablaze. These weren't men but burning spectres from hell. We ran forward, covering them in blankets before rolling them around on the ground. They lay dead on the sand, their charred and brittle limbs like enormous spent matches.

So utterly exhausted, I couldn't continue. After ten minutes of frantic activity no-one else came running, so we slowed down.

This was my introduction to the war, as unforgiving and brutal as it could be. Just for a moment I thought of all the colourful flags, summer camps, and singing, unable to connect them to what had just happened.

Counting our dead and dying, we cursed the British, and promised revenge. The devastation could not be blamed on our leaders in Berlin but was typical British aggression, exactly what our enemy was capable of, and why I joined the air force along with everyone else, to put a stop to it.

An hour later, slumped on a bench in the remains of the dining hut, covered in filth and coughing badly, so tired I could barely function, I struggled to hold a tin mug of sweet coffee in trembling hands.

An acting corporal from my hut sat next to me so heavily I thought the bench would collapse.

"What a night," he said.

Sensing his eyes on me, too exhausted to acknowledge, I heard him add, "Are you alright?"

I didn't answer.

The fingers of my right hand were being peeled away from the mug and something small pushed into my palm.

"Take this, and in twelve hours take another. I have more, but Wernitz, the doc, will supply as many as you need. It's only Pervitin. Don't worry, you'll feel better."

Turning towards him, I forced a smile. Lifting my palm to my mouth I dropped something in, unconcerned, swilling it down with coffee.

Ten minutes later the amphetamines began. I spent the next four hours until dawn shovelling debris, helping to recover the remains of my comrades. From the body parts we found, and from a roll call of the missing, four had been killed and fifteen badly injured.

I unwrapped the tiny parcel the corporal had given me and took another, and twelve hours after that, another.

A day or so after the raid, I'm not exactly sure when, I ate bread and sausage with Werner and told him about the Pervitin.

He smiled and showed me the right pocket of his overalls, furtively revealing the top half of a new Pervitin tube, like a schoolboy hiding contraband from a teacher.

"Everyone uses them; I started a couple of days ago. I didn't know whether to tell you."

I worked on two 109s all the next day and continuously for two further nights without stopping other than for food and the latrine. When released, I passed out on my bed and slept for sixteen hours solid.

On waking, I visited the doctor, a middle-aged captain by the name of Wernitz, as the corporal had said.

He knew exactly my reason for being there and, without even asking, handed me a full tube of Pervitin with an odd kind of willing reluctance.

"These are yours. Give your body time to catch up every now and then. Drink some schnapps and sleep for as long as you can in between, alright?"

He looked away and began writing notes, ignoring me, his way of telling me he'd finished.

9

Campagne-les-Guines France
July 1940

My time in Holland passed in a haze of sweat and exhaustion, until JG54 left for France. After loading everything we could into what became an odd column of vehicles, we trundled south for an uncomfortable journey, finally stopping at the Pas de Calais.

German aeroplanes filled the sky, day and night. Our forces had taken as much of France as we wanted. The focus now centred on England; I knew crossing the Channel might be rough, and the water cold, so I hoped I'd get a lift in an aeroplane rather than a boat.

"We'll soon be sitting in an English pub, drinking pints of their awful warm beer," joked Peter, miming the actions.

"Yes," agreed Johann. "Mr Churchill will be humbled in captivity, if he hasn't already run away to America. We will allow King George to carry on but with our flag over Buckingham Palace."

We all laughed, fiercely proud to be part of it, readily believing the certainty in everything our government told us.

We settled at Campagne-les-Guines near Calais, which sounded wonderful. The scenery certainly lived up to its name, but the airfield sloped on an uneven grass strip, surrounded by tall hedgerows and trees with very few permanent buildings. Apparently, many others in the area were so riddled with molehills and rabbit burrows it was a mystery why they had been chosen at all.

Many of the pilots included us in their birthday celebrations, and some flew in champagne using our Arado Ar66. JG54 were honoured to provide the fighter escort for the Fuhrer's flight when he passed nearby on his way to Paris. Sadly he didn't land anywhere near us so we didn't see him, but we still felt privileged to be part of it.

We all crammed into that French field, surrounded by mature woodland, including Captain von Bonin's Group and, to my surprise, I found myself one of the dedicated ground crew chosen to work on his aeroplane, a 109 E3. I noticed a curious cartoon mouse, holding a pistol, painted on the fuselage under the cockpit on the left side, and I meant to ask him about it but never did. It had double white chevrons behind this, also uniquely identifying the pilot, and he wore the magnificent Spanish Cross, from his time with the Condor Legion.

We lived in spacious tents made of thick canvas held up by sturdy wooden poles, pitched ourselves on the western side of the airfield near the trees. Close to the aeroplanes, it immediately reminded me of my camping days in the Hitler Youth. We slept in the ubiquitous army camp beds, comfortable and warm enough.

I shared my new home with three other 'black men', as we were known (because of our dark overalls), all with similar backgrounds, but Peter, Johann, and Gerhard were Austrian. Their accents were different to mine and, with me being the only German, they took the mickey out of me constantly. I had no idea I even had an accent. I seem to remember someone warning me about the number of Austrians in JG54.

Each tent had a steel bunker stove with a chimney pipe sent up through a purpose-built hole in the canvas roof. The bunker stove measured forty centimetres high and fifteen round, weighing ten kilos, so we could easily move it around. We didn't need to use it for warmth in France but hung our mess tins on the outside to heat the contents. Someone always had coffee simmering away, so our tent had a homely smell, disguising the inevitable odours from four men living closely under canvas.

We didn't want to think about winter, or living in a tent anywhere other than France, and in the summer, why would we? We were at the centre of the war, the British were our only remaining adversary, soon we would occupy England as another part of Greater Germany, and the war would be over.

"Guess what our next task is?" said Peter.

"Latrine tents, probably," I replied without much enthusiasm, for a job that had to be done. Each consisted of a pair of wooden seats over holes in the ground, which were then rotated, buried, and moved.

No flush toilets or running water, but large wooden barrels and steel tanks suspended on a framework, allowing adequate water to flow into the shower heads, always cold but which we used whenever we liked. We took it in turns to fill these tanks from taps in the main buildings, using a lorry and a system of hose pipes with a syphoning method that worked brilliantly. We surveyed our encampment proudly, our resourcefulness a testament to all our training as youngsters.

A new wooden building had been started for the CO, the adjutant, First Lieutenant Otto Kath, and other admin staff, such as the new technical officer Lieutenant Pichon Kalau von Hofe. Our previous technical officer, Lieutenant Albrecht Drefl, was missing, apparently shot down over England.

The signals officer had a tent but, due to protests about his radio equipment getting damp, a small hut was constructed specially for him. Staff from the vehicle platoon, repair platoon, and admin clerks filled the other tents.

We were all keen to see the completion of the large wooden cookhouse; meanwhile, an enormous marquee became our dining room and mess, soon nicknamed the circus tent.

I wondered if this comfortable living would continue when we arrived in England, and whether the English would be as indifferent to us as the French. We were met with smiles and happy faces most of the time and found a fantastic bistro bar near the airfield where they served two courses with wine for twenty francs, the equivalent to only one German mark. Unbelievable value and we usually had to book in advance due to its popularity. We all loved it, not just because of the great food and wine but also the two lovely waitresses who clearly enjoyed flirting. Still unused to girls, as most of us were, I noticed a few of my older comrades took them for long walks on summer evenings, and I can only guess why.

My regular pay had increased, supplemented by one-off payments of thirty-five marks war service pay, and another thirty-five in Front pay. The bistro being the only place where we could spend it, the proprietor, a rather swarthy, round-shouldered man in his thirties with greasy black hair, must have absolutely loved us. No wonder he always smiled.

In August our 109s were increasingly busy on escort duties, the enthusiastic pilots bounding across the grass into their cockpits, always with broad smiles, before heading over the Channel. Although not formally briefed as to what they were doing, they happily told us about escorting Ju88s and Stukas, attacking British shipping, and engaging in free hunts for any enemy fighters daring to challenge them over the sea.

We confidently expected little or no resistance with the invasion beginning very soon.

10

In the first days of August our Technical Officer Albrecht Drefl was confirmed as a POW in England, after disappearing over Kent.

On the afternoon of 5th August I watched as a 109 E3 flew in from the west, trailing smoke, just missing the trees before crash-landing. The pilot, a young sergeant, was hauled out alive but badly injured. Although not based at our airfield, we were probably the nearest he could find.

The condition of this aeroplane shocked us all. The entire fuselage and most of the wings were riddled with so many bullet holes from British .303 machine guns I could not understand how it had reached us. The pilot had obviously been extremely unlucky to have clashed with the only remaining Spitfires in the RAF.

To our astonishment, only a few days later, someone I knew quite well, First Lieutenant Reinhard Seiler, failed to return from a free hunt over the Channel. He had been seen crashing into the sea in hopefully a survivable ditching. Perhaps he had mechanical trouble and his engine had failed.

In that same week another of our pilots ditched in the sea, and another crash-landed in a ploughed field near us, badly injured. A word appeared with increasing regularity on the pilot's duty board: *Vermisst,* meaning 'missing'.

It didn't always mean the worst, of course; our rescue boats patrolled the Channel day and night, mostly with great success. Despite our rescue planes being painted white, with huge red crosses on the wings, and clearly not involved in combat, the British behaved in an outrageous manner by shooting them down.

When we hauled the 109 E3 into the trees to begin work on it, a lieutenant approached us. "It's irreparable," he said. "Break it up for parts."

We looked at one other, surprised, but then Johann added, "Look at that crack behind the pilot's seat, all the way around the fuselage. Its back is broken, as well as the hundreds of bullet holes. It's an E3 problem, and irreparable."

I'd never seen this before.

In reply to the British fighter menace, the CO decided to send our 109s further into England in more aggressive free hunts.

We worked hard all night so every 109 would be available, and the pilots set off at first light in high spirits.

The airfield seemed unusually quiet for a while, apart from a visiting Fieseler 156 Storch, drifting in silently from the east like a leaf in the summer breeze. We gazed eagerly at the cockpit for any high-ranking visitors, but the pilot was alone and just needed fuel.

We slept until roused when the first 109 returned, trailing smoke and overshooting the field, finally coming to rest in the rough before the hedge and the road. The pilot, a sergeant, had sustained serious wounds. Others began returning, some unscathed but most displaying the tell-tale signs of combat with RAF fighters: hundreds of .303 bullet holes.

Two failed to return that morning, listed as *Vermisst*. One had been seen crash-landing in an English wheat field, and the other pilot was last seen wrestling with his dinghy after ditching in the Channel; not what we had been expecting.

In the next few days, to our continuing surprise three more of our pilots returned badly injured in damaged aeroplanes, causing us a great deal of work. Every daylight hour was used including the cover of light-proof tents. My colleagues and I slept whenever we could, between consuming Pervitin at an alarming rate.

Early in the morning of 12th August, on another cloudless day, as I was perched on the nose of a 109 examining the spinner, a fighter aeroplane thundered over our tents at less than ten metres, shaking the tops of the trees. Were we under attack? As quickly as I could I edged my way back along the cowling onto the wing, ready to begin the emergency drill.

Post-mounted MG15s, in sandbagged dugouts, were dotted all around the airfield and the one nearest us was empty. About to run over, I recognised the low flyer as a 109. After a steep turn at low level, as the left wingtip skimmed the long grass at the far end of the field, the undercarriage appeared. In the next moment it touched down gently in a perfect landing. This pilot clearly had total mastery of his machine.

A 109 E, an Emil, taxied towards the circus tent, where it came to a stop. Aeroplanes should not park there, in full view, and if the CO saw it, he would have strong words with the pilot, unless he was injured.

Even from across the field I could see it wasn't a JG54 aeroplane. It had very few identifying marks apart from an astonishing array of victory tallies on the tail fin. We looked curiously at one another as Werner and Karl walked towards it as the engine shut down.

When the canopy opened, a man dressed in a white flying suit hauled himself out. He put on his cap, taking care to place it at a casually jaunty angle, before inserting a long cigar between his teeth.

The CO appeared, walking towards him across the grass, smiling. The two men embraced, shaking hands vigorously like best friends, patting one another on the back, before the CO led the visitor away.

"It's Galland," Johann shouted, nodding, rubbing his hands with a cloth as though preparing to shake hands with him.

We all stared as the CO escorted his guest towards the circus tent where they were joined by other pilots. I heard loud voices and laughter before it went quiet.

Twenty minutes later, a smiling Adolf Galland, commander of No. 3 Group, JG26, emerged surrounded by pilots, putting on his leather flying gloves while walking back to his aeroplane in his brilliant white overalls. We knew he'd recently been awarded the Knight's Cross, because we'd read it in the latest issue of *The Eagle*, but we couldn't see if he was wearing it, due to his non-regulation red polka-dot scarf!

A very eager group of ground crew, including Werner and Karl, ran up to start his aeroplane, but he ushered them away with a casual wave, climbed in, stowed his cap, closed the canopy, and started up. He taxied straight onto the centre of the grass and took off, heading south-west.

We never discovered the purpose of his visit, but Galland held great influence with Command and I later found out losses in his own squadron had so far been nowhere near ours, so perhaps this was Captain Mettig's way of letting him know.

The next day a lieutenant pilot arrived as a passenger in a Me108 to a very warm welcome from other pilots, who immediately dragged him into the circus tent before he'd even seen the CO.

I was passing dispersal when one of the pilots shouted, "Goetz! There's someone here who wants to meet you!"

Mystified, as I had never seen the new pilot before, I suspected them of playing a practical joke, or perhaps some sort of disciplinary action. I needn't have worried. In a throng of loud pilots, the new arrival raised his glass in my direction when I stepped into the tent.

"Thank you for the schnapps, Goetz!" he said, as the entire tent erupted in laughter. "Martin and I drank the whole bloody bottle when he visited me in hospital. I insist you have a drink with me." He patted my right shoulder and poured a small measure.

As glasses were raised someone cheered, "Welcome back, Hans!"

He shook my hand, and immediately after I'd swilled the contents, he smiled and turned to follow a conversation with another officer, indicating my dismissal. Still having no idea of his identity, I returned to my duties, fixing British bullet holes in the wing of a 109.

When several of us managed to eat together we had serious conversations about our mounting losses, and I could see the concern on their faces. Things were not going quite to plan, and the prospect of drinking warm beer in an English pub looked unlikely, at least for a while.

11

Sergeant Schunk returned the next afternoon claiming he'd shot down a Spitfire, but nobody believed him or could verify it. Arguments followed, some heated. Tempers were getting shorter. Then on 15th August we lost four more pilots, two killed and two missing in the sea.

The new pilot who greeted me on arrival had confirmation of a Hurricane shot down over the Channel, and I realised my connection when I found out he was Lieutenant Hans Schmoller-Haldy, the pilot who had benefitted from the schnapps the Ju88 pilot had given me. I wouldn't say we became friends, but we were certainly on nodding terms, and he sometimes approached me for advice about his aeroplane, though I never did any work on it. Pleasant enough, as most officers were, he referred to me by my first name, surprising me one afternoon when he crossed the airfield on foot specifically to hand me a bottle of Moet champagne.

"Now we're even," he said.

Pleasantly surprised, I shared it that night with my Austrian colleagues after we'd fixed a persistent oil leak on a DB601.

In the early hours of 17th August, when I'd not long fallen asleep, we were all woken up by the horrendous sound of bombs falling on our airfield. Memories of Bergen filled my head and I prepared for the worst, but fortunately it only lasted a few seconds.

After some initial confusion, at daylight we realised only two 109s were damaged. No-one had been killed or even injured, but the significance was more concerning. RAF aircraft, possibly Blenheims, had crossed the Channel, apparently unmolested, found us in the dark, dropped their bombs and escaped back to England probably without loss. They weren't supposed to be able to do this. I could see consternation in the faces of my colleagues.

On our worst day so far, Sunday 18th August, each group in JG54 lost more aeroplanes and pilots to crash-landings and ditchings.

We read in the latest *Eagle* magazine that the RAF was virtually defeated and cleared from the skies, with long lists of destroyed British aeroplanes. Clearly this inaccurate information needed updating. Evidently the invasion of England would be postponed, perhaps until the spring.

While discussing the situation, we heard rumours that High Command blamed our pilots for failing to destroy the RAF, thereby causing the delay, and so changes had to be made. How outrageous! We wondered what would happen, until early on 25th August I noticed a gathering around the CO, outside his quarters, in bright sunshine. Perched on ladders, with my top half under the open engine cowling of a 109 under camouflage nets, if I pulled my head out and over the DB601, I could easily see them. It looked serious, so I jumped down and walked a little closer.

Captain Mettig saluted other officers, a small leather bag in his left hand, before walking towards his 109. After handshakes and more saluting, he climbed in and closed the canopy before taxiing across the grass and taking off.

That night we heard he'd gone, transferred, and I was sorry to see him go, surprised he hadn't formally announced it. He seemed a decent man, but obviously his results spoke for themselves.

Captain Hans 'Hannes' Trautloft arrived the next day in his own brand new 109 F, with three others following on behind after some low passes at high speed over the airfield: a dashing young leader roaring in with new pilots and aeroplanes. What better way to announce your arrival? I thought it strange the old leader had not been given the opportunity to hand over command directly to the new one.

We became proficient on the 109 E, and at last the F version, when the Friedrichs arrived. The tailplane struts were gone, as were the guns in the wings, replaced by the cannon in the spinner and engine-mounted guns. This would make our work on the engines different. The wingtips had rounded ends as opposed to square, but these were detachable.

Without even unpacking his belongings, the new CO briefed the pilots in the circus tent before gathering the rest of us under the shade of the trees away from the late morning sun. He looked ten years younger than Mettig, with a small unlit cigar in one corner of his mouth that he occasionally rolled around from one side to the other.

Speaking with a commanding presence, he told us a little about his background and, like Captain von Bonin, he had flown in Spain with the Condor Legion, where he gained five victories, then another in the skies above Poland, and recently five RAF aeroplanes with JG51 in Holland.

This man is different, I thought.

He clearly had a great passion for aeroplanes, adding, "And I paid for my own flying lessons before joining up. Some of you may find it curious, but I'm a fluent Russian speaker."

We did indeed.

Despite the arrival of a new CO, our losses continued.

"Can't we repaint our aeroplanes to match the English countryside?" asked one of the pilots.

"Or the filthy brown of the English Channel?" another said, though I think this was an uncomfortable joke.

We were happy to try anything, but whatever we did, our aeroplanes and pilots were still lost.

Lieutenant Colonel Held died after an apparently fierce dogfight with a Spitfire over southern England. At the end of the month, Sergeants Schottle and Kleeman went missing over the Channel, and Lieutenants Roth and Ziegler disappeared into the English countryside, all four being written up as *Vermisst* on the duty board.

Some of our best pilots; most of us knew them well. Schottle and Kleeman were particularly popular because they had started out as ground crew, thoroughly understanding the pressures we faced.

The only consolation, when pilots were reported missing over England, was that the same thing would apply as happened to our pilots captured by the French early in the war; when we invaded we got them back. The invasion of England had only been postponed and so we'd see them again in the summer of 1941.

Our pilots told us of dogfights with the British, some admitting the Spitfire could out-turn a 109 E. Others disputed this, as they did the supposedly superior rate of climb by the latest versions, and such conversations were all we heard, often becoming heated. They all said that our new CO was always at the forefront when leading the squadron into combat and his aeroplane sustained plenty of damage from British .303 bullets.

Many continued claiming kills, including Spitfires, but No. 3 Group lost five more pilots in the first week of September and another I knew, Sergeant Fritz Hotzelmann, a really nice chap with a great sense of humour, was apparently seen bailing out over Maidstone. Although honoured to call some of these pilots my friends, I was losing them far too quickly.

The RAF was always there, apparently, waiting. On his return from one engagement, the CO told us in all seriousness, "You should have seen it… the sky was full of roundels."

How could they still fight if we were destroying so many?

On the afternoon of 6th September welcome relief came when Captain von Bonin shouted at me from the cockpit as soon as he'd shut down his engine. At first I thought he had a problem with his aeroplane and wanted to admonish me, because I could see fresh British bullet holes all along the fuselage, but no.

He smiled between shouts of: "Get a lorry, quickly, Goetz. Come with me, all of you!"

Fiddling with his map, he beckoned another pilot over. "Was it here?" he demanded, impatiently.

The other pilot glanced at the map, nodding.

"Then it's less than five kilometres away," he shouted, as excited as a schoolboy.

12

Johann drove a huge Mercedes lorry and, from my seat in the back, I could hear him struggling with the gears.

As we laughed, someone shouted, "Don't they have Mercedes lorries in Austria?"

He was probably nervous, having both Captain von Bonin and the CO Captain Trautloft in the front with him, shouting to hurry up. With ten of us in the back, including my old friend Werner, a car crammed with pilots also followed on behind.

Fifteen minutes into the journey, in a country lane, we stopped, turned around ninety degrees to the left, and began driving into long grass.

Then I heard the CO's voice: "There it is!"

We jumped out to find the CO already stepping onto the wing, the aeroplane lying flat after a perfect belly landing.

Our pilots had been ordered to destroy any of our aeroplanes they saw crash-landed in England, so we were initially wary in case the RAF had similar orders, but we quickly forgot this.

It was the first time I'd seen a Spitfire close up and, like everyone else, I found it very exciting. It had the code letters XT – D on the fuselage and serial number X4260 under the tailplane. No doubt our intelligence officers would know exactly what these meant.

When someone asked the CO how he knew about it, he replied, "Because I shot the bloody thing down, that's how!" and he laughed, accepting flattering comments. "He took us on, all on his own, either stupid or brave, or perhaps both," he added, to much hilarity.

Expecting to find the grisly mess of a bullet-riddled corpse in the cockpit, to our surprise we saw nothing; the pilot had apparently been captured alive when he landed. It had no bullet holes in the cockpit, and the only sign of damage was what appeared to be a catastrophic oil leak from somewhere underneath, luckily with no fire.

The CO climbed inside, settling himself in and handling the controls as though in the air, running through the instruments and tapping a few of them with an index finger, muttering, "Ah, yes," and, "Right, of course," while nodding, occasionally shaking his head.

When he climbed out, the rest of us crowded around to take a look. The instrument panel seemed very chaotic and I couldn't see an altimeter anywhere, until Johann pointed it out.

"I've seen one before. It's in feet, not metres."

How confusing; it looked more like a clock than an altimeter.

We played with this Spitfire like boys in a toyshop, and we mechanics wanted to remove the cowling immediately and take a look at the Merlin engine, but several stern army field police prevented us.

With a recovery unit apparently on its way, our trophy would be taken away for detailed examination.

The CO made an interesting suggestion. "Why don't we keep it and rebuild it? It's my kill after all."

He received enthusiastic nodding of heads and shouts of, "Yes!" from other pilots.

"Someone get back to the airfield quickly and bring some transport," he ordered, so two pilots jumped in the car and raced off across the grass. I then heard him speaking to the army police.

"I am hereby requisitioning this aeroplane for intelligence and evaluation purposes."

They looked surprised but, out-ranked, outnumbered, and convincingly out-officiated, they relented.

We tried very hard not to laugh.

After twenty minutes we climbed aboard the lorry and returned to the airfield. Later that afternoon, pilots and ground crew alike crowded into the circus tent to see an unusual guest being entertained by the CO as a visiting VIP.

The Spitfire pilot, shaken but unhurt after his crash-landing, looked particularly incongruous in his RAF uniform, holding a large glass of red wine. There was a friendly, convivial atmosphere as flying tales and cigarettes were exchanged in a beautiful late summer evening as everyone spilled out onto the grass.

Surprised at how many English speakers we had, I suspected he was more than a little shocked at this treatment, and I saw flashes of suspicion on his face, with the occasional glance over his shoulder.

But we were all genuinely curious and disappointed, if not surprised, he'd only tell us his name and rank: Pilot Officer

John Caister, nothing else. Sure enough, though, the markings on his aeroplane told us he was from 603 Squadron, but he repeatedly denied this, much to our amusement.

Johann spoke fantastic English and I kept nudging him, asking, "What did he say?" as he interpreted. Hands simulated aeroplanes chasing through the sky, and I understood Caister when he shouted, "The Spitfire is faster!" to which someone immediately replied in English with, "But we caught up with you, didn't we?" to tremendous laughter, as the two languages mixed and overlapped.

All young men in our early twenties, we discussed aeroplanes in a few odd moments with the war forgotten.

After numerous glasses of wine, perhaps in the vain hope he might tell us something useful, Caister was sent to bed under close guard and taken away first thing in the morning, probably with a sore head. I doubt he'd forget his first evening as a prisoner of war.

We were all naïve enough at the time to believe everyone captured as a POW would receive such benevolent treatment.

I thought nothing more of this until mid-morning when, to wild shouts of approval, the same Spitfire appeared at our airfield on the back of a huge lorry, lifted up by crane and placed onto jacks close to the trees. How thrilling to be given another close look but, sadly, I wasn't chosen to work on it initially, as half a dozen of my colleagues managed to get it standing upright on its own undercarriage before inspecting the engine. All three propeller blades had been bent and removed for repair or replacement, if they could be found.

For several days this Spitfire stood amongst our 109s in the tree line still bearing its RAF markings, until we had to repaint it, or at least cover up the roundels. This aeroplane became an enjoyable project for the black men of JG54, and I'm happy to say, including myself later on, in between our usual duties.

Later in September, something unusual happened. It was an ordinary morning, with a hint of autumn in the air, as I climbed onto the wing of Captain von Bonin's 109, prior to starting it up.

"Don't bother," said my superior. "All the pilots are having a special briefing with the entire command staff and CO."

We worked on other aeroplanes in the morning sunshine, waiting, trying to guess the outcome. Would the invasion be going ahead after all? Or perhaps a new date had been fixed?

Eventually they emerged from the circus tent with glum faces and shaking of heads; clearly bad news. The morning's initial operation had changed, requiring yet another briefing before the pilots returned to their aeroplanes.

Once I'd started the engine, I checked the magnetos, temperatures and pressures as usual before throttling back to climb out.

As I strapped the captain into his seat he said, without looking at me, "We have to stay with the bombers. We have to stay with them, all the bloody time."

He slammed the canopy shut so heavily I thought it would break, before throttling up and taking off, probably still shaking his head as his wheels left the grass.

This would be the major topic of conversation for days afterwards. Someone in the High Command had decided our pilots should avoid free hunts over England and stay close to the bombers, with so many of both being shot down. A fighter is a hunter relying on speed and surprise, so how ridiculous, but the pressure to change something, anything, was obviously too great.

On 9th September No. 3 Group claimed three Spitfires but lost two pilots in the Channel. That narrow strip of filthy, brown sea was becoming a curse on us all.

13

THE NEXT MORNING I STARTED CAPTAIN VON BONIN'S aeroplane as usual, after Gerhard cranked it up, and taxied it a short distance from the trees, checking the engine and the controls. Between the four of us I spent more time in the cockpit than anyone else, dreaming of becoming a flyer. We all knew how to start them up and shut them down, but none of us had done any more with the 109. I considered these start-ups and short taxis my reward, spending a few minutes imagining I was a fighter pilot.

There'd been issues with the coolant system so I sat with the engine running for a few minutes, idling and revving alternately, to make sure. If it overheated then I knew I'd not done my job. All fiercely proud of our technical ability, none of us ever wanted to let down our pilots.

After releasing the brakes, I turned it ninety degrees so I wouldn't blow away our tents, and checked it again, this time with more power, holding it firmly on the brakes. All was fine.

The captain walked towards me and then stopped, watching for a moment before climbing onto the wing. I throttled back so as not to blow him away, as is the custom, then as I strapped him in he asked, "Have you ever done any flying, Paul?"

I shook my head in surprise.

"You handle my Emil well; you should give it some thought."

What flattery, but I didn't tell him I'd already considered it, though not seriously. Perhaps I should. Hubertus von Bonin was quite a few years old than me and had a fatherly relationship with us. He was keen to get everyone flying; perhaps because his father and both his brothers were air force pilots. It wouldn't have surprised me to find out his mother also flew aeroplanes. But the main reason, of course, was that we'd lost so many pilots, now could be the right time to apply, knowing that he might help.

As autumn progressed, the atmosphere in JG54 changed. We had a custom to put a lighted candle at the dinner table in the place of a missing or deceased colleague, and JG54 were burning far too many. Each pilot almost always had a bottle of schnapps in his possessions, to be opened, and a toast made to the absent friend.

As losses continued, a curious illness circulated among the pilots, known as Channel Sickness, the symptoms being vomiting and chronic loss of appetite. Pilot morale plunged, with most becoming short-tempered and irritable. Stress and fatigue were the cause, but heavy use of alcohol and Pervitin didn't help.

This creeping malaise even affected the aeroplanes; more faults were discovered after take-off, causing pilots to return, problems which miraculously repaired themselves soon after landing.

In an effort to raise morale and unify all the groups in the squadron, the CO, Captain Trautloft, from Thuringia in Weimar, the 'Green Heart of Germany', decided every JG54 aeroplane would display a green heart emblem on the fuselage, so we painted one near every cockpit. Pilots were still permitted their own personal badges, as well as individual squadron insignia, and so JG54 soon became known as the 'Green Hearts', of which we were all very proud.

An incident in September didn't surprise me as much as it did others. A JG54 pilot from No. 3 Group, Lieutenant Hans-Ekkehard Bob brought his E3 back across the Channel with a badly damaged radiator, in a way that I like to think I might also have tried; his damaged engine began overheating so he shut it down completely and allowed it to glide, to cool it down, before restarting, applying power, then shutting it down again, in a bold gamble. Luckily he had almost four thousand metres in hand, so he kept repeating the process and managed to get home safely. What he did seemed obvious to me, as a mechanic, but I'd never been in combat, so I wondered if I'd have the presence of mind and courage to do the same. I made a note and stored it in my head for future reference.

In the last week of September we moved again, this time much further north. We loved our time in France, but the summer had finished, and the invasion of England had been postponed, though no-one had told us as much. I realised I hadn't heard it mentioned for several weeks, like a great idea slowly becoming unfashionable.

Heavy autumnal dew lay on the grass the morning we loaded our vehicles, and it felt like we had finished our summer camp, before perhaps returning to the real world. I found the French countryside particularly enchanting as the rising sun cast a golden glow over the fields and our encampment under the trees. We rolled up our tents and personal belongings, wondering where we'd be when we unpacked them.

For my personal effects I'd acquired an old champagne crate, a sturdy wooden box with rope handles at either end, more aesthetically pleasing than a steel ammunition box, yet still fully functional. I found it one afternoon outside the circus tent and claimed it on the spot. I'd then carved my name and rank into the lid during one of the long hot summer afternoons, and it became a tangible memory of France.

We only left behind the irretrievably damaged aeroplanes and parts, and the airfield remained fully serviceable; we weren't retreating, we hadn't lost any battles, merely moving.

*

JG54 was split up, sent to various bases across Holland and as far north as Denmark, mainly on the coast, to counter the threat from British bombers. I remained with No. 1 Group and Captain von Bonin, ending up at Jever in northern Germany near Wilhelmshaven, after an arduous trip in a long convoy.

Despite the losses, we'd all been happy in France, and as my first proper posting, it remained very special.

This move became the prompting I needed to change my role in the air force. After breakfast on my first full day at Jever, I sought out the adjutant, Lieutenant Otto Kath, and made my formal request. I knew Lieutenant Kath fairly well and had discussed aeroplanes at length with him several times. Without further questioning, he took some papers from his desk drawer, quickly running over them with his pen, ticking and underlining paragraphs here and there, before signing the bottom and indicating for me to follow him.

Despite the fact Captain Trautloft was the CO, and reasonably separate from us mechanics, he knew my name and even addressed me as Paul when we entered his office. He barely looked at my application before signing and thumping it firmly at the bottom with the squadron stamp.

"I am happy to do this for you, but I want you back here with us when you get your pilot's badge, do you understand? That's an order."

I thought he was serious, almost angry, until a smile broke across his face while thrusting out his right hand.

"Come back to us, Paul, so you will continue being an asset to JG54."

"I'll try my best, sir," I replied, flattered, though we all knew it wouldn't be my decision. If successful, I hoped I'd be able to return.

"At least you won't have to travel thousands of kilometres to the east, as I did," he said.

I had no idea what he meant.

"This will be submitted today, with the mail," he added. "It won't take long, I can tell you that."

He was right. Less than three weeks later I received a summons at 1100 hours one bleak October morning. I knocked on his office door and entered, finding the CO and Lieutenant Kath engaged in a loud but good-natured conversation, the CO at his desk and the latter enjoying a comfortable armchair. Voices were raised to compensate for the heavy rain on the wooden roof, and it streamed down the windows as though the guttering was missing.

The rain and low cloud had been incessant for days, flooding our tent twice as our welcome to Jever, and keeping all aeroplanes firmly on the ground, including those of the RAF. Inclement weather could always be counted on to be the greatest peacemaker with fighter pilots.

A coffee pot simmered quietly on a bunker stove in the corner, filling the warm room with a pleasant bistro smell. The CO's pipe, hanging precariously from the left side of his mouth, occasionally produced wispy clouds of sweet blue-grey smoke, adding to the mix. Numerous open books scattered across the desk made it look more like a headmaster's study than a squadron office.

"Sit down, Goetz," he said, warmly, pointing to a luxuriant dining chair, obviously a French souvenir. He took a small bottle of schnapps from his desk drawer and poured three glasses.

"You leave this afternoon, weather permitting," he said, as the three of us each raised a glass to Germany.

I would finally be leaving, and at such short notice.

The buoyant mood wasn't just for me, though, as news had come through that two of our pilots, Captain Dietrich Hrabak of No. 2 Group and Lieutenant Hans Philipp of No. 4 Group, were each to be awarded the Knight's Cross, the first in JG54.

We raised another toast, prompted by the CO.

"Here's to our new dicks, Hrabak and Philipp, I hope they get neck ache!"

They both laughed, as I did, although not entirely sure why.

As I left, the schnapps swirled around in my head, making me elated. I had to pack; I had to tell my comrades, and my parents. How thrilling! In a hasty decision I gave all my Pervitin to my comrades. These things had become an essential part of life, but now I was leaving the front line, no longer working round-the-clock shifts. Even the knowledge I had some with me, sensing their presence in the right-hand trouser pocket, had provided reassurance, but I wouldn't need them any longer, would I?

My comrades took them willingly, questioning my judgment. I shrugged but in my naivety didn't listen.

Two hours later, in a Heinkel 111, my champagne crate of meagre possessions at my feet and kit bag full of uniforms, I was en route to Dortmund and the nearby glider flying school at Schuren.

At last I would become a pilot.

14

Schuren Glider School North Rhine-Westphalia Germany

October 1940

I found the thick canvas sling in the tubular steel seat surprisingly comfortable. Boxes and bags littered the Heinkel, with graffiti on the fuselage walls in black ink, and wires hanging down, so my battered old box fitted in perfectly. The only passenger, and not confined to my seat, I stood up carefully and leaned against the left side of the fuselage, peering out the window.

All I could see was a Jumo V12 in the enormous wing, hauling us south through the grey October sky. The cloud base had been high enough for the aeroplane to stop and pick me up, even though the rain continued and the wheels splashed through deep puddles in the grass, the trailing edge of the wing looking like the lip of a waterfall as we took off.

With no bomb racks of any kind, and no-one at the top dorsal gun, I could see the legs of a man lying prone in the ventral gun position below me. The aeroplane seemed to glide in the air as the undercarriage clunked into place underneath. I crouched down, expecting to see the gunner asleep or perhaps reading a magazine, but he was diligently scanning the sky behind, his right hand fixed on the grip of the MG15, a reminder that we were aboard a fighting aeroplane, and not on a pleasure flight.

I didn't disturb him or any other crewmen and returned to my seat.

Sensing the rise and fall in turbulent air, while watching the ground far below through the murky weather, I realised this was the reason I had joined the air force, to be up there, looking down. Aeroplanes have a magic all their own and I wanted it more than ever. I felt hugely privileged to be on my way to flying school and I imagined sleek high-speed gliders at Schuren, reaching incredible distances and great heights, so I could barely contain my excitement.

Of course, sadness tinged my joy, at leaving my Austrian friends behind: Peter, Johann, and Gerhard, and also Gunter, Karl, and Werner, with whom I'd travelled to France in the Ju88. Many of them were also considering a change, so who knows, I may see them at a flying school, or even if I returned to JG54 as a pilot. Imagine that? How fantastic would that be? I never even considered returning as a failed pilot, back as ground crew, just as I had left.

Many things whizzed around in my head about my time so far in the air force. Apart from a few of the senior officers whose aeroplanes I had maintained, I'd become friends with the younger pilots too, and some I'd never forget.

I'd discussed engines at length with a new NCO pilot from Silesia called Otto Kittel, who shared my fascination for the mechanics of aeroplanes.

"You should go for pilot training, Paul," he'd say to me countless times. "You'd absolutely love it."

Having only recently finished his own flying training, his enthusiasm for aeroplanes was utterly infectious.

The landing at Dortmund was a little bumpy and we shut down near the main hangars, where ground staff began helping the crew unload. This must have been their final destination, and luckily the rain had stopped, so I stood with my box of possessions on the tarmac wondering what to do. After a great flight I felt abandoned, with nowhere to go. The crew, uninterested in my plight, offered no help or advice, their brief being to pick me up and bring me here and nothing more, so with increasing frustration I made my way across the airfield in search of the main gate. I had to get a lift directly to Schuren, or failing that, a bus into Dortmund town and a connection to the flying school. It started raining heavily again, and the poor soul guarding the gate looked as miserable as me.

Luckily, within a few minutes, I hitched a lift in the cab of an air force lorry heading for the town. The rather belligerent driver flatly refused to make a small detour to Schuren, even though it would have been easy, and I began to wonder if everyone I'd encounter would be this unhelpful.

At the bus station I took a local civilian bus towards the airfield, packed with noisy women and children, and found the journey increasingly tiresome. I wanted to shout at the children but somehow managed to control myself. All the windows had steamed up, except for those the children had been drawing on, making a terrible mess.

The bus smelled of wet clothing and damp shoe leather, and I had no clue where we were so I asked the driver, a thick-set man with enormous hands, to drop me as close to the airfield as possible. He grudgingly agreed and ordered me to sit down. How dare he tell me what to do? Did he not realise I was going to be a fighter pilot?

I almost had an argument about his attitude until I realised mine was probably as bad. After twenty minutes the bus pulled over near some forested hills, and the driver shouted so loudly everyone turned to look at me, the only person in uniform. I dragged my possessions down the aisle, forcing a thank-you, before jumping off, as it began raining even harder. The bus immediately turned right down a narrow lane with high hedges both sides and disappeared. I stood by the road, seemingly in the middle of nowhere, the skin on my face tightening as the rain fell horizontally straight at me. I wondered if I could possibly become any more miserable and surprised myself at how low I felt, as though I'd burst into tears at any moment. My hands were shaking too, which I couldn't understand but put down to nerves or excitement. An illogical rage filled me and I was consumed with bitterness.

Trudging along the road, dragging my champagne crate and my heavy kit bag containing no less than six spare uniforms, I chuntered obscenities until I saw a cluster of buildings in the trees at one end of a gently sloping field. It looked vaguely like an airfield, so I picked up my pace, searching for a way in.

The deep rumbling of a powerful engine approached behind me, and the wheels of an enormous five-ton Henschel lorry almost crushed me.

About to wave my fist at the idiot driver, I stopped as he opened the window halfway and shouted, "Schuren?"

I nodded, before running around the other side to climb aboard, dragging my possessions after me, and thanking him profusely. Although immaculate, the huge cab reeked of diesel and engine oil, the way such vehicles do, but at least it was warm and dry.

"You're lucky I'm here, young man," the driver remarked. "We can't have a handsome young chap like you getting soaked, can we?"

I thanked him again, forgetting the fact that I'd wanted to thump him only a few moments before. He was wearing air force overalls, the same rank as me, but much older, probably in his mid-thirties, and by the way he struggled with the hefty double de-clutching, and the enormous steering wheel, clearly unfamiliar with the vehicle.

The engine stretched out far in front of the cab and the vehicle was so wide it filled the road entirely, so nothing could have passed if we'd met oncoming traffic. After two hundred metres we turned sharp left and the buildings became clearer, revealing themselves amongst the trees, through the heavy rain.

A sign at the gate indicated we had arrived at Schuren Gliding School and my driver pulled over outside the largest building.

Three biplanes stood together at the edge of the field with tarpaulin covering the cockpits and weighted ropes tying down the wings. I didn't see any gliders.

My rage had suddenly turned to deep apathy and I didn't want to leave the warmth of the cab, but the driver switched off the engine, turned to me, and smiled. "Here we are then," before jumping out and slamming the door.

He ran to my side, helping me with my things, something he didn't have to do, and I noticed the pilot's badge on his uniform. I was in awe of anyone wearing such a thing.

"My name is Klaus," he said, "Klaus Hager," scowling a little against the rain on his face, now worse than ever, offering me his hand with mild impatience.

"Goetz, Paul Goetz," I replied, shaking it.

"Go in there and find a bed," he ordered, moving off. "I'll see you later."

15

A GROUP OF NEW COMRADES WERE PLAYING CARDS around a glowing bunker stove, and after introductions I found an unoccupied bed where I carefully abandoned my belongings.

I knew I should report to the CO on arrival so, a few moments later, I stood in the corridor of a large wooden building, my uniform dripping puddles around my feet.

Klaus appeared from the commander's office, laughing. He shut the door behind him and put an arm on my shoulder, drawing me away.

"I have to go in there," I protested, to which Klaus shook his head.

"No, you don't, I've told him you're here. Let's get something to eat and you can tell me all about yourself."

The rain had eased so we walked at a more leisurely pace across the finely cut grass towards another wooden building, the dining hall, and wonderful cooking smells.

"You've come from a front-line squadron, is that right?" he said, loading large steaming potatoes onto his enamelled air force plate, followed by meat and vegetables. I did the same, wondering how he knew this much about me, but he didn't wait for a response before continuing. I must have appeared miserable in my soaking uniform because he clearly wanted to cheer me up.

"Don't get disheartened by what you see here at Schuren, Paul. There will be far better aeroplanes for you later, but first you must learn to do what the birds do, just the way they do it."

I nodded without really understanding as we found a table in the increasingly busy dining hall, sitting opposite one another.

"Who was your CO?" he said, tucking into his potatoes.

"Trautloft," I replied, worried he'd choke on his food he looked so shocked.

"The Green Hearts? JG54?"

"Yes, in Holland, briefly, then France, and then at Jever," I replied, pleasantly surprised our new emblem had already become so widely known, but it was the squadron's reputation that was becoming famous, and that of the CO, with everything else following on.

"I knew him," he said, obviously delighted, staring wistfully at the windows, now rapidly fogging over, thanks to all the hot meals and wet coats, as though looking directly into the past. He then caught me by surprise with his next comment: "In Russia."

He could see the puzzlement on my face and in return I saw the pleasure on his at providing an explanation.

"Before the war a few of us learnt to fly over there, right in the middle of nowhere at a place called Lipetsk, between Moscow and Stalingrad. I bet you didn't know this, did you?"

He laughed, with a brief shake of his head. "What a shithole it was too," he said. "But we had no choice, of course, because of the Versailles Treaty."

I suddenly realised.

"He told us he could speak Russian," I said, "but he didn't tell us why."

I stood up to get more food. Loading my plate with meat and potatoes, I realised I was incredibly hungry and couldn't fill my stomach.

When I sat down again he continued, making no comment at my appetite. "We were all sworn to secrecy, obviously, but it's hardly a secret now," he said, shaking his head. He spoke quickly, in a staccato manner, firing his words like bullets from an MG15.

"The airfield was a mini-Germany far from home, and it's amazing how the Russians let us take over as we did, but it was all hush-hush. We didn't wear uniforms, the aeroplanes were all Dutch with Spanish markings, and we had mainly Russian ground crew. It worked really well and we got on with the locals, even though they weren't supposed to socialise with us. In fact, some of the women were very obliging, if that's what you wanted, know what I mean?" He winked.

"We had a lot of fun, but the town… and Voronezh, my God, it was primitive; no running water anywhere, no proper roads, and I never saw one flushing toilet." He cursed in German before uttering a few words in a language I didn't know, presumably Russian, before laughing again.

After finishing our meal, at his invitation, I followed him to his quarters in a separate barrack behind the main buildings. He walked as briskly as he spoke and I had trouble keeping up.

On the narrow, wooden step before the main door, he stopped abruptly, staring at the sky, with one hand on the door handle. I wondered if he'd heard something but then I watched as he followed the clouds with a reverential gaze as though reading a religious text. As if by divine intervention the clouds retreated, patches of blue appeared, and it stopped raining.

He smiled with a nod, as though knowing it would happen.

Pilots in France did this a lot, and it was the first time I realised they have as much respect for the weather as they do their aeroplanes.

Three men inside gave me a warm welcome, as did the huge cast-iron stove in the middle of the room, twice the size of the ordinary bunker stove, with lots of mess tins simmering away on the top.

Someone thrust a glass tumbler into my hand with loud clinking, as a bottle of schnapps made its way around.

Almost obscured in clouds of blue-grey pipe smoke which dispersed a little in the draught from the door, the oldest emerged from the fog, his legs on a stool, as though relaxing at home.

Sweet tobacco smoke competed with the wet dog smell of my woollen uniform, and they offered me a variety of cigarettes. I took one without thinking, as Klaus raised his glass with a shout:"*Nazdrovie!*"

The others laughed.

One shouted,"Damned Ruski," as we repeated the process several times in quick succession.

Very soon I felt quite drunk, while still holding the unlit cigarette.

"So, what's the difference between the Emil and the Friedrich?" one demanded.

The others were looking through their own fog of smoke, so I felt obliged to answer. "Apart from the guns," I retorted, raising my eyebrows, "and the cockpit filled with the breech of the nose cannon?"

Klaus smiled. "Don't bully our young guest, Hans. He's not a mechanic anymore; he's an aviator like us. Isn't that right, Paul?" he said, raising his glass again.

As they all lifted their arms I noticed every one wearing a pilot's badge. It seemed they were all flyers, but more than that, I didn't know it yet, but they were our instructors.

In the next half hour I told them about my war, of the Blenheims attacking the airfield in France, the raid on Bergen, and our mounting losses over the Channel. With much shaking of heads, they looked at one another, eyebrows raised in disbelief.

"They told us that it was the unseasonal poor weather that delayed the invasion of England," Klaus said, frowning and nodding at the other two, Erwin and Gustav, who seemed only a little older than me.

Hans, the oldest, was still ruminating with his pipe, observing, occasionally raising his eyebrows at each of us in turn.

"We heard about losses, but nothing on the scale to which you are describing," Gustav said, with seriousness bordering on solemnity.

Why didn't they know all about this? Surely we were all in the same organisation and so it would have become common knowledge? Perhaps they'd been too busy to read *The Eagle*, but then I remembered I hadn't seen it mentioned in there either. I wondered for a moment if they believed me.

"We'd heard rumours, but now you have confirmed it," Gustav added.

Hans became involved, using his pipe to make his point, aiming it at people with his right hand. "This is just a minor setback!" he shouted. "The Fuhrer is the greatest military tactician in history. Look at what he has achieved in just a few months of war!"

They all spoke quickly, trying to put their own points across with sharp bursts of anger between them as the increasingly heated discussion developed into an argument about tactics and Spitfires.

Klaus shook his head and winked at me as it continued beyond half an hour. He came over and suggested that perhaps we should all turn in. "We have an early start in the morning," he said, as I carefully placed the unlit cigarette into my pocket and left.

In France, and latterly at Jever, it had been easy to wake up under canvas; that's just the way it happens when camping. The wind, the birds, and the partial outdoors nature of it all conspired together. But now in a sprung bed and decent mattress with a building around me, I needed rousing by my new colleagues. I felt extremely tired even though I'd slept well, and wondered for a moment whether I could be coming down with flu or some other problem. My limbs ached so much; I felt feverish, and incredibly apathetic. I had a mild headache from the schnapps the night before, but I'd never felt as bad as this.

Karl, a slightly built Bavarian in the next bed, threw me a pair of goggles. "I arrived yesterday and they gave me two pairs," he said, smiling.

I hadn't yet been issued with anything, so I thanked him and stuffed them in my pocket, dragging my feet like lead weights as we all left for breakfast.

I couldn't fault the food: plenty of fresh bread, eggs, and sausage, with endless mugs of coffee. Despite not feeling well, I returned for extra bread and could still eat more. What on earth could be wrong with me?

16

With little wind, ideal for flying, I hoped I wouldn't puke up my huge breakfast. We assembled in another wooden building, sitting together in a row of folding army chairs. Sunshine streamed in through the windows, warming the room beyond anything the single bunker stove could hope to achieve.

The conversations among our new group of fifteen were muted in apprehensive excitement. Posters of aeroplane wings in cross-section covered the walls, with long lines of arrows striking the black shapes, flowing over the top and underneath. Lift, weight, thrust, and drag: the universal principles of flight.

An officer in full uniform strode in, so we all stood up instinctively. He told us to sit, and gave us the usual welcome, informal and friendly, as Klaus, Hans, Erwin, and Gustav arrived.

After only a few minutes the officer nodded to Klaus, before departing with no shouting, heel-clicking, or Hitler salutes. We didn't even stand up.

Klaus revealed a blackboard and drew various shapes, similar to the pictures on the walls.

I had a burning question which I fired at him at the first opportunity. "If an aeroplane needs thrust to work against the drag," I said, "then where does a glider get its power from, without an engine?"

"Good question," he said, smiling. "The answer, of course, is the weight. Unlike a powered aeroplane, a glider is almost always descending, with its nose below the horizon, unless picking up a thermal or an up-current of air, so the weight is the thrust."

I think I understood this, but I could see blank looks amongst my comrades.

Hans sat at the front, facing us, and lit his pipe.

Someone asked how an aeroplane wing creates lift and so, with a nod from Klaus, Hans reached up to the lectern and took a sheet of paper. He turned in his chair so that we saw him from the side, then he took a long draw on his pipe and, holding the sheet of paper in front of his face with the fingers and thumbs of both hands, he blew thick tobacco smoke over the top of the paper. As if by magic, it rose, the smoke flowing quickly over the top surface, before twisting away in spirals off the end of the paper. As his breath slowly ran out, the paper dropped again. I'd never seen a clearer demonstration of lift on an aeroplane wing.

A ripple of applause followed, Hans acknowledging the audience with a gentle nod, almost a bow, before smiling at Klaus.

Like a lot of theory, it's always better understood in practice, when such things as sink rates, pitch, yaw, and roll can be experienced for real. I was relieved when we broke for coffee in the afternoon and didn't return to the classroom.

We were divided into four groups, seemingly at random, with me in Klaus's group.

Led to the biggest hangar, we helped to haul the doors open. A wooden crate stood near the door, full of miscellaneous equipment, and we huddled around, picking up helmets, gloves, and goggles. We each took a new book from a pile on the table and signed for it, the most important book a pilot could possess: the logbook.

Stuffing mine into my coat, I put something on my head that resembled a black leather plant pot and slipped on some gloves which were badly frayed around the wrist. Then we were led over to the back of the hangar, an area of jumbled tubular steel, wood planks, and wing shapes covered in stretched canvas.

What on earth are these contraptions? I thought. Thankfully next to these were four recognisable shapes: two seat gliders.

Each group took hold of a glider and pulled them outside onto the grass, in line abreast, as two of the biplanes which I recognised as Fw44s, were started up and began trundling across the field. How wonderful it felt to be out in the fresh air, as whenever I sat down for any length of time, I almost fell asleep. I still wondered if I could be getting a dose of influenza, as I kept alternately sweating and shivering.

Discussions followed, with nodding glances towards us, before Klaus sat in the back of the first glider, instructing me to sit in the front.

"Put your hands and feet on the controls, but I'm in charge until I say otherwise, alright?" Klaus said.

"Understood, Mr Hager," I shouted back rather abruptly.

Someone attached a cable to a hook underneath, and as the biplane fifty metres in front moved, it immediately took up the slack. We were tugged along the grass quite jerkily at first, but then smoother and at ever-increasing speed. Almost at the same moment as the biplane's wheels lifted from the grass we became airborne.

Climbing rapidly, we flew straight forward, ever higher, for about a kilometre before I heard a bang from underneath, as the cable released and fell away.

The biplane turned 180 degrees, dropping almost vertically towards the airfield, the cable flailing around behind like the lead on an errant dog.

Silence reigned, except for the rushing of air around my head and over the airframe. The nose had settled a few centimetres below the horizon and remained there, after rising suddenly on the cable release.

"What do you think?" was the first shout from behind.

"Fantastic!" was the only thought in my head.

The Grunau's open cockpit had a small Perspex windscreen in front, with the instrument panel missing. What on earth? No familiar references: magneto switches, fuel gauge, oil temperature and pressure gauges, booster pump switches, RPM gauge, all missing; but then I noticed a tiny altimeter and an ASI, airspeed indicator, looking particularly lonely, sitting together like orphan twins just under the windscreen.

It's a glider, I said to myself.

But this didn't help because the instruments remaining were the ones I'd never used before. A length of string, five centimetres long, flapped about on the nose in front, telling me wind strength and direction: primitive but effective.

From sheer habit my eyes remained inside the cockpit, ignoring the outside until the next shout from behind: "Look where we are, keep a track of where we are going!"

I realised too late that the airfield had disappeared. Turning left, descending all the time, I wondered how we would find it and what would happen if we ran out of height. Not panic as such, more a sense of happy bewilderment.

We couldn't apply power to give us a quick burst of height. Thinking of Hans-Ekkehard Bob's rollercoaster flight back across the channel in his 109, I now marvelled at his achievement. I realised this was like chess; you must anticipate every move long before it happened, because there's no second chance.

When we turned left again, as if by a miracle, I saw the airfield ahead and we descended quicker. I felt a clunk as something was pulled, and the glider fell as we aimed for the end of the field.

A shout came from behind: "Air brakes!" as the nose remained in the same place on the horizon, until a few metres above the field, when we levelled out and touched down with a gentle bump, bouncing along at speed, until we stopped and the right wing sank slowly onto the grass.

Klaus broke the silence. "Enjoy that?"

It had all happened too quickly, just a few minutes, and so I didn't know what to say, simply replying with, "Can we do it again, Mr Hager?"

He laughed, slapping the canvas side of the glider with his right hand before replying. "Yes, of course, but for God's sake call me Klaus, alright? I'm not an officer and we are the same rank, after all."

I nodded, my head swirling with information. I thought I'd have absolutely no chance taking everything in, and I'd be sent back as a failure or even worse, to a flak unit.

A tractor appeared and towed us back to the threshold area. We were hooked on and bounded along the grass, and up again. I pulled the cable release toggle this time when I saw we were three hundred metres above the far end of the field.

The next time we were dragged into the air, I flew the take-off, the cable release, and most of the circuit. After that I landed it, using the air brakes, which popped out the top of the wings, causing us to drop so dramatically. From then on I did everything, in between corrections and shouts of derision from behind.

I didn't want to stop being dragged skyward, until the early winter darkness prevented us from doing any more. At the end of my first flying day, utterly exhausted and after an enormous meal, I slept for twelve hours solid.

17

CLASSROOM WORK FOLLOWED ALL THE NEXT DAY, during which I struggled to stay awake, even in the cold room. On the third day I realised I had finally recovered from the flu, or whatever had taken hold of me. Thankfully my energy had returned to normal, and it hadn't developed into anything more serious. Recent inexplicable feelings of anxiety had disappeared too, making me much calmer.

We flew the two-seat gliders in circuits around the airfield with the instructors, until the landmarks and turning points became automatic. Schuren was perched on higher ground, surrounded by woods, and occasionally the wind would grab hold of the aeroplane and push it down, or conversely hurl us upwards.

Every time this happened Klaus would yell, "Feel that? *Feel* the aeroplane in the sky, *feel* how it moves and how the air acts on it. It's no different in a fighter, so understand these principles and how it works."

We'd translate all these experiences into the classroom, and how the control surfaces change the airflow over the aeroplane.

A few days of heavy freezing rain and strong winds prevented our flying until a fine, frosty November morning when we were formally introduced to the odd bits of tubular steel and wood in the hangar. We hauled out one of the contraptions referred to as a Grunau 9, made by the same manufacturer as the larger two-seat glider, and the next thing I would be flying. It looked like something a group of children had made for a school project one rainy afternoon. I saw only one seat, if you could call it that. The time had come for us to fly our first solo, clearly too dangerous to risk the loss of a proper glider!

This winged beam of wood had no instruments and my body formed most of the nose and all the weight. Until I saw a cable hook at the front, I wondered if I should run with it strapped to my back and jump off the nearest cliff. There were what appeared to be rudder pedals and a control column, and I could see where the cables ran to the control surfaces, if you could call them that.

We had to move a hundred metres to the side, away from the main grass strip, where I sat down and strapped in.

Klaus stood nearby, waving at someone down the airfield about three hundred metres away, dragging something towards us. "It's just the same, Paul, but you won't get anywhere near as high as with a tow, probably two hundred metres or so, if you're lucky. Stay over the airfield in a shorter circuit and land back here. Remember to cut it short, always close to the field, keeping an eye out for your height. You'll be fine, you know exactly what to do. Enjoy it."

The Grunau 9 was held steady by several people before, to my astonishment, they hooked me up to an enormous rubber band suspended between two distant posts. I was being launched into the air by catapult!

Someone shouted at me, "Ready?"

I nodded and yelled back. I couldn't change my mind even if I wanted to.

Hurled forwards, I skimmed across the grass at great speed, becoming airborne within a few seconds, rising so steeply my head hit the frame behind my seat. The rush of cold air briefly took my breath away, but thankfully I was wearing a hat and gloves as well as my greatcoat. With no cable release, the elastic chord simply fell away when perpendicular to the ground.

Reality can never match a description. I settled with my feet just below the horizon, turning left, sailing down the length of the airfield so close to the roof of the dining hall I feared I'd never make it: ending my days smashing through the wall of the CO's office. What an ignominious end to my flying career, crashing through his window and impaling him onto the back wall behind his desk.

Somehow still in the air, I made a gentle turn back towards the field, in preparation for landing. Klaus had been right; I doubt I'd been higher than 150 metres. This insane contraption was as much a test of nerve as flying skills.

With no air brakes, the Grunau 9 had to be flown right down onto the ground. Aided by a prevailing ice-cold headwind, I reached the end of the field with about ten metres to spare. The padded seat didn't feel very thick as I thumped down hard on the frozen grass.

Eventually skidding to a halt, to my surprise I couldn't stop laughing, really deep, heaving laughs, so powerful I almost choked. Everyone must have heard. It was a mixture of relief and pure enjoyment. I'd been so used to sitting in 109s and now I'd flown my first solo, astride a string-bag contraption that looked like the earliest aeroplane ever made.

Before I could say anything, I felt my glider being hauled back a hundred metres, hooked up again and slung back into the air, with me laughing all the way: real, basic flying that I'd never forget.

I don't know how many flights I had in this wonderfully dangerous contraption, probably hundreds. I recorded most in my logbook, and on some afternoons, a small group remained behind with Klaus and Hans, to stretch the day as much as possible, slinging one another airborne every few minutes with some highly unofficial flying. What fabulous fun.

Though I never gave it any serious thought, it wasn't without risk. Sadly I was first on the scene when a fellow student, Franz, appeared to misjudge his approach and hit the ground hard, digging the distorted frame of the glider deep into the grass. Some of the timber had snapped on impact, sticking in his body in various places. Both his feet were hanging by skin, his throat open at the neck with an odd pale-yellow tube clearly visible, though no bleeding. Astonishingly his eyes opened. Because he'd been a doctor in civilian life he told us what we should do to alleviate his pain. As others arrived I held onto his feet and immediately regretted it when one came off in my hand.

He died when lifted onto a stretcher, next to the wreckage of the glider.

Klaus later told me he believed Franz had been caught in a phenomenon called wind shear: a huge rolling wave of air that, by chance, swirled around at the end of the field as he passed through it, pushing him unavoidably into the ground.

That afternoon a cold front hurtled in from the east, with freezing rain and strong winds putting a stop to everything.

We then had much more ground school, mainly in meteorology, learning to read the sky as well as complex weather charts, along with technical aerodynamics. We had fewer trips in both types of glider, but as autumn turned to winter the flying inevitably became less frequent anyway. Gliders are obviously more susceptible to poor weather, particularly strong wind.

As Christmas approached we did very little flying. On these quiet days we occasionally left the airfield and took the bus into Dortmund, where we'd sometimes meet local girls. Perhaps they were used to seeing trainee pilots, but we rarely saw the same girls twice, and when we did, they didn't seem very interested in us. I suspect we probably behaved in such an arrogant manner we put them off.

I wrote letters home, and to Inge, spending a lot of time with Klaus and the other instructors in their barrack.

Klaus even offered me a bed next to his, but I declined. I didn't want to miss the activity with my fellow students.

Our instructors had all flown 109s in combat at various squadrons, and a host of other aeroplanes, before being selected to teach at Schuren. They told the usual flying stories experienced pilots will always tell you: miraculous crosswind landings, lucky escapes, bad weather, fantastic navigation, brilliant flights, and comparisons in performance between aeroplanes. I joined in with some of it, mainly the technical aspects regarding the engines, which they were keen to hear, but I was still very much a novice.

On one such evening in their quarters, after Erwin had lit his pipe, he leaned forwards, offering me something in his left hand, a small packet I immediately recognised as Pervitin. I took it, holding it in both hands. The others looked on in silence as I realised I hadn't taken any for weeks, since before I'd left Jever, so I handed it back, thanking him.

"That's fine," he said, slipping the unopened tube into his pocket. "You've done well. I presume you were taking them in France? We still use them," he groaned, looking around at the others, nodding in sympathy. "It's difficult to stop when you've been used to it as long as we have. The tiredness, the hunger, the aches and pains, not to mention the mood swings – they are too much to bear if you come off them, so it's easier to carry on."

We then raised our glasses to the war and our ultimate victory, with Pervitin never discussed again.

18

Everyone spoke about the war, particularly after the 16th December 1940, when the British bombed the German city of Manheim, killing dozens of civilians, and destroying houses and schools. We heard about this despicable act on state radio and it angered us all. More than anything we wondered why our night fighters hadn't intercepted them.

Reprisals by our air force followed with raids on Liverpool and London. Surely the British would now come to their senses and seek an armistice? If they did, we all agreed the war would be over very quickly. Our government repeatedly offered an olive branch, but they consistently refused to make peace. I had no idea the British were such aggressive people. But of course they had a huge Empire, which meant they had conquered millions by force of arms.

I kept in touch with friends in JG54, mainly the Austrians with whom I'd shared the tent in France: Peter, Johann, and

Gerhard. December was a quiet time for them because large-scale fighter operations over the Channel had paused, and a lot of pilots were away on leave, most of them skiing at Kitzbuhl, so they told me.

Here at Schuren, we cut down a three-metre pine and dragged it into the dining hall. The day before Christmas Eve many of us were granted leave to return home for a few days.

As a non-operational member of the air force, a man between jobs, neither ground crew nor pilot, for the moment I was essential but unused, like an understudy waiting to perform.

After breakfast I packed a small bag, buttoned the collar of my greatcoat to the neck and set off in freezing rain with a group of comrades to jump on the first bus we came across. The huge, grumpy driver was the same man who had dropped me off months before.

On the long unremarkable train journey home from Dortmund everyone seemed to be in uniform, the whole country mobilised.

My mother hugged me. "You've changed; you look much older," she said, "and tired-looking."

We forget our parents know us better than we do ourselves.

In return they were smaller and frailer, though I didn't tell them.

Home seemed more cluttered than I remembered, and my father particularly cheerful, smiling more than usual. He told me the newsreels were full of optimism and the war would soon be over, once England had been subdued in the coming year. I nodded in agreement, sincerely hoping him to be right. He gratefully accepted the cigarettes I'd saved for him, and still couldn't understand how and why I didn't smoke.

We didn't discuss the fine details of what I'd been doing. I didn't tell them about the Pervitin that I and everyone else had been addicted to for months, despite the fact that some of my comrades were supplied by their parents, who sent them packets from home. Neither did I mention the scale of our losses in France, of which they were clearly unaware. I convinced myself that it was not for the public to be informed of such operational matters. I simply told them how much I enjoyed flying, the details of my first solo flight, and my anticipation of the next stage. I could only stay two nights before my return to Schuren, where I hoped my posting orders would soon come through.

*

We had a party, of sorts, on a bitterly cold mid-January night before I left Schuren for good. Our instructors, Klaus, Hans, Erwin, and Gustav, stormed into our barrack, each one holding a bottle of schnapps, as we toasted one another extravagantly, ruthlessly taking the mickey out of everyone present, the way men do.

Taking it in turns, we each stood in the middle of the room near the stove to make a short speech or tell a joke or funny story, so I told them about how I couldn't stop laughing all through my first flight in the string-bag Grunau 9. To my astonishment most of the others said they had been exactly the same.

All fourteen of us survivors would soon be leaving, so marking our departure was important. These were happy days, some of the very best; by comparison to what was coming, they were wonderful.

Klaus and I would meet again years later in the most awful circumstances, but for now, none of us had any idea such a dreadful fate lay ahead.

At Quakenbruck, the home of Pilot Training Regiment 82, I arrived as an NCO trainee, one of the people I'd seen during my basic training while rolling around in the mud. I'd been promoted to Acting Corporal, which didn't mean a lot, other than no guard duty at night for a while, and I had to stitch my V-shaped stripe onto the arms of my uniform.

The accommodation was a little less basic, and after two days other keen, young men like me arrived, some of whom had been at Schuren with me: Walter, Ernst, and Rolf.

We began flying the next day, straight after breakfast and an informal handshake with the instructor. Walking across the grass, we exchanged names, before Sergeant Armin Scholl threw me a leather flying helmet.

"Get in," he shouted, before climbing aboard the nearest aeroplane, followed by, "strap in, tight."

Shaking with cold and excitement, I lowered myself into the front seat of the Arado AR66 biplane. Familiar with the start-up procedure, although much quicker than a 109, I placed my hands and feet lightly on the controls, as instructed.

Aeroplanes are all pretty similar, so we checked the engine temperatures and pressures as it warmed up, then the controls to ensure full and free movement, before gently applying full throttle.

Bouncing along the grass, we were airborne quickly, climbing ever higher into the bleak January grey. Levelling off at a thousand metres, below the cloud base, without saying a word, we banked hard over to the right and kept on turning until completely inverted. My entire body hung on the shoulder straps and, when I looked up, the airfield was above us.

Heading straight for the ground, we then pulled up vertically, throttling back, standing still in the air, before the left wings dropped and we began spinning earthward ever faster like a sycamore seed from the highest branch. We then climbed back up to a thousand metres, repeating the process.

This continued for thirty minutes.

I couldn't say why; perhaps he was trying to kill me. Maybe it was meant to frighten the pupil into screaming for mercy and applying for a flak unit, but not me. I wanted more, and to do it for myself.

We landed and he shut down the engine.

Sergeant Scholl unstrapped and climbed out, not saying a word, so I followed. I wondered if I'd upset him in some way.

He stood near the aeroplane, smiling, lighting a cigarette, and waiting. He was well built and I suppose handsome, with a fresh complexion which stood out above the whiteness of his silk scarf.

While trying hard to appear adult, I sensed my nose running thanks to the icy wind, with a drip that was about to fall, so I touched it with my glove.

"Come," he said, leading the way to the dispersal hut.

I warmed my hands in front of the huge stove, glowing bright red like my face a few seconds later. An enormous woman, probably my mother's age, served hot drinks as Sergeant Scholl put an arm around her vast waist, kissing her on the cheek.

She giggled.

Then he turned to me. "Too many times I reached the aerobatic stage to be showered in puke, so I wanted to check," he said, handing me a coffee. "I'd spend a week up there teaching, only to find the first time we did any real flying they'd decide it wasn't for them and they'd piss off," he said, still serious.

I laughed. "You're safe with me," I said, smiling.

"Not that puking is always the sign of a bad pilot; it isn't," he said, "but when they get to a month into the process and they are still handling the aeroplane like they're wrestling it into submission, then there's something not right. You get so you can tell, when you see as many as I do."

"I don't blame you," I replied, taking a sip, watching him closely as he leaned forward, looking outside.

Our aeroplane waited a hundred metres away, calling us back, with plenty of fuel in the tank.

After I'd finished my coffee, my instructor shrugged, looked at me and then outside. "Do you know how to start it?" he asked.

With probably the widest smile he'd ever seen I nodded.

"Then go out there and get on with it while I talk to Hanna." He winked at her.

She giggled again.

"I'll join you when I've finished."

This time, determined to impress, I walked around the aeroplane, checked the control surfaces and engine oil, making sure he could see me, before climbing aboard and strapping in.

19

The engine started without a problem, being still a touch warm and much simpler than a 109.

Sergeant Scholl jumped onto the wing, so I eased the throttle back as he climbed in.

"Left-hand circuits at 350 metres," he shouted, tapping me on the shoulder. "You do everything unless I tell you otherwise."

After releasing the brakes, I taxied to the end of the field, and we took off.

Ten minutes later I landed it, a little bouncy, with too many adjustments of the throttle, but it was safe, and I grinned with pride. I'd done it all.

We repeated this several times until freezing rain and low cloud stopped all flying. Used to a powered aeroplane on the ground, and a glider in the air, I merely combined the two.

That night it took me a while to get to sleep, reliving this fantastic day in my head a hundred times.

We did the same the next day, and the day after, and one morning, as we climbed through two hundred metres while still taking off, I heard a shout from behind: "Your engine has failed – what you are going to do?"

Sergeant Scholl closed the throttle completely, so I sprang into emergency mode: nose down, set the glide speed, and pick a suitable field to land. Once established in the glide he tapped my shoulder and I applied full throttle again. We were told never to attempt turning back towards the airfield, as there wouldn't be enough height to do so safely, despite that being the most natural temptation.

I always imagined taking a powered aeroplane up on my own would be a momentous occasion, but my first solo in the Ar66 was an oddly routine event. I'm not saying I didn't find it exciting, it certainly was, but it felt natural. Besides, I'd already been up on my own in the Grunau 9 which, on reflection, had thrilled me just as much.

After a perfect circuit I landed, still a little bumpy but alright. As I taxied towards dispersal Sergeant Scholl indicated for me to do another, so I happily obliged. After a better landing I taxied to the hut and shut it down.

Sergeant Scholl grabbed my hand, shaking it warmly. "Well done, young man," he said, "you are now a real flyer."

The Ar66 became so familiar that I almost heaved a sigh of relief when given an Ar68 instead. Also a biplane, and darkly camouflaged, it appeared more war-like, but much more than this, it was armed. Although not involved in any shooting yet, I couldn't help feeling that guns transformed an aeroplane into something entirely different.

With so many different types at our disposal, we could try as many as we wanted. As new pilots, we learnt a lot about adaptability, perhaps the intention. In the next few weeks I flew a Gotha Go145, an old Heinkel He51 single-seater, and a Henschel Hs123, all very similar.

Our navigation was tested with ever longer trips and landings at many different airfields, both solo and with an instructor.

Now on first-name terms, Armin and I discussed aeroplanes and tactics, and at any time while flying he would still occasionally shout, "Paul, your engine has failed," after closing the throttle.

At some of the many airfields we'd stay for a few hours chatting to staff in the canteens; it seemed Armin knew everyone, particularly the ladies.

Encouraged to practise engine failures on our own, I did so frequently. On one occasion I made it so real I briefly touched down in a field, startling the life out of a farmer and his horse, before reapplying full power and climbing away. I could see him shouting, waving his fist, so I turned around and did it again, while pretending to shoot him to pieces. What fun.

Flying around the country in my own aeroplane, as though entirely alone in the world, it never occurred to me that an enemy might want to shoot me down.

After the A2 training stage, the B1 and B2 followed, with instruments and more of the real flying, aerobatics. Not just for fun, of course; you gained a thorough understanding of how an aeroplane behaved in high-stress manoeuvres, and I thoroughly enjoyed every moment.

I found night flying challenging, like learning to fly all over again. So naïve; I hadn't realised this would be as important.

Almost as a formality, while busy enjoying my flying, I gained my pilot's licence. What a wonderful document, bearing a photograph of my smiling face and the stamp of

Pilot Training Regiment 82; everything I'd been working for. I'd achieved my dream, but suddenly I wanted more. How ungrateful.

I wrote to my parents, and a week later they replied, with my mother repeating several times how proud my father was. Wondering when I'd see them again, I pictured them at home, reading my letter.

In April I said goodbye to Armin and the others when I moved to Fighter Training School Number 1 at Werneuchen near Berlin, hitching a lift in an Arado Ar96, a monoplane trainer. I'd get to know this aeroplane incredibly well in the next few months.

Some of my comrades from Schuren were now at bomber bases, and only Rolf came with me to Werneuchen.

"You've been promoted to full corporal," said the adjutant on my arrival.

What a pleasant surprise.

We were accommodated in a smaller barrack with just two others, in another step up. That evening a group of us were welcomed to the base by the commander, Colonel Theodor Osterkamp, a thin-faced, highly decorated veteran of the Great War. He spoke with fatherly warmth, as though we were his grandchildren.

Proudly wearing my pilot's badge, I sewed the new double stripes on my sleeves, sending the old ones to my parents with the good news.

Flying became more serious as we flew the Ar96 in groups of four, learning the dynamics of formation flying, then the Bucker Bu181, and Bu131, both monoplanes with enclosed cockpits and side-by-side seats, rather than behind one another. This was better for communicating with the instructor, so more popular, and for the first time, we used an aircraft radio, or R/T.

My next treat was to fly one of several old Fw44s, the type that had towed the gliders at Schuren: a lovely aeroplane to fly, I used any excuse to take one up, and wished I could return to Schuren to help out launching their gliders!

We started gunnery practice, which I loved, and continually amazed myself that I could hit the paper targets only a metre and a half wide, plus lines of scrap vehicles, as I roared overhead at twenty metres. My aeroplane became my weapon, but I still only fired at empty objects and paper. I didn't think about combat situations when the target would have a man inside it. We didn't discuss this at all.

*

The RAF had become a lot quieter since we'd subdued them the previous summer. With no more large-scale daytime engagements, as the spring days of 1941 lengthened, we wondered when the delayed invasion of England would begin.

We'd just taken Crete to add to most of Europe, so everything seemed very much in our favour. We still thought the British would seek an armistice as surely they had no choice, and the war would quietly end.

Happy, secure, and prosperous, Europe's citizens lived in a community of nations under strong German order, with life returning to normal now hostilities in our new territories had ceased.

But in June a lot of squadrons began moving around the country, filling the skies in huge numbers like migrating birds. I heard JG54 were on the move again, the entire fighter wing, according to letters from my old friends, but they didn't tell me where, despite writing with great excitement.

Major roads everywhere seemed constantly filled with long columns of vehicles, troops, and armour, and all kinds of military equipment jammed the rail network. We could find only one common factor in all this movement: everything was heading east.

20

Rumours are common in the air force. We heard a great many about this build-up, the most persistent being the most logical: we had a non-aggression pact with Russia so we assumed they would allow us to pass through their territory so we could attack the British in Iraq, and ultimately take the oil fields and the Suez Canal. This made a lot of sense.

We all have days when we remember exactly where we were and what we were doing when a momentous event occurs.

On the morning of 22nd June 1941 I was alone in a summer sky with just fair-weather cumulus for company, three thousand metres above Berlin. The view of the ground from an Fw56 is superb, and I was trying unsuccessfully to take photographs with my new Agfa Isolette, later writing in my logbook 'Familiarisation on type' as an excuse for the trip.

Only when I landed did I find out. Like most people, I was firstly surprised and then shocked.

What about the treaty with Russia?

Comrades in our air force were now bombing Russian airfields and cities from Leningrad to Crimea as Operation Barbarossa began.

"Self-defence," said the adjutant when we asked why. "The Red Army has been poised to attack in huge numbers. Their troops have been massing in Poland, so we had to act."

Although angered that it had to happen, we couldn't help being concerned. After all, the Soviet Union was a huge country. But areas such as Ukraine could provide Germany with much needed wheat and other crops, and general lebensraum or living space for our people.

With the British still hostile in the west, we were now operating on two fronts, as well as in North Africa, but our leaders assured us of a speedy victory, stating our flag would be flying above the Kremlin by Christmas.

But what happened to the invasion of England? Had it been cancelled altogether?

This was still possible later, because the Red Army was nothing more than a badly led, poorly equipped rabble of peasant farmers. As the first few days passed and the speed of our conquest was clear, this proved to be true, and any concerns disappeared.

The newsreels showed thousands of scruffy, dejected Russians shuffling into captivity, and it seemed the East really was populated by Bolshevik simpletons with no brains or stomach for fighting. We were told this repeatedly, and now the newsreels proved it.

*

Apart from these astonishing events, I particularly enjoyed the last week of June. After some brilliant flights in a two-seat

Me108, my instructor gave me the best news.

"You're now capable of flying solo in a 109."

I couldn't believe it.

Parked near the edge of the grass on the concrete stood a 109 E1 with the DB601 engine I knew so well. Obviously an old machine, it had no personal markings or badges of any sort, but to me it looked wonderful.

Max, my latest instructor, stood on the wing holding the crank as I lowered myself inside. As soon as I settled into the seat the aeroplane felt as though it had been specially made for me. I'd been in so many 109s, but this was entirely different. I remembered the happy days in France and even earlier at the Daimler-Benz factory, and it all seemed so very long ago and such a lengthy process to get here.

Max cranked the inertia wheel and I engaged the starter. He jumped down as the engine fired. I gave a thumbs-up before closing the canopy. Checking the temperatures and pressures, the magnetos, and fuel, I gave it a few moments to warm up before releasing the brakes. I turned on the radio to listen out for traffic before taxiing to the end of the field. Ten degrees of flap and a final check on the engine and controls.

All set.

As I slowly applied full throttle, within a few seconds the wheels lifted off. All the aeroplanes I'd flown up until then had been trainers, many quite elderly biplanes, and so this was something entirely different. After stowing the undercarriage and flaps, I turned left in a gentle fifteen-degree bank in the circuit, and then again onto the downwind leg. I lowered the undercarriage, giving myself a few hundred extra metres, before I turned into the base leg with the field on my left. At such low RPM the DB601 merely hummed quietly, almost idling, like a tiger yearning for release. With a slightly longer final approach, I lowered the flaps for landing, as the automatic leading-edge slats appeared, and I touched down with the gentlest bump.

I'd flown a 109!

I pulled over and sat with the engine running as Max jumped up onto the wing. "Do another circuit, and if there aren't any problems take it up for some general handling, but come back within an hour."

I nodded in a very casual, understated manner, completely disguising my excitement, turned the aeroplane around, and took off.

After the next circuit I kept the throttle almost wide open in a climbing orbit until I reached four thousand metres above Werneuchen.

The handling, responsiveness, and power were breathtaking, and I hurled the aeroplane around through a variety of manoeuvres, comparing it with everything else I'd flown so far.

Nothing came close.

I wanted to stay up there all day, dodging the clouds and performing aerobatics.

After forty-five minutes I brought it back, writing my first 109 flights in my logbook with the entry proudly entitled 'Type conversion – Messerschmitt 109', the first of so many with that aeroplane.

We never really get the opportunity to take a step back from the busiest times in our lives to fully appreciate what we are doing, but I did on this occasion.

After shutting down the engine, I opened the canopy and climbed out. Walking across the grass, I looked back as the Werneuchen ground crew took over. I found Max in the crew room where he countersigned my logbook before handing me a small bottle of schnapps.

"Enjoy that?" he said, smiling, watching me take a few long gulps.

"My first hour and a half on a 109," I said, handing back the bottle. "Absolutely fantastic."

From then on, with continued exciting news from Russia, our training accelerated, becoming more aggressive.

As my handling of the 109 improved, we practised shooting at targets in the air, and a variety on the ground. My accuracy improved and I handled the 109 as well in the air as on the ground as a mechanic. I had huge confidence in this aeroplane, as we all did, and we couldn't wait to try it out for real. We practised extreme low flying, not once thinking of the danger.

Newsreels showed grateful citizens lining the roads in the Baltic States and Ukraine, embracing our soldiers, handing them gifts and flowers, pleased to be liberated from the Soviets. This even happened in Russia, as our forces yet again swept away everything before them.

The fantastic summer made it all easy, of course, and on one of the hottest days in August, the adjutant pinned up the postings list on the noticeboard.

I hoped for France, to return as a fighter pilot, but was only slightly disappointed to be given an operational training wing of No. 3 Squadron, at Bergen in Holland, another airfield I'd known before. My first thought was the air raid I'd been caught up in, and so the likelihood of encountering RAF aeroplanes seemed high. I had a very brief flash of nervous excitement.

21

Bergen would be my home for the next three months, flying 109s on combat training patrols, as an introduction to operational life before my first proper combat post. After the usual goodbyes to Max and the others, I flew there in a Bucker Bu181, the pilot allowing me to fly it most of the way so I could practise my navigation. I had forgotten just how near the sea Bergen lay, and as the Bu181 turned around and took off again I noticed the airfield had been rebuilt and expanded.

The adjutant, now a man called Bauer, greeted me. "Be at the briefing in the morning, prompt, and ready to fly."

I saw Captain Wernitz, who first issued me the Pervitin, leaving the CO's office lighting a cigarette, cupping his hands against the sea breeze. At least for now, I decided not to become one of his regular customers.

After my first meal, I played cards with my new comrades. Further news came through on the forces radio of our latest successes; we were marching across Russia at incredible speed and we'd definitely be in Moscow by Christmas. By the time any of us arrived, we would merely be engaged in a policing role, after the war was won. Perhaps then, with Russia subdued, the British really would sue for peace, because if they didn't, all our efforts could be concentrated to force it on them.

In between heated debates about the war I won the first few card games but then lost the rest, as though my new friends had been luring me in to lose fifty pfennigs in every game.

Roused at 0600 hours, with three others, our flight commander, a lieutenant, briefed us in the dispersal hut. Maps of the Dutch coast were pinned all around the walls and he gave me a personal copy. "Today we will patrol the coast fifty kilometres in each direction. You are my Katschmarek, Goetz; we don't expect any Indians this morning, but stay close, alright?"

I nodded.

Straight into the slang terms which thankfully I understood, as I'd heard them used frequently by pilots in JG54; *Katschmarek* sounded Polish, but here it meant 'wingman', and 'Indians' meant enemy fighters.

After breakfast two of the ground crew started my aeroplane, an E3, and then helped strap me in. Judging by the paint chipped around the gun button and other controls, it had obviously been around for a while.

As I checked the engine and the controls I thought, *This is it. This is the beginning. I could face the enemy today.*

I checked my oxygen, turned on the radio, and closed the canopy. My hands were shaking. With a strong breeze coming in from the sea, we taxied to the bottom end of the field before turning to face it. With full power, we trundled across the grass in pairs. Wheels up, hanging on to the lieutenant's right wing in a climbing turn north, we followed the coastline at a thousand metres.

So far so good, I thought.

After ten minutes we turned out to sea, then down the coast, passing Bergen and flying further south, turning back after ten minutes. We did this three times before flying inland in preparation for landing. We touched down in pairs and shut down our engines, my first routine coastal patrol completed.

My experiences in France should have told me what to expect as a pilot, but I had often been too busy to notice, with my head stuck under the engine cowling of a 109. However, as pilots, we spent the next few hours reading newspapers, listening to the radio, and playing cards. Some of my colleagues were excellent skat players, so I became wary of playing for money.

Despite being on the front line, nothing happened all that first day, and I felt an odd mix of relief and disappointment. I wanted my first engagement with the enemy for several reasons; I needed to know how it would be, of course, but more importantly how would I cope? You can never tell these things until they actually happen.

The next day, we flew the same uneventful routine patrol in the morning.

On my third day in the early afternoon, the air was filled with the sound of DB601s starting up, as the alarm sounded.

Enemy aeroplanes had been sighted heading our way; our group were on standby, so we strapped in and took off.

Flying straight out over the water, I saw a single aeroplane, a twin-engined bomber, definitely not one of ours, heading due west at about six hundred metres. I shouted rather too excitedly over the R/T, thrilled that I'd seen it first as we turned towards it at speed.

"Well spotted, Goetz," the lieutenant replied over the R/T. "It's a Wellington. Let's get him!"

22

Tracer bullets arced towards us from the rear gunner's turret as the pilot banked the Wellington hard to the south-west. No doubt there'd be panic among the crew on seeing 109s fast approaching, hence the turn towards low cloud.

My lieutenant fired as soon as we came to within a few hundred metres, so I did the same, more in hope than expectation. To my surprise the right engine began trailing smoke as the Wellington vanished into cloud. I had no idea whether I'd contributed to the damage, but the chase had been exhilarating.

But I had problems of my own. My oil temperature was far too high and worsening rapidly.

At ten kilometres from land, I announced my problem over the R/T.

"Return to Bergen immediately," shouted the lieutenant.

He stayed on my left, while the other two continued pursuing the enemy, in case he broke cover.

My engine started rough running as the oil temperature dropped well into the red, and I wondered if the Wellington's tail gunner had been lucky, hitting my radiator. Losing power, I began preparations to ditch in the sea.

Then I remembered Hans-Ekkehard Bob's rollercoaster trip back across the Channel. I daren't shut down my engine altogether as he had, so I pulled back on the throttle and applied power again, hoping for a boost in height, but nothing happened. I didn't have his four thousand metres; I barely had one, and it was disappearing fast.

A 109 was not designed to land on water. I've known pilots tell of how unforgiving it is, saying they'd prefer a ploughed field than a cold and choppy sea. With renewed determination I decided to get as far as I could, avoiding the water if possible.

Another minute passed with no flames or smoke, so I held the aeroplane steady, the engine continuing to turn the propeller with at least some power, slowing my descent.

The coast now a mere couple of kilometres away, I still had three hundred metres in hand. It seemed I'd probably make the beach but not the airfield. I knew from my training that in a forced landing the worst thing you can do is be indecisive; it's best to make a decision and stick to it. I'd have enough speed and height to make a decent forced landing on the sand or shallow water, so I committed myself to this.

Curiously the tension eased once I'd made this decision, and at a hundred metres I realised I'd reach the wide sandy beach after all. I turned to line up with the coastline and tried lowering the undercarriage and flaps, but nothing happened. I gently eased the stick forward to avoid a stall, coming in faster and lower than usual. For a moment I flew over the sand at ten metres and 150kph, easing back on the stick as the underside made contact, tailwheel first.

The propeller was still turning, so all three blades hurled sand over the nose and cockpit. The engine fell silent as I closed the throttle, sliding along in a surprisingly smooth crash-landing. As it came to rest I quickly turned off all the switches, unstrapped, and climbed out.

There was silence apart from a little gurgling from the engine, protesting at being dumped on the beach, but no fire. I stood nearby, removed my goggles and leather flying helmet, staring at my aeroplane.

The other two 109s from my flight roared overhead, wheels down, ready for landing. I sat on the nearest dune, overlooking the scene for twenty minutes, until a car appeared, weaving around towards me, driven by my lieutenant, with Captain Wernitz by his side.

The latter jumped out and ran up, clutching his medical bag. I realised that, despite being shaken, I had survived without even a scratch.

Expecting a reprimand, I stood up and saluted, shaking my head.

To my surprise, the lieutenant, an affable man by the name of Joachim Kirschner shouted, "Well done, young man!" and after slapping me on the back and almost knocking me over, he produced a hip flask of schnapps which the three of us happily drained in a few seconds. We stood chatting amiably on the beach as though this was a daily occurrence. Perhaps they were as relieved as me that it had gone so well, and I was still alive.

That night I was toasted repeatedly in the mess.

The CO approached and, in sudden reverential silence, handed me a pair of black overalls. "Here you are, Goetz. You damaged it, so you can bloody well fix it, right?"

I clicked my heels in response, standing rigidly to attention. "Yes, sir!" I shouted.

The whole room erupted in raucous laughter.

"Relax, young man," he said, "I'm joking. In fact, you can be proud of yourself. The Wellington ditched in the sea, so between the three of you we can claim a victory, well done."

I smiled with relief as the CO shook my hand.

"Don't make a habit of ditching, though; we don't want another bloody Quax Schnorrer on our hands!" as the whole room erupted with laughter again.

I had no idea what this meant, and no-one would tell me.

We divided the victory equally between us.

My first kill, even if only a third.

A few days later the ground crew recovered the 109 from the beach and lifted it onto jacks. I rushed over to look for the bullet holes, expecting to find the engine badly damaged. After five minutes I couldn't find any combat damage at all. Pleased I hadn't allowed my aeroplane to be a target, I wondered why an engine could do this without warning. They developed problems, of course, but now I considered, with some prescience, what might happen if I had an engine failure over the sea or even hostile territory.

Close friendships were made in these three months, particularly with Reinhold Hoffmann, Anton Dobele, and Helmut Missner. Reinhold was from Silesia, but Anton and Helmut grew up in Wurttemberg near Stuttgart. We had similar backgrounds and shared a great passion for aeroplanes, though Anton was older, having been with the Condor Legion in Spain as ground crew. We didn't always fly together but, during October, the four of us sometimes flew as one flight with either Anton or Reinhold as leader, and we felt invincible.

We had frequent visits from veteran fighter pilots who didn't just teach the usual routines, but a lot of things that do not appear in flying manuals: real combat survival. This included using the terrain to your advantage, ultra-low-level flying, evading ground fire, evasive action when attacked from behind, and how to monitor your instruments quickly, whilst also looking outside during high-stress combat. So many times we learnt how to maintain the advantage, and this meant seeing the enemy long before he saw you. We remembered every word these veterans told us.

Many featured in our magazines and newsreels. Treated like movie stars, with their decorations glinting on their finest uniforms, they even had brooding photos of themselves which they signed and handed out at the slightest request. Everyone aspired to gain twenty, thirty, or fifty combat kills in order to be awarded the Knight's Cross; this became our main obsession.

One such pilot flew in to Bergen early in September in a new-looking 109 F, a Friedrich, greeted by all our senior officers in turn like a true dignitary. When he entered the mess we all saw Hans Philipp's Knight's Cross with Oak Leaves around his neck, making him one of a very small elite. He'd been given the award only a few days before, by Hitler personally in his Wolf's Lair headquarters in East Prussia. Now on business leave, he toured the country for photographs and autographs.

He addressed a packed room, immediately reliving some of his astonishing tally of sixty-two combat victories. Some were unique, however, because he told us from his own experience how the enemy would try to shoot down a 109.

"How do you know this, sir?" asked one of the pilots.

"Because I shot down five 109s of the JKRV, the Yugoslav Royal Air Force, in April," he replied, to loud applause and laughter.

In the next few weeks before the weather closed in, we made contact with the enemy several times, pursuing him back across the North Sea, but were forbidden from flying any further than fifty kilometres, so to our disappointment most escaped.

Despite the fact we weren't shooting down many aeroplanes, these patrols gave us great experience and by the time the first chill of November arrived, we considered ourselves ready for anything.

Our training continued, however, and just when I thought we might spend Christmas at Bergen, postings came through in the first week of December.

Pinned up on the noticeboard in the dining hall, an exuberant crowd of pilots gathered, jostling to see. Some lucky blighters were being sent to France and others remained in Holland.

Anton and I were posted together to a place called Gatchina. I'd never heard of it, and neither had Anton. The best part was the name of the squadron: No. 1 Group, JG54. My old friends! I thumped the air with my right fist, grinning like a delirious child.

Anton scanned the list for details. With nothing more about the location, we looked at other postings; perhaps it's in Poland, Norway, or somewhere along the Baltic coast. Reinhold, Helmut, and a few others were not yet listed, and so I asked aloud, almost absent-mindedly, "Where the hell is Gatchina?"

After a brief silence the crowd began dispersing, before a lean, thin-faced acting corporal standing close by spoke up.

"I have a brother there," he said. "It's near Leningrad, in Russia."

Part 2

1

Russia

December 1941

Standing at a map of Europe in the dispersal hut, we examined it closely. Most was German, of course, with Russia recently added. The new sections caused the map to run more than halfway along the wall, requiring dozens of additional pins. On the far right-hand side, at the very edge of the world, one word stood out larger than all the others: 'Leningrad'.

We could see no trace of anywhere called Gatchina, and my first thought while staring at it all was, *How are we going to get there?*

With four days in hand before heading east, details remained vague until our final night. We'd be flying there, not as pilots but as passengers, in long hops all the way, taking off at 0800 hours the next day.

Our daily patrols had continued without incident until the last afternoon and I wrote some very excited letters, one to my parents and another to Inge. On our final evening we played cards and discussed our postings. Eager to get started, everyone cursed the delays, demanding we should simply fly the aeroplanes we already had straight into combat, but of course these were reserved for the next trainees.

The remaining postings had come through. Some would be joining us at Gatchina, but not until the following week, with thankfully Reinhold and Helmut amongst them.

We drank far too much in celebration on that last night and in the morning we watched bleary-eyed as our transport, an elderly Ju52, touched down and lumbered towards us across the grass. We were each handed a small Russian phrase book with our typed orders, and I wondered whether I'd ever need it, and in what possible circumstances.

Climbing aboard, we all tried hard not to appear hungover. Three army officers were already seated inside, poring over maps, one of them nodding by way of acknowledgment.

Like an elderly aunt with heavy shopping, the aeroplane waddled slowly and clumsily to the bottom of the field. Little wonder that the already obsolete Ju52, with its corrugated metal fuselage, was affectionately known as the 'Auntie Ju'.

We turned around and bounced along the grass, slowly gathering speed, finally taking off in a shallow climb over the sea before a gentle climbing turn east.

The cold cabin, Spartan and uncomfortable, reminded us it was an operational troop carrier, with no luxuries. Two loaded MG15s hung either side of the fuselage, the barrels of which stuck out through small openings. With no other crew, presumably, if we were attacked, any one of us would have to grab hold and start shooting. I found a blanket and took an extra coat from my kit bag, leaned my back on the fuselage side, and, despite the noise, nodded off.

Our first stop, Berlin, where recent heavy snow made

the city look beautiful from above. We approached low and slow on long finals. After a perfect landing the engines were shut down while we took on more fuel and the army officers departed. We had thirty minutes to find the food service canteen before taking off again.

On our return, as well as food and ammunition, two young SS officers boarded for the next stage. Curiously, in the centre of the fuselage, dozens of enormous paint tins had been stacked, all identical, one of which had clearly been opened, as a run of bright yellow had dried before reaching the bottom of the can. I wondered why this would be needed at the front line, and in such huge quantities.

After two hours' flying, mostly in darkness, we landed at 1700 hours at what looked like a municipal airport in the middle of a city. There had been a partial blackout in Berlin but not here, everywhere being brightly lit. When the engines shut down we rightly assumed this was our stop for the night. It couldn't possibly be Gatchina. No, East Prussia.

We enjoyed the hospitality of a transport squadron and slept well in one of their barracks until roused in the morning, in what seemed the middle of the night, to eat breakfast of meat and bread. The East Prussian accent is difficult to understand, so I felt relief when we were called to gather our things and re-board the same aeroplane. 0900 hours and still dark, the first signs of light began filling the cabin as we climbed eastwards towards the dawn.

A dark grey, inhospitable mass stretched away to our left and it took me a few moments to recognise the Baltic Sea; I shuddered with dread at the thought of ditching in such freezing water. Ahead, and to our right, the ground rolled away on an endless white treadmill, and I wondered how our forces had managed to capture such a vast expanse. Biting cold penetrated the cabin, despite our complaints, but the heaters were set to maximum. I never knew the inside of an aeroplane could be so cold.

After more than three long hours of linear snow-covered terrain, like flying over an enormous blank sheet of paper, wondering if we would soon stop for fuel, the engines changed pitch, we turned ninety degrees and then again, as though joining a circuit. The pilot eased back the throttles and lowered the huge flaps for landing.

A railway line ran parallel to the right side of the airfield with a series of small frozen lakes near a town, Gatchina, perhaps, to the right of those. It all looked picturesque, like anywhere else following continuous snowfalls. We thumped down heavily, with no bounce, and taxied to a row of buildings under construction. One had a newly tiled roof and windows, from which dim yellow lights showed signs of life. We rolled to a stop, the engines shutting down, as we gathered our belongings.

Before one of the SS officers opened the door he buttoned his greatcoat collar high up over his face, pulling his cap down hard onto his head. Finally he put on a pair of thick fur mittens, clearly not army issue. Where did he get those from? Looking ridiculous, he then pulled open the door and lowered the step before climbing out. He'd obviously been before.

The aeroplane had been cold but, even before I fully reached the outside, I sensed a penetrating chill that passed through my skin, deep into my cheekbones. My entire uniform suddenly seemed paper-thin, as though I was naked.

The SS officers walked briskly from the aeroplane in step with one another, as I floundered around, instinctively turning my back to the prevailing wind, placing my belongings on the ground before I dropped them, fumbling for the top buttons of my coat. Despite my leather gloves, my fingers were already seizing up and I struggled to grip anything, eventually succeeding, after taking twice the usual time.

Fiddling with his coat and gathering up the collar, Anton shook his head, clearly feeling the same.

We followed the two SS officers towards the building from which a huge chimney produced great clouds of smoke, like a steam engine, that were immediately caught in the breeze, whirling around in front of us before vanishing with a reassuring smell of woodsmoke. A few seconds behind, we burst in as though chased by a wolf.

We didn't even know whose building we had entered, and didn't care, we were so thankful to get out of the wind. Luckily it was a packed food service canteen for pilots, the windows obliterated with layers of frozen condensation, where a huge log burner piled high with blazing wood battled to keep out the cold.

A smiling acting corporal in a cook's apron leaned over the counter, handing us coffee in tin mugs, his forage cap at an impossible angle on his greasy head. I gripped the mug tightly in both hands while taking a sip through clouds of steam.

"First time in Russia?" he said, still smiling.

"Yes." I nodded, managing a swallow of coffee as he laughed.

"What's wrong with you? It's lovely and warm today; it's only minus twenty-five!"

A ripple of laughter followed as I realised we were the subject of amusement.

"Don't worry, you'll get used to it," he said, as his breath drifted towards us in an enormous cloud, joining the steam from our drinks.

The room seemed warm, almost tropical, compared to outside, but still very cold. My senses tricked me, and I shook my head, doubting I'd ever get used to it.

Suddenly I thought of my wonderful life under the trees at Campagne-les-Guines, long afternoons in the sun outside the bistro, and the horrific prospect of living here in these temperatures, and in a tent. Anton's face reflected my own thoughts and I couldn't help smiling, as he did. Eventually we started laughing. You know when you smile at someone else's misfortune, because it's funny; he was smiling at mine and I reciprocated. We were stuck thousands of kilometres from home in snow and ice and could do nothing about it, so we laughed.

Someone threw open the door, letting in a blast of cold air that made us all flinch, and an army corporal stood in the doorway, shouting, "Anyone for the palace? I'm leaving now. I can take ten."

I looked blankly at Anton, as he did at me.

The cook threw us both a serious look. "Where are you heading?" he asked.

"Gatchina," I replied, puzzled.

"You need to go with him then. You're pilots, aren't you? That's where he's going, the palace at Gatchina. What are your names? I'll tell them you are coming."

Anton obliged with our details and we quickly sipped as much of the wonderful coffee as we could before loading our things into the back of a lorry and climbing aboard with the others. The 'palace' was obviously a cynical euphemism for our quarters, and so I expected the worst: a dark sub-zero canvas-covered hole in the ground surrounded by frozen sandbags.

We drew the tarpaulin rope together as tightly as we could, but there were still gaps from which the icy wind jabbed at our faces, poking us in the eyes like sharpened sticks. Through the same holes I caught the odd glimpse of the airfield.

Despite the relatively fine weather – it wasn't raining or snowing – the sun was nowhere to be seen, with just a vague hint of something lighter very low on the horizon, like a dim streetlamp covered in a blanket.

In less than an hour this midday sun would be gone, and we'd be smothered by freezing night, in the early afternoon.

As I prepared myself for the draughty tent, buried in snow, I realised my teeth were chattering uncontrollably. I'd never experienced anything quite like it. With extra socks from the stores at Bergen, along with an additional summer greatcoat and two sets of air force thermal underwear, most of which I had on to save carrying them, I realised to my utter dismay that they still weren't enough.

2

THE LORRY TRUNDLED DOWN A LONG SERVICE ROAD parallel with the runway, rattling over what sounded like multiple sets of railway lines, and off the airfield. No-one spoke, due to the noise and, in any case, most faces were obscured by high-buttoned collars and tightly worn headgear.

After driving for about five minutes on a straight road we began to slow down. The vehicle lurched to the side as the tyres lost their grip, and we finally stopped with a slide of at least two or three metres. As I struggled to unfasten the tarpaulin with my numbed fingers, the driver's ruddy face appeared and he quickly finished the job.

We dragged our possessions from the lorry and, for a moment, Anton and I stood dumbfounded. Despite apparently being in the middle of nowhere, in what we were told would be a bleak and empty Russia, we had pulled up outside a fabulous building as huge as it was opulent.

What is this astonishing place?

With an intricate stone facade of three floors, dozens of enormous windows, castle turrets at each corner, and rows of chimneys, it looked like a French chateau.

Stepping inside the grand entrance hall, the others from the lorry dispersed in every direction as a young SS private clicked his heels in front of us.

"Pilots Dobell and Goetz?" he asked, with a practised fake smile. "Follow me, please."

He led us across the hallway, up a grand marble staircase onto the first floor, down a wide spacious corridor, and into a room about ten metres square with a distant high ceiling and fireplace big enough to walk in. Enormous logs burned fiercely, making the huge space extremely comfortable.

Our guide behaved as though the entire building had been gifted to him personally, he seemed so proud of it.

"This is your room, gentlemen," he said, beaming. "Welcome to Gatchina. There is bedding in the store on the ground floor, where you will also find flush toilets, washing facilities, and the canteen."

His smile evaporated, replaced by a serious, almost puzzled expression, no doubt aware of our shock at such fabulous accommodation. "This is the old czar's summer palace, where Catherine the Great once lived," he said, pausing for a moment before staring at us. "But it's ours now."

He clicked his heels and turned, before leaving with a limp that had been more pronounced when he'd climbed the stairs. A silver wound badge hung on his tunic, so I made the obvious connection. I thought about asking him if he knew my old school friend, Heinrich, because I'd heard he'd successfully enrolled in the SS, but dismissed the idea.

For a moment Anton and I stood in awe. I'd never been inside any building quite like it, or even *seen* anything like this, other than in photographs of grand palaces, perhaps in

Paris and other great cities. The walls and doors had damage, with the occasional bullet hole in the ceiling, and we'd passed Russian graffiti in the corridors, which had obviously been carelessly daubed onto the walls with a paintbrush. Despite the grandeur, it seemed anything portable of value had been removed, including carpets and rugs. The roof looked intact, also the windows and, adequately spacious and dry, an army could have been housed in it.

Half the air force lived there, or so it seemed, by the uniforms of bomber squadrons, army, and SS. I had brief glimpses of smiling secretaries in black pencil skirts, white blouses, black ties, and heels. My opinion of Russia was changing rapidly, and that of my deployment. I couldn't wait to write home and tell my parents.

Two army camp beds looked slept in, with the standard blue and white check pattern blankets, already taken, with two more folded up against one wall, presumably ours. After formally claiming them, Anton and I left our things and decided to find some blankets.

Starting on the ground floor, we turned left along a curved corridor with ornate plasterwork around the high ceiling, and every step drew us closer to wonderful cooking smells and rattling plates.

From a narrow passage into a straight, wider corridor, we discovered kitchens, packed with busy cooks, and further down, enormous pipes leading through the walls into a series of steam rooms, where we found not only flush toilets but hot showers, and a row of sinks with mirrors above, all running with condensation.

Incredibly warm, like a sauna, we were immediately impressed. We found a uniform store where an army private made us sign for six blankets, and we returned to the main entrance to get our bearings.

Following another curved corridor at the other side, we entered a block of rooms occupied mainly by army personnel and SS, who clearly didn't appreciate our curiosity, so we turned around. To our surprise we came across another marble staircase leading up to the first floor at a shallow angle, with ornate dark wood banister rails either side of the wide shiny steps.

The first floor was similar to the ground floor but with magnificent gilded ceiling plaster, everything linked by corridors with their high ornate ceilings. I wondered how I had not known about this place before.

It became clear the palace was divided into three main sections: the central building with three floors, and the two large square sections at each side. Marks on the walls indicated where pictures had been, and in some cases the plaster had come away when the Russians had obviously pulled them down in haste. On the top floor, huge oil paintings remained, covered in a veneer of dust, obviously too large to be removed. I soon found out that other treasure had been hidden in the vast cellar, sealed behind piles of rubble, in the hope we wouldn't find it.

Looking out through the windows at the front of the palace, I saw the frozen water I'd seen from the air: narrow lakes running right to left, with a road leading to a bridge over the water into the town. In Catherine the Great's time visitors would drive their carriages up the long, straight entrance road and into the huge courtyard with the lake on one side and the beautiful ornate façade ahead.

Most of the ground floor had mezzanine tiles, some of which had been badly scratched, either by the Russians in their hasty departure or by us when we first arrived. I could only imagine how wonderful it must have looked before the war; I had an odd thought that, afterwards, when it was all over, I'd invite my parents to stay in one of the hundreds of rooms. Such thoughts now seem so utterly absurd, a clear indication of my naivety back then.

The courtyard at the front of the main façade was at least a hundred metres across and, where horse-drawn carriages would once have been, now a parking area existed for German army lorries, half-tracks, and staff cars. Vehicles arrived and departed constantly, mostly at the other side where the army were located.

After ten minutes of wandering around this astonishing place, we remembered we were supposed to report to the CO on arrival, so we dumped our blankets and told the other newcomers in the next room to come with us.

Along the same corridor a door had 'Captain Trautloft', and 'Briefing Room' pinned to it on a sheet of paper. I knocked and, hearing an echoing shout from inside, opened it. The CO and two other pilots, both officers, were leaning over a map spread across an enormous desk.

Another remarkable room of astonishing grandeur, about ten metres across with a ceiling so high it probably risked being obscured by low cloud in poor weather. A fireplace, also large enough to walk into, crackled with huge blazing logs and, despite its size, the room seemed pleasantly warm. With jackets unfastened, they were all smoking in what seemed a very informal gathering.

The CO remembered all six of us as we stood to attention, naming us and shaking our hands in turn. "You came back to us then, Goetz," he said with a smile, pointing to his desk, catching the eye of one of the officers, who pulled open a drawer, removing a full bottle of schnapps. A tray of shot glasses emerged, each soon filled to the brim.

"To the Green Hearts," he shouted, as we all tipped them back, downing the contents in one.

He then turned towards the map. From where I stood, one thing dominated the entire top half: written in German gothic script, the name of a huge sprawling city a few kilometres away.

After briefly studying our faces, Capt Trautloft spoke with an odd solemnity.

"Gentlemen, welcome to the Leningrad Front."

3

"We've been here since 13ᵗʰ September," he said. "I doubt the German army ever had a palace like this before, but Gatchina is Army Group North HQ, so you'll see a lot of activity. From our point of view we have four main operational bases: Siverskaya, Staraya Russa, Ryelbitzi, and Krasnogvardeisk, just down the road; the palace is Gatchina, but the airfield is Krasnogvardeisk. You might also hear it called the Palace Airfield too, to add to the confusion."

The two officers laughed.

"We have bomber squadrons here and at Siverskaya, KG77 and KG1 mainly, with a lot of army reconnaissance, weather reconnaissance, and training units cluttering up the airfield, so watch out for them. We have supply services, transport units, signals units, and medical services, but not enough flak units, so I've asked for more."

He pointed at the map, encouraging us to come forward

for a closer look, so we gathered around. I immediately noticed Staraya Russa and Ryelbitzi, some distance south, near Lake Ilmen along the Volkhov River, with the other two close to the southern edge of Leningrad.

A thick red mark ran from the city all the way down across Russia in a wavy line, as though drawn by a drunk, with areas rubbed out and reapplied several times. I found the same word written in three places: 'Front', each with recent dates.

Many other dots populated the map, names like Mga, Lyuban, Szuizy, and Dno, spread along the left side of the Volkhov, our side of the river, all listed as forward airfields. To my surprise much of the land surrounding the river on either side was marked by huge tufts of grass: marshland, frozen solid now, but in summer, a soggy, impassable bog. For pilots this meant forced landings would have to be made wheels up, with taking off again impossible. Obviously my first concern, with the only consolation being that such areas of marshland would be inhospitable to armies of both sides for part of the year, particularly vehicles.

A thick black line completely encircled the city of Leningrad.

I leaned closer and the CO noticed.

"With the help of our allies, the Finns in the north, we have Leningrad totally surrounded," he said, "and it has been for several weeks already." He paused, looking around.

"We in the Northern Sector have four hundred kilometres of front line to cover, gentlemen," he continued, stepping back, glass in hand, "from Leningrad right down to Demyansk, here." He tapped the bottom edge of the map, almost off the end of his desk.

"Below that, it's the Central Sector, then further down, the Southern Sector and Stalingrad. Two thousand Russian aeroplanes were destroyed on day one of Barbarossa, but please don't underestimate the enemy. The bastards bombed the airfield here on 12th October during the night. They only damaged an old Go-145 biplane belonging to a courier squadron, but they made sure we knew they are still around. They had more success at Siverskaya, though; they've bombed our airfield there twice; the first time at the end of October and again in early November, when they damaged a few Ju88s." He paused. "But they haven't been back since."

The two officers laughed.

He smiled before continuing, "I've tangled with him quite a few times. He can be very determined, even if his machines are poor, and he will ram you if he gets the chance."

He tapped the map with his right hand as though knocking on a door. "We defeated the French, gentlemen, and we will soon defeat our last remaining adversary in the west, the British. But remember this. Here in the east the Russians are our enemies, not our adversaries. There is a huge difference. We are not here merely to fight them; we are here to kill them. We give them no quarter, and expect none in return."

His expression became more serious. "We have to keep Ivan busy, away from our ground forces, and you'll get to know how we do this in due course."

He glanced at the tall three-metre window on his left, looking up at the sky. "At the moment our biggest problem is the weather. A week ago, on 5th December, it was minus forty-five degrees."

At the faintly audible gasps, he shook his head. "Nothing worked, and thankfully the weather was too bad even for Ivan, apart from a few, determined to kill themselves, but you see my point."

My thoughts turned to what he told us. How could we maintain the advantage with so much area to cover, and in such conditions? While trying to remember everything said, I still couldn't get over the luxurious surroundings after anticipating so much worse.

"It's not so much the snow that causes the problems; at least you can see it. Freezing rain and the subsequent icing is the worst. It settles on your aeroplane and turns solid in seconds, adding so much weight you end up trundling into the rough and straight into the trees. That is, of course, if you're still on the ground. You will be operating from any of our airfields, but we will always make sure you can return here at some point occasionally, so don't worry about that."

He lit a cigar, and the smell and the décor convinced me for a moment I was in a fashionable Berlin hotel rather than close to the front line.

"We are repairing the buildings at the airfield down the road which Ivan damaged, and also at Siverskaya, but for now you will live here and travel to the airfield for operations. Make the most of the palace; I hear they already have the roof on one of the airfield barracks."

Although he received a laugh, a few heads shook, too.

The CO then addressed me directly. "I wanted to ask you, Goetz, as a brilliant mechanic, why would a wing break off a 109 in flight?"

Surprised, and deeply embarrassed, I couldn't answer, but he carried on anyway. "We lost Arnold Lignitz over the city a couple of months ago when this happened. I've never seen it personally, but I've heard of it before."

I shrugged, mainly because I had no idea, although I had also heard of it happening to a few Friedrichs, the 'F' version of the 109.

He could see I had no answer. "Not to worry; he was seen bailing out so he's no doubt on his way back to us as we speak." He laughed, as did the others.

"So, gentlemen, it's not Ivan that's causing us the biggest problem at the moment. We've lost twelve aeroplanes this month, almost all of them to this damned weather, with pilots skidding across the airfields at Siverskaya, and down the road here at Krasnogvardeisk. They get lost in the snow, run out of fuel, freeze up, crash on landing or even taking off, so be careful."

He sat down in a huge chair behind his packing crate desk, indicating for us to stand at ease or sit wherever we could. I shared a box with a fresh-faced young man who had been sitting opposite me in the Ju52.

"We've had a lot of ground fire from our own forces, which is unavoidable, I suppose, given the circumstances. It's dark most of the bloody time at the moment, and when it's light it's still pretty dark, and only then for a couple of hours. I'm trying to reduce this friendly fire, but be aware of it. I've had an idea that might help, and have requested some yellow paint; I'm hoping this will arrive soon. Black crosses on yellow and white aeroplanes should stop us getting shot down by our own bloody troops," he said, laughing.

I wanted to tell him some of the paint had arrived in the Ju52 with us, but he continued. "Krasnogvardeisk has three runways, gentlemen, all quite forgiving when frozen because they are made of packed earth and grass, but then bloody awful in the wet when it all turns to mud, as you can imagine. As I've already mentioned, we are rebuilding the accommodation huts, along with all the hangars that Ivan tried to destroy before he left, so we'll have it looking like the first-class airfield it once was in no time."

He looked around at our eager fresh faces before continuing in a more serious tone, glancing back at the map. "Anyway, High Command ordered a cessation of operations last Monday, the 8th, but then the very next day Ivan threw everything at us and recaptured Tikhvin, pushing our ground forces back to the river, as though he knew we'd stood down."

He paused, and with a very distinct frown, rubbed his chin with his right hand, tapping the map just to the east of Leningrad. "This was the first time since Barbarossa that Ivan has successfully pushed us back on the ground anywhere in Russia, did you know that? It certainly rattled senior commanders in Berlin, even though it was only a few kilometres and a pretty insignificant place. But we haven't managed to take it back yet."

He shook his head and leaned across the map, spreading both hands across in a sweeping motion, as though flattening out any hills in the landscape. "So now the Volkhov River is mostly the front line; please remember that. Keep a close eye on your fuel, gentlemen, and don't go too far over the edge of the world. We can't afford to lose you or your aeroplane simply because you weren't paying attention."

He touched the wavy red line on the paper with his right index finger. "The same applies to operations over the Gulf and Lake Ladoga; keep checking your fuel. The lake is three hundred kilometres long, north to south, and a hundred wide, more like a sea. Don't leave it until the fuel warning light comes on; as you all know, in the Friedrich, it should indicate seventy litres, giving you plenty of warning, but it can also come on at ten, which is far too late, so my advice is, don't trust it. You know your aeroplanes, so speak to the ground crew."

In absolute silence he looked each of us in the eyes. "If you're way over the other side of the Volkhov with only ten litres of fuel you'll be eating *kulesh* and stale bread for dinner in some Ruski shithole with a bayonet – or something worse – stuck up your arse."

We laughed, but the prospect of capture was unthinkable to all of us.

"We were successful in stopping their ships in the lake, but now it's frozen the swine are running supplies across in vehicles, so you will find the ice road a decent ongoing target. Our ground forces are not attempting to take the city as such; it is being blockaded and forced into submission, so the idea goes."

Looking at our blank faces, he knew we were all wonderfully unaware of what we'd be facing.

If I'd known then what I know now, I'd have asked a hundred questions, but hindsight is a gift none of us possess. We were filled with bright optimism and huge self-confidence in our own abilities, our aeroplanes, and our sense of purpose. Everything was going well at the end of 1941, even though the loss of Tikhvin was unexpected. We would have to find out for ourselves what flying in minus forty-five degrees of frost would be like against an often suicidal enemy, mostly in the dark.

The CO ended his talk with one final instruction: "Your training is over, gentlemen, you are now fully operational. The next time you are at the airfield, please hand your logbooks in to the *Startkladde* clerk in the adjutant's office, and make sure you liaise with him after every operational flight, understood? This way we can keep an accurate tally of your kills."

Every squadron had one of these famous books. I'd seen one at Bergen, where my quarter-kill was registered, and so now I had my chance to use it regularly.

Considering Capt Trautloft was the overall commander of JG54 and all its groups in the entire fighter wing, we considered this to be an informal briefing, more like a welcome chat, and it ended with us being at least a little clearer in our minds of what was expected.

From Gatchina to Siverskaya and all the way down to Staraya Russa, we were all Green Hearts, the many different groups within it flying together as one. He immediately infected us with his self-confidence, expressed with apparent integrity and charisma the way good leaders do. As new pilots, eager to get started but also just as keen to seek reassurance and inspiration, of which the CO had plenty, we all knew from that moment we would follow him anywhere.

4

At 1100 hours on Monday 15th December 1941 I arrived at dispersal for my first operational flight in Russia. I spotted two black men preparing to venture outside, and one of them asked, almost in passing, about my experiences with the Friedrich.

"I haven't flown one yet," I said.

He mumbled something through his thick woollen balaclava that I could barely hear, removed a glove, and rolled his right index finger at me, indicating to follow him out the door.

With my chin pressed firmly onto my chest against a biting wind, I followed him to the aeroplane, our boots crunching loudly on the frozen snow, shattering the surface like broken glass. Where there was no snow, I slid around on the ice, making no traction at all. How on earth could I take off in this?

The cockpit provided immediate relief from the icy blast as the same tall figure loomed over, helping with my straps. Bound so tightly with clothing, I couldn't see his face or even communicate, other than a few grunts and hand signals. I wore as much clothing as I dared. If I wore too little I'd freeze to death; if I wore too much I'd be unable to move, or even fit in.

The 109 cockpit is quite tight in a summer shirt, so I had to find the right balance, if indeed I could. The breach of the nose cannon protruded right back into the cockpit between my feet, so already it didn't feel particularly spacious.

The tightly bound man reached into the cockpit, pointing to a new switch. "Radiator cut-off!" he shouted, rather comically, like a talking bear.

I nodded. To be honest I knew already. If one radiator sustained damage I could isolate the other, which was a brilliant idea. In fact I knew all the differences between the Emil and the Friedrich. The leading-edge slats were shorter too, and the rounded detachable wingtips. I would still have liked a short familiarisation trip first, as perhaps I should have, but it wasn't to be.

Despite the time of day, the heaviest grey sky lay around us like thick camouflage netting, bringing the cloud base below five hundred metres.

After heating my engine, I felt a brief blast of warm air from the petrol generator as it was withdrawn, as someone turned the crank. I primed the engine heavily, set the throttle, and started her up. The crank man jumped down and I slammed the canopy shut. Within a few minutes I sensed warmth in the cockpit.

The other three now had their engines running and our flight leader, a lieutenant, not much older than me, by the name of Gunter Scheel, put me as his *Katschmarek*, on his right. They moved off and as soon as I released the brakes, to my horror, the aeroplane slid sideways as much as it rolled forwards. This had never happened to me before and it struck terror into my guts. I saw my aeroplane running off the edge of the field, straight into frozen walls of cleared snow.

Remaining as calm as possible, I throttled right back in an effort to regain control and, a few seconds later, the sliding stopped. Sitting for a moment with the throttle almost closed, the prop wind-milling gently, I sweated profusely. *How insane is this?*

What if I lost control on take-off at 150kph and slid into a ditch? I remembered the CO telling us they had lost more pilots on the ground than in combat, so I thought I would definitely be next.

To my astonishment the others moved towards the end of the field, onto the threshold area, ready for take-off, apparently without any problems, so I had to follow. I loosened the throttle, making tiny adjustments to the power in an effort to gain traction, while tapping the brakes gently, rushing an engine and controls check before lowering ten degrees of flap. Being the only new man of the four, I watched the others closely, realising they were sliding on the ice too, but using it in their taxiing, anticipating it like a racing driver sliding sideways around bends.

I'll never get the hang of this, I thought.

Any other airfield at another time would have pronounced the runway unsafe. Clearly I had a lot to learn.

A squadron of Stukas took off without incident, for which we were the escort. Gunter gave a thumbs-up and applied full power, so I stayed with him. Passing 100kph, my pounding heart almost choking my throat, by some miracle, I was still rolling straight. To my relief the tailwheel lifted and then at 150, the main wheels were lighter on the ice. I gently held the nose down as long as I dared, before easing back on the stick, passing 160, and I was airborne.

Raising the undercarriage, I realised my hands had warmed up. This had been by far the most nerve-wracking take-off in my life, worse than my first sling-shot trip in the Grunau 9. I thought of the next time I would have to do it, forgetting that I'd somehow have to land back on the ice soon.

Climbing to three thousand metres, my 109 behaved well, and I breathed a sigh of relief to be back at the controls, suddenly realising I had become over-obsessed with the fuel gauge; I disciplined myself to avoid checking it every thirty seconds! I had full tanks, so forget it.

Heading north-east, the Stukas flew below us at two thousand metres, and we watched as they trundled towards their target. We heard shouts over the R/T before they commenced their attack, screaming down, releasing their bombs as huge chunks of frozen earth were hurled skywards, followed by dense clouds of filthy, brown smoke.

After a few moments, scanning the dim grey sky for the enemy, the otherwise featureless landscape changed into odd squares and long strips of grey. This fragmented chessboard, the shattered ruins of Leningrad, looked oddly quiet for such a populous city, empty and lifeless, now with its southern edge burning.

We realised we'd strayed too close when the sky filled with bursting flak, obscuring everything, so we turned around, following the Stukas south-west. We'd only been in the air a few minutes. Gatchina was so close to the city, and now we lingered overhead while the Stukas touched down in pairs.

After the first had landed, the second veered off to the right towards a huge wall of cleared snow fifty metres away. We watched as it crashed into the ice, the propeller hurling frozen chunks of debris high into the air until the engine stopped.

The aeroplane sat embedded up to the wings in a near-vertical position, tail suspended four metres above the ice. The crew climbed out, apparently uninjured, assisted by a gathering crowd.

Before assuming the pilot to be an idiot, I withheld judgment because I hadn't tried it yet. My turn next.

5

Nearing the landing area, I held off as long as possible, and once the main wheels touched, I kept up the back pressure, resisting the temptation to apply the brakes. I rolled on, quickly passing the usual length of time a 109 should stop.

As every metre passed, remaining straight, success loomed closer. When the aeroplane finally slowed to a brisk walk, I touched the brakes gently. The throttle now closed, the prop wind-milled lazily as I dared turning back to park where I'd started. It slid a little, but using gentle braking and a touch of throttle, I rolled to a standstill. What a relief! Despite landing straight into wind, I'd probably used two hundred metres more than usual. Crosswind operations on ice must therefore be impossible, or so I thought.

After securing my aeroplane, I made a point of thanking the two black men who'd helped me. I found them in the dispersal hut where I received congratulations for surviving my first flight. They seemed genuinely surprised I'd made it. Relieved I hadn't run out of fuel, or joined the Stuka in the ice, I realised I hadn't given the Red Air Force a single thought. I'd been more concerned about the conditions, flying a Friedrich for the first time, and proving myself to everyone else, than contact with the enemy. But it had been as much to do with luck as skill.

While waiting in the adjutant's office, logbook in hand, I heard the Stuka pilot's discussion. One side of his brakes had frozen solid, so the pilot's brief use of his aeroplane as a snowplough was entirely beyond his control.

Barely an hour after landing, darkness fell.

I didn't fly another op until two days later, when Gunter took the same group south for a landing at Siverskaya, as part of our familiarisation of the area.

The aeroplane was started for me on what seemed a lovely warm day, but yet again I was fooled; it only felt warm because the temperature had risen to minus ten. Unwrapped and exposed, I actually saw the smiling faces of the ground crew, and spoke to the man who had first helped me, Adelbert, as he strapped me in. Taking advantage of the relatively mild conditions, Bert, as he liked to be known, told me he and the rest of the ground crews had been up early every morning, painting our aeroplanes with new paint; under the wingtips and the underside of the engine cowlings were now bright yellow.

A band of yellow also ran around the fuselage, making the black cross stand out. He cursed because it had dripped everywhere: on his gloves, all the way up his right sleeve and dots on his face like a severe dose of chicken pox.

"We had to keep it hot all the time, like soup. It hasn't dried, it's just bloody frozen. I bet it will all peel off in the spring," he shouted. "And whose brilliant idea was it, anyway?"

Hiding a smile, I shrugged and, once out of sight, laughed out loud. They'd been busy. He and his team had already been working solidly for two days, removing the wheel fairings from all the Stukas, to stop the brakes freezing. To be safe, all our 109s had the same treatment, after reports of ice building up. The fairings were now a neat pile at the back of a hangar, ready for the summer.

For take-off I decided I'd do everything exactly the same as before. With a favourable headwind, straight down the runway, I gently applied full throttle, hoping for the best. I gave a huge sigh of relief into my oxygen mask when the tailwheel lifted just before the main wheels, with a very slight shaking of my head. I'd cheated death again.

We'd barely climbed to a thousand metres, heading due south, before we flew over Siverskaya airfield and lowered our naked undercarriage legs for landing. I was immediately impressed by the size of Siverskaya's smooth runway, beautifully cleared of snow, with all the service roads, taxiways, hangars, and other buildings. As good as anything in Germany; I wondered if our forces had built it.

Sadly, as soon as my wheels touched, I realised the impacted sand and gravel surface was glazed over with ice, making it incredibly difficult to keep straight. I held the tailwheel off as long as possible, again resisting the brakes, allowing the aeroplane to roll as far as it wanted before intervening. The runway is long enough for heavy transport aircraft, so I shouldn't run out, and after a great deal of luck and perspiration, I managed a turn back along a wide taxiway, after the others.

We shut down our engines and followed Gunter into the crew room near dispersal. This fantastic brick building had two welcoming bunker stoves and a small canteen serving hot food and drink from a huge masonry oven. We sat together at a small table, warming ourselves with coffee, while Gunter chatted to friends. I knew some faces but couldn't remember names. Some of these pilots could possibly have been in France when I was there.

Aircraft recognition posters covered the walls, Russian aircraft I'd heard of but quite a few new ones, and some familiar names and shapes I thought I'd never see here, namely the Spitfire and Hurricane. I felt an odd rush of excitement and trepidation at the prospect of facing one of these in combat, as my comrades' confrontations over the English Channel were still in my mind. These aeroplanes wouldn't be handled as well as those in the west, though, obviously, so it would be a great opportunity to shoot them down.

Without warning, someone thumped my right shoulder, spilling my coffee over the table, scalding my fingers. I immediately stood up, incensed, and turned around to give the offender an angry rebuke.

A lieutenant pilot stood there with a sarcastic grin.

"What the hell?" I protested, making my anger clearly apparent.

"Do they really let you fly our aeroplanes all on your own?" he said, with a stupid grin. "At least you'll know how to fix them when you break them," he added, laughing.

I couldn't thump an officer, so I resisted, just as recognition dawned when he offered his right hand.

I instinctively took it. "Otto Kittel," I said, shaking it firmly.

"Yes, Ivan hasn't got me yet, Paul," he replied, more seriously. "Let me get you another coffee. Sorry about that." He moved past, ordering one for himself too.

"Jever, September '40, wasn't it? Trautloft was the CO there too, wasn't he? You left to go to Schuren. How did you get on with those Grunau 9s?"

He laughed, really loudly.

"I should have warned you about those, but hey, we all had to do it, and actually they were good fun, weren't they?"

I shook my head, still surprised. A thinner Otto had also lost some hair, and the skin on his face hung lower over his cheeks, like heavily creased blackout curtains, making him look ten years older. He probably thought the same about me too; one of those odd things when you meet old friends after a year or two, you can't help making assessments. I noticed the Iron Cross First Class on his uniform, so he'd obviously been very busy.

I'd hardly managed to get a word in before Gunter rounded up our little group. "There's a front coming in fast; we have to go," he said, nodding at Otto, calling him 'Bruno'.

Back in my aeroplane, I grinned, really pleased I'd found Otto, or more accurately he'd found me, at the very edge of the civilised world. His appearance shocked me, and I had my doubts that I'd have recognised him.

At Krasnogvardeisk we all landed safely, intermittently sliding around on the frozen mud with reckless routine as though we'd done it for years.

We shut down our engines as heavy snow rolled in on a blue-black wave ten thousand metres high. The ground crews skidded about, frantically covering the engines and canopies as our boots became ice-skates.

The adjutant's office and his schnapps warmed us up in the debrief, and twenty minutes later we jumped aboard a lorry for the palace, laughing and joking, edging our way through falling snow as thick as fog. It piled high quickly, and on arrival, once the engine had been turned off, a snow-whispered silence unique to heavy falls, enveloped us.

"No more flying today," announced the CO, "and probably for some time to come."

6

Our roommates, Horst and Erich, both sergeant pilots, had lit the fire and all afternoon the four of us played skat, occasionally exchanging air force stories and childhood reminiscences.

I told them about Otto and they both smiled, also calling him Bruno.

"If you want to know how to shoot down a cement bomber, ask Bruno; he's got..." Erich paused, looking across at Horst, "four, five, is it?"

"He's got more than a dozen kills to his name already, mostly cement bombers," Horst said, smiling. "I don't know how he does it, but maybe it's because they are the only thing he shoots at. He likes the challenge. I saw one a week ago, and I swear both the crew were dead, but the damned thing just kept on flying."

I smiled at the nickname the IL-2 Sturmovik had acquired, *the cement bomber*, because they were so hard to shoot down.

As everyone no doubt thought, I hoped I'd have no problem when I encountered one for the first time.

Horst and Erich had been in Russia for several months and their enthusiasm was infectious. Erich told us of so many exciting encounters with Ivan's antiquated Red Air Force aeroplanes.

"There's plenty to shoot at and most are hopeless," he said, laughing. "We've saved some for you, though, Paul, so don't worry."

With sullen, expressionless faces, they both offered the same warnings senior officers had repeatedly given, namely about watching the fuel gauges and landing in hostile territory.

Quietly spoken, almost reserved, Horst didn't reveal much about his time in Russia despite being there the longest. He'd arrived at the palace in September when first occupied, and had lived alone in this huge room for weeks. I wondered if he was naturally quiet or just tired. We soon found him to be a good card player, though, and the only time I saw him smile was when he took quite a bit of money from the rest of us.

During a brief pause in one of these first games, Horst disappeared to the latrine and Erich leaned forwards. "He shouts in the night sometimes," he said, almost in a whisper, while calmly shuffling the cards.

Speaking with a hint of humour he continued in a more serious tone. "You need to be aware of it," he said, "because he's probably due for another soon."

He must have noticed I had no idea what he meant. "He made me swear not to tell anyone why, so I won't. If he wants to tell you, then that's up to him, but until then..." He shrugged, pausing briefly before dealing the cards again, finally adding, "I know others involved who are just the same."

Horst returned and the subject was dropped as we resumed our game, so I forgot about it.

The overall commander of JG54, Captain Trautloft, was well known to me, but not the current leader of No. 1 Group, to which I had been assigned. On the afternoon of 20th December 1941 this position changed hands, and I joined a gathering of pilots in a huge ballroom on the first floor of the palace to witness the handover. You could easily imagine an orchestra seated at one end of the vast room with dancing under tall chandeliers. The walls and ceiling were white with a wispy blue shade like a hazy summer sky, a stark contrast to the earthy brown of the dark wood floor.

I'd never seen such a gathering of so many JG54 pilots; the only ones missing were those in the air or on standby at the airfields. Instinctively we gathered near the fire as huge logs, a metre long, burned fiercely, piled on top of one another as though an entire tree had been loaded into the flames. A dim, ethereal grey filled the room from the windows behind, the brightest part of the shortest winter day. The faces of those nearest the fire were scarlet and orange, and our crisp clean uniforms reflected the general optimism as jokes were exchanged and flying experiences recalled in an increasingly noisy gathering.

Everyone quietened as Capt Trautloft entered with other officers. Heel clicks and salutes spread around the room like falling dominoes until we were all standing rigid, in silence, with our right arms raised. Such a spontaneous gesture of respect for the CO I hadn't seen for a long time.

With a quick glance at the assembly, and briefest acknowledgement with his right hand, he spoke. "Please relax, gentlemen, thank you," as arms and shoulders dropped with a few suspended conversations quietly resuming.

Capt Trautloft shook hands warmly with the current squadron leader, Capt Erich von Selle, patting him on the back, before the incumbent Capt Franz Eckerle stepped forward. I'd never met von Selle, but Eckerle had been in France, and I'd seen him occasionally, though we'd never spoken at length and usually only about engines. I knew he'd been in Russia since the beginning, guiding JG54 through Operation Barbarossa while I happily chased clouds over Berlin.

As part of the ground crew I didn't get the opportunity to meet everyone, but as I was now a pilot, this had changed. Some remembered my face and were quick to welcome me with sincere congratulations, but others whom I had met previously appeared to ignore me. I suppose this is the same in every profession.

While chatting to Horst, applause and cheering erupted when a man I recognised as Capt Reinhard Seiler appeared among the faces near the CO. How thrilling to see him, as the last I'd heard, he ditched in the English Channel the previous summer. We gathered around in a huge semi-circle as the room hushed.

"What's going on?" I whispered to the man beside me.

He shook his head.

Capt Trautloft said, "How was Berlin?" briefly taking hold of the cross hanging around Seiler's neck, a Knight's Cross, awarded for his forty-second aerial victory. He'd actually met Adolf Hitler in person and shaken his hand. This is the celebration.

He made a short speech about his trip to Berlin, meeting a particular famous person, and his war so far, briefly mentioning his swim in the English Channel on 11th August 1940. More applause and handshakes followed. Afterwards I made a point of shaking his hand, pleased he remembered me.

Captain Erich von Selle would be leaving us for a new position at JG1 in Holland. It's incredible to think now that such was my youthful enthusiasm and naivety that I actually felt sorry for him, having to leave Russia.

7

The weather closed in with heavy snow and cloud base down to a hundred metres so most routine flying could not take place. Some of the more experienced pilots still took off, however, mainly to counter the threat of suicidal Russians in their antiquated open-top biplanes, which kept on appearing, by some miracle, unaffected by the conditions.

With other pilots, I went to Krasnogvardeisk airfield most days where we started the engines of our aeroplanes between snowstorms, more in hope than anticipation, and twice I assisted the maintenance of one, even if only for a few minutes.

Like most aeroplanes remaining out in the open, mine now had huge portable plywood screens around the front, like a cheap garden shed, forward of the cockpit, large enough to open the engine cowlings but still bitterly cold inside. I could barely hold any tools, never mind use them, glad to be a pilot and not ground crew.

The night before Christmas Eve I was startled awake in the early hours, convinced we were being attacked by angry Russians banging on the doors of the palace. Someone close shouted orders while screaming abuse in both German and Russian as I instinctively fumbled under my bed in the pitch dark for my P08 pistol.

In my haste I couldn't find the damned thing and imagined hurling myself at the invaders barefoot, armed only with a bottle of schnapps and an angry expression. The shouting moved to our room, the owner of the voice running to and fro from the door to the windows and back again. Another voice joined in, and I recognised Erich's, much calmer, following the first. After an exchange of words in a mumbled conversation, the first shouted again, screaming, in an awful wail as though in pain. Then I recognised the owner: Horst.

The light came on to reveal Erich at the switch by the door, whilst Horst stood in the middle of the room, apparently wide awake, legs apart, genitals hanging heavily in his off-white air force underwear. His hair a mess, his eyes staring wildly from dark sockets in an ashen-grey face, the most alarming sight was the P08 pistol in his right hand, index finger on the trigger.

"Horst, get back to bed!" Erich ordered, acknowledging me with the briefest nod. Horst turned to face him, raised his arm, and pointed the P08 directly at Erich's forehead.

They were only three metres apart and he couldn't miss.

"It's over, finished," Erich said, no longer shouting but with a reassuring calmness while still not moving. "You can get back into bed, Horst, honestly you can; it's alright now."

Anton sat up in the next bed to me, indicating his readiness to intervene, but I slowly shook my head.

Horst's trigger finger moved and I expected a bang, followed by Erich's brains spattered against the wall, but instead Horst looked around and then down at his feet, as the gun hand slowly lowered to his side.

"Yes," Horst finally said, nodding as though acknowledging a well-known truth, shuffling back towards his bed as he repeated, "Yes."

He sat on the edge as Erich repeated, "It's over, Horst; it's gone, hasn't it?" as he shuffled towards him, adding, "It wasn't your fault anyway, was it?"

He sat to his right as the bed dipped heavily, reaching over and delicately taking hold of the P08.

Horst lay back and Erich pulled up the blankets, covering him like a parent with an anxious child.

"I'm sorry," Erich whispered. "I usually move his P08 to the other side of his bed, out of reach, but I forgot last night; it's been so long since the last one."

I took a deep breath and moved to sit up as Anton sprang out of bed and rushed over to Erich.

"What the hell?" he said, within a few centimetres of Erich's face. Erich shrugged, placing Horst's P08 on the floor. What could he say? It was the first time Anton and I had seen it, but he had warned us.

In the morning nobody said anything, and Horst woke up apparently oblivious. I wanted to ask him but didn't. From then on I told Erich I'd remind him every night to hide the P08.

*

We knew it was Christmas Eve because we had stollen cake with every meal, and even without meals, with coffee, extra schnapps, and cigarettes. We each received a bottle of good quality schnapps as a gift from the German people.

As though deliberately delayed, our mail arrived in huge bundles, perfect timing indeed. *The Eagle*, our air force magazine, had a Christmas tree on the cover, and four pine trees brought in on a lorry were dragged inside the palace and placed at various locations, making some areas feel just like home. What a wonderful smell.

Pilots gathered in a grand first-floor room where the walls were lined with white marble. Initially known as the white hall, it was filled with furniture of all sizes, including a pool table, as well as a small grand piano missing most of the lid. This astonishing room became known as 'The Casino', not just because it had the atmosphere of one but because the air force often used this nickname.

It became our pilots' mess, populated by groups of card players engrossed in their games, with plenty of books, magazines, a gramophone, and, crucially, a well-stocked bar – a marvellous place, always extremely popular.

One of the huge pine trees stood in the corner opposite the homely, roaring fire. A huge pile of rough-cut logs were stacked up all along one wall, a metre deep and two metres high, but like all the huge fires in the palace it consumed wood at an alarming rate. The pine smell and woodsmoke mixed with tobacco reminded me so much of home.

Apart from the kitchens, this was probably the only communal room where the fire never went out, and so you could always guarantee a warm welcome. Several tables were laid with sausage, fresh bread, butter, huge slabs of stollen cake, layered in icing sugar, and four cooks from downstairs with radiant faces struggled to carry two great ceramic bowls of hot, mulled wine.

The casino gramophone crackled into life as Lili Marlene sang Christmas songs, soon drowned out by loud conversations and laughter. Captain Trautloft appeared in the doorway with a familiar face, Lieutenant Hans Philipp, probably investigating the noise, and both were immediately mobbed by pilots telling them something I couldn't quite hear.

Five minutes later they both reappeared, with Lieutenant Philipp lugging a huge piano accordion on a wide leather strap around his neck. Spontaneous loud applause and cheering erupted, with space cleared near the fire.

Sitting on the edge of a dining chair with the accordion on his knees, he whistled and worked the concertina, his fingers dancing amongst the keys with expert precision. The brass castors of the lidless piano squealed in protest as they dragged it across the floor, leaving three smooth lines in the dust. Two officers played a duet and others sang along. The CO took on conducting duties with great enthusiasm and everyone clapped in time, until the entire room was caught up in the Christmas spirit.

It didn't seem odd that some of the senior officers of JG54 Fighter Wing entertained their staff like this; they were so well-liked and respected they could have done anything and we would have joined in.

For a while we completely forgot what we were doing in Russia.

8

After an hour I volunteered to fetch more refreshments, and anxious not to miss anything I ran along the corridors and down the stairs to the kitchens. Though we were meant to be observing a blackout, the back door was propped open as crates were being unloaded from a lorry.

Huge snowflakes whirled around in the doorway, lured inside by the light and the warmth, where they melted away in tiny puddles on the blue and white tiles. With the CO's compliments I took a crate of schnapps from a gruff sergeant and ran back up the wide marble staircase.

As I reached the top, pausing to catch my breath, the music and singing echoing down the corridor took me back to Germany, to a Christmas function in Elmshorn long before the war. It felt as though I'd never been to Russia, or France, and Europe was still at peace. But the war brought me 1,500 kilometres from home, and I suddenly had a brief but very bleak thought that I'd never see it again. I shrugged this off and returned to the party, now a very loud gathering of fresh-faced, inebriated young men, almost all of whom were either still teenagers or in their early twenties.

The next day, nursing a bad head, I wrote more letters to my parents and to Inge. She had stopped mentioning her brother and from my experience in the air force this could only mean one thing. I decided not to ask, trying to keep our communications as light as possible.

We wondered what life would be like in Germany. Mixed news came from the west: the RAF had become active again, bombing our bases in Holland and Denmark, and even German cities, but only at night. They couldn't bomb during the day because they'd all be shot down. I found it ominous that, after all Goering's promises, they were still capable, and more than ever, so it seemed. The enemy were being shot down in large numbers, the same as here in Russia, so we were surprised they still kept on coming.

Everything in Germany was fine, always confirmed when we asked those who had recently visited Berlin. Our forces' radio kept us in touch with world events and in the first week of December, the Japanese joined the war on our side, after destroying the entire American fleet at Pearl Harbor. Any war in the Pacific would not affect us, and even though the Americans had declared war on Germany, they would find it difficult, if not impossible, to cross the Atlantic with so many of our U-Boats on patrol. The Americans would be busy countering an invasion on the west coast, so their entering the war would not affect us at all.

Low cloud with heavy snow persisted until the last day of the year when it finally lifted as high pressure returned, presenting us with a beautiful clear sky and very little wind.

Ten of us climbed aboard the lorry and we filled the

briefing room hut at airfield dispersal, keen to make the most of the daylight. I was to be the wingman for Sergeant Karl 'Quax' Schnorrer, a thin-faced, slightly built man with a wide easy smile.

After introductions I remembered my time at Bergen and the tenuous connection when someone had accused me of being 'another Quax', so I couldn't resist asking about it.

He looked blank at first but then smiled. "I crash-landed my 109 three times on my first trips," he said, putting on his gloves, "so they called me Quax, after the comedy film character."

I told him I'd heard the story after my own crash-landing on the beach, and he patted me on the back. "We did it in training, Paul, so we don't have to do it now, eh?"

As though they had also been waiting for good weather and even before we could get into our aeroplanes, we were alerted to Russian aeroplanes approaching the front line, so four of us immediately took off in line astern on freshly cleared snow.

Clinging to Karl's right wing as we climbed eastwards, dipping the nose occasionally to look ahead, we constantly searched the sky. Karl had been in Russia a few weeks longer than me and was desperate to make his first kill, and it showed. He threw his aeroplane around as though being pursued all the time and I found it difficult to keep up, even before sighting the enemy.

Approaching the southern tip of Lake Ladoga at three thousand metres I heard a shout over the R/T: "Indians dead ahead, below us and turning south!"

Looking down, a cluster of dots in the near distance crossed our front from left to right. As we neared them, I thought they were our own Me110s until I heard another shout – "Pe-2s" – as Karl lowered the nose of his aeroplane, applying full power.

On his right wing, as we closed in at high speed, we had total surprise. The Russians made no attempt at evasive manoeuvres but remained on their heading as we raced at them, the recoil from my guns rattling the entire airframe. Karl turned to pursue one, firing intermittently, getting up close behind as it trailed smoke, when huge parts broke off, spinning towards us. His target flipped over onto its back, pausing momentarily before heading directly earthwards.

No movement came from the cockpit, and it struck the frozen earth hard and exploded.

Karl cheered with delight at his first kill and I was pleased I'd done my job as his wingman.

The other Pe-2s headed east, safe behind a barrage of their own flak, so we broke away, landing back at Krasnogvardeisk airfield without loss. Trembling with excitement, my veins flush with raw adrenalin, I jumped onto the ice.

Refuelled and rearmed, we waited for another call, but darkness fell again soon after, and much to our disappointment Ivan failed to reappear, so we returned to the palace.

Anton had been flying in an op to the south and he beamed when he told us he had secured his first confirmed kill, also a Pe-2, so we had extra schnapps as we celebrated this with the arrival of 1942. The war was progressing entirely in our favour, exactly as our leaders had promised, with our forces poised at the very gates of Moscow. Pilots in the Central Sector reported seeing the Kremlin spires, so we were all confident that 1942 would see the city as ours and, with it, total Russian capitulation, ending the war in the east.

Some Central Sector aeroplanes were already displaying a curious new badge, the three domed spires of the Moscow Air District Command. It seemed we were already there. We drank schnapps and vodka, raising our glasses to the New Year with great optimism. We all wondered when we'd be able to visit Moscow and see the sights. What would happen to Stalin? If he was captured alive perhaps he would be put on trial for provoking war with Germany?

In the morning, eight of us took off at 1000 hours, joined by four 109s from No. 3 Group at Siverskaya for a free hunt in pairs across the front line. I flew with Anton and very soon we all became involved in a mix at two thousand metres with Polikarpov I-16 Ratas west of the River Volkhov. Dozens buzzed around like flies, looking odd with their stubby little fuselage and huge radial engine. To our surprise they were flown well, so we took them seriously, chasing them around for what seemed hours, getting up as close as possible, in a sky filled with dog-fighting aeroplanes.

Our CO of No. 1 Group, Captain Eckerle, pursued a pair one after the other who couldn't shake him off, and I saw both aeroplanes go down, trailing smoke and exploding on the ground. Several others smashed into the frozen earth with the briefest puff of smoke and shower of ice and snow. Great drifting arcs of brown smoke and shallow black pockmarks on the face of the landscape were all that remained of our enemy.

Two surviving Ratas turned east, fast and low, and we watched as they ran, tempting us to follow. But we knew their tricks; they would often try leading us deep into their territory, knowing we would become short of fuel; this caught a few of our pilots who were then captured after a forced landing.

I wanted to pursue them and take the risk. When the adrenalin is flowing it's hard to resist, but the CO's voice was unequivocal: "Disengage."

We didn't lose anyone in this encounter and I found it a real thrill, just what I had imagined aerial combat to be like. I was sure I had damaged at least one of them, and amongst all the excitement, Anton came back with another kill to his name.

9

At Krasnogvardeisk, or the Palace Airfield as we more often called it now, the CO caught my eye.

"Please accompany me to the adjutant's office near dispersal," he said.

What an honour!

"Yes, I witnessed your two kills, sir," I said, guessing the reason as he led me into the office. I was to act as his official confirmation.

A thin corporal with round glasses sat behind a small work desk, immediately adjacent to a stove. Behind him a blackboard, fixed to the wall, showed a list of names and numbers which, at first, I thought to be a nominal roll of pilots. Then I noticed it was a kill list, with the grand total against each pilot's name, like a squadron scoreboard.

The corporal stood bolt upright for a moment, before sitting back down, reaching for a thick ledger book by his side, opening it several pages in. Taking a ruler and an ink pen, he drew a line across the page under the last entry, before beginning the new one.

"Aircraft type?" he demanded, without looking up, then, "Aircraft number?"

Captain Eckerle answered every question promptly.

"Were you the pilot, sir?" he said, finally looking up as the CO nodded. "Take-off time and landing time, please."

We stood over the desk as the clerk wrote the details with what appeared to be an ancient quill, in an old script I could hardly read.

"Purpose of the flight?" he asked, followed by, "Any contact with the enemy?"

His quill now poised over the final column on the page, without hesitation I jumped in. "Yes, Captain Eckerle shot down two Ratas. I saw them go down."

The CO smiled. "Thank you, Goetz," he said.

The clerk's quill glided smoothly across the page before he dotted the end and asked, "Was this over enemy territory?"

"Yes," the CO replied.

"Any losses?"

"None," he said, and an exaggerated zero was written in a tiny space at the end.

"Excellent, thank you, gentlemen."

The clerk rolled blotting paper across the page before closing it reverently with a delicate thud. The front cover was inscribed with the air force eagle and swastika in gold leaf, with one word underneath: *Startkladde*.

*

At breakfast on 3rd January we heard that Siverskaya had been bombed during the night. We were all stunned. How dare they fly over our territory? One or two pilots claimed they'd heard it, but it was thirty kilometres away, and to my shame I didn't. I'd slept soundly after quite a few drinks in the casino.

Very few flak artillery units were in the area and no night fighters, and so Russian losses were probably nil. The coldest weather had returned, regularly dropping to minus forty-five, and frankly I wondered how the enemy could operate in such conditions, with some of their older aeroplanes having open cockpits.

The news that ten of our aeroplanes had been destroyed, including two Fieseler 156 Storch machines, caused a great deal of anger. Luckily the human casualties were light, but it seemed they could overfly our airfields at night at any time with total impunity.

Captain Trautloft arranged a meeting of Group COs to see what could be done. The next night at around 0300 hours I heard the intruders: a rhythmic clattering of primitive Russian aero engines passing overhead at about two thousand metres, heading west. Perhaps there were more of them, rattling across the freezing sky with the mechanical rhythm of a sewing machine in thick cotton. They slowed occasionally, then speeded up, fading away and getting louder again, like my mother's foot easing up and down on the treadle. For a few moments I was at home, listening to her machine, with the smell of coal burning in the grate, and my father's tobacco smoke drifting through the house, eventually drawn up the chimney by the fire.

The dull thud of distant bombs exploding threw me back to the present. It was Siverskaya again, as a flak battery opened up with a distinctive pom-pom and tracer raking the sky.

Others woke up and I heard mumbled comments such as, "Shit," and, "Bastards."

In the morning we realised these recent attacks were part of a wider Russian plan. We were scrambled at 0900 hours, before first light, to counter an advance by their ground troops around Staraya Russa. The CO admitted with dismay that they had smashed a hole in the front line more than ten kilometres wide, so we were to throw everything we had at them.

These were my first ground attack operations and I remembered the paper targets at Werneuchen and the high-speed low-level approach. This time it would be real.

After a flight of almost two hundred kilometres we landed at Ryelbitzi to collect fuel and white-painted butterfly bombs. A mere strip in the Russian landscape, this airfield's facilities were primitive, compared to Gatchina and Siverskaya. The front line was fluid but as we closed in, their flak came up to greet us: ferocious and accurate.

We dropped down to fifty metres in line abreast, as vehicles and troops scattered for cover we roared in, firing all our cannons and machine guns.

Flak burst all around with small arms fire pinging on the metal skin of my aeroplane, and I realised I was holding the controls far too tightly as though hanging on for my life. I could hardly breathe as my chest pounded, because I knew that if I took a major hit at this height and speed, I'd be unable to get out and I'd be gone in an instant, maybe without even knowing it. I held on and hoped my speed would get me through it, aware that my colleagues were doing exactly the same.

My munitions ripped vehicles open like tin cans. I can only imagine what a cannon shell does to a man, and thankfully I was flying too fast to see. To my horror I then flew directly into a bright orange ball, and my aeroplane shook violently as flames surrounded the cockpit.

I'd been hit by flak. My mother would read an air force telegram informing her I was *Vermisst*, my fragmented charred remains lost for all eternity in the anonymous Russian landscape.

10

Holding on tightly, I instinctively pulled up the nose, trying to delay the inevitable. If on fire, I'd only have a few moments before I hit the ground. Too low to bail out, I turned back to our own lines. In an extraordinary moment of calm I glanced around the instrument panel, surprised to see everything fine.

I'd flown directly into a flak burst, yet I was still in the air. Half a second earlier and this would not have been the case; passing through it just a millisecond after the explosion, I'd dodged most of it, merely hurtling through fire and disturbed air.

Shaking uncontrollably, I gripped the controls ever tighter to keep my hands still. I felt warm liquid around my legs. Was it blood, oil, or fuel? Had I been I hit after all? I searched for a leak or a hole somewhere in the cockpit, and in myself, because my uniform was soaking. I had to find the problem fast or

I'd be in serious trouble. If it was blood in such a quantity, I'd probably pass out, and if it was fuel my aeroplane could explode at any moment.

I opened the throttle, the engine responding, and gained height. Between repeated instrument checks I saw the others and turned to follow. With no smoke, and no apparent damage to my aeroplane, how was my uniform wet?

We landed at Ryelbitzi. I shut down my engine and climbed out, shaking, abandoning my parachute in the cockpit, before heading straight for the crew room where a huge brick stove had nudged it above freezing. A thin layer of ice shone on my trousers. In a mix of shame and surprise I realised nothing had been leaking in the cockpit other than me, and it wasn't blood.

Standing as close to the stove as I dared, I unbuttoned my coat and tunic. Steam rose from my uniform in such dense clouds it looked as though I was on fire. The pungent smell of warm urine rose up, almost making me sick. I'd come too close to the heat too quickly, and chilblain needles jabbed at my hands and legs. Feeling self-conscious, I knew I had to dry out or I would most probably freeze.

Daring to look around, I expected shocked faces and ridicule, but the room was filled with red-faced steaming bodies like mine, waiting patiently for hot coffee and a few moments by the stove. No-one noticed.

Conversation was subdued with none of the high spirits that usually follow an op. I felt utterly wretched and my main thoughts were of getting back to the palace safely and taking a shower.

After standing around in this condition for almost an hour, we finally took off, calmed and a little drier, landing back at the Palace Airfield without loss. I sent my uniform to be washed, and almost drowned myself in a steamy hot shower.

Is that what happens when you die in combat? You piss yourself, or shit yourself, returning in your last moments to the incontinent state when first born? If it wasn't so real, the irony would be hilarious. Of course, I didn't discuss this with anyone. It never occurred to me that others may have experienced the same. I tried to forget it, and hopefully prepare myself if it happened again.

*

We repeated this type of op every day, expecting Ivan to retreat, but he didn't. I didn't fly through a flak burst again, but I learned to cope with the likely prospect of my own sudden death at 300kph, because I would probably be unaware of it, except perhaps for the briefest moment of hopelessness. Not only this, I had survived the last time, so I only had to repeat what I had done before. Why should it turn out any different? I was flying faster and lower every time, not being braver but in order to get the job done as quickly as possible. Others were doing exactly the same.

Despite how many hundreds of vehicles we destroyed, and men we killed, they kept on appearing. Where were they all coming from? Clearly we needed reinforcements in order to kill more of them.

At the end of the week Captain Hrabak's No. 2 Group joined us straight from Germany, now billeted at a rough airfield eighty kilometres west of Staraya Russa called Dno. They had the new 109 F4 and, after a few days, with their help, we finally began to make an impact, or so we thought. By this time the Red Army had pushed forward almost sixty kilometres in some places before we stopped them. We had killed thousands, probably tens of thousands, but they kept on coming.

There's no doubt we were all concerned. The troops on the ground were fighting in dreadful conditions in the open, while suffering constant bombing by night. We heard a rumour they wouldn't bomb Gatchina because they didn't want to damage the palace. If so, then more fool them.

We needed additional troops urgently, and I saw admin clerks and air force cooks with glum faces, boarding vehicles at the rear of the palace, hugging brand-new Mauser rifles. I thanked God for being a pilot. I'd be sleeping on a warm camp bed in a luxurious palace, not in a frozen trench in minus thirty degrees.

In the late morning of 15th January a group of pilots from Staraya Russa and Ryelbitzi arrived in high spirits but looking particularly drawn. They immediately filed into our hot showers, emerging freshly shaven wearing clean uniforms. Our well-equipped uniform store on the ground floor, managed by two elderly sergeants, could provide any item for anyone, provided they had a requisition, signed in triplicate, bearing their squadron stamp. For convenience, there was a delousing room for air force personnel next door, but luckily this had yet to find much use.

The army had stores of their own at the other side and their delousing facilities were more popular. The problem of lice was taken very seriously, due to the risk of typhus, and bonfires of condemned louse-ridden field grey uniforms became an increasingly common sight.

Senior officers among the visiting pilots had a closed-door meeting for half an hour with Captain Trautloft, before we were all ordered to attend the great hall. Dozens of folding chairs had been set out and as soon as I entered, I noticed a huge new blackboard fixed to the wall on the right of the fireplace, similar to the one I'd seen in the adjutant's office at the airfield.

An acting corporal chalked names and numbers: JG54 written in full, Jadgeschwader 54 in bold gothic print, surrounded by the spreading wings of the air force eagle clutching a swastika.

As the room filled with pilots, I caught up with Otto Kittel again, and a few other familiar faces, among them Helmut Missner and Reinhold Hoffman, whom I'd met at Bergen. I loved seeing them again and realised how lucky I'd been when they told me they'd been at Ryelbitzi since leaving Bergen. They'd seen the palace only briefly before and so they took the mickey out of me mercilessly for never having roughed it as they had.

The room hushed as the CO began with a couple of announcements, the first of which he modestly mentioned almost in passing, the fact he'd been promoted to major.

Holding his new rank insignia in his hands, he said, half-joking, "Anyone good at sewing? The private who usually looks after me is now in a trench near Lake Ilmen."

After applause and laughter, he then raised the issue for which the meeting had been called. No-one had lit the fire, the usual firestarter probably in the same trench on the Volkhov, so the weak winter sun, barely above the horizon, made no impact in the room, despite the huge windows.

Several men were smoking but they stubbed out their cigarettes into the once-beautiful, polished wood floor when the CO began.

11

"Gentlemen, I'll be brief. I need twenty volunteers," he said, scanning our faces in his usual manner, "to have a crack at Ivan on his damned night flights."

I smiled, nodding, seeing others equally pleased. Most of our ops were in such poor daylight as to be almost dark anyway, and even on these day flights we'd been taking off or landing in darkness, the days being so short. But Ivan was coming over at two or three o'clock in the morning, so this specific problem had to be addressed.

I wanted to have a go at this, even though I didn't know if I'd be any good at flying in total darkness all the time, and always in the middle of the night. It seemed everyone else thought the same, because all present volunteered.

The CO beamed.

Facing the task of rotating everyone on night duty, unless someone acquired a particular skill or taste for it, meant they'd remain as night owls.

"Provision will be made for sleeping in the day," he said, "for those pilots who prefer fighting at night a formal rota will be drawn up." He nodded to the adjutant.

Nobody knew how successful the permanent night ops would be or how long they would last; no other German fighter squadron had yet done anything like this in Russia. We had become an experiment to be observed very closely.

I wasn't rostered for the first ones, but as soon as they began, they clearly caught Ivan by surprise, as his losses quickly mounted. His elderly sewing machine biplanes fell like autumn leaves all around us. Some of the crews were captured alive and we were astonished to find many were women; two of these 'Night Witches', as we called them, were led through the palace, roped together like animals, into the custody of the SS. I stood metres away when one of them lost her headgear and thick blonde hair cascaded over her shoulders and we briefly made eye contact. She was gorgeous. I never saw either of them again and have no idea what happened.

Despite not having much night-flying training I'd already flown many hours in darkness since arriving in Russia so looked forward to having a crack at it on a permanent basis. When my turn arrived, I felt quite confident as I strapped into my machine.

Eight of us took off into a clear frozen night at 0200 hours, heading east at two thousand metres, Ivan's usual cruising height. Despite the intense cold my underclothes were already damp with sweat.

My first night being incredibly clear, like nothing I'd experienced before, I was surprised at how much I could see; the white landscape reflected the bright moonlight, and Ivan was careless by showing lights from many kilometres away.

Not long into the flight came a shout of, "Indians, dead ahead!" as a formation of silhouettes cruised across our path, heading south-west, probably for Staraya Russa. I couldn't believe our luck, and Ivan's carelessness.

In typical Red Air Force fashion they didn't break formation or try running but allowed us to get close up on their tails, as though volunteering for target practice. My flight leader and I blasted away at the lumbering black shapes, occasionally lit by flashes from their engine exhausts and from hits on their airframes.

I was wingman to Lieutenant Erwin Leykauf, who flew so close behind the enemy that he could have chopped his tail off with his prop, or reached out and punched Ivan on the nose.

The black shapes now identified as Ilyushin IL-4s, the first one lit the sky so brightly I saw the red star on the tail, with the cannon in the nose of Leykauf's 109 thumping away from only fifty metres. The IL-4 banked hard over to the right, not in a smartly executed, evasive manoeuvre, but more like the wide arc of a pebble thrown from a bridge, dropping into a vertical dive from which it never recovered. I lost sight of it for a few seconds until a fireball lit the frozen snow when it struck the ground.

Sticking to my leader's right wing, guided by the light from his exhaust, I joined in the attack on two more, unbelievably still holding formation. Another Il-4 lit the sky bright orange, but then I heard a bang from under my feet. The upper turrets of both Il-4s flashed in my direction. It seemed one of the bastards had got a lucky shot somewhere on my airframe.

The gunners in both IL-4s were still firing, and as they did so their faces lit up, framed by leather headsets. The closest seemed to be showing his teeth as he hauled his gun around the sky, firing wildly. They couldn't see us any better than we could see them, but they only needed to be lucky again and I'd be in serious trouble. To my horror there came another bang from under my seat, and as my DB601 made terrible noises I'd never heard before, I assumed the worst.

Practice engine failures were never like this in training. I had to make an immediate assessment, and in particular, the survivability of my aeroplane. Is there any oil or coolant burning? Is it still controllable? Do I have power? With no detectable fire or even smoke, I still had control, and power, so now I had to think of my location and my chances.

Lights from the city of Volkhov were close by, so I must have been some distance into hostile territory. In the middle of the night, and at minus forty degrees, if I bailed out into the freezing slipstream, my hands would be too cold to open my parachute, and I'd probably freeze instantly. If I landed behind the lines, even if I survived, I'd most likely be shot on sight.

My lower bowels began loosening as a wave of terror I'd never known before took a firm hold.

12

Desperately trying to remain calm and in control of both myself and my aeroplane, I throttled back and checked the instruments thoroughly. In the pale green cockpit light everything appeared normal as the engine sounded reasonable again. Although not right, at least it seemed to be functioning. Prepared for any variation in pitch or deviation in temperatures and pressures, I remembered my fuel gauge; to my astonishment it was frighteningly low. Before I reported my predicament, Lieutenant Leykauf signalled over the R/T that they were heading for home. While distracted I'd rather stupidly lost sight of him and the Il-4s, suddenly totally alone.

The engine began rough running again. With my usual calmness I calculated that with the Palace Airfield at least two hundred kilometres away, I didn't have nearly enough fuel to make it back, even if my engine continued, which was doubtful. Although curiously relieved the calculation had been made, I was now committed to some sort of forced landing behind the lines. The exact location of my inevitable contact with the ground would depend on whatever fuel and power I had left. My obvious goal would be to reach as far west as possible.

Why the loss of fuel? I should have had more than enough. I made a detailed estimation as to how far I could go with what I had, at least some distance back over our lines, or so I thought. Straining to see in the poor light, I quickly flipped my map open on my knee and saw the reflection of my face in the canopy, now a mirror against the blackness, my green complexion hauntingly appropriate.

With an odd name I first thought to be an abbreviation, Mga was about halfway home. Landing there seemed a wonderful idea. One of our forward landing grounds, west of the town bearing the same name but close to the front, it was kept precisely for the reason I now found myself in. Luckily we still had it, as far as I knew. I imagined a successful landing, quickly refuelling, and taking off again. Everything would be fine.

After informing Lieutenant Leykauf, he calmly sent a message to Mga airfield on my behalf. I'd never considered my radio might be damaged. I received a brief acknowledgement: "Roger that, we'll get the garden fence ready for him."

Reassuring air force slang, nice to hear.

About to curse my bad luck and solitude, suddenly the silhouette of a 109 appeared a few metres off my right wing. A ghoulish pale green Lieutenant Leykauf smiled and waved. "You'll be okay at Mga," he crackled over the R/T. "The runway is 050 and 230, so take your pick; we're not that far away now. They'll light it up for you, so don't worry, you can't miss it."

Erwin was only a year or two older than me and the amount of reassurance he gave me was priceless.

Ten minutes later, with my low fuel warning light staring me in the face like an angry teacher, I still couldn't see an airfield in the frozen darkness, and imagined trying to put down blindly into an uneven Russian field, wheels up and engine silent in a dead stick landing. My cockpit now warm, I wondered if it was me or perhaps there were flames underneath my feet trying to get in.

Very faint flickering lights appeared. Could this be Mga? With perfect timing the R/T crackled again. "There it is, Goetz, get down safely and we'll see you tomorrow," shouted Lieutenant Leykauf, finally adding, "Good luck," before powering away into the darkness.

Following the direction indicator, I lined up on 230 degrees and what I now realised were parallel lines of dimly flickering oil lamps. To my relief I still had power, so I throttled back, raising the nose before selecting the undercarriage lever. Nothing happened. My first thought wasn't one of terror at yet another wheels-up landing but of frustration. *Not again!* I thought, angrily. The flaps didn't come down either, so I had to land much lower and faster to compensate.

Keeping the aeroplane steady on a flapless approach was going well and at the last moment, instead of landing on the cleared runway, I decided to touch down next to it, in what I hoped would be deep snow. This was an instantaneous decision based on the fact the snow could minimise damage to both myself and the aeroplane. Although risky, I hoped the nose wouldn't dig in immediately, sending me tumbling over in a violent ground loop.

Quickly tightening my straps, with the two lines of flickering yellow lamps now on my left, the prop began clipping the snow.

To my surprise I didn't sink slowly as planned but rode along on a frozen crust at 150kph. I held off as long as possible with firm back pressure before an increasing roar of metal on ice as the tail and then the whole fuselage made contact.

For a few moments I continued sliding, but then, as my speed decayed, the increasing weight forced the aeroplane through the ice, juddering violently.

The prop had stopped and the snow underneath gripped the aeroplane like rice pudding, so I shut my eyes and hung on. The nose dug further in and I came to a halt surprisingly quickly, with my head lurching forwards and my body held firmly in the straps.

I immediately turned off the fuel and all the switches.

The lamps to my left and the stars above had gone. It took me a moment to realise the canopy was covered in snow and my seat leaned forwards at quite a steep angle. The nose had obviously dug in with the tail sticking up like a flag.

Silence reigned in my igloo, the type of vacuous quiet that only thick snow creates. My rapid breathing and hot breath fogged the Perspex as an overwhelming desire to pee came over me. I resisted because I knew it was just the cold telling me to go when I really didn't need to. My bladder had been playing these rotten tricks on me ever since I'd arrived in Russia.

A flare gun lay near my right hand, and I wanted to use it but was buried, so I knew it wouldn't go anywhere but straight back into my face. I was trapped and wondered what the hell to do.

Sensing the rumbling of a vehicle close behind, I waited. Unfastening the leather holster on my belt, I took out my P08 just in case, but as the vehicle stopped I heard muffled shouting in German a few metres away. "You missed the fucking runway, you dumb shit," or similar, to which I laughed, and almost cried with relief.

Two pairs of fur mittens scrubbed at the snow on the canopy before they threw it open and I was hauled out by two enormous figures wrapped in so much animal fur they looked like grizzly bears. While being restrained as though under arrest, they threw me into the back of a lorry, without any introductions, and five minutes later from a series of grunts, I understood I had to follow the two bears down some makeshift steps towards a vertical hole in a wall of snow.

They dragged a door across the ice, and then another door opened two metres further inside, after which I entered a place I can only describe as a brightly lit cave, ten metres wide and barely two metres high.

13

The two bears immediately began removing their fur, revealing a sergeant major and a second lieutenant. Two blazing bunker stoves stood close to one another, covered in mess tins and coffee pots, next to a huge pile of logs. The smell of damp earth, boiled food, coffee, body odour, and tobacco was overpowering.

After unbuttoning my coat I removed my gloves, stuffing them into my pocket. I looked around, wondering what to do.

"Welcome to Mga, and thanks for waking us up, young man," the lieutenant said, throwing a log into each of the stoves. "Get the schnapps, will you, Karl?" The sergeant major disappeared for a moment into what appeared to be a corridor dug into the earth, returning with a half-empty bottle and three glasses.

I didn't know what to say, so just said, "Sorry," rather pathetically.

"Are you alright?" the sergeant major asked, scanning my uniform for blood and broken body parts.

I nodded, realising I was uninjured.

"You missed the runway," he said, sardonically, filling the glasses.

"I know," I murmured. "It was deliberate, I hope you don't mind. I didn't want to damage my aeroplane too much and thought the snow might help."

The lieutenant looked surprised and nodded. "Good man," he replied, "Then I think you did well, considering."

He threw back his glass, swallowing the schnapps in one. "Fucking cold, isn't it?" he added, staring at me.

Why was he telling me the obvious?

Before I could say anything, the sergeant major jumped in, sounding a little less sympathetic. "What was wrong? Did you get shot up?"

He put his glass down on an upturned packing crate table and lit a huge briar pipe.

The air in the earth cave was bad enough without great clouds of his pipe smoke fogging up the place. But the German smoke made the Russian mud feel less inhospitable.

The muffled hum of a diesel generator somewhere outside stalled for a second, causing a string of bulbs hanging from the ceiling to flicker. The wire to these lights was held in place with bits of bent metal, like aeroplane parts, and above the stoves, the mud was dry and cracked where the chimney pipes disappeared. There were boards to walk on but I could see bits of the ceiling on the floor.

A rough wooden gun rack leaned against the wall near the door, containing new-looking MP40 machine pistols, all loaded, and next to this a row of Mauser rifles, some stick grenades and miscellaneous uniforms. The other side of the room was clearly a trophy wall, covered from floor to ceiling with bits of enemy aircraft, the largest of which was an entire tail fin, about two metres high, dominating the room with its bright red star.

"I was hit, I think, I don't know exactly where, but I lost fuel and my landing gear gave up," I said, trying to sound like a veteran. "Fractured fuel line and hydraulics, I should think," I added, a little more confidently.

The lieutenant had the German Cross in gold on his right breast pocket and an Iron Cross Second Class on his left. Odd that these remained on his uniform, despite the fact it seemed to be falling to bits everywhere else.

He nodded, leaning back in a padded chair that looked home-made from rough un-planed wood, worn smooth at the arms.

The schnapps made my head spin, and I felt nauseous. I was going to be sick right in front of my rescuers. How damned ungrateful. I tried thinking about other things.

A gramophone with a few records lay on the table, and next to that two open packets of Pervitin, the tablets scattered around like children's sweets. Although tempted, just looking at them exhausted me.

"You did well, young man," the lieutenant repeated, nodding at the sergeant major, now obscured in a cloud of smoke. "You'll be our guest tonight, and for as long as it takes, I'm afraid, until we can either get your aeroplane repaired or we get you back to…" He stopped. "Where are you based?"

"Krasnogvardeisk," I said, looking at the mud walls, feeling guilty, deliberately not mentioning Gatchina Palace.

"The palace?" the sergeant major asked through the cloud, shaking his head.

I was about to answer when they both finished their drinks quite suddenly, and the lieutenant nodded to the sergeant after checking his watch.

"We'll find you a bed then, if you follow me."

The sergeant major stood up, hands on hips, waiting. As I rose I almost fell over from a massive rush of blood to the head. When it cleared I no longer felt sick but incredibly hungry. I followed him along a tunnel corridor deeper into the earth, down more steps, and along another corridor, not quite high enough to walk fully upright.

Immediately off to the left an army field kitchen stood on its wheels, occupying most of the space in a brightly lit cave. I'd been wondering where the cooking smells came from.

Pausing briefly at a blanket-covered archway on the right, he turned and lifted the blanket, revealing a dimly lit and very smelly little cave.

"Latrines," he said, pointing to a long wooden plank at the back with three holes side by side, each big enough for a backside. "These are only for night soil, and are emptied every morning. The proper latrines are in the shed outside, but if you don't want a frozen arse you'll use these." He grinned.

A wire with single bulb hung from the ceiling and dozens of ripped copies of *The Eagle* magazine lay on the floor, with a dented white enamelled tin bowl at one end for hand-washing. The concentrated smell of urine and faeces, added to all the other odours drew the oxygen from my lungs, and I instinctively backed off. Despite the stench, when the time came, I knew I would not expose anything of mine to a minus forty-five-degree wind.

Numerous other small cave-like rooms to the left and right had obviously been dug out of the mud by hand, in which figures slept on rough timber beds. We passed a radio room where transmitter equipment covered one entire wall, and I recognised some Dora-2 army field radios, similar to the ones we'd used in training. The bigger equipment hummed quietly, poised like a well-mannered child waiting to speak. A single radio operator sat facing the equipment, wearing a headset, oblivious to our presence, flicking through a magazine.

The air became staler the further we went, until we reached a small dark cave in which I could barely see a heap of blankets and a thin mattress on two packing crates end to end.

"My name is Fritz, by the way, Fritz Tegtmeier," my guide said, "and the lieutenant is Gerhard Loos, the duty officer. Get your head down and we'll see you in the morning."

He smiled before turning around to walk back up the tunnel. I watched as he moved, unhurried and with a practised stoop, his pipe smoke whirling around the back of his head like wingtip vortices.

Moving over to the bed, I released a deep sigh of relief.

I'm lying in a mud cave deep in the earth, I thought, *alive, uninjured, warm, and dry.*

The nearest bulb flickered in the corridor several metres away. Though exhausted I lay awake half an hour in the dark, uncomfortably cold, until I found three more blankets in an ammo box. After wrapping myself up like an Egyptian mummy I finally dozed, thinking about the action which had caused me to be shot down, though not for long because, within a few minutes, I fell asleep.

14

A LOT OF PEOPLE WERE TALKING; I HEARD MUSIC, and laughter. Lili Marlene bounced around the walls, sounding like she had a nasty cough, the vinyl so badly pitted. Where the hell could I be?

Above me I saw dark mud, damp and smelly, like a riverbank, and nearby a doorway supported by rough timber planks, leading into a bleak tunnel. For a moment I felt uneasy, until suddenly remembering. An odd seriousness came over me, telling me to get up and do something, though I had no idea what.

Then I thought of my next letter home.

Dear Mama and Papa. I was shot down but I'm alright because two German bears rescued me by dragging me into their cave.

I laughed out loud. It would be an interesting letter.

With no natural light, I had to believe my watch saying 0700 hours.

Wonderful smells of hot food and coffee mixed with the damp mud.

Intermittent radio traffic drifted down the tunnel from the communications room, competing with Lili's juddering voice, along with quick bursts of dramatic classical music and shouting.

After putting on my belt, I stuck my head into the tunnel. Instead of returning to the entrance, I turned right, to see how far it went. A few metres away, at the end stood a tall, home-made bookcase, heaving with books and magazines, all curled at the corners in the damp atmosphere. The entrance to the final cave was obscured by two blankets suspended across the doorway. Among many copies of *The Eagle* I spotted some fantastic books I couldn't resist flicking through, as the blanket door was thrown to one side and a sergeant emerged, hoisting up his trousers and buttoning his flies. He'd obviously just put them back on, so I wondered if it could be another latrine.

Younger than me and clearly surprised I was there, having almost bumped into me, he paused briefly as though about to offer some explanation, which he didn't. Before the curtain fell, I saw another man on an army camp bed, the only one in the room, smoking, virtually naked.

The sergeant stared at the floor, not looking at me again, before walking briskly away up the tunnel towards the light. At the time I was still too naïve to realise what had just been happening.

After collecting my things, I wandered towards the entrance and stopped at the field kitchen. Standing in the doorway, I probably looked as hungry as I felt, because a fat, balding sergeant shouted from behind it, "Help yourself," as though reading my mind.

The mud walls streamed with moisture and the chimney had been extended to run up through the ceiling. It never occurred to me how they'd managed to get something as huge as the field kitchen into this tiny space. Despite the dubious cleanliness, whatever it was smelled delicious, but I thought I'd better make myself known to the CO before eating.

The classical music from the radio room had stopped, replaced by loud static and occasional rapid bursts of Russian from someone sounding both excited and anxious. Two men, wearing headsets, crouched on long metal ammo boxes in front of the wall of receivers, and one appeared to be translating while the other frantically scribbled away in a notepad. The Russian was often high-pitched and distant, as though a thousand metres up in a very noisy aeroplane.

I knew very little Russian, but I heard *nemetsky* several times, meaning 'German', and *messer*, their generic slang for the 109. How anyone could understand anything else was beyond me, the man spoke so quickly. I wished I understood more than a couple of words and, at that moment, I decided it might be in my interests to learn, just in case.

Back in the entrance near the main door, a dozen or more men sat around packing crates, hunched over bowls of hot stew. They wore pilot badges and I noticed leather headsets and maps lying around.

With no CO's office or anyone else to report to, I returned to the field kitchen. As soon as I'd picked up a white enamelled bowl it was filled with stew by a thin corporal using a huge ladle. He nodded politely.

"Come back if you want any more," he said, as I grabbed a few slices of black bread and made my way to a table near the entrance.

I tasted meat in the mixture, so tender it crumbled in the mouth: as good as anything I'd eaten at the palace.

The sergeant from the end room stood chatting to Lieutenant Loos, occasionally glancing in my direction as though I was the subject of discussion. I didn't know it yet, but the sergeant was in charge of recovering my aeroplane and repairing it. I wondered what would happen and how long I'd be there. It would be conditional on the weather and what state my 109 might be in; if it could be repaired would I have to wait here all the time, and what if it couldn't be repaired at all, then what?

With no personal possessions or change of clothes, and in need of a shave, I felt untidy, but looking around at the others, I looked clean and smart by comparison. We were all JG54, the Green Hearts, but this was the front line and nowhere near palatial accommodation. I needed to get back as soon as possible, and so when I'd finished eating, I decided I'd speak to Lieutenant Loos.

After returning my bowl and spoon, I realised I'd lost sight of him, and found out he'd gone outside to assess the damage to my aeroplane. Should I follow, perhaps to offer a more detailed explanation? I picked up a coffee and waited.

This part of the dugout clearly had several functions; as well as a living area and dining room, it was also a briefing room and dispersal hut.

Several pilots in full kit with parachutes gathered around a map, all smoking. One passed around a hip flask, probably containing schnapps, or 'target water', as we called it.

An alarm sounded and four of them rushed out into the cold, buttoning up their thick coats as Lieutenant Loos returned, peeling off his bear skin.

Aeroplane engines started up nearby and, in only a few minutes, they moved away, ready for take-off. I then heard a commotion down the corridor so followed others to the radio room.

Lieutenant Loos stood over the radio operator as a crowd gathered.

Bleak news: Ivan had pushed forward even further, bypassing Kholm and Demyansk while pressing on westwards. I sensed a great deal of anxiety, unusually close to panic.

More pilots took their kit and ventured outside, Lieutenant Loos being one of them. I was useless without an aeroplane, and there were none available. Before he disappeared, he caught my eye.

"We must get you back to Gatchina," he said, to which I nodded, shouting an enthusiastic, "Yes!"

I didn't know what else to say.

When he'd gone, I put on my jacket and opened the doors. The fresh air took my breath away, and the cold, fierce as usual, seared my face and lungs as I trudged across fresh snow to find my aeroplane. The sky in the north-east was a deep undulating blue grey like a wild ocean, menacingly heavy with snow, and the strengthening wind nipped at my eyelids, trying to freeze them shut.

Three hundred metres down the field the tail of my 109, the only thing visible, stuck out like a shark fin. Unless recovered soon, another snowfall would completely cover it.

With my back to the wind, nose running like a broken tap and starting to freeze, I stared, desperately needing a pee.

An overwhelming sense of helplessness swept over me and, back indoors, I stood at the bookcase trying to distract myself. Several had fallen down the back onto the floor, and the title of one intrigued me, a tattered and rather bleak-looking hardback with a plain grey sleeve, and the words *'Im Westen nichts Neues'* in old German script completely filled the cover. *Nothing New in the West* had obviously been very well used; always the sign of a good book. I picked it up absent-mindedly and took it to the latrine.

Looking out for splinters, my backside carefully perched over the first hole in the rough wood, I flicked through the book. It was a novel about the First World War, a German book even though the author's name, Erich Maria Remarque, sounded French. I'd never even heard of it, but it looked interesting, so I began reading.

As I ripped up a copy of *Die Aktion*, the anti-communist periodical, finishing what I needed to do, a young private stuck his head around the doorway. "Are you Corporal Goetz?" he said, to which I nodded.

"Be ready at dispersal in two hours. A Storch is picking you up."

Wonderful news.

Within an hour all the pilots had returned safely ahead of a ferocious storm I'd seen building earlier, rolling towards us like a huge blue-white wall. Every available man, including me, rushed out to cover the aeroplanes as much as possible and, when the inevitable news came that my lift had turned back to the Palace Airfield, I shrugged.

It seemed I'd have to spend another night living in the mud like a Russian earthworm.

15

After a surprisingly good evening meal and a few games of cards with a crowded but convivial mix of ground crew and pilots, I decided to take a wander down the mud corridor towards the radio room.

Classical music echoed from a receiver and from somewhere I heard Lieutenant Loos shouting, "Turn that shit off, Weber!"

As I reached the entrance the radio operator turned it down but not completely.

He'd been the man translating Russian, now occasionally flicking switches and turning dials without even looking up from his magazine. The quiet music began building to a crescendo very dramatically as I saw him tapping a finger, gently nudging the volume back up.

I stepped over and sat next to him. Totally engrossed in the music, when he saw me, he almost fell off the ammo box.

"Shit, I thought you were Loos. He doesn't like me tuning into this, but hey, it's great music. Lili Marlene is nice, and Dr Goebbels is very informative, of course, but not all the time, eh?"

He smiled briefly, nodding to the rhythm as he turned it down a touch, glancing at the doorway. "They play this whole thing every four hours, every day, starting at midnight. You can set your watch by it."

I checked mine: 1815 hours.

"They play other stuff too, but this is the only one they play like clockwork. It's probably because they think it's patriotic, but I know different. The composer hates Stalin and it's obvious in the music, but of course he's too thick to realise. Isn't it brilliant?"

He probably saw how puzzled I looked, turning the volume up again as the music had grown softer. "I was in an orchestra before the war," he said, by way of explanation. "I'd never heard it on German radio."

He took a cigarette from a green Eckstein pack and offered me one, which I declined.

"Doesn't Lieutenant Loos like classical music?" I asked, curious.

Moving closer, he looked at the door again. "He probably does, but he knows what this is, so he tells me to turn it off, because he has to."

What did he mean?

"It's the Red Army Radio," he said, smiling. "I tell him I listen to it for intelligence reasons, as one of the few Russian speakers in this place, but it's my only chance to hear this music, because of course, it's contemporary Russian, so it's banned at home." He shook his head.

As I looked around at the equipment he stuck his right hand at me. "Hans Weber," he said, as I noticed the radio antenna badge on his uniform.

"Paul Goetz," I said, shaking his hand.

"You're the pilot who arrived in the night, aren't you?"

"Yes, the first time I've had to ditch in the darkness, and in snow," I said, shaking my head with a wry smile.

"I know. I was the one on duty when Lieutenant Leykauf called up on the R/T. You're lucky."

He resumed his reading, perhaps anticipating I'd move away, but I didn't.

After a few moments he turned to me, looking curious. "What can I do for you?" he said, above the sound of a particularly beautiful section of the music.

"You speak Russian?" I enquired, edging closer.

"Pretty well," he replied. "I was in Russia before the war."

I resisted the temptation to ask him why.

"There's a few of us in here who do, but not as well as me."

As if guessing what I was thinking, he went on to explain. "I toured this area with an orchestra. We played Leningrad a dozen times. They loved us, we were always packed out; German stuff mostly, of course, Beethoven and Brahms, and a lot of Wagner. I had to learn the language because I did most of the arranging with the venues and local officials, which was always a bloody nightmare."

"I wish I knew Russian," I said, genuinely envious, tempting him.

He stared through his round glasses and reached for another cigarette, lighting up without offering me one. "You should know..." he said, inhaling, "a few words at least," he nodded, "in case, God forbid, you are shot down behind the lines."

He ripped a page from his air force notepad as he exhaled and wrote as though preparing a shopping list, alternately chewing the end of his pencil and drawing on his cigarette.

Several minutes later he handed me the completed note. "These are essentials," he said. "They won't do you any harm to know, anyway." He paused, smiling. "That is assuming they don't shoot you on the spot before you even get a chance to speak." He laughed. "Or you shoot yourself."

He could see I wasn't amused. "We had a captured Russian in here a week ago, an officer of the Volkhov Guards Division, and he told us about Hans Strelow, seen going down in that particular sector." He paused. "You didn't know him, did you?"

He looked at me with a concerned expression, so I shook my head.

"He survived a perfect crash-landing in his 109 and the Russians were keen to get hold of him for intelligence, but when he saw them he ran back to his aeroplane, jumped into the cockpit, set it alight with a flare and blew his brains out with his P08, cremating himself in the process. Apparently they were really disappointed."

I tried to remain expressionless, attempting to hide the shock of what I'd just heard, but my eyebrows involuntarily rose in horror. Initially listed as *Vermisst*, then confirmed deceased, this was very definitely not the way I wanted to go.

With great care and very cleverly, Hans had written the Russian words in their Cyrillic letters, with the German translations in phonetic sounds. The Luftwaffe eagle embossed in the notepaper looked particularly incongruous, overwritten with Russian script.

Some of the words and phrases could indeed be useful, such as: 'Don't shoot' – *Ne strelyay*, 'Pilot' – *Pilot*, and one that I was surprised to find, *Ya podchinyayus* – 'I surrender.'

"You've written 'pilot,'" I said, pointing to the note.

He smiled. "That's what they call it, though they say it a little different, but you'd be understood."

I folded the note twice, slipping it into a rarely used inside pocket, already aware of its separateness and a desire to keep it safe. I wanted to learn every word.

Half an hour later the music ended with a tremendous crescendo as Hans nodded along. Suddenly Morse code streamed in through one of the receivers and he immediately picked up his pen and began writing, in Russian, and with that my very brief language lesson terminated.

I stood up to leave and, with a pause in the stream of dots and dashes, I asked, "What is that music, anyway?"

"Shostakovich, Fifth Symphony." He smiled, with obvious pride. "Written and first performed in Leningrad in 1937. I met him there, Dmitri Shostakovich."

Retreating to my dark hole, I took the nearest bulb from the corridor, replacing it with the dead one in my cave. I had light, but the corridor now looked and smelled like an unlit alley in the worst part of a rough city. I lay back on my bed against the mud wall and continued my book, *Nothing New in the West*, the text on the faded pages now as bright as daylight.

The Russian shopping list was burning my pocket so I took it out and began reading. Words like *fashist* and *natsistskiy* were self-explanatory, but phrases like *Mne nuzhna pomoshch* I repeated in my head, 'I need help', and *golodny*, 'hungry', words to use after assuming I'd survived a crash and had not been shot immediately.

The storm persisted all the next day and the dugout filled with anxious pilots and exhausted ground crew, concerned for the aeroplanes and the state of the runway. A weather update told us the storm was part of a deep slow-moving low-pressure system that would probably take days to clear, so we sat around and waited.

I passed my time as best I could, by reading magazines, writing letters, and playing cards. We discussed aeroplanes, home, and the war. Despite the cold and distance from home, our spirits were generally high. Curious about the place, I frequently asked about it.

"We are not actually based here permanently," said one of them, dealing the cards. "Most of us are like you, trapped in the bloody snow."

"There are more flak units than aeroplanes," said another, a sergeant pilot and the best card player I've ever met, winning every game. He stared at his cards with astonishing intensity.

"The army is here in huge numbers too," the first said. "There's a major railway junction down the road that Ivan keeps trying to take from us."

Laughter was followed by cursing as the sergeant won yet again.

My book also kept me occupied and I frequently sat with Hans for more Russian lessons. I found him oddly keen to pass on his knowledge, with me as anxious to learn. Strange thoughts began filling my head when Mr Shostakovich came around: imagining myself, perhaps working as a teacher after the war, or touring Russia with Hans and his orchestra in a calm, quiet world.

On the morning of the third day I made myself useful when the poor weather eased and, between Russian lessons, I assisted in clearing snow from the aeroplanes. Another metre had fallen, and the ground crew were constantly busy with an elderly but effective Russian snowplough along the taxiways and runway. My 109 had now completely disappeared, despite obvious efforts to reach it with the snowplough.

By midday the sky cleared and at 1200 hours a Storch landed delicately on its long thin legs like a pure white dragonfly, blending in perfectly with the surroundings. My lift home.

I had a few hurried minutes to say goodbye to my new friends, Gerhard Loos, Fritz Tegtmeier, Hans Weber, and others, before I crunched across the frozen snow towards the aeroplane.

By now I had half a dozen pages of cherished Russian language notes. The pilot was busy at the controls doing a running start, his face obscured by his greatcoat collar, pulled right up over his leather headset.

"Get in quick, for Christ's sake, I'm freezing," he ordered, his hands on the controls, easing the power back as I climbed aboard.

16

"Sorry, but I daren't switch it off because we'd never get the damned thing started again," he shouted, his voice familiar.

As soon as I'd strapped in we taxied towards the newly cleared runway before applying full power.

Once airborne, the flaps were stowed and the cabin heat applied, warming up just enough to avoid freezing to death. The Storch cockpit is primitive and very narrow but can carry two passengers seated in tandem directly behind the pilot, and when he turned around and shouted, "Welcome back!" I recognised Erich. I felt obliged to tell him about the crash, shouting above the engine noise, and when I'd finished, he shrugged.

"It happens," he said, before settling the aeroplane into level flight on a heading for the Palace Airfield.

A tailwind pushed us along gently like a sailboat, and we

chatted as best we could, landing only thirty minutes later. After engine shutdown, I wondered if I could take the Storch up for a few minutes later that day. I'd never flown one before and it looked a great little aeroplane to fly, so I asked Erich about it.

He shook his head. "They told us you needed picking up, so I volunteered. They won't let you take one up just for fun, sorry." He laughed. "Those days are gone. You need to put your name down on the rescue list. You're my second one of these pick-ups. Pleasure flying is finished, I'm afraid. Fuel is becoming a problem, remember, so this is the only way to get any flying other than combat."

Just then a pair of 109s touched down, apparently our escort from Mga.

The palace had the appearance of a huge wasps' nest continually prodded with a stick as people and vehicles rushed around amongst piles of box files and papers burning fiercely in the front courtyard. The vast corridors echoed with rapid footsteps and loud conversations like a crowded church before a Sunday service. I hadn't realised how bad things had become, and reported to the adjutant immediately to find out when I would be flying again, or indeed whether we were retreating.

When I saw the duty board in the corridor I gasped, amused to see a clearly inaccurate word against my name: '*Vermisst*'.

"Goetz!" the adjutant shouted as I knocked, walking straight in, my surprise turning to mild anger. "Not joined the Red Army after all then?" he said, smiling.

"Erwin Leykauf saw me go down at Mga, so where did you think I was, sir?" I retorted, with consternation, trying not to sound rude.

"Yes, he saw you go down, but you vanished in the dark. Did you not think to keep your radio on and let us know?

Nobody confirmed you'd made it. You could have been dead in a field for all we knew." His smile was replaced by a withering look, throwing me onto the defensive.

"Didn't anyone at Mga let you know?" I asked, genuinely intrigued at how my own demise had come about. "They sent a plane for me so someone must have known."

"No, they didn't, not until their radio operator, Weber, got in touch with us today. I suppose they should have told us immediately, but they didn't, so that's that. Until we formally hear otherwise, that's precisely what you would forever remain, missing," he said, shaking his head.

I wondered why Hans had only sent the message that morning, but then the weather had been so hopeless.

"What happened, Goetz? Why did you have to put down there?"

He stood up, scrubbing *Vermisst* from my name on the office duty board and then in a few short steps the one in the corridor.

"Engine trouble, sir. I think it was hit a couple of times."

"So where is your aeroplane now?"

"Under two metres of snow at Mga airfield," I said, guiltily.

"So I heard," he groaned, shaking his head.

Why did he ask if he already knew? I wanted to explain, or perhaps give my excuses, but loud shouts came from outside, as dozens of SS troops crowded around a convoy of vehicles just arrived.

Anxious to find out more, I asked, "Are we retreating?"

"Retreating?" he said, looking quizzical. "Christ no, whatever gave you that idea?" With no humour in his voice, he looked as though I'd just hurled an insult.

"The bonfires; and everyone running around?"

"That? No, that's just the SS clearing out their closet. General Keller and his staff are due here in a couple of days for an inspection. Apparently Goering is anxious to get an urgent appraisal, so no, we are not retreating. Don't mention that word to the CO either; he gets a bit touchy about it. There's a briefing for all pilots tonight, so you're just in time, Goetz."

He picked up the telephone receiver, engaging in conversation immediately, so I left.

In the casino my friends gathered around as though I'd become a hero.

"We were sure you were hiding in the snow eating rabbits and raw potatoes," one said, shaking my hand firmly as others jostled around.

"Knowing his luck, Goetz would be picked up by a gorgeous blonde with huge bosoms who'd shag him half to death," Anton said, slapping my back so hard I almost fell over.

"It wasn't that, was it?" Anton asked as the others laughed.

"No, not quite," I said, "I've been at Mga, the forward airfield," accepting a swig on a new bottle of schnapps while enjoying the attention.

"Never been," someone said, to general nodding of heads, followed by, "What's it like?"

"No, I've never had to use it either," someone else said, sarcastically, to more laughter.

I shook my head, before replying with a wide smile, "It's fantastic, honestly. There's a well-stocked bar, lots of obliging Russian girls, and the rooms are even better than the palace, but you'll just have to find that out for yourself."

They all laughed, knowing full well I was lying.

Having survived two crash-landings in a 109, I discovered a few others had had similar problems while I'd been away.

Reinhold told of his first kill, but Anton overheard, giving him a wry smile. "Only one?"

His tally had now doubled to four. Others jumped in,

telling me they'd reached half a dozen, and some were now well into double figures.

Sitting down facing a roaring fire with a glass of schnapps, I glanced at the high ceiling with its finely detailed plasterwork, acknowledging my good luck. My comrades gave me far too much to drink, in what I realised was collective relief that one of us had returned safely. I wasn't conceited enough to imagine it was all about me, more about the fact another of us had beaten the odds, aware that these same odds were increasingly stacked against us.

A couple of hours later, I staggered up the marble staircase, pleased to see my champagne crate still intact under my bed. Thankfully a pilot's personal possessions were sacrosanct; unless he was definitely confirmed as gone his schnapps and everything else remained untouched.

Two letters waited, one from my mother and the other from Inge, so I decided to savour opening them until I'd taken a shower. Down on the ground floor, the busy kitchens sent cooking smells through the corridors, and thick, undulating clouds of steam rolled along the ceiling like boiling cumulus, so I knew there'd be plenty of hot water. I stood under the flow, very relieved to be back.

The steam filled my lungs, drawing out the smells from the Mga dugout and revitalising my soul. There had been washing facilities at Mga, but nothing like this and for a moment as the hot water perfectly warmed my bones, I had a guilty sense that the war was happening elsewhere.

Pausing at the Russian graffiti near the main entrance, I took out my list and stared at it, attempting to translate the Cyrillic script.

Despite it being carelessly daubed in red paint, I pieced it together.

'FASCIST PIGS – YOU WILL ALL DIE IN RUSSIA!'

17

I don't know why, but I never told anyone the German translation. Someone must have found out, though, because a few weeks later it had been painted over. Occasionally still visible in certain light, the ghostly promise refused to be subdued.

Moments later I stood in the great hall with dozens of other pilots as the CO appeared.

"Gentlemen, we have a job to do," he said with an uncertain frown, an expression I'd never seen on his face before. There wasn't much light in the churchy gloom of the hall as the February night turned the windows into dusty mirrors, with the four army light bulbs turning faces a pasty yellow.

"Ivan has now completely surrounded Demyansk and Kholm. Our ground forces are therefore trapped."

He paused as our expressions reflected the seriousness.

"It has been decided we are to help air drop supplies, as surrender is obviously not an option."

Murmurings of agreement broke the silence, rising to a crescendo of support. The adjutant and two others fixed a huge map to the wall, made of several stuck together, carelessly bashing nails into the corners with a hammer. Bits of plaster flew off, scattering across the floor like troops running for cover. He cursed several times, thumping it repeatedly as cracks appeared which spread several metres around.

Finally it stayed up, the Russian Front in all its vastness from Leningrad to Stalingrad, mocking us with its sheer size. I'd never before seen a single map showing the entirety of western Russia without half of it hanging over a desk, and for the first time, I sensed an element of doubt. I wondered if anyone else thought the same; looking around, I didn't detect any.

The CO positioned himself adjacent to it, facing us. "Half of you must go down to Dno, Staraya Russa, and Ryelbitzi. I'll ask for volunteers first, but I may need to volunteer you myself."

A welcome ripple of laughter lasted longer than the CO had anticipated, perhaps prompted by nervous excitement.

"Some of JG3 are now there, as are Hrabak's No. 2 Group, as you know. Not only do we have to protect our ground forces trapped here," he said, tapping the red circled area now known as the Demyansk Pocket, "we will have hundreds of transport aircraft to look after too." He paused, scanning our faces, as he always did.

With raised fatherly eyebrows, he continued. "Gentlemen, I do not want any of these transport aircraft to be shot down. Is that clearly understood? Not a single one."

The room remained silent.

"Our troops need every kilo of food and ammunition."

In perfect unison, as though we'd been practising, we all nodded our heads with a very firm, "Yes, sir," in reply.

"To those of you who remain here, you will not have an easy time. You will double your usual number of ops, including the night ops, which I'm pleased to say have been a tremendous success, so these will also continue, while in the daytime we must convince Ivan we are still at full strength. You will all be very busy indeed."

Finally he asked for a show of hands from volunteers. I don't know what he was expecting, but every right arm in the room shot up.

He seemed impressed, and more than a little humbled.

We saw no option. What else could we do? Our ground forces desperately needed help.

The CO and adjutant then drew up a list of names in no particular order, with everyone taking a turn in due course.

The meeting broke up with loud conversations about how we would smash Ivan's encirclement; we were absolutely confident.

*

In a letter already a month old, my mother stated my Hitler Youth friend, Heinrich Berger, had been killed. His parents were told few details other than it had happened 'somewhere in Russia'. She had met his mother Helen buying groceries, and apparently told my mother ten times before my mother managed to get away, saying in her letter that she thought Helen had 'turned a bit odd'.

He'd been successful in joining the SS as he'd always wanted, and now he'd gone. Heinrich had never married, or even had a girlfriend, as far as I knew; his only passion in life had been National Socialism.

Hanging up my jacket by my bed, I felt the book from Mga in my pocket. I didn't want to read it, so I put it in my champagne crate. Maybe there'd be a time when I would catch up with it again.

At dawn we were woken by the revving of vehicle engines, doors slamming and barking orders from the courtyard below, and I stepped over to the window to investigate. Members of the SS were screaming at one another as though in a shouting competition. One poor soul was roundly admonished, before an officer turned on several others standing rigidly to attention beside odd-looking vehicles.

Half a dozen Mercedes vans with rigid sides and their back doors wide open were being swept from inside, the liquid contents pouring out.

"Idiot!" the officer shouted repeatedly, "Not here!" to some frantic salutes, followed by shouts of, "Get them out of here, now," his orders bouncing off the walls right across the courtyard, as he occasionally glanced in our direction.

The drivers started their engines and drove away like a dismal circus. As they passed closer to our room, I saw two sets of shutters on each side of the larger vehicles and one on each of the smaller, but the doors were still open, pinned to the sides. There were no windows, so why the fake shutters? Even more curious were thick clouds of exhaust fumes from *inside* the rear of the vans.

Should I have worried about this? Important issues were on my mind so, no, I didn't. Being posted south into the middle of the war, I had to collect all my things, such as uniforms, shaving kit and personal effects, get to the airfield, and claim another aeroplane. The adjutant told me I would have a choice of several. The duty board at the palace was now missing half the usual names, including mine because of my trip south.

My canvas bag packed with a spare uniform and personal effects, I shoved my champagne crate back under my bed, determined I would return. We took a lorry to the airfield where I found an ageing 109 F, looking as though the white camouflage paint had been thrown over it and spread by a blind man using his stick. Black exhaust stains covered half the fuselage and, as I stood looking, a ground crew member shouted me over to dispersal.

"It's just come from Meukuhren, the training base. We were going to clean it up, but we didn't have time, sorry about that," he said, forcing a smile. "But it's otherwise in first-class condition, fully armed and fuelled."

He disappeared back inside and emerged a few moments later with a crank handle in his gloved hands.

I found a parachute in the dispersal hut, strapped it on, waddled over the ice to the 109, and climbed in.

It was a warm day, only minus ten or thereabouts, and beautifully sunny. We'd already had the jokes about the strange orange ball low down in the sky, hiding behind the trees that we'd not seen for such a long time. After start-up I looked around at the others and waited, allowing my machine to warm up.

A few minutes later four of us slithered across the ice and applied full power, roaring down the runway in pairs into the freezing air. Despite its age and obvious well-used condition, this Friedrich seemed a nice aeroplane, mainly because of the brilliant cabin heater.

We'd been instructed to fly close to the front line while travelling to Staraya Russa, part of our new tactic to impress Ivan, and this soon proved dangerous. It's okay making yourself known, but when you do so you obviously become a target. Ground fire weaved its way up in great arcs in many different calibres, some of which appeared to be coming from our own lines. I heard contacts on my airframe several times, so we applied more power, sped up, and flew lower.

The four of us made it through unscathed, but before final approach to Staraya Russa I heard frantic shouts on the R/T: "Abort! Abort! They are shelling the airfield!"

We landed at Dno instead. It was worse than I thought.

18

Dno looked a mess: so many trying to land at such a poor airfield. Two aeroplanes parked unattended caught my eye immediately: new Focke-Wulf 190 fighters. I made a mental note to ask about them.

We secured our 109s and made our way to the only brick building and what we hoped was a crew room, close to the runway. Two roaring stoves made it quite tropical inside, at least warmer than zero. There we met pilots from JG3 and made ourselves known to their CO, Lieutenant Colonel Gunther Lutzow, as a matter of courtesy. He sat among pilots, relaxing with a coffee. I'd heard of Gunther Lutzow because of his great reputation, not only as a fighter pilot but as a first-class leader.

The four of us stood to attention as he kindly rose to his feet.

The magnificent Spanish Cross in Gold hung on his right breast pocket and the Knight's Cross of the Iron Cross with

Oak Leaves and Swords at his neck. Although older than us, probably in his thirties and well known to the High Command, when he looked directly at me he seemed surprisingly young, and small in stature. We'd all heard so much about him and seen photos in *The Eagle*, often with other aces like Ernst Udet and Werner Molders, we knew he'd already shot down a hundred enemy aeroplanes in combat. So, for some reason, I expected a loud, domineering character, but he came across as warm and friendly, quietly spoken and modest, shaking our hands in turn, ordering us a drink, telling an over-attentive sergeant to make sure we found somewhere warm and comfortable to sleep.

He asked where we were from and where we'd learnt to fly, and our favourite aeroplane: a very engaging man and all four of us liked him immediately.

Before we left him, he told us that, despite wearing flying gear, he wasn't supposed to be operational, working with Command, inspecting fighter activity with his friend Adolf.

"No, not him," he said, shaking his head, "my friend Adolf Galland."

Our immediate CO, Captain Franz Eckerle, commander of No. 1 Group, had been awarded the Knight's Cross for thirty kills only a few months before. Typically, he had gone out on an op, but a lieutenant deputised with a very informal welcome.

Four of us were to remain at Dno for the foreseeable future, but this could be flexible, as everything now seemed. We may find ourselves at Ryelbitzi for a week or Staraya Russa, as part of the plan to make Ivan believe there were many more of us.

We followed a thin sergeant shuffling his feet along a narrow path of cleared snow, into a large wooden hut our engineers had built the previous autumn.

The bunker stove in the centre obviously couldn't cope, and we had no running water or flush toilets; they'd most likely freeze up anyway. Washing facilities were in a small brick building nearby, consisting of lukewarm water fed from a metal tank over a stove. The latrines consisted of holes in the ground in an unheated wooden shed.

Our first ops briefing took us by surprise. We were not escorting the transports; we'd be engaged on free hunts, in pairs, around the landing grounds at Demyansk and Kholm. Perhaps the memory of escorting bombers over England remained fresh in the minds of the high command.

Franz Eckerle, also an immediately likeable man, often spoke with a wry smile and sharp wit; despite his status as one of JG54's best fighter pilots we found him approachable and ordinary, unlike others who are always keen to remind you of their achievements. He'd been in Russia from the start and had a vast knowledge of the area. "Don't go near here," he said, pointing to the map, and, "Avoid this if you can, the flak is always bad," and, "If you get this far over the line with less than half tanks you'd better be able to speak Russian."

He joked, making light of potential disaster, seeming optimistic, with a great sense of humour, but he clearly had a serious side.

"We are to sweep Ivan from the skies, gentlemen, so engage the enemy wherever you find him, and shoot him down, but do it together, at least in pairs. Don't go off on your own. The Ivan you destroy in the air cannot attack the transports or our men on the ground."

What simple logic, and a relief we would not be languishing close to the Ju52s as they lumbered across the freezing sky.

Finally he ended with, "Good hunting, gentlemen. Enjoy your flying, watch out for each other, and let's make sure we are successful."

*

On 21st January 1942, the days were finally lengthening, and after a freezing cold first night in the shed, as we called it, we took off at 0900 hours, flying in two pairs, heading for the air corridor west of Demyansk.

As if waiting for the Ju52s, we found ten or more white-painted I-16 Rata fighters at two thousand metres, circling like vultures over Demyansk. We approached head-on at high speed, breaking them up, scattering some eastwards, but most engaged with us, and we happily obliged.

Throwing my aeroplane around like I'd never done before, I chased the tails of the stubby radial-engined fighters, and it quickly turned into a set of individual dogfights, each waiting for the other man to make the first fatal error. I blasted away as two went down in flames, which I like to think I had a part in, but I suspect they were Captain Eckerle's latest victories.

After fifteen minutes the sky cleared, timed to perfection as the Ju52s lumbered into view, their undersides painted black, landing quickly. Despite the Russian flak around the Demyansk pocket they all arrived safely to unload precious cargo.

This was to be my experience at Dno for several days, on two ops a day, with each the same. I damaged more Ratas and shot down a few, but each new day they reappeared in the same numbers, as if by magic. So we kept on shooting them down.

We rectified the cold problem in our hut by organising the installation of another stove, which the engineers fixed up with a makeshift chimney through the wall. Lots of things were 'organised', from stoves to blankets and extra food, most of the time it was a simple euphemism for theft, but of course we didn't see it like that!

Trees had to be cut down continually to feed these beasts and, not even waiting for the wood to dry out, we threw it straight in. We found coal too: filthy stuff, lumps of tar that stank and made a mess of everything but burned incredibly well.

For several days I saw the Fw190 fighters standing idle, regularly cleared of snow, but never flying, so I asked one of Dno's officers why they weren't engaged in combat.

"Because they're not ready," he groaned, shaking his head. "The engines are unreliable," he added, much to my surprise.

I knew so much about the BMW 801, and I thought it a superb engine.

"Of course it's a great aeroplane, a lot better in these conditions than the 109, but it's not ready yet. They are both going back later this week."

The new fighters stood a few metres apart in the snow, separate from the 109s, like unwanted Christmas presents.

This news about the Fw190s came as a disappointment. I'd read great things about it in *The Eagle* only a month before, how it would be the best fighter in the world once it became fully operational. I didn't mention that I knew about this engine and didn't offer any advice. Whatever teething problems it had, I didn't remember them back at the factory.

Our 109s and their tired engines weren't being replaced as quickly as we would have liked. We heard we'd soon be getting the new 109 G, but again, not in the numbers we wanted. We also needed the Fw190 to keep pace with Ivan, but this wasn't forthcoming yet either.

After a week we switched to protecting Kholm and continued our success without loss until the second week of February. On the morning of the 14th during a successful op against the enemy's ground forces, I saw a 109 take a nasty hit to the engine from ground fire. We had all been lucky so far and I found it surprising more of us hadn't been hit. With too much smoke and flame for it not to be serious, the pilot was forced into an immediate crash-landing; to my horror

I realised we were a long distance inside hostile territory. Despite the flak, we circled, ensuring he'd come down safely in deep snow, sliding across a field, to eventually stop in a similar manner to my own recent crash-landing.

I saw the pilot climb out, apparently uninjured, as a huge number of Red Army troops waded through the snow towards him. The flak intensified and we had to watch our fuel, so were forced to leave. Perhaps by some miracle he could get away, reach our own lines, or try to get into the Kholm pocket?

I'd never felt such intense helplessness as when we abandoned our CO Franz Eckerle to those Bolshevik wolves.

19

With the CO formally listed as *Vermisst*, a few days passed before we had a replacement, in case he returned. In the meantime we kept up the pressure on Ivan's ground forces, while protecting the transports daily.

On 23rd February a 109 made a particularly hard landing at Dno after an op around Demyansk. When the aeroplane came to a stop and the engine shut down, the pilot made no move to get out. We recognised it from the markings, and ran across the ice to help. The pilot's injuries were so severe, even his thick flying jacket was soaked in blood. Barely conscious, he looked up at us with the strained expression of an abandoned puppy. At least he'd made it back, but Hans Schmoller-Haldy would need more than a bottle of schnapps if he reached the hospital alive. By the time we had lifted him out and into an ambulance he'd passed out, and his coat was frozen solid around him like a red ceramic pot.

Ryelbitzi became our next home, from where we continued fighter sweeps over the Demyansk corridor. With accommodation similar to the hut at Dno, I had become accustomed to living a temporary existence from one cold wooden shed to another.

Another half-kill was mine when two of us downed a Pe-2, and then my first full kill, when I caught a lone Rata that frankly seemed to be flown by a dead or dying pilot, making no effort to escape, allowing me to turn his engine into a fireball. The poor bastard didn't even try bailing out, despite having plenty of time. Perhaps he had been injured in a previous encounter and I'd merely finished him off.

Others increased their tally at an incredible rate, including my old Gatchina roommate Anton Dobele, who downed another three. As the weather improved and we flew more in daylight, so the kills increased. We joked they should build more factories so we could destroy more of them, but they were obviously already doing this.

In early March the first signs of a thaw appeared, as temperatures at midday sometimes rose to zero. After months of severe frost, this seemed positively balmy. On the 7th we lost one of our 109s, but not the pilot; the Palace Airfield had been bombed during the night, the first time since November, and it came as a shock, even though it only lasted a few minutes. Nothing else was damaged and we all heard the explosions but dismissed it as something else. When we saw the airfield we came to the conclusion it had been a lucky hit by a single daring pilot.

On 12th March we received two related items of important news. The first being the name of our new CO, Captain Hans Philipp, promoted to lead No. 1 Group from No. 4 Group. He and his famous piano accordion were well liked. This meant that Franz Eckerle would definitely not be returning. We were informed he had been awarded the Oak Leaves to his Knight's Cross posthumously, for his fifty-nine victories. Intelligence sources confirmed the horde of Russians wading through the snow had shot him as soon as they reached him. Being a fluent Russian speaker, I can only imagine his earnest attempts at communication being ignored.

This news devastated us. As a popular officer, it made us even more fearful of captivity. A palpable sense of dread gripped us when flying over the lines, and I suspect it could only be the same for our opponents, who rarely ventured far into our territory. The merit in killing an enemy pilot, particularly one so high-ranking and valuable as Franz Eckerle, defies understanding. This must have been typical of the savage Bolshevik beast.

By the middle of March a tentative land corridor had been established to relieve Demyansk, and so with the pressure easing, I returned to Gatchina with seven others. Our part in the operation had been a great success, along with the entire airlift of supplies, which would continue throughout the summer. We now knew that any German army trapped behind the lines could be successfully supplied from the air.

The Palace Airfield became very busy with 109s after a training wing attached to JG54 became fully operational. Due to the unpredictably harsh weather, all flying training would now be conducted in either Lower Silesia or in France at Bergerac or Toulouse. We joked among ourselves as to how we could get more training, in France obviously, as the thought of it filled us with excitement.

Soon after my return, I spent an hour enjoying the palace facilities: flush toilets, warm rooms, a hot shower, and a decent shave. We had a celebration in the casino when news came through that five of our pilots had been awarded the Knight's Cross. More dicks with sore necks, as they were known:

Anton Dobele, Otto Kittel, Hans-Joachim Krochinski, Rudy Rademacher, and Wilhelm Schilling.

The eager recipients stood in line as the CO shook their hands, beaming with pride, a photographer from *The Eagle* snapping away, forcing them into ridiculous poses, but never having to shout for a smile because these were there already, in abundance. With plenty of schnapps, sausage and black bread, music, and even champagne, a great atmosphere reigned, also prompted by the relief of the Demyansk pocket and the halt to Ivan's advance.

It was finished off with the CO congratulating Max Ostermann, awarded the Oak Leaves, or cauliflower, as we called them, to his Knight's Cross, for sixty-two victories.

Before everyone dispersed the adjutant announced the CO had been awarded the Swords to his Knight's Cross, the first of the Green Hearts to be so honoured.

The numbers on the scoreboard by the fire increased rapidly and, as a squadron, we accumulated so many kills the air force had a problem to think up new rewards. The Iron Cross and then the Knight's Cross had been sufficient, for thirty kills, but quite a few exceeded this, hence the Oak Leaves and then the Swords.

After the death of Franz Eckerle, some stopped wearing their medals on ops. Although not an official order, it became common practice. To be captured as an ordinary airman seemed better than as a decorated war hero.

The early spring thaw in the last days of March brought its own problems: mud. With few proper roads, everything grass was churning up like ploughed fields, so the ground crews and engineers laid planks of wood and birch branches in the busiest taxiways. We couldn't afford to lose any aeroplanes but quite a few sank, up-ending on their props, putting them out of action for days. The fairings on our undercarriage struts were due to be fixed back on, but this had been delayed. I noticed quite a few Stukas never put them back on at all, even in summer.

By now every airfield had been stripped of trees for hundreds of metres all around, mainly for firewood and pathways. We avoided cutting down the tallest near the buildings to provide cover from the air. But the mud was unlike anything before; pilots walked on their toes to their aeroplanes like ballerinas, staying on the grass wherever possible. I laughed at first, thinking it to be the vanity of shiny boots, until I realised. Any mud clinging to the soles would eventually dry out and fall off, sometimes in huge chunks, and so the next negative 'G' meant flying around with all this in the cockpit. It happened to me once, and never again. Some big pieces could potentially damage the controls. From then on I happily joined the tip-toe club. I also began wearing a scarf to stop any dirt going down my neck, in addition to the woollen one I'd worn to keep out the cold.

We operated from Siverskaya as much as we could, because of their pre-war Red Air Force strip of impacted sand and gravel, a nightmare when covered in ice but now absolutely ideal, far superior to anything else.

Most of the buildings were brick-built, but the washing facilities and latrines were still primitive. I formed the opinion that Gatchina Palace had the only flush toilets in the whole of Russia!

From here we launched strafing attacks on new targets in the north, such as the Soviet fleet in Kronstadt Harbour, and vessels in Lake Ladoga, now the ice road had melted. These targets were over a hundred kilometres from Siverskaya, and if we engaged enemy fighters, we watched our fuel gauges with religious intensity.

Again we were astonished at the sheer numbers of enemy we encountered; Ivan kept on sending them up and we continued shooting them down. Such became the normality of this situation that the rare occasions we were not outnumbered, these were the surprises.

By the end of March I had gained another kill and Anton another three; the CO reached his hundredth. When a new friend of mine, Rudolf Klemm, shot down a Yak-1 west of Leningrad, we had more celebrations, for this had taken JG54's total group tally to an unbelievable two thousand confirmed kills. I thought of the air force clerks at each of our squadrons filling in the tally of kills in their *Startkladde*. They must have been the busiest in the entire German air force.

At Siverskaya, around this time, our war in Russia revealed itself in an undeniable manner. I can only describe it as I saw it, not as a rumour but as an incident that actually happened.

20

Ironically, it took place on a beautiful early spring morning. We'd just returned from an op in the north and were refuelling and rearming, when a small convoy of army and SS arrived, among them three of the odd-looking vans with the fake windows. Chatting in the packed dispersal building, I saw them park nearby.

An SS major jumped out the first vehicle, a battered, well-used *kubelwagen*, slamming the door behind him, which to his annoyance bounced open again before closing. He shook his head and marched straight for us.

"Where is your commanding officer?" he barked at no-one in particular, while standing in the doorway.

Officers of higher rank than him stood nearby but his aggressive manner persisted.

Even though our CO was at the palace, by chance, the most senior air force officer present, Lieutenant Colonel Lutzow, was typically engrossed in conversation with a mixed group of fighter pilots, his own 109 parked outside. He made himself known to the major, who promptly clicked his heels, throwing up a sharp Hitler salute, the like of which I'd not seen for many months. I remember thinking how incongruous it seemed amongst all our mud.

"We need some of your men, Colonel," he said, looking around the quietened room at bemused pilots, ground crew, cooks, and engineers.

Obviously unimpressed by the lack of response, he continued. "We have an important action a few kilometres from here we must complete today, so we need your assistance."

Lieutenant Colonel Lutzow approached him, standing within a metre, staring into his eyes. The major was much younger, but his drawn face and dark sunken eyes made him look as though he'd never slept, ageing him twenty years. Thin and fidgety, he obviously had a similar chemical habit I once had, with dried mud on his boots underneath a fresh layer, as though he'd been digging.

"What exactly do you want these men for, Major?" the lieutenant colonel asked.

The major glanced around, clearly wondering whether to proceed or not, almost as though about to impart a secret. "We have an action to clear the area of saboteurs and partisans, ten kilometres away," he said, with renewed vigour.

"What do you mean, exactly?"

"Liquidation of enemies of Germany."

"Russians? Prisoners of war? Are they not taken to Germany for labour?"

"Not these, Colonel. These are saboteurs, and partisans, for immediate liquidation."

I sensed an instantaneous change in atmosphere. A few still talking stopped.

"How many, and who are they?" Lieutenant Colonel Lutzow asked, his gaze fixed.

The major took a slip of paper from his pocket and began reading. "There are 253 Jewish saboteurs, one hundred Jewish looters, and fifty-six Jewish partisans, not including females and their children."

A brief pause followed.

"So how many, altogether, Major?"

"Seven hundred and twenty."

Another pause.

"Let me see," the lieutenant colonel said, taking the note, scanning it before handing it back. "So, correct me if I'm wrong, Major, that means 311 of these saboteurs are women and children?"

The major checked before nodding. "That is correct," he said, in a dispassionate business-like manner loaded with insincerity, as though selling a car he knew wouldn't run.

Lieutenant Colonel Lutzow fixed his gaze at the major's face before looking down briefly at the floor between them. He flushed red before staring back at him.

"Tell me, Major, how does a babe-in-arms blow up a railway bridge, or steal German army property?"

He said nothing. His face twitched as though a fly had landed on his cheek, but otherwise didn't move.

"Enemy combatants and saboteurs we can help you with," the lieutenant colonel said, "but how are women and children enemies of Germany?"

He took a step back, finally turning away from the major, who answered, in a much lower, almost hushed tone. "I have my orders, Colonel. We *all* have our orders."

Lieutenant Colonel Lutzow glanced out the window before ordering everyone outside. In continued silence, we all stepped into the spring sunshine, gathering in front of the building.

One or two were still smoking, some holding coffee mugs, and most stood at ease but in quiet reverence, aware something important was happening.

It was almost warm enough to remove our heavy coats, but not quite.

The major had followed us outside, standing by the lieutenant colonel's side, no doubt expecting us to be ordered to go with him, as I suspect we all did.

The lieutenant colonel began, and we all listened.

"Gentlemen, we are soldiers, and so it is our job to kill the enemy. We kill him wherever he is, whatever he is doing, as part of our duty."

The major began to relax, with just a hint of a smile on his face. It seemed he would get the help he needed.

Lieutenant Colonel Lutzow continued. "We are fighting this war for reasons we believe in, and as such it is our honour to do so."

I looked around at the gathering, increasing all the time. Fifty became a hundred or more, as everyone present listened with absolute concentration.

"Partisans and other non-uniformed combatants do not enjoy the privileges bestowed by the Geneva Conventions and other rules of warfare. But what the major is engaged in, gentlemen, is not warfare, and it is certainly not honourable. What he wants you to do is murder, plain and simple, of women and children, for which one day you may face a reckoning, if not with yourself but to some higher authority, whether that is almighty God or otherwise."

His voice grew louder, and I detected trembling hands, perhaps with anger or frustration. As he paused, a dog barked, probably half a kilometre away, but it seemed close, being the only sound.

The major remained silent, with a distinct sulk forming on

his weary face as Lieutenant Colonel Lutzow continued.

"I am telling you all now, that you are indeed free to volunteer for this action and go with the major, but if any one of you does so, I will remove my uniform right here, and I will never wear it again."

He turned to make sure he was addressing everyone present, and as he did so his Knight's Cross with Oak Leaves and Swords at his neck, Germany's highest honour, caught the sunlight, flashing around the crowd like the beam from a lighthouse on a dark night.

No-one said a word, and nobody moved.

A moment's silence that seemed like an hour and still no-one moved. Someone shuffled, but then nothing.

When clear there were no volunteers Lieutenant Colonel Lutzow spoke again.

"You have your answer, Major."

He faced him. Filled with an obvious pride, and making perfectly sure everyone could hear, he addressed the visitor again.

"Now, Major, will you kindly get off my airfield."

21

Without even saluting, the major stomped across the concrete and jumped back into his car. He waved at the other drivers and they turned in a wide arc onto the grass, before driving away in clouds of diesel smoke. The assembled crowd began dispersing in silence.

Lieutenant Colonel Lutzow and several other officers left, heading across the concrete for the adjutant's office, in hushed but animated conversation. We all knew the risk he took by upsetting the SS, they had powerful friends in Berlin, but like me, most of us were stunned at what we had been asked to do.

I never knew such things as 'actions' really happened, even though I'd heard rumours, and this was the closest I'd ever come. In my naivety, I assumed, because we didn't help, it didn't take place, and therefore my conscience was clear along with everyone else's.

The whole incident remained prominent in my mind for some time. A few days later when back at the palace I asked my roommates Horst and Erich, who had not been at Siverskaya, if they'd ever been required for an action by the SS.

Erich said no, even asking what I meant, and Horst wouldn't answer, choosing to ignore me.

I looked at him, about to repeat my question, when he replied. "It's nothing to do with me," he said in a stern rebuke like that of a guilty thief before a judge.

He lay on his bed, head buried in the latest *Eagle*, ironically with a full-colour photograph of an Fw190 on the cover and a caption saying how brilliant it was. His surprising answer demanded another question, I couldn't leave hanging.

"What?" I said, turning towards him, hoping my gaze would penetrate the cover, but he didn't reply. "What, Horst, what has nothing to do with you?" I repeated. I wanted to leave it at that, but I'd cast my line and he took the bait.

"You've really no idea," he retorted, dropping the magazine on his lap. "I'm glad for your sake you didn't do it."

He stared, as though gazing right through me into the wall, and reached under his bed, hauling out his steel ammo box and a bottle of vodka. He flicked off the cap and, holding it vertically, with the neck deep in his mouth, he drained a quarter of it in one before standing it on the floor.

"What?" I said again.

He shrugged, rolling over on his bed, facing the other way.

"Maybe I'll tell you one day," he mumbled, "when this damned war is over."

I stood up to move over towards him, but Erich raised his right arm, indicating for me to sit down, shaking his head, so I did.

A few minutes later, Horst was unconscious, snoring loudly.

I lay awake, wondering about Horst. Perhaps he needed leave, but then we all did. Thoughts of home persisted, and when I might be there again. I considered getting up for a wander around the anonymous corridors, but I must have slept. Roused for ops at 0600 hours, I felt exhausted.

*

Ornamental fruit trees grew all around the palace, many in full bloom, now it was April. At the Palace Airfield any remaining trees were bursting into leaf: blossom falling like pink snow, gathering in long shallow drifts in an increasingly warm breeze.

In the middle of April 1942 we were ordered to attend the uniform store at the palace or, failing that, ask a comrade to collect a personal item on our behalf. A special gift from high command, every soldier in the German forces in the east irrespective of rank received the same. We speculated: a bottle of schnapps, tobacco, perhaps, or even a cash bonus, but no. We got a small packet in brown paper from a huge box that had been airlifted to us from Germany. I had to sign for it and laughed when I pulled the wrapping apart to reveal a new pair of army underpants.

Ivan made three daring but pointless attacks on the Palace Airfield in the latter half of April. On the 15th a group of Il-16 Ratas flew over but were seen off by our flak units. They caused only minor damage to a 109, with no-one hurt. Then on the 18th a dozen ancient Polikarpov I-153 biplanes trundled overhead, while most of us were on an op, and tried unsuccessfully to strafe the airfield but were also seen off. Those who saw it stated they had come down from the north, probably from the Baltic Fleet. We suspected they were more interested in seeing what we had, because the next day the airfield was attacked by more of the same, plus I-16 Rata fighters.

Again, most of us were on an op and were told it had been the usual inept performance, bordering on the comical. The only losses we sustained were two Ju88s from Reconnaissance Group 122, damaged after our flak units shot down a Rata which crashed into them.

Our ground forces had finally been ordered to take Leningrad, so renewed efforts were made in support. Escorting Stukas and Heinkel 111s, we continued shooting down enemy aeroplanes at an astonishing rate. Where were they getting them all from?

Finally, in May, the Eleventh Army Corps in the Demyansk and Kholm pockets were fully relieved as our forces captured thousands of Russians. Two more of our pilots, Hans Beisswenger and Horst Hannig (not my roommate), both received the Knight's Cross for forty-seven and forty-eight kills respectively. By now I had six, and in any other theatre of war at another time, I would have been lauded as an ace, but not here, where most had at least double figures, and rising rapidly.

We held a celebration for Hans and Horst in the casino, during which the adjutant moderated the tone by adding an intelligence briefing. He did this occasionally, mainly because he knew it would be the only time we were all together. He held black ink drawings of aeroplane shapes, the first one in front of his chest, the outline of an impressive, sleek single-engined fighter.

"Not a Russian, surely?" I said.

"No, it's not a Spitfire," he replied with a smile.

Several leaned in for a closer look.

"Gentlemen, you will no doubt see many of these soon," passing it to the gathering. "Take a good look. It's a MiG-3, and it's not quite the usual Russian shit. You might see more American Curtiss P-40s and Airacobras coming in through Murmansk too, but the MiG-3 on first accounts is faster, so beware."

He held up a drawing of another apparent improvement in the inventory of the Red Air Force: a sleek single-engine fighter with a radial engine.

"It seems Mr Lavochkin has fallen out with Mr Gorbunov and Mr Gudkov and gone into production on his own. The La-GG3 has therefore changed into the La-5. Either that or Stalin has had them both shot for producing shit aeroplanes." Spontaneous laughter erupted, but we were seriously interested.

"The La-5 is still a heavy wooden contraption that burns well, like the La-GG3, but we found one a few days ago and discovered it actually has a radio, amazingly enough, and a new fourteen-cylinder engine, so be aware of it."

He left the drawings with us before the briefing dispersed with instructions to pin them to the wall, and this new information immediately became the centre of our conversation. I don't think it worried any of us. It had been so far rare to encounter a Russian aeroplane flown well, so our relatively low opinion of Red Air Force pilots continued.

Our only concern was the sheer numbers we were beginning to face, and even in the hands of a poor pilot, a good aeroplane can be a real threat.

At dawn on 26th May a number of Il-16 Ratas flew over the Palace Airfield but the flak was too heavy and they disappeared without doing anything.

Over the next few days the Russian forces around the Volkhov on the south of Lake Ladoga collapsed and thousands more prisoners were taken. Where were we to put them all?

In the first week of fabulous June weather, with long sunny days reminiscent of France, many of us found sleep a problem.

Even in the middle of the night, it was never totally dark. On one such sunny morning, some of our Mediterranean allies landed at the Palace Airfield. At first I thought they were Ju52s until I saw the markings of the *Regia Aeronautica*.

Like us they were a long way from home and, despite the fact we knew they were involved with us in Russia, we were still surprised to see them. Our op for that day was to escort all four of these Italian Savoia-Marchetti SM79 torpedo bombers in an attack on shipping in Lake Ladoga.

I'd never seen one so close and it took eight of us to provide safe passage to the lake, where they hurled a few bombs and torpedoes around before we brought them back without incident. I noticed Russian aeroplanes shadowing us from across the lake, but thankfully they didn't engage.

On our return I walked over to one of these aeroplanes and spoke to the crew, intending to have a look inside. It had smooth aesthetic lines, typically Italian, and I asked where I might find the pilot. Only one of them spoke a few words of German, promptly standing to attention as though I wanted to inspect them. To my astonishment the same man then addressed me in English, to which I shrugged, shook my head, and replied in German. Perhaps I should have tried Russian?

After helping me climb aboard I found the windows had curtains neatly tied back, folding chairs and a table, like Hitler's Ju52 in the newsreels – far too tidy to be an operational aeroplane.

They were cheery, highly decorated fellows, and when they left I felt an odd sense of bewilderment. What on earth were they doing here? They only stayed one night and in the morning they took off again, heading south. I never saw them again.

22

We continued harassing Ivan on the ground and in the air during the fine weather, and most of our aeroplanes now had the undercarriage fairings reapplied. We flew long days, often taking off at 0300 hours, and flying ops until 2200 hours.

On the morning of 10th June, to our utter consternation, bombs began falling all around us. It was 0245 hours and almost dawn on a quiet night with no sound of approaching aeroplanes, so where had they come from?

The briefing hut groaned at every shockwave and would surely disintegrate in a mass of splinters as chunks of earth and shrapnel showered down onto the roof. Windows were blown in, sending shards of flying glass across the room. We lay flat on the floor, covered in blankets, with the ground shaking every few moments, listening out for aeroplane engines, but we couldn't hear any.

"They're not bombs," someone shouted.

To our horror we realised we were being shelled.

They hit the airfield dozens of times, and couldn't have known the result of their shelling from such long range, but clearly counted on the psychological effect. How could it be possible?

Two 109 F4s were destroyed and one Klemm K135 weather reconnaissance aeroplane, infuriating us. A few minutes later we took off and roamed the countryside around the Volkhov River looking for the guns, but never found them.

At the end of June 1942 our Great Summer Offensive began; it started so well we dared to think we could finally take Leningrad and Moscow, ending the war in the east.

Fresh troops arrived and our airfields were crowded with all types of new aeroplanes in a very exciting time.

In July the new 109 Gs appeared at the Palace Airfield. The Gustav, as we called it, had been eagerly awaited, and a small crowd gathered around the first one, when Lieutenant Max-Helmuth Ostermann jumped in, taking it up for evaluation.

Small in stature, quietly spoken and very popular with all members of the squadron, Max – as he insisted we call him, ignoring his rank – had an unusually large number of friends amongst ordinary ground crew. Despite this easy-going manner, I'd seen him in combat, where he was a prodigious and determined killer. Clearly he liked the Gustav a lot because, when he returned half an hour later, he claimed it as his own, asking the ground crew to personalise it for him.

Other Gustavs arrived almost every day and all our old Friedrichs were eventually sent west for training squadrons.

I never flew a G1 because I soon had my Friedrich replaced with a G3. The bigger wheels and stronger undercarriage on all Gustavs were very welcome, but I noticed the extra weight affected performance, despite the engine being upgraded from a 601 to the more powerful 605. The cannon in the nose remained the same but the two guns on the top were upgraded to a higher calibre, which again added weight. Not only that, but the belt feed for these two new guns required bumps on the airframe, which I thought ruined the sleek lines of the 109. Both the Friedrich and Gustav had permanently rounded wingtips compared to the square ends of the Emil, which we began to see fewer of at the front line, and the new Gustav soon acquired the nickname 'the bump' due to those unfortunate lumps. But they were all 109s and great aeroplanes, far superior to anything the enemy had.

Only a few days later, on standby at the airfield, I sat outside the crew room enjoying the sunshine when Ostermann's wingman, Heinrich Bosin landed alone, trailing smoke from the engine of his Gustav. Where was Ostermann? They always flew together and I knew they had taken off in high spirits an hour earlier on a free hunt. When Bosin didn't immediately get out after shutting it down we expected trouble.

A few pilots made their way over as the ground crew opened the canopy, giving us a welcome sign that he was alright. I walked towards them and noticed shiny black grass underneath where oil was leaking.

Bosin, a sergeant, climbed out and jumped off the wing, shaking his head, looking at the engine and at the sky to the east.

We sat him down in the crew room as a small crowd gathered.

"He's gone," he said, accepting a bottle of schnapps, trying unsuccessfully to light a cigarette. "We saw nine Indians, so we took them on. Max got one almost immediately, I saw it go down. They were Curtiss P40s."

Somebody lit his cigarette as others appeared in the doorway, shuffling in, and eager to hear. After taking a long pull on the cigarette, in a tobacco smoke fog, he began to speak while exhaling.

"We were just about to have another go when we were bounced from above, by more P40s, I think; I'm not sure, ten or more, easily. I was hit, as you can see, but I saw Max's cockpit burst into flames. He went straight down. It was all over in a few seconds. He can't have known anything about it. No 'chute and no landing. He's gone."

He looked at our blank faces as we briefly stared at one another. The second time in three months Ostermann had been shot down; he'd survived the last one with a bullet in his shoulder. He'd also recently achieved his one hundredth kill.

The next day the CO of No. 7 Group, Captain Carl Sattig, whom I'd seen a few times at various airfields, failed to return from an op south of Kholm, in hostile territory. No-one saw him go down.

The dreaded word *Vermisst* appeared next to his name on the duty board, a word synonymous with loss and death. They didn't list Ostermann as missing; his name was simply wiped off altogether and, from that moment on, no longer discussed. When you're gone, you're history.

*

Fighter Wing JG54 had 140 pilots in July 1942, forty-seven of them officers, seventy-eight NCOs, like me, and fifteen of airman rank. We were supported by hundreds of ground staff, all of whom were vital in keeping us airborne. It sounds like a lot of people but at any one time we only had around ninety serviceable aeroplanes, with the rest in need of constant attention, and our numbers were continually falling. With this we were expected to cover the entire Northern Sector of the

Russian Front from the Gulf of Finland all the way south beyond Kholm.

The Red Army and its air force probed our defences in huge numbers, almost on a twenty-four-hour basis. We countered them with our night fighter operations, so much easier due to the brevity of darkness, becoming fully light again at around 0300 hours. Because of this we had as much success as in the daytime, but we couldn't help notice their numbers continued increasing.

The roll-out of the new 109 G nearly complete, it took me some time to get used to the gun button on the stick, where you could either fire the machine guns or the cannons, or both, requiring dexterity in the fingers that took practice, like playing a piano.

Our chief armourer, a huge personality by the name of Ernst Brunns, bounded into the dispersal hut one morning, hurling something at us from the doorway as though lobbing a stick grenade. I didn't know whether to catch it or dive for cover.

The object was caught by another pilot, who laughed when he recognised the control column of a 109 G. Fed up with hearing us moan, Brunns had acquired a new one complete with gun buttons for us to practice on.

"Sort it out with this," he shouted, leaving without waiting for thanks.

After many hours I eventually managed to flick the safety off with my thumb, then press either and not both, purely by touch, thereby saving precious time and ammunition.

We joked about it but found it essential. Before this, the first few times I tried it, I failed to fire anything at all, and the lucky Russian must have thought I'd run out of ammunition.

One fantastic July morning a familiar face appeared at the door to our room at the palace.

"Paul Goetz, how would you like to be a guest at my wedding?" Otto Kittel said, beaming with pride. No doubt I looked astounded, trying to think how this could be possible.

"Let me guess," I replied, "you're marrying a Russian peasant girl, no, a Russian aristocrat, and you're leaving the air force to live with her in Gatchina?"

He smiled, shaking his head.

I guessed again. "Oh I see, you're marrying Goering's daughter and we are all flying to Berlin for the ceremony?"

He laughed. "Not quite."

He swung his cap around on the end of his right index finger. "But if you can be at the Palace Airfield tomorrow at 1100 hours, you can see me get married."

Nodding like an idiot, I agreed to something I thought impossible.

"I'd be delighted, of course," I said, standing up, shaking his hand.

"Good, then it's all settled. Don't be late, it's timed to the minute!" he shouted, disappearing down the corridor.

Erich, the only other person present, was just as baffled. I hadn't seen Otto with a woman, so any romance in Russia must have been extremely secretive.

The next day, to my surprise, I had been scrubbed off the duty board, along with the CO and any other pilot close to the groom.

I had a shower, a shave, and put on my best uniform. At 1030 hours a group of fellow guests and I boarded a lorry for the airfield. I hadn't looked and felt this smart in years. On such a lovely summer's day, with a gentle breeze, warm air curved its way around the vehicle into the back, hurling summer smells of dry grass and wildflowers with it.

The lorry pulled over onto an area of freshly cut grass at the top end of the airfield, where a small table was draped with our flag, as several officers stood around chatting and smoking. With ten minutes remaining we could still see no sign of the bride and groom, but then, just before 1100 hours, the CO pulled up in a black car with the groom.

They stood at the table and the ceremony began. But who was he marrying, and where was she?

As the ceremony began we gathered around, and it appeared just like any other, but without the bride. It seemed she would not be appearing in person.

"In this distance marriage," the CO began, "we are witness to the joining of Anne Marie and Otto."

He paused, glancing at his watch, nodding to Otto, who looked around, smiling, in a brand-new air force steel helmet and dress uniform. The formal vows and racial declarations were read out by a very tall air force pastor, and then the groom signed some papers, countersigned by the CO, all smiling for a photographer who constantly fussed around, fiddling with his camera and glancing up at the sun.

"Anne Marie will have now signed the same papers in the presence of her family," the pastor said, "and other witnesses, including the mayor of Kronsdorf, so I now declare you man and wife."

He reached over the table and shook hands with Otto, who turned for a photograph. A sparklingly clean 109 G stood behind, dominating most of the photographs, and a cork popped as an officer I'd never seen before stepped forward with champagne glasses.

The CO gave a toast to the married couple, and everyone shook Otto's hand. It was the first wedding I'd ever attended, and with not a woman anywhere in sight.

23

An interesting house guest arrived in July. His high status clearly evident, he came escorted by attentive SS officers, rather than ordinary troops with fixed bayonets and glum faces. He disappeared into the army side of the palace for a few days then frequently strolled around the grounds, always deep in conversation with groups of German staff officers.

Standing at least a head height above everyone else, this VIP wore a uniform that looked Russian but not entirely Soviet. General Andrey Vlasov, Commander of the Second Soviet Shock Army, was captured on the 12th July near Leningrad when his entire army was surrounded.

We heard rumours he had expressed hatred for Stalin, and immediately offered his services to Germany. As a result he was treated with dignity and respect. We didn't think him a traitor; many of us thought changing side was inevitable. Who wouldn't want to be part of the most successful military force in history?

A few days later a group of staff officers from the Central Sector arrived in a Ju52. To our astonishment that night they all entered the casino, along with Vlasov. It looked odd, seeing a Red Army general in our mess, drinking schnapps, and understandably he created a huge amount of interest.

"He's going to raise an army of Russians to fight Stalin with us," Anton told me with a grin, probably as a joke, but there must have been some truth in it, judging by his treatment. "I heard them talking. The German captain with the glasses is Wilfried Strik-Strikfeldt, from the General Staff."

"Do you think it might be possible?" I said, leaning around Anton's shoulder to gain a better view as the casino filled up.

"Of course!" he replied. "Most Russians hate Stalin as much as we do so why not?"

I thought seriously about this; there were already many thousands of Russian POWs in our custody, so if they were allowed to fight Stalin with us the war would be over even sooner.

With his round, black-framed spectacles, receding hairline and smiling, easy manner Vlasov looked more like the headmaster of a boy's school than a veteran army general. Despite this, his stature gave him a commanding presence and Captain Strik-Strikfeldt never left his side.

Sadly, our incongruous VIP didn't stay long as two days later I saw him and Strikfeldt climb aboard the same Ju52 heading west.

Flicking through the next copy of *The Signal* magazine, I saw Vlasov relaxing in the company of Dr Goebbels and other senior Nazis. The article reported that after leaving Gatchina, he went to Berlin, via a brief stay in a prison camp at Vinnitsa in central Ukraine. The rumours that many Russians despised Stalin and his cronies were confirmed; soon we would be fighting with millions of Russians and not against them, striving for a free Russia. What a fantastic idea.

*

August gave us a taste of Russia I thought I'd never see: my cockpit hotter than a glass house. We flew with the small Perspex side panels open most of the time, but it was still baking hot, and worse than July. When we encountered the enemy, many flew with their canopies wide open, something we dreamed about but could never do, as the 109 canopy opened on hinges rather than sliding, like most other fighters.

On the ground, we were plagued by mosquitoes from the marshlands and forests surrounding us; though not too bad at the palace, other airfields were intolerable. At least they couldn't chase us up into the sky.

Now the barrack huts were fully operational I spent more time living at Siverskaya between ops, and one such evening, near the end of the month, the CO, Hannes Trautloft, had a visit from one of his best friends.

I'd seen Adolf Galland in France, and he flew in aboard a Ju52 with other officers, spending the first few hours in the command post, emerging for dinner at 1800 hours.

They gathered around the front of the command post for photographs, everyone dwarfed by one of the two famous stuffed bears standing by the road. I wondered where these animals had come from but, clearly, they were uniquely Russian, hence the photographs, taken by an officious magazine photographer. I doubt there were many other German airfields with such things, one being more than two metres tall.

Now a staff officer, Galland gathered information for Berlin, but still mixed with us, eating the same, at least for one night, before staying at the palace for a few days.

The front line in our sector remained fairly static over the summer, but at the beginning of September 1942 Ivan tried yet again to relieve Leningrad.

Bitter fighting resumed and one beautiful morning, while visiting Gatchina, I saw the palace courtyard filling up with a variety of vehicles unloading casualties from the front. Filthy, exhausted troops, looking utterly wretched, had clearly been having a tough time. The palace was an ideal place to recover and we made room for them all around the ground floor and in huge tents at the back.

Our own visits to the palace became less frequent; living in barracks at the airfield we spent more time in the air than ever before, supporting ground forces with low-level strafing attacks. These continued several times a day for almost a month until Ivan gave up again and thousands more enemy soldiers were captured. As far as I know they were all taken by train to Germany for labour in our factories and fields. I never saw any Russian casualties amongst our wounded and assumed they were being treated elsewhere, perhaps in the field before transportation. They were our vanquished enemy, so I spent little time thinking of their welfare. Perhaps I should have asked, but I didn't. None of us did.

With the Northern Sector stable again, we heard rumours of leave, confirmed when I heard some pilots had already gone. When summoned to the adjutant's office early the next morning, I guessed the reason, and to my surprise, I also found I'd been promoted to Senior Corporal, with an increase in pay from thirty-five to forty marks a month. I took my ten-day pass with glee, thinking I'd be spending over a week at home.

"Get cleaned up at the palace and report to Gatchina railway station at 1800 hours this evening," he said.

It seemed I'd not be flying home in a day but catching a train.

How long this would take, I had no idea, certainly more than a day or so. Although overjoyed to be going home, I baulked at the delay. As compensation I had an extra twenty-one marks special 'Front Pay' supplement.

I was due to take part in the ops that morning; when I reminded the adjutant I'd been granted leave he stood me down. A pilot should never be sent into combat with a leave pass in his pocket; it's tempting fate.

My uniforms and boots cleaned, as part of the conditions of leave, I gathered up all the Reemtsma cigarettes for my father, my book, and a bottle of schnapps, before relaxing in the casino, reading *Eagle* magazines.

At 1700 hours five of us climbed into the back of a lorry bound for Gatchina station. With mail taking at least three or four weeks to reach home, my parents would have no idea, so it would be a wonderful surprise. The train arrived promptly, astounding me at its size and condition. The Russian carriages were filthy, with broken windows and holes in the floor and ceiling. Only a few of the lights worked so at night there would be nothing to do but sleep.

Most of the last six carriages were packed with wounded and, at first, we were told we would have to sit with them until, at the last moment, seats were found in a forward compartment. A carriage in the middle and one at the end had anti-aircraft batteries, and parts of the train looked as though they'd been recently hit, with bullet holes and splintered wood hanging from the sides. I found a seat and, as we sat waiting to depart, felt as vulnerable as at Bergen during the air raid.

Within minutes of us setting off, I fell asleep. The rhythm and the sunshine through the filthy windows sent me off like a baby. When I woke up, darkness had fallen. I curled up, resting my head on the window, and passed out again.

Morning came, with us still trundling west, a little faster now, as the sun rose behind us. We had soup and bread, with the occasional dried sausage, enough to keep us going, usually served around midday.

After another uncomfortable night, just after sunrise, we stopped at a large station called Heiligenbeil in Prussia, where we were told to get out. Medics in blood-stained white coats stepped down from the rear carriages with heavy buckets and armfuls of soiled bandages, returning to the train with boxes and empty buckets.

The distinct aroma of army disinfectant weaved its way along the train as the overnight dead, wrapped in blankets, were carried off, and spirited quickly away, loaded into the back of an Opel lorry, three and then four deep. Twenty minutes later we were trundling along again and I began to resent this entire train.

The toilet at the end of my carriage was simply a hole in the floor, the surroundings slippery with waste. I tried the one at the other end which, only a little better, I deemed usable.

Unbelievably, four field police came in, checking identity papers and leave passes with their usual abrupt rudeness, before a pair of quivering army privates handed out bread and sausage to anyone who wanted it, followed by cold coffee. Hungrily I ate as much as possible, finishing my meal with some of my own schnapps before falling asleep again.

After brief stops at Konigsberg and then Marienburg, much of it spent sleeping, on the third night, the train finally reached the old border with Poland and Germany. Everyone had to get off to re-board a German train because of the difference in the track gauge.

How luxurious to find clean seats, working lights, and flush toilets with running water in clean wash basins.

Four days after boarding, I finally arrived in Berlin. My homeland looked orderly and prosperous after Russia, with everyone clean and smartly dressed. Surprised to see bomb damage in Berlin and air-raid shelters, I didn't realise the worst was yet to come.

The remainder of my journey on local trains and trolley-busses passed comfortably, and I soon arrived at my parents' front door.

My mother burst into tears and wouldn't let me go. "He's here! My boy is here!" over and over as my father looked on with a wide grin.

When my mother finally released me, I could breathe again, while my father grabbed my hand in a formal handshake, which evolved into a firm hug on the front step.

Of course I looked a lot older and thinner, but my parents did too, though I didn't tell them. My father accepted the cigarettes, still astonished I hadn't yet started smoking.

I opened my bottle of schnapps, and even my mother joined in the toast.

None of us knew what to dedicate the drink to until my father simply said, "To the future, whatever that will be," as we took our first sip.

24

My mother immediately set about washing everything even before I'd finished my bath. We'd been ordered to wear the best uniforms available, but all mine were showing signs of wear.

Afterwards I put on the spare uniform I'd brought with me and, as soon as I'd finished my meal, I fell asleep in my father's favourite chair.

Home was a time capsule, as though Russia had never happened. Although the same, everything seemed much smaller. The ornaments I'd known for years, but hadn't taken much notice of, made the house look cluttered, and the rugs under my bare feet were incredibly spongy, like thick seaweed on a sandy beach.

My father only occasionally asked about the war, perhaps remembering his own time as a soldier, and the fact he never discussed it at length. I told him just enough about the aeroplanes and roughly our whereabouts.

"Leningrad?" he said, bewildered. "Fifteen hundred kilometres away? It took us a year to move fifty metres in 1916."

He'd seen it in the newsreels, but to hear it from his own son confirmed the astonishing achievement. He laughed when I told him I'd crash-landed twice, and I wasn't sure if he was serious when he asked, "Do they make you pay for these aeroplanes you keep damaging?"

Long walks kept me occupied, but I didn't see any of my old friends, assuming them to be elsewhere, as I had been, perhaps hundreds of kilometres away, serving their country. The war hadn't reached this part of Germany, and as yet, I was my parents' only real link to it, so to them it seemed a distant conflict.

With the weather unseasonably warm, I sat outside in the afternoons on the bench my father had made five summers before, reading my book.

Mother stood in the doorway, watching and smiling. "What are you reading?"

"*Nothing New in the West*," I said, showing her the cover.

"That's your father's favourite. He has a copy in the cupboard by our bed."

I'd never seen him with it, but of course it made perfect sense. I don't know why, but I didn't discuss it; I didn't even want him to see me reading it.

Because the journey had taken four days I could only stay for two. My time at home therefore flashed by like one single sunny afternoon. For a while I thoroughly enjoyed being a boy again, with childish dreams of flying aeroplanes in clear blue German skies. Home-cooking smells filled my lungs and smothered me like a warm blanket, and the reassuring bass tones of my father's voice, only occasionally replying to my mother, were a unique reminder of childhood.

The tears in my mother's eyes came from somewhere deep

as I stood on the step in my crisp uniform, her creases in my trousers razor-sharp. She reached up to brush fluff from my shoulder as my father patted my back.

"Our boy is the most handsome in all Germany, isn't he, Ulrich?" she said, dabbing her eyes.

He leaned forwards and spoke directly into my ear so my mother wouldn't hear him. "Make sure you come back to us, Paul. Your mother wouldn't be able to cope…" He stopped and turned away.

For a moment I wanted to drop my bag and run inside.

*

After settling into one of the last seats on the packed train, I contented myself with watching Germany disappear. Wide awake, I found it extremely tedious.

Taking out my shopping list of Russian phrases, I burned every word into my head. With a pencil I re-wrote the Cyrillic script until I was able to recognise them all.

As we changed trains again at the former border, I noticed the ruined buildings in detail for the first time: shell craters, huge numbers of smashed Red Army tanks and vehicles, and when the train stopped at smaller stations, graveyards with rows of wooden crosses topped with German helmets.

The soup and bread tasted better on the return journey, but it still took another four days, with me eventually reaching Gatchina on the morning of my tenth leave day.

I hitched a lift to the Palace Airfield in the cab of a huge five-ton Henschel lorry. The driver, a Dutchman from Amsterdam, spent the entire ten-minute journey telling me how much he hated Bolshevism, so hadn't hesitated in joining the German army. On reflection, I think he was either trying to impress me or reassure himself, or both.

At the Palace Airfield dispersal I couldn't find my name on the Siverskaya duties list so immediately hitched a lift to the palace. The marble corridors had an odd calmness about them, and I had a familiar sense of belonging as I ran up the wide staircase. It didn't feel like home, of course, more what I imagined a favourite hotel to be, one that a person returns to every year. Echoing conversations emanated from open doors, steamy cooking smells and tobacco smoke lingering everywhere.

I found my bed still there so, without delay, I unpacked and took a shower. Then I sought out the much more comprehensive palace duty board for the whole of JG54, covered in names; most pilots had returned from postings in the south and far north.

I was scheduled for flying duties in thirty-six hours, with just about everybody else, not from Krasnogvardeisk or Siverskaya, but the forward airfield at Mga, where I had once crash-landed. I had to report there by noon the next day, 5th September, taking a designated aeroplane from the Palace Airfield.

Later that night the familiar comfort of comrades overwhelmed me, and I drank to excess, between long games of skat in the casino. While sitting in a lounge chair, several comrades jumped on me, spilling my beer. We all fell forwards onto the floor, where we rolled around, trying to gain the advantage over one another, demanding a submission, cursing with our best foul language, as others drew around in hysterics, shouting encouragement. Someone grabbed me by the hair, but I broke free, no doubt leaving the offender with a fine clump from the back of my head. I laughed so much I lost all the strength in my arms and was pinned into the wood floor by six pilots, almost crushing the breath from me.

Erich shouted, "Give me your hand!" as he hauled me out from under the mass of writhing bodies.

I stood up and was pursued around the room until Gunter Scheel, now an officer, stepped in to declare a truce.

I thanked Gunter for saving my life and all six of my tormentors then bought me a drink and spent twenty minutes reliving the incident, followed by talk of home, parents, and Germany.

In the morning I threw my bag into the cockpit of a 109 G I'd flown several times before, daring to call it mine. Officers usually claimed the best machines, and maybe, because this Gustav was already oil-streaked and in need of a good clean, they allowed me to claim it. The cockpit revealed the true age of the machine, however, with fresh leather and new-looking controls and switches.

Four of us took off together, heading east. I was flying with my roommates from the palace; though we'd all faced the enemy many times, this was the first occasion the four of us had flown together. It seemed strange to see Mga in the tail end of summer after my last enforced visit in the middle of a deep freeze.

We landed in pairs, shutting down our engines near the trees as close to dispersal as we dared.

We ate in newly constructed timber huts near the woods, with dense camouflage netting stretched over the roof of each building, and lines of sandbags, up to chest height, guarding the doors. Sandbagged machine-gun posts were dotted around, all pointing to the east, the crews constantly watching.

We had an hour to kill before briefing, so when I found out many were still occupying the rabbit-warren dugout, I walked two hundred metres to take a look.

25

A LONE FIGURE SAT CROUCHED ON AN AMMO BOX JUST outside the door, propped open with a Mauser rifle. Static crackled from a Dora radio, the man obviously struggling to get anything from it. An array of tools lay around him with bits of wire and a sprinkling of nuts and bolts.

Hearing my approach, he turned around to reveal the black, round glasses on the face of Hans Weber. A larger air force radio set stood on a metal table within his reach, active with local traffic, loud enough to counter the clangourous throb of the sandbagged diesel generator twenty metres away.

The entire bunker system was almost invisible, covered with tall summer grasses, giant weeds, and thick strands of wild wheat, perhaps why it remained popular.

To my surprise he didn't recognise me.

"I'll be with you in a minute," he shouted, after a quick glance, like a distracted shopkeeper.

"*Privyet*, Hans," I said – 'hello' in Russian.

Still unaware, he stopped. He looked at the Mauser in the doorway. Surely my Russian accent wasn't that good?

To avoid a problem I introduced myself, seeing a loaded MP40 machine pistol at his feet.

"Goetz, you bastard, I could have shot you dead. How are you?"

"Do you want a reply in German or Russian?" I asked, laughing.

"*Zhazh du shchiy?*" he said, testing, to which I replied in German.

"No, I'm not thirsty, thank you, but I'll have a coffee if you have any," to which he smiled, shaking his head.

"I don't have any here, but there's some in the kitchen, so off you go, and get me one too, will you?" he ordered, returning to the radio.

The same fat sergeant and wiry corporal clattered about in the field kitchen; the first had even less hair, the latter thinner than ever. A badly dented army kettle whistled on a hotplate, so I picked up two enamelled mugs.

The sergeant nodded as I filled them with heaped spoons of Abea pressed coffee from a 5kg tin, followed by hot water. Nobody challenged me, the mere familiarity in my action providing the necessary permission.

As I walked back towards the door, the tunnel entrance appeared uncharacteristically bright, as warm sunshine streamed in, and a tremendous surge of well-being came over me as though I'd just taken a hundred Pervitin tablets.

Hans and I sat on an ammo box each, sipping coffee, staring out across the airfield in the dappled shade of thick camouflage netting. The grass had grown a metre high, except for the taxiways and landing strip, which were regularly cut, but tall poppies, daisies, and buttercups, resplendent amongst the grass, made the airfield look more like a wildflower meadow than a combat zone. Sunshine flickered all around, amplifying the red in our faces, turning us into characters from an impressionist painting.

Hans offered a green pack of Eckstein cigarettes and I have no idea why, but I took one, lodging it firmly between my lips. He reached forward with a match, and I inhaled, too much at first, resulting in a series of brief coughs, so I took another sip of coffee. The nicotine rush caused dizziness and mild euphoria, so I inhaled again, repeating it. Now I understood the popularity of smoking: like tiny but instantaneous hits of Pervitin.

Hans had no idea this was my first cigarette.

"You learnt everything then?" he said, peering over the top of his glasses.

"Yes, everything," I replied, my head spinning, "although I haven't had to use any of it yet."

"Let's hope it stays that way, but I doubt it."

He turned fully towards me. "We are in trouble, Paul."

He stared as though reading my face, perhaps expecting surprise. "They didn't all retreat over the horizon to Siberia and disappear forever. I listen to what they say, not their scripted official broadcasts, but what they talk about between themselves. You can learn far more from this than anything else. Do you know what's the most telling? It's *how* they talk to one another that's different, Paul, particularly about us. They are not afraid of us, not in the slightest."

He turned back to the radio, but only stared. "We will all need to speak Russian. We are in their country, after all," he said, flicking cigarette ash into a wide crack in the earth.

A skylark sang sweetly, undisturbed by a pair of 109s coming in to land, the sound of their quietly idling engines carried over to us on the warm breeze. I heard the shrill of a grasshopper and watched as a butterfly drifted close; when it tried gaining height to fly away, it became entangled in the netting. It struggled, testing the net again and again until, eventually, it found an opening and flew off.

"A group of them came wandering onto the airfield, right here, last week," Hans said, pointing at the trees on the eastern side. "They gave themselves up straight away, luckily, all ten of them, to me. I was on my own, and I only had that," he said, pointing at the Mauser.

"I managed to get a few words in before the field police and SS came. One of them claimed to have been a musician before the war, but frankly I didn't believe him. They were in some sort of convict battalion and they told me if they went back to their own lines, their officers would shoot them. Pretty ruthless, eh? This is what we are up against, Paul."

He took a long pull on his cigarette before another sip of coffee, exhaling over the chipped enamelled mug, giving the impression the contents were on fire.

"Odd-looking fellows with their brown skin, round faces and eyes like Chinamen, with weird accents I'd never heard before. They were stocky, thick-set, and looked bloody strong. That's why I keep this with me now," he said, nodding at the loaded MP40. "One of them told me there were millions of them, from all across Russia and the Far East, just waiting."

"Waiting for what?"

"To come here, of course, push us out, or kill us, or both. He didn't seem to care. What was remarkable was that he told me this very casually, as though I should already know, and that it was entirely inevitable." Shaking his head, he turned back to the radio, touched the tuning dial as it crackled.

"What happened to them?"

"You don't want to know, Paul," he said, shaking his head.

"Yes, I do."

"They were interrogated, of course, if you can call it that, for all of five minutes. I don't know if they revealed anything of value or even if they talked. The SS just seemed to argue amongst themselves, shouting, so I don't think they were given much of a chance. You'd think they would be bundled onto a train and sent to work in one of our factories or in the fields, wouldn't you?"

"Or given the chance to fight with us," I said, remembering General Vlasov and taking another sip of coffee. This suggestion either didn't register with Hans, or he didn't hear it, because he gave no reaction. "So where are they?" I asked, pressing.

"They were all stood in a line and shot, just there, near the generator, and dumped amongst those trees." He nodded to his right, and carried on tinkering with the radio, as if he'd just told me a weather report, or the cookhouse menu.

My cigarette fell onto the dry earth, still smouldering. So this was what we had come to, such a casual attitude to death. Then I realised, with a dark sinking feeling deep in the pit of my stomach, that the idea of the Russians fighting with us on a grand scale as allies would never happen.

I suspect I knew what this meant for us, even then. I should have asked Hans about it, but I had no idea of his involvement at the time.

"I thought there were rules," I said, still hopelessly naïve.

"About prisoners of war?" Hans removed his glasses, wiping the lenses with a corner of his shirt, before putting them back on. "The Russians never signed the Geneva Treaty, and so I don't think we are bothering either." He turned back to the radio. "To be honest, from what I've heard, I don't think we ever bothered while we've been here," he said, turning the dial to the left, "unless it suited us."

He paused, nodding at the open door. "The Russian POWs built this, about a hundred of them, in a week. I don't know what happened to them after that; they were just taken away." He shrugged. "Should we care? They're not German and civilised like us; they are sub-human *Untermensch*, remember?"

A familiar sound drifted from the speaker. I checked my watch: 1200 hours, the first notes of Shostakovich's Fifth Symphony.

"Listen to this wonderful music, Paul," he said. "Listen to it. It's so damned civilised."

He winked, acknowledging the irony.

26

When I wandered back inside with the mugs, I noticed the previously damp walls, now shades of yellow, dried and crumbling, had been causing problems, with cave-ins patched up with rough timber. The bookcase still stood at the end, and I remembered I'd finished the book so should have brought it back, but oddly enough I didn't want to part with it. Being a connection with my father, I knew it would never be returned.

The briefing imminent, I said goodbye to Hans, shaking his hand before walking briskly across the airfield. I'd heard everything Hans had said but hadn't listened to a word.

The 109 I had abandoned had gone, perhaps scrapped for parts or rebuilt and sent to a training squadron.

*

Instead of flying free hunts in pairs we were ordered to look out for a group of Sturmoviks, Yak 1s, and I-16 Ratas that had recently attacked the Palace Airfield, probably heading our way. Due to their usual ineptitude, only minor damage had been caused, but we still wanted to teach these Russians a lesson.

Eight of us took off and almost immediately a group of Sturmoviks tried luring us north-east across their lines. It must have been the same ones, so we took a few shots at them, but all kinds of flak came up, so we turned away. A year ago we would have waited, in case the Ratas and Yak-1s appeared, but standing patrols were now forbidden, due to the increasing fuel problems.

A few days later, after more similar ops and visits to Hans, I returned to the Palace Airfield.

On a grey day of heavy September rain, when the long-dry earth produced a heady smell of new dampness, we were briefed in the main hall by the CO, now promoted lieutenant colonel after the briefest time as major. He told us we were being reorganised and would be joined by four squadrons from JG51, two from JG77, and more from JG3, who had already been flying with us for a while. We were to change our tactics by flying further south and landing at other airfields more often, in a concerted pro-active attempt at fooling Ivan as to our numbers. It seemed we could be sent anywhere at short notice in support of the ground forces, no matter how far and for however long.

We wondered about the wisdom of this fire-brigade type of operation as it would inevitably use more fuel and the vastly increased distances put men and machines at greater risk, but this was a decision made way above our heads.

To help us keep track of time on these long flights, any aeroplane not already having a clock would have one fitted.

We all wore a watch, but it's quicker and easier to glance at a dial in front of you than fumble about with your sleeve.

The briefing ended on a lighter note when the CO asked if Lieutenant Hans Heter was present.

"Here!" came a shout, as a vaguely familiar face raised a hand, and he nudged his way forward.

"Congratulations, Hans," the CO said, handing him a laurel wreath, "for your fifty-third victory."

I'd never seen a laurel wreath given for fifty-three victories and wondered what the CO was doing, but after applause and a modest cheer, he continued. "Fifty-three combat victories, six at night, but that's not what the wreath is for." He smiled. "This is to mark a totally unprecedented achievement by any fighter wing in the history of aerial warfare."

We waited for what this could be.

"Your fifty-third victory is JG54's three thousandth kill, so congratulations to you all."

A sergeant added this figure to the scoreboard on the wall, and it looked utterly extraordinary. Such a huge number of enemy aeroplanes destroyed in combat by one fighter wing. What an unbelievable achievement.

My current tally had risen to eight, which still seemed poor compared to most, but with me often being a *Katschmarek*, a wingman, my job was to watch out for the leader so he could do most of the killing; these pilots relied on a good wingman.

Photographers from *The Eagle* and *The Signal* took dozens of pictures, and huge propaganda features were later made of this extraordinary achievement. Any air force in the world would have been rightly proud.

*

We hadn't seen Ivan over the Palace Airfield for three weeks until 29th September. Sturmoviks sped in at low level, destroying two Stukas and damaging a 109 G from JG77. As usual we were incensed, not only because they'd reached us but for the fact they managed to escape unmolested.

The CO summoned the officer in charge of the flak units, his voice carrying as he admonished the poor man.

Throughout September and October 1942 our ops mainly supported ground forces and Ivan sent more aeroplanes to stop us, which we continued shooting down. I claimed another kill, a Rata, and saw the pilot jump from his aeroplane, floating down into his own lines. I'm sure he waved a fist at me as he drifted to safety, but I didn't hang around to confirm this!

On 25th October a new lieutenant, who had rapidly increased his tally over the summer with JG54, became CO of No. 1 Group. Walter Nowotny took over when Major Hrabak and Lieutenant Lange, two of our highly regarded officers, were posted south to the Stalingrad Front.

Most days became cloudy and wet, causing havoc with mud, and the nights increasingly cold as the first snow arrived between heavy freezing rains. We all dreaded the oncoming winter and hoped to have never seen another in Russia. With stalemate all along the front, our forces were busy at Stalingrad, and we were nowhere near to taking Leningrad, or Moscow, and as every day passed the Red Air Force grew larger.

Flying greater distances meant we experienced frequent changes in weather. In late autumn we could encounter four seasons in one flight, only adding to our problems, putting extra strain on us and our machines. Now based at Siverskaya most of the time, I alternated between occasional nights at the palace and days at Ryelbitzi and Staraya Russa. All designed to make Ivan think there were many more of us. It may have fooled him for a while, but it exhausted us.

At Siverskaya I fired my pistol at a Russian for the first time. He was running towards me and wouldn't stop, despite my shouts, so I drew my P08 and shot him.

27

My target fell on his face. Walking towards him, I lowered my arm. Suddenly the man I thought dead began moving, so I levelled my pistol at him again.

"*Ne strelyay, comrade!*" he shouted, pleadingly, and then 'don't shoot!' in German, now on his feet, arms raised high enough to touch the low cloud. I'd been checking my aeroplane before an early morning op when this idiot had come running towards me from the trees. Not wearing a uniform of any sort or carrying weapons, when I shouted, "Stop!" he'd ignored me, living proof of my ineptitude with a pistol.

Unharmed, he stood before me, rambling away in Russian, and surprisingly, I understood more than I anticipated, even though he spoke incredibly quickly. Just then another figure appeared from the trees, running towards us. The first held his hands out, turning his head, shouting at the other, and the second slowed to a walking pace before eventually reaching us.

The first looked in late middle age and the other a teenage boy, perhaps father and son. We stood near the tail of my aeroplane ten metres apart and, for a moment, I had no idea what to do or say until I heard an engine approaching from behind.

My shot had created interest as a pair of field police raced up on a motorcycle and sidecar, bounding across the grass, shouting at the two men in broken Russian.

The man in the sidecar gripped an MG34 and drew back the slide as though about to use it.

To my amazement the older of the two men said, "Sorry we are late; my apologies," in reasonable German as the man in the sidecar smiled, letting go of the pistol grip as it rocked like a see-saw with the weight of the ammunition.

"Over there, quickly, and get on with it!" the motorcyclist, an army sergeant, shouted, lifting his hands off the controls, leaning back on his seat with the engine idling.

The two Russians moved off towards our accommodation block in a swift march, chatting to one another, the older one berating the youngster with a hard slap on the back of the head.

"Local volunteers, working for us," the sergeant said, "so try not to kill them," he added, grinning.

"At least not until we've finished with them." The man in the sidecar laughed, slapping the breech of the MG34.

"They live through there," the sergeant said, pointing at the woods. "We even pay them, apparently." He shook his head in obvious disapproval.

Only then did I notice there were no fences around the airfield, and realised the horse and cart I'd frequently seen carrying ammunition and other provisions was probably locally owned.

If those two idiots had told me who they were I would probably not have tried to kill them. I shook my head. I'd seen civilians wandering around, both men and women, but had never assumed they were locals working for us, allowed to come and go as they pleased, not as vanquished slave labourers but as volunteers. The war continued to amaze me.

*

On 19th November an ace from JG2 in the west arrived to become CO of No. 2 Group. Captain Hans 'Assi' Hahn flew in to the Palace Airfield in a sparkling new 109 G, full of enthusiasm, despite the return of dark winter days and near permanent sub-zero temperatures. He'd never been there before, making his name over the English Channel against the British and, as an ace pilot, he featured several times in our air force magazines. Meeting him was an event in itself and again I imagined a much bigger character than the relatively short, stocky man with a wide, toothy smile and round face.

A convivial man, generous with his advice at shooting down the enemy, but more importantly with combat survival tips, one of the first things he asked was, "I only shoot down Spitfires, so do they have any here?" to much amusement. I hadn't seen one yet; apparently the Russians had some for high-altitude reconnaissance.

A few days after Hahn's arrival I had brief contact with the enemy over the southern suburbs of Leningrad. We usually stayed well clear, due to the heavy flak, but we had been drawn in when eight of us couldn't resist taking on an entire squadron of Sturmoviks, as they circled the city. It was only the second time I'd flown with Sergeant Peter Siegler, a popular member of No. 3 Group, and very skilled card player as I recently found out to my cost.

While I stuck to Peter's wing as we approached, he assured me he knew of only one way of attacking them successfully.

Others had warned me they were difficult to shoot down and the only way to do it was to hit it underneath in the radiator. Their pilots knew this, so whenever they saw us they would drop down as low as possible so we couldn't get underneath, in real cat-and-mouse stuff. It meant only one chance.

Alongside Peter I fired everything I had into the fuselage as the rear gunner shot at me continuously. Even though I know I hit the target – bits were falling off – the damned thing just kept on going. The crew must have been surrounded by armour plate, along with the engine and fuel tanks. Any other aeroplane would have disintegrated when hit by so many 20mm cannon shells.

Passing over one of these ferociously keen rear gunners, or *klappertopps*, as we called them, Peter was hit, ironically underneath, in his engine, which began trailing smoke.

A shout came over the R/T: "I'm okay but I need to get out."

His aeroplane rolled slowly over onto its back, giving birth to a curled-up figure tumbling in freefall before the parachute opened, and Peter began a slow descent towards the empty city streets.

On my return I reported what had happened and Peter was formally listed as *Vermisst*. Very optimistic, I fully expected he'd find his way back within a few days.

But, that night, Horst shocked me into reality over a few drinks. He knew Peter better than I did, and when I told him he shrugged.

"He's dead," he murmured, with ice-cold detachment.

As he poured me a drink I said, "There's every chance he could evade capture, hide, or at worst be taken prisoner, for intelligence reasons."

He looked at me, shaking his head, and I thought for a moment he would laugh. "Still not with us, are you, Paul," he said with a wry smile, taking the bottle and pouring another. His speech was slurred as though he'd been drinking for a while already.

"There were more than two million people in Leningrad when we arrived in September '41 and we've been deliberately starving them ever since. What do you think they are eating now? Thousands must be dead, starved to death, thanks to us. Imagine how desperate they are?"

He could see I'd never given it any serious thought, until now.

"Imagine half your family dead from starvation. You've already eaten the cat, the family dog, and every rat you can find, and you are even considering eating your mother, you're so hungry. Suddenly an enemy pilot comes floating down from the sky wanting to say hello. What would you do? I'd give him five minutes, ten at the most. Probably the time it takes him to fire his P08 before running out of bullets."

The naïve picture in my head of him chatting with the locals dissipated, replaced by a desperately bleak image of Peter standing in the street, drawing his pistol, as starving, vengeful locals emerged from bomb-damaged ruins.

On 3rd December Horst's suspicions were confirmed when Peter was posthumously awarded the Knight's Cross for his forty-eight victories. Intelligence sources revealed he had indeed been slaughtered somewhere in the southern suburbs of Leningrad. I can only imagine what they did to him.

His name wiped from the duty board, we burned a candle that night but never discussed him again.

I swore I would never allow myself to be captured alive.

28

As Christmas 1942 approached we were busier than ever, Ivan continually pushing towards Leningrad and all the way down the line to Demyansk as we kept blasting him back. In the Southern Sector we expected the announcement that Stalingrad was finally ours, and once taken we could concentrate on Moscow and Leningrad.

Locally our worst enemy was the weather, with our aeroplanes constantly freezing up again, but this time we were better prepared. We had many more 'dwarfs', petrol-engined hot air blowers, and more of the ingenious wooden huts covering the engines. Even so, I can't imagine how the black men did anything in such temperatures.

American-built Airacobra fighters appeared for the first time and, when flown well, were reasonable opponents. The cannon and machine guns in the nose made our two aeroplanes an even match on firepower, but the first ones I met weren't flown very well. I didn't manage to shoot one down, but I reported damaging three, which remained unconfirmed.

Most of our major servicing was done at Siverskaya, mainly because the Red Air Force were kind enough to leave us excellent hangars, which they had only partially destroyed before leaving. Our black men could shut the doors from the wind, but the cold always penetrated. I sometimes spent a few hours with them, discovering that, even in the hangars, exposed hands would freeze, the fingers becoming as articulate as a bundle of sticks. You couldn't work on the intricacies of an engine while wearing fur mittens, so some of the pilots donated their leather gloves. The hot-air blowers were often brought inside to raise the temperature to near zero, before shutting them down, aware that fuel was becoming increasingly precious.

Christmas stollen arrived in huge cases, along with Knorr oxtail soup and wonderful Dr Oetker's puddings, all the way from Germany. I had a first taste of what I thought to be a special kind of Christmas hot drink, until I found out it was coffee substitute made from figs. Few liked it, mainly due to the taste but more because of its effects on the bowels. If you could find a little sugar I thought it a really tasty drink. Occasionally we enjoyed captured British or American food, no doubt reaching the Russians through the Arctic convoys at Murmansk, but this was rare.

We may have been better prepared to look after our aeroplanes, but the food generally worsened, with very few fresh vegetables and no fruit at all, most of it originating in tins, too heavy to fly in to us in any great quantity.

Local farms had long since given up most of their animals, and for the first time in the war I was sometimes hungry, even after meals.

We thought about home on Christmas Eve. My last letter from my parents had arrived a month ago, and they said everything was fine, but I knew the British were still bombing German cities, and we'd heard the Americans might soon be joining them, but so far this hadn't happened. Perhaps they were too busy fighting our allies in the Pacific.

Letters from Inge became less frequent. She told me the factory was still working to full capacity, despite recent issues. At first I had no idea what she meant, and then I guessed. She and her parents lived close by, so I feared for her safety. Inge also asked if I'd met any Russians, because there were hundreds now working in the factory. She enquired whether I would be getting leave to visit her. I couldn't tell her because I didn't know. Her last letter seemed business-like, signed in a formal manner, like a doctor to a patient.

In addition to the occasional newspapers and magazines from home we followed the progress of the war on the radio. We knew Rommel had made a tactical withdrawal from North Africa; a good move because it had been a sideshow anyway, and now all the resources of the Afrika Korps could be put to better use.

When Christmas came none of my comrades mentioned leave, even though I'm sure it was on everyone's mind. It seemed the only way to get a flight to Germany would be if you were wounded with a 'home shot', as we called it, or to receive a medal, or both. We'd heard rumours of trips west for conversion to the new Fw190, but so far it hadn't happened, for anyone.

The air force gave me a gift on Christmas Eve, however, notifying me of my promotion to sergeant, and I was delighted to send my corporal stripes home. My pay had now risen by five marks to forty-five a month.

On Christmas Day Ivan remained mostly quiet and we were able to gather together in the evening to sing carols and tell jokes. The musicians amongst us played harmonicas and piano accordions, and we all drank our superior cognac, a gift from the air force.

*

January 1943 arrived amidst great celebrations and renewed determination to make this our last winter in Russia. I was back at Siverskaya most of the time, where we had long since adapted the buildings to suit, one of them filled with chairs and the back wall painted white: our cinema.

Another much smaller building had a tiled floor, drainage holes, very few windows, and an enormous coal-basket stove. Some men had served in the far north of Norway and recognised it straight away. We found coal, and pilots of JG54 enjoyed rolling around naked in the snow after twenty minutes' roasting in a sauna. When I tried it the weather had turned relatively mild; I cannot imagine surviving the shock of anything colder than minus ten.

I now lived with three others in a small wooden hut the Russians had constructed before the war around a huge brick-built stove which took up almost an entire wall. Our engineers had replaced the shattered roof and it seemed to have once been occupied by Red Air Force pilots.

An army camp bed occupied each corner, with two blankets nailed above the door to provide extra draught-proofing, and we did everything we could to keep the fire going.

The freshly cut logs, still heavy with sap, hissed loudly in the flames, but they still burned well. We were very impressed with our Russian masonry stove because even if the fire went out it remained warm for many hours, ideal if we were away from our hut unexpectedly. Not only this, we used it for many things from boiling a kettle, heating pots of food, to drying clothes, but it consumed forests of trees.

With no running water or flush toilets, we screened off a small area at the back of the hut for privacy with a wooden frame of blankets, so we had water, a mirror, a hand basin, and a bucket.

Forced to venture further into the woods for fuel, luckily we found an old local man with his Panje pony to gather it for us. Every German airfield in Russia had an old man and a cart. With an array of tools, including band saws and axes, it seemed unlikely that someone of his stature could bring down trees.

He looked similar to the man I'd almost shot, particularly when accompanied by a teenager whom I assumed to be his son or grandson. I often wondered where they lived and how they could come and go whenever they wanted. Friendly and happy to trade vodka for schnapps, he even supplied us with potatoes and meat, though we had no idea what sort.

The best part of Siverskaya was who I was living with in our little hut, as we called it: Reinhold Hoffmann and Helmut Missner, my old friends from Bergen, and Fritz Tegtmeier, whom I'd met at Mga, when he dragged me from my snowbound 109. All sergeants now, we drew strength and inspiration from each other. Fritz, the oldest at twenty-five, had been awarded an air force goblet a few months before after a successful summer at Mga. Astonishingly, he said he missed the place, complaining our building was cold compared to the squalid earth dugout.

I also had the good fortune to bump into Peter, one of my Austrian friends from France, still working on aeroplanes. The other two from my tent, Johann and Gerhard, had remained in the west.

Ivan began yet another attempt to reach Leningrad, just when our patrols in the Central Sector began. There were demands even further south; the Stalingrad Front absorbed far more men and materials than anticipated. We did our utmost but with increasing difficulty.

On 6th January Hans Philipp shot down seven in a single day, bringing his total to 146 confirmed kills. More pilots were awarded the Knight's Cross as Sergeant Zweigart claimed his fifty-fourth kill and Lieutenant Rupp his fiftieth. Max Stotz was enjoying a tremendous run, claiming his 150th kill, and the new CO of No. 2 Group 'Assi' Hahn his 130th. The numbers were phenomenal and yet they still kept on coming. How could this be possible?

29

We all knew our ground crew at Siverskaya, and most of the time mine was Karl from Silesia, who I'd told all about my background. He was passionate about the technical side of aero engines, as I was, and so the time I spent in the hangar with him passed incredibly quickly. He had a great sense of humour and as such he was good company, really valuing my assistance, though his knowledge of the Daimler-Benz engine was far superior.

I was getting to know my own aeroplane, all the nuances a particular machine has, and it began to feel part of me, almost an extension of my own self. But I couldn't fail to notice that everything we had, both machines and people, were deteriorating rapidly, with replacements scarce.

In the second week of January we had the fantastic news we'd all been waiting for: JG54 pilots were being sent for conversion onto the new Fw190. I waited my turn, remembering the verdict on the aeroplane I was given months ago. I raised this with Karl, who informed me the A1 was indeed unreliable, now addressed in the A3 and A4.

Pilots were sent west in no particular order and within a few days new Fw190s began appearing to a huge amount of interest. Two were rolled into the hangar at Siverskaya for pre-combat checks and I was among a small crowd gathered around, keen to get a first look. The cowlings were opened and it was the first time I'd seen the BMW engine since training days.

As soon as they were checked over, fuelled and armed, the two pilots who had brought them in, my friend Otto Kittel and Helmut Brandt, fresh from their conversion courses, climbed back in with boyish grins, starting them up and heading east into the grey winter sky for some hunting.

That same afternoon I flew with the adjutant of No. 1 Group, Lieutenant Edwin Dutel, as his wingman for the first time; he was terrifying. Having almost bumped into me at dispersal, he took hold of my arm. "Come on, Goetz, you're with me, you're my *Katschmarek*."

From that moment I was playing catch-up even walking to our aeroplanes.

Dutel had a reputation for low flying but no-one had warned me he flew lower than anyone I'd ever seen before, and of course I was expected to keep up, hurtling along at 400kph ten metres over the enemy.

We had to climb or fly around trees; we were so low we could even see the startled faces of friends and foe alike as we roared over their heads. One lucky shot from any kind of weapon and we'd be finished in an instant. It was exhilarating, of course, but my uniform was soaking and I couldn't afford even a split second's lapse of concentration.

My first trip with Edwin Dutel was successful, but I consider it pure luck that we both survived.

The ice road across Lake Ladoga was back in use, so we were dropping oil bombs, a potent mix of high explosive and petrol that would hopefully melt the ice, making it impassable. I'm not sure this ever worked as intended, but a huge petrol bomb skimming the ground and exploding at a 100kph was certainly a fearsome weapon. We also dropped hundreds of the small white-painted SD-2 butterfly bombs that would be lost in the snow, only to explode when stepped on.

The weather closed in again as a deep depression a thousand kilometres wide rolled in from the east and everything was grounded.

After several days of very heavy snow it was 26th January when we strafed the column of troops shuffling along the ice road, tearing apart the wretched lines of men trapped in their own frozen hell from where we despatched them. None of us discussed it, other than that it had been successful.

As if by retribution the next day one of No. 3 Group's new Fw190 A4s was damaged at the Palace Airfield by a hit from a Russian aeroplane. No-one saw it pass overhead, confirming the opinion they'd just been lucky.

The duty board at Siverskaya was in the briefing room near dispersal where the CO and adjutant had their offices. On 2nd February three names were cursed with the awful word *Vermisst*: Helmut Brandt, Gunther Götze, and Karl Kulka. I knew all three and they were some of the first to convert to the Fw190. As far as I knew none of them had ever been shot down in a 109. We were all desperate for news, but no-one saw what happened to Karl and Gunther. Anton was flying with Helmut and he told me he saw him lower his undercarriage and land on the Lake Ladoga ice.

"We'd just tangled with four Ratas, shooting two of them down, and Helmut just landed, right there, I've no idea why. His aeroplane seemed okay, there was no smoke trail and he didn't say anything over the R/T. I can only assume he had engine problems."

This was a worry. His chances of getting back were slim, particularly now the Red Army had retaken Schlusselberg on the southern edge, and so he'd just landed straight into captivity, handing them a nearly new Fw190. I thought of the early reputation the A1 had for unreliability, and I admit I was concerned.

The next day four of us flew to the Palace Airfield on standby where just after landing we heard shocking, unbelievable news. It was broadcast several times on the army radio and I missed the first one, but we gathered around in huge numbers to hear it repeated.

"The Battle of Stalingrad is over," a sombre voice told us. "The Sixth Army under Field Marshall Paulus fought courageously to the bitter end as expected but they have been annihilated by overwhelming numbers. They died to save Germany."

We looked at one another in stunned silence. There'd been an army broadcast from Stalingrad only a few weeks before telling us the fighting was tough but everything was going well, so what had gone wrong?

"What happened to Manstein?" someone said. "He was supposed to relieve them…"

"The airlift was working well, supplies were getting through, just like at Demyansk," someone else said.

"Demyansk was six divisions, there were twenty in Stalingrad," a forlorn voice muttered.

Thousands of German troops were in the city, an entire army, so what had happened? In addition to this there were hundreds of transports flying in supplies, and as far as we knew it had been successful, so where were they now?

Surely it wasn't true? We simply couldn't believe it. The scale of the loss was incomprehensible, and as yet we had not considered the wider implications. There were no official denials as the message was repeated and so we were forced to accept the truth.

Desperate to learn the fate of our comrades, when a pair of white-painted Ju52s landed at the Palace Airfield, apparently from the south, we were extremely curious. Sure enough, the passengers were pilots and army officers who had escaped the Stalingrad pocket; I hitched a lift to the palace where they were being taken for recuperation.

Their middle-aged appearance and over-sized dilapidated clothing hanging from skeletal frames drew immediate interest, and sympathy. After delousing and new uniforms we saw them in the casino where they spent most of their time fast asleep in the chairs nearest the fire, like old men.

When awake and suitably persuaded with enough schnapps they spoke to us.

"We couldn't undertake high-G manoeuvres," one of them said, "because we were so hungry we'd simply pass out."

Everyone in earshot stopped to listen as the room fell silent.

"We only had enough fuel for one op a day and barely any ammunition," another murmured, "maybe a two-second burst, but that was it." His eyes were deeply sunken in his head, his long thin fingers yellow and black from frostbite, as were parts of his face.

"JG3 were down to three serviceable 109s in the end," another said, before a long pause. He stared into the fire. "But we were lucky, we escaped."

Another gaunt face spoke. "We had to leave all our ground crew behind in that hell-hole. God only knows what happened to them."

One looked at me directly as I sat opposite, barely two metres away. He leaned forward, looking around briefly, an elderly man in his twenties passing a dark secret.

"Do you ever speak to the infantry?" he whispered.

I shook my head. "We see them here occasionally coming and going, wounded mainly, but that's all. Why?"

"Do you talk to them about what's happening at the front?"

I shrugged, shaking my head again, wondering why he was asking. He smiled as he tried rolling a cigarette, but the tobacco fell around his legs onto the floor. He couldn't bend his brittle fingers, as dextrous as twigs that might snap at any moment. I leaned forward with a packet of Reemtsma and he took one, which I lit for him. I gave him the packet.

Someone called out for drinks and he indicated that he wanted a beer.

"I don't want it cold," he said. "Warm it up, just a little, please," he shouted. "My stomach..." his voice as weak as his fingers.

He then began a conversation with his colleague in the next chair and I was abandoned.

We bought them drinks and made sure they were comfortable, but in a few days they were gone, flown back out, maybe for some home leave. I returned to Siverskaya and those of us who'd spoken to these Stalingraders didn't dwell on what we had heard. It seemed they had been incredibly unlucky.

We'd never known such conditions, and none of us thought it would ever happen to us.

30

On 19th February 1943 pilots gathered in the crew room at Siverskaya on the instructions of the CO and new adjutant Edwin Dutel, in the first such meeting since Stalingrad. A laurel wreath was handed to Otto Kittel, who looked surprised, as I did. Otto had secured another confirmed kill which in itself was not unusual, but this had taken JG54's grand total of aerial combat kills to four thousand.

The CO unveiled a huge Green Heart on the wall with the number four thousand written across the centre. A lot of schnapps followed, with an unusually decent meal at a long table draped in white cloth and garlands. We shared jokes, speeches, mutual back-slapping and congratulations, and shaking of heads at this astonishing figure. It was all great news after the setback at Stalingrad, which we now tried hard to forget, and those with cigars took them out as the schnapps and brandy were liberally passed around.

As a finale the CO rose to his feet, cigar in one hand and schnapps in the other.

"There will be no let-up, here, gentlemen," he said, scanning the room. "Our job is to stop Ivan, to kill him wherever we find him, because this remains our sacred duty, so let us continue, and with God's help we will succeed." He paused before adding, "Never forget the most important fact, that we have God on our side."

The room fell into absolute silence. It was just the reassurance we had been waiting for, and we loved it. Brief and succinct, but very welcome, and the CO knew it.

We'd all had time to reflect on the setback in the south, and to use it as an opportunity to regroup and organise the fight-back.

He rose to his feet, glass in hand, signalling for the rest of us to follow. "To victory!" he shouted.

We all instinctively stood bolt upright and replied with the same, loud, confident cry, draining our drinks in one. This was probably the last occasion every one of us still believed it.

In the next few days more rumours circulated, this time of an offensive planned for the summer, as in 1942. Perhaps Leningrad would be taken, and because we had come to within a few kilometres of Moscow, perhaps this was back as an objective again.

Meanwhile, emboldened by his success at Stalingrad, Ivan increased his offensive sorties all across the front. None of us wanted to admit the undisputable fact that we were losing the initiative, the key to successful warfare.

Front-line troops were bombarded with another weapon, just as insidious as the cold: Ivan dropped thousands of leaflets promising fair treatment and hot soup if they laid down their weapons. We were banned from reading them, but I saw one of these scraps of Russian nonsense in the briefing room. In poor German Stalingrad was mentioned several times, with promises of favourable treatment. It did nothing for me. But then I wasn't stuck out in the open, freezing to death.

To my surprise another leaflet appeared soon after, entirely in Russian, one of hundreds that had drifted across the airfield from the east. It wasn't until I saw boxes of them at dispersal I realised they were ours.

"Brothers and sisters! Fellow countrymen! Officers and soldiers of the Red Army! Cease fighting this criminal war! Turn your arms against the dictator Stalin and his Bolshevik criminals!"

Luckily it was written in simple language and so I understood much of it. The last line read: "The Committee for the Liberation of the Peoples of Russia," signed, "General Andrey Andreyevitch Vlasov."

To my astonishment I saw his unmistakable figure a day later. German officers were escorting him around Siverskaya airfield as though on a tour of inspection; Hans Weber was with them, probably for his language skills. When they boarded the aeroplane heading north Hans went with them. I'm not sure he saw me.

*

On 21st February four of us were ordered to the CO's office, with no idea why.

"You're going to Heiligenbeil, in East Prussia, tomorrow," he told us, projecting the usual fatherly enthusiasm into his voice. "We'd fly you there in a Ju52 but they want our old aeroplanes for training. It's nine hundred kilometres so you are scheduled to stop at Jakobstadt," he said, unfolding a map, aiming his right index finger near Riga on the coast, about halfway.

Obviously a surprise, reflected in an odd sense of urgency in the CO's voice.

"It's 120 kilometres south-east of the city, they are used to seeing us so they'll have fuel for you and your aeroplanes, if you want it," he said, smiling, "but don't stay too long, an hour at the most, because I want you at Heiligenbeil before dark. Take your time, throttle back, and don't tangle with anything on the way, alright?"

We knew it was unlikely we'd meet the enemy so far behind the lines, but it wasn't impossible.

He still hadn't told us why we were going, until then.

"Your Gustavs will stay at Heiligenbeil for training, and you'll return with brand-new Fw190 A3s or even A4s. So good luck, gentlemen, and see you when you get back."

How fantastic! New aeroplanes, Fw190s! It was a short, professional briefing and we each took a map with a diagram of both airfields including the landing strip, R/T frequencies, fuel points, and dispersals. We finished with a quick shot of French cognac and a toast to victory.

We hoped it would be Germany, or even France where we'd heard others had been sent for training, but sadly not. Even so we were fired up with excitement at flying the new Fw190.

At 0900 hours I took off with the others heading south-west, settling at seven hundred metres in a beautiful clear sky on a heading of 260 degrees. We flew in the usual finger four, even though we weren't anticipating any combat. There were other emergency airfields marked on the map, but our flight to Jakobstadt was easy and uneventful.

Their grass strip was a little uneven and badly maintained, and I saw very few aeroplanes other than wreckage of some old biplanes, which I was astonished to find were British Gloster Gladiators in Red Air Force markings. Two Storch reconnaissance machines stood at dispersal, with a lot of activity, mainly army personnel and their vehicles in various states of repair.

Fuelled by two air force personnel communicating in a series of grunts, after offering us nothing to eat or drink we decided we'd take off as soon as we were ready. Thankfully even the weather was kind with a rare anti-cyclone centred over the Gulf of Finland. The next stage was just as easy and we found Heiligenbeil without difficulty.

The airfield looked like a sprawling city with a landing strip in the middle. There were hangars everywhere, probably ten in all, interspersed with other buildings of all sizes, and I realised this must have been where I had stopped in the Ju52 on the way to Gatchina. Neat rows of Fw190s stood close to the hangars next to filthy old 109s standing out in the snow like so much scrap metal.

Anton, Helmut, Fritz, and I took our small bags and made ourselves known at dispersal. A corporal waved us over to a car and we gratefully climbed in out of the cold. He was a cheerful young man with a squeaky voice; the car reeked of cigars, the ash from which had smudged into the black leather upholstery. It was obviously the station taxi for pilots and officers.

Dropped into a warm spacious barrack of twenty or more beds, mostly unoccupied, we claimed ours then made our way to dinner. As we crossed the airfield on foot we saw a ragged crowd of a hundred or more men under the guard of SS with MP40s and dogs, filing through a gate in a barbed-wire fence. They were led to a large wooden door into an enormous factory at the rear of the hangars. With barely enough clothing, many had filthy strips of cloth on their feet for boots.

They hurried into the building, no doubt keen to find warmth, and I wondered who they were and what they were doing there.

*

Amongst the crowd, Grisha Bogdanov pushed his way forwards out the cold. He had been captured on the road between Mga and Volkhov two weeks before, during Operation Iskra, one of the Red Army's many failed attempts at breaking the siege of Leningrad. Their captors chanced upon them by accident as they slept huddled together near the road in a Rachel, a natural trench three metres deep. They were yelled at in a language no-one understood that was neither German nor Russian. Adding to the indignity of capture was the fact that Grisha and his comrades were seized by a group of Spaniards, so hungry they stole every scrap of food in their bread bags. They even took Grisha's boots. He was forced to tie bits of cloth and uniform around his feet to prevent them from being consumed by frostbite.

Twenty-seven men of the Spanish Blue Division, Franco's anti-communist volunteers, captured fifty Red Army soldiers and their walking wounded from the 372nd Rifle Division. Forced out into the open, they all stood together in a freezing blizzard for several minutes before their officer, Captain Francisco Soriano, finally made a decision to march west towards Mga.

Grisha feared the worst; the Spanish had a reputation no better than the Germans when it came to treatment of prisoners, and maybe they were lucky, because so far this officer seemed reasonable. They marched in darkness and minus thirty degrees for hours, finally covering the twenty-five kilometres to Mga railway station, where they were handed over to the SS.

Grisha climbed into the cattle trucks with a hundred others, but the wounded, numbering about twenty, were not allowed on the train. To the familiar clattering of MP40 machine pistols they were shot and left by the track.

31

Grisha arrived at Heiligenbeil the following morning, put to work immediately in a huge dimly lit warehouse. Though freezing cold inside, at least it was under cover and out of the wind. His first job, lifting heavy machine parts on his back across the floor, he found incredibly difficult. An obvious test of fitness, those incapable of doing so for twelve hours with no rest and nothing to eat or drink were dragged away and never seen again.

At least the work kept him warm. They were allowed a few hours' rest in the night on the bare concrete floor before resuming early each morning. Those too sick to continue were removed.

At the end of the third day a huge vat of lukewarm water was wheeled into the warehouse. Pale green, it had the same smell and consistency of pond water. Apparently pea soup, each man had an enamel mug to keep.

Grisha was moved to an adjacent factory where he then became a lathe operator, nothing too technical at first, perhaps another test, but which he managed perfectly. That night, and every night from then on, the survivors were escorted across the airfield to an unheated secure barrack where they slept on the wood floor with one blanket each.

If someone died in the night they would be stripped, leaving a naked corpse for the Germans. This is how Grisha gained a decent pair of boots and a scarf. He didn't care that everything was alive with lice because he was too.

*

In the dining hall with my hot meal and huge mug of steaming coffee, I asked a food service corporal about this ragged band of men. He shrugged his shoulders with a curious look.

"Ruskis, POWs, of course," he said, as though I should know. He continued looking at me suspiciously.

When I asked, "What are they doing here?" he merely shook his head and laughed.

I couldn't think of a single reason why they would be here at an active airfield, but he seemed to take pride in his answer.

"They work in the factories; they do anything we tell them. They are the best cheap labour," he said, with a smirk. "We even feed them," he added, as his colleague interjected with one word: "Sometimes."

A fairly decent sleep followed in a warm barrack, and after breakfast we were ordered to dispersal at 0900 hours. Ten of us sat in a briefing room when a lieutenant entered, telling us to remain seated.

"Heiligenbeil is a factory airfield, gentlemen, as you might have gathered."

He positioned himself at a wall map of the airfield. "Refuelling points are here, and here," he said, touching the paper at areas in front of the hangars on the north side. "We keep ammunition here, serviced by vehicles at this point," he said, tapping the map with his right index finger. "These are repair hangars, here, and service hangars, here and here." The last was the closest to the building I noticed the POWs had entered, so I stuck my hand up.

"What about the Russian POWs?" as others looked at me and then at the lieutenant.

"They are not all sent to Germany. We put them to work here. They are useful, and they know the penalties for escape or sabotage," he said, sternly.

It occurred to me they would have ample opportunity for both. These weren't local civilian volunteers, they were battle-hardened combatants, no doubt bearing a grudge, or merely thinking of their duty.

What would I do in their situation? I couldn't imagine it, not even for a moment, mainly because I didn't want to. No doubt they were involved in menial tasks only, with no opportunities for sabotage, this was obvious. Surely we wouldn't be stupid enough to allow anything else. I forced this issue to the back of my mind and stared at the map.

At the southern end was a cluster of more than a hundred buildings, like a small town, half a dozen with *RK* written on them in red, *Russisch Kriegsgfangener*, Russian prisoners of war. Our accommodation was at the opposite, north-west side of the airfield, like the affluent side of a city.

"Your aeroplanes are here, ready for you," he said, tapping the map at dispersal. "They've just been serviced and you'll find them fuelled and armed."

The lieutenant gave a nod to a sergeant pilot I'd never seen before, who rose to his feet. They exchanged a few words and the sergeant began addressing us.

"The Fw190 A4, gentlemen: remember these figures. Stall speed clean is 205kph, take-off 170kph, approach speed

300kph, gear and flaps, 220–250, and touch down with flaps is 170. Lock the tailwheel by pulling back on the stick and wait until the engine is warm before taxiing for take-off. Mags, throttle, and circuit breakers are all in the same position as the 109. Watch your oil and coolant temperatures; don't be too keen to start taxiing until they've reached optimum, particularly in this weather." He glanced at the window, probably more out of instinct than reason.

"Here, these will help," he said, handing around sheets of paper with figures, diagrams and checklists.

"You all know the 109 well, but this is a far superior, modern fighter, you'll love it," he added, finally smiling. "Circuits today, enough for you to feel comfortable, and that's all. Do *not* lose sight of the airfield."

He nodded at the lieutenant before pointing to the door. We donned our flying gear and collected parachutes before climbing into the back of an Opel Blitz lorry.

Across the airfield they came into view, standing tall on their wide legs like pure white swans, black crosses on their wings: a staggered line of Fw190 A4s.

Parachute on, I climbed onto the wing as two black men helped. One of them with extremely bad teeth ran through the switches, comparing each one with the 109, or not, as the case may be, and then the controls. He obviously knew both aeroplanes well and I was grateful. With a pre-flight checklist on my knee he was kind enough to go through it with me, step by step.

"This one is a nice aeroplane, Sarge," he said, nodding before looking across at the others. "One or two have had fuel-flow problems and seem a bit temperamental, but this one's fine. By the way, don't open the canopy in flight; you're likely to lose it if you do, sorry."

I wouldn't want to in February, but the summer would be

interesting, to say the least. The canopy was huge and likely to attract every ray of sunshine. But now I was shaking with cold, or was it excitement, or both?

"I'll leave you to it then, Sarge," he said, hauling the canopy up. "You'll be fine, enjoy it!" shouting as he jumped.

So here it is, I thought, *the Focke-Wulf 190*. Settling back in the seat with the pre-start and take-off checklists on my knee, I began.

To my surprise I was nervous. It wasn't just the cold. This was the first new type I'd flown for a long time. How many different aeroplanes did I know, perhaps a dozen? So this was just one more.

Having always flown aeroplanes where the controls were well-worn, with paint chipped off handles and buttons, it was obvious this was straight from the factory, with a wonderful smell of fresh leather and clean oil like a new car, adding to my anticipation.

"Right, concentrate," I said, out loud, running through the checklist. Here goes: canopy closed and locked. Brakes on, fuel pumps on front and rear. Oxygen on; I checked the flow and secured my mask. Giro uncaged; waddling a little before finally standing still. Fuel on. Mags on both. I noticed this was the same as the 109. Throttle set, again, noting with some reassurance that this was just about the same too, probably nodding as I did so. Trim for take-off. I then turned the starter to the left, counted fifteen seconds before turning it back to the right as the inertia whirled and the BMW started with a thunderous roar.

32

Holding on the brakes, I waited as the oil and coolant temperatures slowly rose. It seemed pretty warm at Heiligenbeil, probably only a few degrees below zero, and even though there was full sun, it still took a while. I turned on the radio, an FuG16, the same as in the 109 G, and listened for traffic.

Two others were already lining up, so as soon as the oil reached forty degrees and the coolant sixty, I took a quick glance around. I locked the tailwheel and released the main brakes, testing them immediately to find them sharp and effective. After opening the radiator flaps I lowered some wing flaps. The controls full and free, I made a final check of the engine before lining up.

As I eased the throttle forward the aeroplane accelerated smoothly, with only a gentle bounce along the grass. The wide undercarriage immediately felt more stable than the 109, and as I passed 160kph I applied firmer back pressure, lifting off at 170. At a hundred metres I stowed the flaps and undercarriage. Although there was little wind, my first impressions were that the aeroplane seemed steady, more so than the 109.

Banking left into the circuit, and again for the downwind leg, I lowered the undercarriage after slowing below 300kph, giving myself plenty of space for a long final approach. I then lowered the flaps as soon as my speed dropped to 220. Holding the aeroplane steady with slight adjustments of a stiff throttle lever with my left hand, I flew over the hedge at 170, holding off and touching down. With a clear field ahead, I kept a little flap, eased full power back on, and took off again.

After four more circuits, I received the order to return, so someone else could use the aeroplane. I was enjoying it so much, I would have probably continued until I ran out of fuel! Feeling like a spoilt child handing back a new bicycle, I taxied across to dispersal and shut it down.

Sitting in the quiet cockpit before opening the canopy, I nodded to myself, impressed, pleased with what I'd seen so far, and incredibly excited at the prospect of taking it up to two thousand metres for some real flying.

There followed a discussion about the aeroplane with the instructors where frank opinions were exchanged, and as we were not flying again that day, these friendly discussions were helped with a bottle of schnapps. We all agreed it was an improvement on the 109.

Several pilots pointed out that airfields such as Mga and Ryelbitzi would be safer with the 190's wide undercarriage. The A4 had greater firepower too, with four cannons in the wings and two guns over the engine in the nose (but nothing in the propeller hub), and the increased stability would help in ground attack operations. We were keen to get started.

That night we experienced an unusually buoyant atmosphere in our barrack, a welcome change from recent bad news. We played cards with our hosts, someone brought in a gramophone with a wide variety of music, some odd but fantastic.

"What the hell is that?" I asked, moving closer to the music.

"It's American jazz. Good, isn't it?" one of the sergeant instructors said.

I nodded, having never heard anything like it. The record sleeve showed smiling photographs of the musicians, all black.

"I spent time with JG5 in Finland and Norway, fighting Ivan over Murmansk. I bought these in Helsinki," he said, handing me some others.

To my surprise he stated he knew our old 109 Friedrichs very well.

"We never had any new aeroplanes, we were always given your old ones, most of them still with your damned Green Hearts on the side," he said, lowering the needle onto something called 'Tiger Rag'.

We loved the infectious rhythm, unaware of why we'd never heard it before, assuming it to be new.

We mentioned the night would have been improved with female company. Helmut winked, leaning across with a bottle of schnapps, whispering in my ear as though passing a secret. "When we get back to Siverskaya I can help you out in that department," he mumbled, slapping me on the back. I probably looked confused, so he elaborated. "There's a very obliging peasant woman in one of the hovels near the airfield. She's clean, and pretty; they don't all look like Stalin."

He laughed, winking again, this time in an exaggerated manner the way drunks do. Had he been having a relationship with her? This was strictly against regulations. I thought he was joking so didn't pursue it.

We all continued drinking far too much before finally turning in very late.

The next morning the wind picked up as the weather changed. My head thumped, so, once in the cockpit, I turned on the oxygen and inhaled deeply with the mask fixed to my face, rectifying my hangover.

We were told to recap on circuits before another briefing, so I did two more before shutting down.

Ten of us listened intently to a second lieutenant pilot telling of his experiences flying the Fw190 in the west.

"The roll rate is superb, better than anything you'll ever encounter out here, unless you face the latest Spitfire, which I doubt. You will have greater acceleration than any other aeroplane in the sky too, so use both of these to your advantage, and even better, it doesn't need much trimming, which is fantastic. If you get in trouble, this aeroplane responds well to the split-S, a quick half roll, steep dive, and full throttle, but you don't need me to remind you how to do this. You are low down in the cockpit with your feet level with your arse, so you won't black out as easily in high-G manoeuvres, and don't forget there's an explosive charge in the canopy release for emergencies, the red button on the right, for use either in the air or on the ground. It makes a hell of a bang, but if you need to get out quickly, I don't think that will be a problem," he said, smiling.

We each had a diagram of the cockpit and a rough plan of the aeroplane had been chalked onto the blackboard.

"Maximum combat endurance with a climb to about 7,500 metres is around one hour and twenty minutes, but a red warning light will indicate when only twenty minutes' flying time remains. Please don't ignore it, gentlemen," he said, raising his voice for that last sentence. "There's more armour plate than the 109, particularly around your arse, and the windscreen is bullet proof," he added, a little more upbeat, to chuckles of approval, as he tapped the blackboard. "The oil tank is armour-plated and both fuel tanks are self-sealing."

He paused, looking around the room with a barely audible sigh. I noticed the cuffs of his faded uniform were frayed in places, the material badly creased over the shoulders, indicating repeated lengthy pressure from parachute straps. A German Cross in gold shone on his right breast pocket opposite his pilot's badge, along with an Iron Cross, and a silver Wound Badge.

"The war is changing, gentlemen, and we are changing with it. This aeroplane has been specifically designed to work well out here; it has better protection for you, and better armament. You will be carrying bombs more often than you did with the 109, anything up to 250kg. It is therefore an ideal ground attack aeroplane, perfect for what you will be called upon to do much more of in the future."

The room had become deathly quiet. We all knew he was right. Since Stalingrad we realised that we had begun fighting a more defensive war, but still a war we hoped to win. With the best aeroplanes and the best pilots, most importantly, we had right and God on our side.

Suggestions of taking Leningrad or even pushing back over the Volkhov to retake Tikhvin were forgotten: accepted losses, at least for now. At first I thought this radical change in thinking might damage morale, but it had the opposite effect. We became more determined to succeed, to push back the Bolshevik hordes forever, thereby safeguarding European civilisation. We had to win. We had no alternative.

33

In the morning I took an A4 up to seven thousand metres. The rate of climb and acceleration were fantastic. A flick roll took less time than thinking about one; it was so light and responsive. In some moments the incredibly powerful BMW801-D engine seemed to be rough running a little, but every time I listened out for the sound, the engine ran perfectly.

We would be returning in these aeroplanes, so I decided to check it out on the long flight home to Siverskaya. If the sound continued, I'd speak to the ground crew. Other than this I couldn't wait to get started.

After one more flight for general handling we found out, to our surprise, that we had finished the course. There had been plans for navigation exercises, formation flying, and ground attack practice with bombs, but these had been scrubbed, due to fuel restrictions. None of us minded because we were all experienced and confident enough in our new machines. We'd dropped bombs before, so it didn't worry us.

After drinks and celebrations the night before, on the morning of departure, I saw another bedraggled line of POWs escorted between buildings. I watched as they entered a huge building past enormous open doors where I saw an assembly line of pre-formed sheet metal, cables, wheels, and tools, with aero engines hanging on chains from girders above. Huge empty crates were piled up outside, each one marked 'BMW'.

*

We took off after breakfast, Saturday 27th February 1943. With a headwind slowing us, we stopped for fuel at Jakobstadt. A tattered mass of Russian uniforms shuffled along a road towards the railway line as a train pulled up, heading west. Two hours later, as we took off again, some were climbing into the train, others lying down in the snow by the track.

I turned away and busied myself in the cockpit.

The aeroplane behaved itself for most of the way home, but then I noticed it rough running again, so on arrival I taxied over to the hangar and shut it down as close as I could, climbed out, and searched for Karl.

"Bring it in," he ordered, before I'd even said anything.

How did he know? I climbed back into the cockpit and released the brakes as four black men gently eased it under cover. Karl opened the cowling and began work immediately. What could he be doing?

Before I had chance to ask, he opened a sturdy cardboard box with 'Siemens' written on the lid.

"The rough running is fouling of the Bosch spark plugs, so we are replacing them all with these. This is what you were going to ask, isn't it?" he said with one of his knowing looks as he grabbed one from the box.

I nodded. Karl truly was a magician.

"These are new, but we are getting plugs from decommissioned Dornier 17s, the Siemens ones from their 801A engines. You won't have any problems after this," he said with assurance. "But I can't do anything about the knocking, that's the shit fuel."

My finely tuned ears had noticed something else, apart from the rough running.

"The fuel is getting worse," Karl groaned. "Octane levels keep going down. We'll be filling the tanks with water soon."

I thanked him and wanted to take it up as soon as he'd finished, but we had no fuel for test flights.

The black men had already made changes to the other engines, and the officers continued taking what they perceived to be the better aeroplanes from NCO pilots like myself. Often, they'd get away with it, but in this case they were all supposedly the same, at least so far.

The first time I looked at the duty board after returning, I noticed the CO of No. 2 Group, Major Hans 'Assi' Hahn, had been listed as *Vermisst*, last seen crash-landing in woods near Demyansk in his 109 G, far behind the lines, the day we left for Heiligenbeil. That dreadful word was now popping up on the duty board with increasing regularity.

On 6th March eight of us took off for a free hunt along the Staraya Russa – Kholm road just south of Lake Ilmen. I was one of four Fw190s from No. 1 Group, with four from No. 2 Group, led by their new CO Captain Heinrich Jung.

We swept in at ultra-low level, firing all our guns at Red Army vehicles which exploded, hurling debris high into the air.

An excited shout came over the R/T as one of our pilots, Sergeant Georg Munderloh, sighted a group of Sturmoviks escorted by a similar number of La-5s, the ones we had been warned about, all heading in our direction. There were probably thirty enemy altogether, so we broke off our ground attack as they moved to take us on.

My first real test of the Fw190, in both ground attack and aerial combat, was superb. Within a few seconds I saw an La-5 burst into flames after being pursued by Munderloh, quickly followed by another as I rattled away at anything with a red star.

The Sturmoviks were still in formation, but the La-5s, with their initial height advantage, were over us like wasps at a picnic. I managed to get behind one and fired a two-second volley, which struck the airframe but didn't bring him down.

For ten minutes utter chaos reigned as the Sturmoviks broke formation, joining the melee, flying straight at us in suicidal fashion, followed by their rear gunners firing continuously. Then I saw an La-5 collide with the right wing of Munderloh's aeroplane, probably deliberately, sending him down in a controlled dive that he managed to pull up, before a very rough crash-landing.

Our ammunition counters soon read zero, so we were forced to return home. I was exhausted, and my uniform soaked.

Only six of us landed back at Siverskaya; in addition to Munderloh, Hans Beisswenger failed to return. The last thing we'd heard had been him shouting up over the R/T, claiming two more kills, but no-one had seen what happened after his 'Yellow 4' was seen heading west at low level, quite a way behind the lines. His prospects looked bleak.

They were the latest pilots entered as *Vermisst* on the duty board. The La-5 colliding with Munderloh had been his twentieth kill, but for Beisswenger the second La-5 he brought down had been his 152nd.

Our immediate CO, Hans Philipp, began enjoying greater success with the new Fw190, as many of us did. His personal tally rose to 180, with half a dozen on a single day. 7th March saw No. 1 Group of JG54 shoot down an astonishing fifty-nine enemy aeroplanes without loss.

While thrilled with our success, it meant the numbers were startling, with just as many facing us the next day, however many we shot down. On 17th March Hans Philipp's total reached a staggering 203 confirmed enemy kills. He held an impromptu celebration in the crew room at the airfield, not just for this but also because it was his twenty-sixth birthday, confirming his status as one of the oldest amongst us.

With such amazing success in our new Fw190s, we believed Ivan would surely soon run out of aeroplanes and pilots.

34

The middle of March saw the return of an old enemy: mud, and our second year experiencing the great thaw. Far worse than that created by autumnal rains, it came so suddenly, making the time between bitter winters and baking hot summers just as hazardous. Our main wheels often sank a metre deep, into the same surface that had been as hard as concrete only days before. Too many precious aeroplanes were damaged when their props struck the mud, and they up-ended, requiring an ignominious rescue for the pilot, and days lost in repairs. All four seasons deliberately conspired against us.

Near the end of March I flew a 109 G5 for the first and only time. Four of them from No. 3 Group had arrived and, on the pretext of an engine check, I took it up for twenty minutes. I knew I shouldn't, but no-one noticed. It was the first time I'd flown an aeroplane with a pressurised cockpit and it seemed incredibly advanced, even against the Fw190 A4.

On 1st April, we had a formal parade at Siverskaya for Hans Philipp: not a belated birthday present but, sadly, a farewell. In the early spring air we assembled in our best uniforms. Hans Philipp told us he had been chosen to command JG1 in the west and would be leaving immediately. This was a huge promotion and an endorsement from the very top.

Everyone in No. 1 Group, JG54, lined up on the grass near dispersal, including the cooks, drivers, signals staff, mechanics, and admin, as the overall CO, Hans Trautloft, made a moving speech.

When Hans Philipp spoke, we understood he would have preferred to stay, but we were soldiers, obliged to follow orders.

Some of our best pilots and all the 109 G5s were taken for Defence of the Reich in the west; not just because of the RAF but a new threat increasing as rapidly as the Red Air Force: the high-altitude American B17 heavy bomber.

An hour after Hans Philipp's parade we scrambled, following reports of Sturmoviks heading our way. Eight of us took off in pairs, heading north-east into an increasingly dark sky: huge rolling towers of blue-black cumulus heavy with rain spread before us up to ten thousand metres. Somewhere in or under this the enemy lurked, waiting, drawing us in.

Over the Volkhov River we made contact with fifteen Sturmoviks and were joined by four 109s from Mga. I stuck with Lieutenant Hans Ademeit as his wingman and we closed in head-on at high speed.

Together we caused damage to three, which typically continued flying, and then we were bounced by a mix of La-GG3s and La-5s from the north, just under the cloud base. Everyone split up and did what they could as the Sturmoviks turned, dropping to a hundred metres, with us in pursuit. Yet more La-GG3s appeared with my first sighting of MiG-3s in a crowded sky; we had been lured into a trap. Eight of us were now trying hard to make an impression on at least thirty enemy aeroplanes, now drifting over our lines and across the river.

Flak burst around us and Hans shouted up over the R/T, "Let's get out of here. There's too much iron in the air!"

So we all began our usual flak waltz, as I heard hits on my airframe, close to the cockpit. I had two thousand metres in hand, so I turned 180 degrees before a quick half roll, steep dive, and full throttle.

Not surprisingly they didn't pursue us into the flak and we all made it back with only a few minor ventilation holes in our aeroplanes.

The next day a similar thing happened, but this time only four of us were bounced by twenty La-GG3s. Again, we were lucky to make it back.

All the time we engaged in this way, we were neglecting our primary role, that of ground attack, helping our troops, so we tried concentrating on this whenever we could. Few of us enjoyed it, due to the risks, with no-one exempt from the danger, however brilliant a pilot.

Several more ops followed for me as Edwin Dutel's wingman. He was one of those people who could never sit still, always busy with something, whether it was trying to get the cooks to improve their meals or, like me, showing a keen interest in the mechanics and our aeroplanes. By now his flying had earned him the nickname 'Low-Level King' and again I struggled to keep up, tearing over the ground at ten metres or less. He seemed to be flying even lower than when I first flew with him back in January. At this height an unseen telegraph pole or even a vehicle on slightly higher ground can mean disaster, and I'd never strained my eyes as much.

He slapped me on the back after every op, laughing at the near misses, which were numerous on each. I'd given up emulating him, skimming the ground, cutting crops with my propeller, because on one occasion I flew right through the top of a tree, lucky to get home with half of it in my engine. From then on I decided to be a little less reckless. As his wingman I could hang back a little higher, maybe twenty metres, as part of my job, and still work effectively.

On one of these low-level attacks near Schlusselberg on 9th April, Edwin's aeroplane made contact with the ground at 300kph. In an instant I saw it sliding across the mud, imagining him hauling back on the stick in an effort to get back into the air, but his prop had already struck. Perhaps if it had been a perfectly flat field with no obstacles he may have been alright, but in the two or three seconds before his aeroplane struck the T34 tank he would have known he had no hope.

His aeroplane exploded just after I passed overhead. Pushing the throttle forward, I pulled up the nose as hard as I dared until all I could see was my own reflection in the cockpit canopy, my propeller whirling a hole through dense grey cloud. I came out almost inverted, even though I thought I was straight and level, and headed for home.

Edwin wasn't listed as *Vermisst* that night, because I saw it, as others did, so he obviously wouldn't have survived. His luck simply ran out.

We opened his schnapps and lit a candle, as was the custom, but after that we never discussed him again.

Earlier that day while we had been busy near Schlusselberg the Palace Airfield had been hit again. We were adamant we hadn't seen any enemy aeroplanes, and indeed it wasn't bombing but more shelling from long-range artillery. This worried us more than anything else, mainly because we couldn't stop it. We suffered no casualties, but in total, eight He46 and four Ar66s, all from reconnaissance squadrons, were destroyed.

A familiar face, Captain Reinhard Seiler, arrived from No. 3 Group to take charge of No. 1 Group. He settled in quickly and I managed a few minutes with him between ops, and a week after his arrival he called a meeting of pilots in the crew room at Siverskaya.

On the first warm day of 1943, the double doors were propped open by a pair of badly dented ammo boxes. A large mongrel dog laid full stretch on the warm concrete, occasionally lifting its head to see who was arriving. Bruno supposedly belonged to one of the pilots, but in reality, we all made a fuss of him. Many of us had grown up with dogs, so he made a tenuous but vital link to home.

Clearly in a good mood, the CO called for Hans Ademeit, who promptly extinguished his cigarette under his flying boot and made his way over.

"Fifty-three victories, Hans. Well done," the CO said, placing a Knight's Cross ribbon over his head, the Iron Cross settling on the recipient's chest to spontaneous applause.

Handshakes were followed by schnapps and the gramophone for patriotic songs.

Aeroplanes from No. 5 Group were being abstracted to an airfield along the Gulf of Finland, halfway to Heiligenbeil, to patrol the anti-submarine nets. Fighter pilots did not relish flying over water, some having bleak memories of the English Channel, and we were all glad it wasn't us. Until a month later, when the pilots returned with tales of fantastic nights out in Helsinki, making us all incredibly jealous.

Continuing our ground attack ops, I had a few lucky escapes until Ivan decided he'd had enough and stopped trying to push us back. We were all relieved to be diverted to escort duties once again, tagging along with Heinkel 111s and Stukas, attacking shipping in Lake Ladoga, and railway lines the other side of the Volkhov. Though preferable to ground attack, this was also risky, of course, flying thirty or forty kilometres behind the lines, but if we could sever their transport links they'd never be able to mount another attack.

We soon engaged in dogfights at altitude with Ratas and La-5s trying to keep them away from our bombers, and I had my first encounter with a Curtiss P40.

In a straight confrontation, I managed to get the better of him in my 190 A4 with a two-second burst into his fuselage from my four cannons. Bits blew off and I must have hit the pilot because he stopped manoeuvring, settling into a shallow dive from which he never recovered. I didn't see a parachute. This took my tally to fifteen.

More P40s crowded in, clearly intent on having a go, so I made an immediate exit as soon as the bombers had done their job. Flak burst all around and I heard a tremendous bang from under my feet, as my engine immediately began rough running.

One word flashed through my head, as I shouted it aloud: "Shit."

35

With the oil pressure dropping, the engine sounded like an old bus struggling up a steep hill. I needed to get down as fast as possible. Luckily I had almost two thousand metres in hand, so I throttled back, aiming the nose due west.

The groaning engine continued turning the propeller, and as every moment passed, it dragged me closer to safety. To my horror I detected a burning smell from under my feet. Fuel vapour could be feeding it, despite the self-sealing tanks, so I considered shutting it off. I knew the aeroplane might simply explode, in which case I'd probably know nothing about it.

At least thirty-five kilometres behind the lines, I made for Mga, where I'd make a wheels-down emergency landing. Churning up the mud in a Russian field would not be a good idea. I'd been lucky on two previous occasions, but crash-landings are not always so easy. I had seen some nasty incidents in France where the pilots had been severely injured.

Using the R/T, I stated Mga as my destination.

Someone shouted, "You won't make it; we're too far south, you'll have to try for Lyuban."

Looking around and at my map, I realised I was on a south-westerly heading, with the Volkhov on my right, so I banked over the river, only to be met by more flak. Applying power slowly, I half expected nothing to happen, but the engine responded, despite obvious problems. I eased the throttle further forward and thankfully the engine continued, but for how long? There were more hits on my airframe, but then as soon as the river disappeared behind me the flak stopped.

My comrades were high above, making their way home, leaving me alone. Just then an Fw190 roared past my right wing, banked around, and settled on my left, Gunter Scheel waving and smiling as though we were on a Sunday-afternoon pleasure flight. I smiled back, immediately reassured. He gave me a thumbs-up before pointing beyond the nose and then down. I knew straight away what he meant. I remembered he'd been to Lyuban before, calling it his 'favourite shithole' because of its lack of facilities. Thanks to Gunter, I now knew my chances were good.

But, as the engine sounded more normal, wisps of smoke drifted up into the cockpit between my legs. I faced the stark reality that my aeroplane was on fire.

A quick glance in the mirror confirmed a thin grey smoke trail swirling behind, the same colour as the clouds. At five hundred metres, if I needed to jump, it would have to be now. Gunter seemed unconcerned at the smoke, indicating with the flat of his right hand in a chopping motion to press on. We passed a railway line, still at five hundred metres, heading due west, anywhere west. Were we back over our lines or not? I had no idea.

A long ten minutes passed, my engine continued and I remained airborne, though now at four hundred metres, falling below 300kph. The map on my knee indicated Lyuban to be dead ahead, but where the hell was it? After five more anxious minutes, with smoke filling the cockpit, I had no choice but to shut down the engine. I tried lowering the undercarriage and luckily it worked. I shut off the fuel and within seconds the engine stopped and the smoke cleared.

There's something about airfields that makes them visible from a great distance, even at relatively low altitudes. Usually a wide grassy area, a large cleared space with absolutely no trees, probably one or two straight lines of grass or other surface of a different shade, perhaps crossing one another at angles, and a small cluster of buildings, usually on one side.

Lyuban appeared straight ahead and to the right. It was odd seeing a stationary propeller blade standing on the nose of my aeroplane in flight, something I'd never experienced before. I lowered flaps in preparation for a dead stick landing, before turning off all the electrical switches.

Flying a fast, heavy glider, I recalled my time at Schuren, anticipating well ahead, keeping the nose down and airspeed up. Dropping too quickly, I thought for a moment I'd end up in a ploughed field. The landing strip was east to west, and as a northerly wind gripped the aeroplane, I cursed my luck that I'd have a crosswind landing to contend with too. Touching the rudder firmly with my right foot, I leaned the aeroplane into the wind, using it to buy a few more seconds.

Over the hedge with ten metres to spare, a few seconds later my wheels touched the grass with a rattling thump, louder than usual in the silence.

Hardly a crash, but a forced landing nonetheless. The

long grass gripped my wheels, stopping me quickly. Smoke thickened in the cockpit and I began choking. With fuel still in the tanks, I had to get out fast.

The canopy wouldn't budge. The runners had probably warped and, for a moment, I stupidly tried to find out what the problem might be, before remembering the explosive canopy release, picturing the lieutenant at Heiligenbeil. I covered my face with my left hand before pressing the button.

The blasts were just a few centimetres from my ears, sending the canopy away. I unstrapped, rolled out onto the wing, and lay on the muddy grass, never as glad to get my uniform so filthy. Gunter flew over once before climbing away to the north-west. I cannot describe how grateful I felt for what he'd done.

No reception committee greeted me as I stood up, watching my aeroplane burn. Someone should have come along to at least put the fire out and save it, but there was no sign of anyone. Was I even at Lyuban?

I walked across the grass in warm sunshine towards brick buildings and heard a crackling sound from behind. The cockpit had become the funnel of a steam train, belching thick black smoke with occasional flashes of yellow flicking over the side. I looked around again for someone to help, but my A4 stood alone in a sea of grass, burning like a Viking long ship.

At a building I took to be a crew room, the door stood open, so I peered inside. No-one. Posters covered the walls, all in Russian, the same as the writing on a tattered noticeboard. I removed my leather flying helmet, unfastened my holster, and drew my P08. I wandered outside; behind this building a Polikarpov I-16 Rata fighter looked ready to go. Instinctively I pressed my back against the wall and raised my pistol. It seemed I'd landed at a Red Air Force airfield.

36

As I approached the next, larger building, perhaps an aircraft hangar, metallic banging came from inside, with several men's voices. Assuming I'd landed in enemy territory, I realised I needed transport, either a car or an aeroplane, and wondered about the Rata. Even if I managed to start it up I'd be pursued on the ground and shot at before I made it to the threshold. But I had to try.

Bracing myself for a confrontation, sweating profusely, I peered into the hangar.

Three men wearing only uniform trousers and no tops, their skin glistening with sweat, leaned over an engine mounted on jacks, a Daimler-Benz. A few metres away a 109 E stood on its wheels with no power plant.

One of the men turned, looking at me. "Oh, it's you," he said, in German with a slight Austrian accent. "What's the gun for?" he added, nudging his friend, who looked around, laughing.

Shaking my head, I smiled with relief.

The other man, his head buried somewhere underneath, intermittently cursed them.

I holstered my P08, glad I wouldn't have to use it, walked over, and knelt down.

"What's wrong with it?" I asked, genuinely interested.

"Oil problem," the balding, older man underneath said, looking up.

"A leak?" I asked.

"No, I wish it was. We could fix it. The problem is we can't get any decent stuff. We've taken everything from the Rata outside, but their lubricants are just as shit." He laughed before standing up, looking across the field. "That's yours?" he said, my A4 now well ablaze.

I nodded.

"Sorry about that," he said, "but we have nothing to put out fires other than a bucket. We could see you'd got out, so that's the most important thing, isn't it?" He wiped his oil-blackened hands on a filthy rag and moved over to a metal cabinet with a slow, easy-going manner the way older people do, as he pulled out a bottle of schnapps.

"They'll fetch you in a few hours, don't worry, they usually do. They know where you are, don't they? We get visitors like you almost every day now. I don't think we'll be here much longer either, to be honest," he said, taking the first swig before passing it to me.

Within seconds of the schnapps hitting my stomach I felt odd as the relief smothered me, drawing all the breath from my body. I sat on a toolbox, fumbling for my cigarettes, and lit one.

"Where's your CO?" I asked, blowing smoke across the hangar towards the open doors. As though I'd just told a hilarious joke, all three laughed spontaneously.

"There's no-one else here, of air force personnel, that is," one said.

"We have some flak units somewhere," another said, jumping in.

"Oh yes, at the far end of the woods," the old man said, shaking his head. "But we never see them."

"And some army just down the road, a field hospital, and troops at the railway station, SS, I think," the youngest said, "so we're not completely alone."

Various aeroplane parts lay around, lots of empty boxes, signs of previous activity.

"We were really busy here until about a year ago," the old man said. "We had bombers, Heinkel 111s and Stukas, just after we took it from the Russians. There's about a dozen Heinkels over there in the woods in bits, including the engines, minus all the oil, of course," he laughed.

I stood up, staring out across the field at my aeroplane, now almost totally destroyed.

"Is there room to land?" he said, "or did you do the clever thing by leaving it right in the middle?"

"I'm not sure," I admitted.

"Then we'll have to shift the bloody thing with the tractor," he groaned, throwing down the cloth before stepping outside.

An elderly diesel engine clattered as a relic of a Russian tractor passed the hangar, dragging a long chain that flattened the grass while jumping around like a snake. The youngest threw himself aboard, clinging onto the left fender. The blackened, smoking wreck was dragged backwards across the grass and abandoned fifty metres from the front of the hangar, still smouldering.

To my surprise I fell asleep sitting in front of the building, leaning against the wall in the sunshine. I had no idea how long for, but shouts from inside woke me.

"Sarge, your taxi's here."

The sun had moved and the temperature had dropped. Two hours had passed. Across the field a Storch trundled towards us across the uneven grass, occasionally revving loudly to overcome the larger clumps.

I stood up, thanking my hosts, who merely grunted before returning to their engine.

Running over to the Storch I was greeted by a beaming Gunter Scheel.

"Great company, aren't they?" he shouted.

"Yes, brilliant," I said, climbing up and strapping in behind.

"I know them too well," he said, "after four visits."

He laughed. Clearly I wasn't as bad a pilot as I thought.

Gunter eased the throttle forward, lined up for take-off, then we bounced across the field on long, bending legs before lifting off, past a nasty little area of scorched grass.

The eighty kilometres to Siverskaya took over an hour; struggling against an increasing northerly headwind, our groundspeed at times was probably no faster than a brisk walk. But I really enjoyed the flight with Gunter, because for a while, as we chugged along at three hundred metres, we had no sign of the war, either between us or outside. We spoke about the Germany of our childhood, about his home in Dannenberg in Lower Saxony, mine in Elmshorn, and our families. It seemed we weren't even flying over Russia; we were two aviation enthusiasts sharing a cross-country trip.

As we approached Siverskaya the war returned and the tone in Gunter's voice became more formal. "We are getting the A5 soon, and it's no doubt you'll have one as a replacement for your A4," he said, lowering the flaps as the Storch drifted gently earthward, floating like a leaf, eventually touching with the gentlest bump. "We'll all be getting it hopefully, but you'll have to wait, because they won't be here for a while yet," he said as we taxied towards the hangars.

"Thanks for the lift," I said, climbing out, clutching my leather headset, the only memento from my A4. I said it as a joke but meant it sincerely.

He made no reply but merely smiled.

Temporarily without an aeroplane, I returned to the palace that night, where I immediately enjoyed a long, hot shower. Anton had left, claimed by JG54's newest ace, Walter Nowotny, and was now his wingman on an almost permanent basis as they spread their talents for killing the enemy as far south as the Central Sector.

My bed and champagne box were still in the old room, as were Horst and Erich, and after a reasonable meal with them, fatigue overcame me and I quickly fell asleep.

*

Stamping of feet and shouting woke me, in what I thought to be an alert. Even before fully awake I found my P08 in my hand, requiring a level of unconscious thought I didn't think I possessed.

Horst was shouting, arguing with ghosts again, as his silhouette roamed the room, taking long swipes at threatening shadows. "You are fucking pigs! You utter bastards! Pigs! Bastards!" between loud, incomprehensible ramblings, and I saw a figure jump up from Erich's bed and check the blackout curtains before turning on the light.

Erich took hold of Horst firmly by the shoulders, and with reassuring words eased him gently towards his bed.

They sat together for a few minutes, Erich's left arm wrapped tightly around his comrade, speaking in gentle, reassuring tones. Horst's mumblings eventually stopped and with Erich's help he lay back.

Erich looked across and smiled, the type of sympathetic

smile you give at funerals, nodding before stepping over to the light switch, casting us back into darkness.

We were up only three hours later, without mentioning it. This time I decided to ask Horst about it, but yet again changed my mind.

I had no ops for a few days, mainly because there were still not enough serviceable aeroplanes, but in any case a deep depression with April showers like I'd never seen before kept everything grounded. The courtyard flooded and all our grass strips became unusable.

Thinking of the dugout at Mga and our troops out in the open, I lay on my bed, admiring the decorative plasterwork on the ceiling, fully aware of my good fortune.

37

Two letters arrived from my parents, but nothing from Inge, as there hadn't been for a while. I wondered if I'd upset her in some way, so I wrote a long letter expressing my concern.

In one of my mother's letters she asked me several times: 'Do you think we will be alright?' and I didn't know if she meant her and my father, or perhaps Germany as a whole. She said the entire country was busier than ever, with Dr Goebbels constantly on the radio in rousing speeches telling everyone to 'hold out'. Some of the best shops had closed and people had to barter for goods in addition to money. What had caused this apparent change? I checked the date and postmark; it was the first letter she had written since the fall of Stalingrad.

As the April days lengthened I lay on my bed one evening reading magazines and intelligence bulletins on Red Air Force aeroplanes. Even though the cloud base touched the roof of the palace the grey light filled the room through the huge windows. I decided to continue reading my book, but when I opened my box it had gone.

Horst trudged into the room and I wondered if it might be the right moment to ask about the nightmares. He sat on his bed, smoking; the skin on his cheekbones stretched tightly to his face when he inhaled, and his eyes retreated into his head. Losing his hair at an alarming rate, he looked utterly exhausted, and I wondered how he managed to fly with such unsteady hands.

"Here, I've finished with it," he said, reaching into his ammo box and handing back my book. "I took it from your champagne box. Hope you don't mind," he added with a smile.

"Not at all, did you enjoy it?"

"I did," he said, glancing at the door, furtively, before continuing.

I wondered why until he spoke in a hushed, conspiratorial tone.

"You know it's illegal, don't you, Paul?"

What? I didn't need to reply for him to realise I had no idea.

"The Nazi Party banned it, because the author is a Jew or something, but even if he isn't, I can understand why they don't like it."

He paused, as though searching his memory.

"Where did you get it?"

"It was behind a bookshelf at Mga," I said, guiltily, like a child caught scrumping.

"It's very…" He stopped mid-sentence, gazing at the book in my hand, shaking his head. "It's very honest about war, and I don't think they like that." He moved back to sit down and lit a cigarette, leaning against the wall, legs outstretched.

I put the book away and lit up. "It certainly does make you think, doesn't it?" I said, blowing smoke across the room, wondering about the direction of our conversation.

"That's why they don't like it, of course," Horst said, tapping his cigarette onto a tin, "and the fact that it's very popular with our enemies."

"I had no idea," I said, genuinely surprised. I wondered if I should do the right thing and burn it immediately, while shouting, "Heil Hitler!" as loud as possible.

"Yes, they call it *All Quiet on the Western Front*. The British and Americans love it."

Erich came in and threw himself on his bed, beaming, obviously bringing good news. "Some new A5s are arriving next week," he said, "weather permitting." He lit a cigarette.

Horst produced a bottle from somewhere in his clothing, like a magician. He offered me a sip, which I accepted. I'd never tasted anything quite so rough. It wasn't vodka, more like something from a chemistry lab, with no flavour, just burn. A small, crooked label bore a few handwritten Russian words in red, probably a warning not to drink.

I took hold of it long enough to see the words and read the figure 90%.

"What have they done to the 190?" Horst said. "Does anyone know?"

"What do you mean?" I asked, detecting sarcasm.

"What's the difference between an A4 and an A5?"

"No idea, yet," I said, deciding to find out as soon as possible.

"It doesn't matter anyway, does it?" Horst said, shaking his head. "We'll never keep them back, not even if we had a thousand or ten thousand A5s."

I was shocked, and he could tell.

"Every day they are stronger and we are weaker," he said,

taking a long gulp, "and God help us when they get here, after what we've been doing."

I knew what he was referring to, not just Leningrad but the special task forces of the SS that I had so luckily avoided. I hadn't forgotten the day Lieutenant Colonel Lutzow managed to keep them away. I reminded Horst of this, and he simply shook his head.

"You were lucky, but how many of their 'special actions' do you think actually happened?" He took a deep breath, exhaling in a long sigh, staring at the floor. "We've no business here, none of us. We should get out now, while we can, and return to Germany."

Erich stood up. "Shut up, Horst, for Christ's sake."

"You've no idea," he continued, mumbling, staring at me. "You should know what's really been going on," he added, louder, fumbling for a cigarette.

"Don't," Erich said, sharply.

"He should know, it's his right. He has no bloody idea, does he?" he retorted, speech slurring.

From the amount he had drunk, I couldn't understand how he even formed words, let alone managed a conversation. He missed the end of his cigarette as the flame from a match burned his finger, but he didn't even flinch. He struck another and pulled so heavily on it, he consumed an entire centimetre as the red glow ran through the tobacco like a high-speed train. Goodness knows how he didn't burst into flames, with the spirit so strong.

"You told me about the ice road slaughter. You think about it a lot, don't you, Paul? You can't forget it, can you?"

He looked me in the eyes across the room. At first I didn't want to admit it, but eventually nodded. Pushed to the back of my mind, it had always been there, and he knew it. They were only Ruskis, Bolshevik scum, the enemy, undeserving of sympathy, but the images remained.

Horst looked vacant. "Well, this was a hundred times worse," he said, "and I'm going to tell you all about it."

Erich sat down, shaking his head.

38

"They came here, to the airfield at Krasnogvardeisk, asking for volunteers to help with an evacuation, as they called it, two SS officers from an *einsatzgruppen*, a special task force."

He clearly wanted to tell me, as though in a church confession, *compelled* to speak, so who was I to stop him?

Erich didn't want him to, but it seemed he'd given up trying to stop him. I wonder if he thought it might help. Judging by recent events and looking at Horst I came to this conclusion.

"It was only a few weeks after we'd arrived," Horst continued, "so it was all a bit chaotic." He shook his head. "There were still partisans all over the place, so we had to be careful, but we were excited about finding this place, as you can imagine. The SS told us we were needed to help with an evacuation of civilians from a village twenty kilometres from here, with some minor action against partisans. Naïve enough to believe them, how stupid we were. Anyway, they weren't short of volunteers, so many in fact that the one lorry they provided filled up quickly. Three of us took a car and followed. The other air force personnel, my comrades, went ahead, drinking schnapps the SS had given them, and singing, for God's sake. After checking the map, I realised I knew where it was, close to woodland we use as a landmark for long finals sometimes, south-east of here, you know?"

I nodded, though I wasn't entirely sure.

"Ten minutes into the journey the car got a flat. I pulled over, found the jack, and began changing it. It didn't take long, about twenty minutes, but the other two were cursing, saying we should turn back as we'd be no help, we were so late, but we didn't. I wish to God we had. It was my idea, as the driver, to press on, a decision I'll regret forever."

He sat upright on his bed, bare feet on the floor, staring across the room. A centimetre of ash dropped from his cigarette, exploding like a tiny silent bomb on the wood floor. He suddenly appeared entirely sober, as though by some miracle all the alcohol had drained away through the soles of his feet.

"I was with Schack and Wenzel, both sergeants. They're down at Staraya Russa now, though I don't really know, because we don't talk. We avoid one another, the way people do when they share a dark secret." He shook his head.

"Anyway, arriving at the village, we were shocked to find it deserted. The others suggested we turn around, but I didn't listen. It was quite a big place and, as we drove through the empty streets, a scruffy-looking SS private with an MP40 waved us down, asking who we were. Like an idiot I told him we'd volunteered to help, to which he nodded and smiled, directing us to some woods. We struggled to get the car up a farmer's track, the underside making constant contact with the ground, perhaps in another strong hint that we shouldn't have bothered. I noticed fresh vehicle tracks and hundreds of footprints in the mud, as though a huge crowd had walked up there recently.

"After a couple of minutes we emerged into an open field where two of those vans with the fake windows were driving around in circles, chasing one another, the drivers revving the engines and laughing. I wondered what the hell they were doing. They had bottles of schnapps in their hands, obviously drunk.

"A single MP40 machine pistol fired in short bursts somewhere near the wood, the distinct rattle echoing in the trees. A mound of earth about thirty metres long and two metres high concealed the origin of the gunfire.

"I couldn't see what it was, but on reflection I knew, or at least suspected, but I really didn't want to believe it, if you know what I mean."

Horst had not taken a drink or lit a cigarette for a while, so I stepped over and reached for his vodka, taking a long gulp, burning the back of my throat and setting my stomach on fire.

He paused for a moment, staring at us, before resuming. "We left the car and began walking, and it was then we first saw a huge crowd of people: men, women, children of all ages, standing around, undressing, while SS men and women screamed at them, using horse whips and rifle butts to keep them together. Huge piles of clothes, all sorted into underclothing and top coats and so on, and a pile of shoes a metre high, hundreds, probably thousands of pairs in all sizes, being added to all the time."

Horst stopped, his gaze now fixed at the same point on the wall across the room. I breathed with relief, not wanting to hear anymore. I knew what was coming, but at the same time I had a macabre curiosity in finding out, so I sat rock still, as did Erich.

"Without screaming or crying, the people calmly finished undressing and stood around in small groups, probably families, totally naked, kissing each other tenderly. They huddled together, the women trying to keep their dignity by covering themselves with their hands, saying something repeatedly to one another which I couldn't make out, so I stupidly edged closer. I heard the words *Do svidaniya*, 'goodbye', in Russian."

He stopped again, looking across at Erich. He didn't say a word, so he carried on.

"Nobody bothered us as we stood watching. Those people knew what was about to happen, but they waited in turn, quietly, as though standing in a bus queue. I couldn't understand it. The SS used their horse whips, pushing them along one at a time, with no pleading or crying out for mercy. You know when you see something that you can't believe, even though it's really happening, you can't bring yourself to look away? We should have left immediately, but like ghoulish idiots, we carried on watching. I noticed one particular group, a family of eight people, a man and a woman, both in their early forties, with their children aged perhaps one, eight, and ten, and two grown-up daughters in their early twenties. An old woman with snow-white hair stood holding the one-year-old, singing to it, occasionally tickling it, making it shriek with joy. The couple watched, tears streaming down their faces. The father held the hand of the ten-year-old boy, speaking to him softly. The boy looked absolutely terrified and shook violently. The father then pointed up at the sky, saying something to the boy as he squeezed his hand. An SS officer then shouted, counting twenty people, including this family, telling them to get behind the mound of earth. One of the young women, tall and slim, very pretty with beautiful, long, black hair caught my gaze. She pointed to her chest, saying, 'Twenty-three years old,' in good German. I looked around, and yes, she was talking to me. At any other time I would have been glad to have spent a night with her; she was gorgeous. An elderly woman with stick-thin legs had to be helped to undress, as though paralysed. I moved over to see the other side of the mound. I saw a huge pit. Dead lay full length in the bottom, pressed so tightly together only the heads were distinguishable at one side.

"The people stepped down and lay on top of the dead and dying. Some spoke tenderly to those still alive, touching them gently. The family lay down together, side by side. It seemed so unreal and calm.

"The SS officer directed an SS sergeant, sitting on the edge of the pit with his legs dangling over the side, smoking, the cigarette hanging loosely from one corner of his mouth, a long piece of ash about to drop. With his tunic unfastened at the neck, he looked a mess. His face flushed bright red; he was sweating profusely. A bottle of schnapps leaned against his right leg, from which he took an occasional swig, and an MP40 machine pistol lay across his lap, as he kept waving the people along. Finally, when the family lay in front of him he fired, raking their backs, their entire bodies convulsing and jerking with every hit as blood poured from their necks. He paused as some of the heads and arms moved, replacing the magazine calmly before firing again, until all movement stopped.

"The pit was already two-thirds full as the next line undressed and struggled down, stepping on the bleeding bodies. Some couldn't help themselves as they evacuated their bowels, trembling and crying.

"Suddenly the SS officer shouted, 'Halt!', waving his pistol around, and then, 'Don't shoot the dog, get it out of there!'

"A girl about ten years old held a puppy in her arms, cradling it like a baby, and when ordered to surrender it, she refused, holding it even tighter, so it had to be forced from her grasp by two SS privates.

"It yelped and the girl screamed.

"The officer said, 'Put it in my car.'

"The girl at the edge of the pit shouted a name, presumably the dog's, sobbing uncontrollably. The officer walked over, drew his pistol and shot her in the face. She fell backwards into the pit like a crumpled blanket.

"The man with the MP40 quickly finished his work."

As I took another drink I looked at Horst, my head spinning from the strong spirit, relieved to be sitting down.

Erich came over, lifted the bottle and took a long drink, pushing it back into my hands before moving to the window, gazing out at the partially flooded courtyard. The rain seemed worse, the failing grey light conspiring with the low cloud to smother the palace.

"It was as quiet as this room is now. After all the crying and chanting there was silence, with a rotten smell of cordite and shit; so many shit themselves as they walked, it lay everywhere. Pigeons about to land in the trees flew over the wood, as though wanting no part of it. I wanted to be up there with them, to get away, but I couldn't move. There must have been a thousand bodies.

"We weren't asked what we were doing, standing in stunned silence. More vehicles arrived and people unloaded. I saw other air force personnel pushing people around. I knew some of them. They had wives and children back home. I recognised a man in a postal uniform who delivers our mail, for God's sake, Alfred, I think his name is, pushing them along, laughing, and clearly enjoying himself. I couldn't believe it. I'd always told myself only the SS engaged in such things, but they couldn't have done it without help."

He stopped for a moment before taking a deep breath. "We were all there, involved, taking part. We helped. I helped.

We were German, in uniform, like the man with the machine pistol, and I did nothing to stop it."

Erich and I still said nothing. I didn't know what to say. I knew how I'd felt immediately after the ice road column on that dreadful winter morning, but I was in my aeroplane; the men I shot didn't speak or look me in the eye.

"Nauseous like never before, I thought I would pass out. I walked back to the car, trying desperately to stay upright, as those odd vans stopped and the back doors were thrown open. You wondered what they were, didn't you, Paul?" Horst looked at me, his face still devoid of expression.

"As if it couldn't get any worse there must have been fifty naked bodies, of all ages, small children and babies in each one, piled on top of one another, gassed by the van's exhaust. Excrement and urine poured out the back because the doors were sealed with rubber, like aeroplane windows, and the breeze sent the smell over to me, gripping my stomach. That was it. Everything I'd eaten for a week came up onto my boots."

He looked down as Erich and I remained silent. I wanted to tell him he wasn't the one pulling the trigger, but I didn't.

"An SS sergeant offered me a bottle of schnapps, and I took a long drink, probably a quarter of the bottle, in one, so much that I almost choked. He could see my hands shaking, and he shrugged, saying, 'They are our enemy, sub-human, this is our duty,' and then, perhaps seeing how distressed I was, he added, 'You get used to it, like working in any slaughterhouse, I suppose.'

"They all had a disinterested hopelessness about them.

"We drove away, none of us saying a word. I expected to be told not to repeat what we had seen; but far from it, a man with a camera snapped constantly, even using a movie camera, smiling as though at a wedding.

"The three of us vowed never to repeat what we had witnessed."

Taking another deep breath, his shoulders dropped as he exhaled, as though telling the story had been a release.

"So that was it, my own part in another successful day for *Einsatzgruppen* Task Force 'A', Tuesday 7th October 1941, at the Krasnogvardeisk Action."

39

Erich and I remained silent. He knew some of it already; I could see him looking across at me, perhaps testing for a reaction, but I had none. What could I say? Should I believe Horst when he said he hadn't taken an active part? Clearly wracked with guilt merely for being there, it seemed this was the source of his nightmares.

Horst lit a cigarette with trembling hands as though he'd just been in combat. Dragging his ammo box from under the bed, he took out more cigarettes, stepped over and took the bottle back, draining the remains.

Erich and I looked at one another and then at Horst, with some concern.

Lying on his bed, he closed his eyes before turning to one side, lifting his legs into a foetal position. I stepped over and gently pulled the bottle away, placing his cigarettes on the floor. I found his P08 and removed the magazine before moving to the window with Erich.

"No wonder the SS had a clear-out before General Keller's visit," I said in a whisper, lighting a cigarette.

"You believe him then?" Erich said. "You think it happened, just like he said?" He looked at me, closely monitoring my face.

"He said it did," I replied, surprised there was any doubt, and edging closer, glancing across at Horst. "Don't you think it's true then?"

"Who knows," Erich said, before drawing on his cigarette. He paused, exhaling, directing the smoke across the room towards Horst, lying quietly on the bed, his back to us.

"He does exaggerate sometimes. Even if it is true, does it really matter? Yes, there may have been children there, and a good-looking woman, but so what? Remember who they are, Paul, as the SS said, they are our enemies, and *Untermensch*, sub-human. Don't forget that."

I knew he didn't mean what he was saying, but merely repeating the official mantra, so it didn't shock me. It had been drilled into all of us, for many years, beginning as children in the Hitler Youth. How we ended up here had been a gradual process.

*

I remember running into the street, marching in double time towards Heinrich's parents' house. Five minutes later there he stood at the end of Market Street, in Elmshorn, taking salutes from passers-by, raising his right arm sharply, thoroughly enjoying himself, as usual. I laughed out loud. He loved it, as I did. We loved everything about it: dedicated Nazis in uniform, fourteen years old.

"I was about to go without you," I remember him saying, shaking his head before taking one more salute as we moved off, marching in perfect time.

Suddenly he stopped, staring at me with a quizzical look. "Do you know what Dr Reinart asked me today?"

I shook my head, wondering why a question from our schoolteacher could be important enough to delay us.

"He said, 'Which is Germany's worst enemy, the Jew or the Bolshevik?'"

Before I could answer, Heinrich laughed. "Do you know what he said? It was brilliant, Paul, and very true, of course. He said a Bolshevik Jew! It's obvious, though, isn't it?"

We both laughed, marching on, Heinrich in his long strides with me at his side, trying to keep up. The parade would start in the town square, but last-minute rehearsals were near the school, where we joined hundreds of others in uniform, all carrying colourful flags and banners, everyone buzzing with excitement at the sheer joy of taking part in the Fuhrer's birthday celebrations.

Like everyone else, this was the only world I knew; I'd been enrolled into the German Youth at ten years old, and at fourteen the Hitler Youth. No discussions and no opt-out policy. Youth groups had already become popular and we had no choice but to wear the new brown shirts; all other groups like the scouts were illegal, though I didn't know this at the time. As a child I couldn't care what colour my shirt was, as long as I had my friends with me, enjoying fantastic adventures together.

From a very early age the Nazis taught us to march, to shoot, and all of us boys were taught boxing while the girls less masculine pastimes. Music became very important; it made our marching so much more fun. We were quickly filled with pride and confidence, and I suppose inevitably arrogance followed.

We felt powerful together and because it was illegal for anyone to strike us or even challenge our uniforms, some boys like Heinrich took advantage, refusing to do their school homework. When the teachers asked why they were told the Hitler Youth meetings took priority and they dared not question it, so it never did get done. The swastika on our arms carried the absolute authority of the State.

Heinrich Berger was my best friend, and one afternoon, while marching together in uniform, he played a trick on an older boy. When he passed us walking the other way, he failed to give us the mandatory salute.

Heinrich turned around and shouted at him, "Hey, you, that's no way to acknowledge the Fuhrer!"

The boy stopped so suddenly he had to correct himself from falling over, and I could see him trembling.

"Go back fifty metres and pass us again, properly this time!"

The boy did as he was told, throwing up a sharp Hitler salute, even turning his head towards us as he passed. What's ironic is the fact that even though neither of us knew him, he was most likely also in the Hitler Youth; he just happened to be in civilian clothes.

When he'd gone Heinrich laughed. "That'll teach him," he said.

I laughed too. I didn't see it as humiliation of another person; I didn't understand such things then. I just knew it was funny. But it also added excitement, a thrill, the power coming from the uniform, and the ideas behind it. 'Whoever wears the uniform is no longer a separate individual but the personification of all who share the belief', so we were told.

Heinrich began behaving like this more often, but it didn't stir me as much. He became obsessed with joining the army and particularly the SS at the first opportunity, and the adults around us happily encouraged him.

Heinrich was so excited when we had a visit at one of our Hitler Youth meetings from a soldier in the SS wearing his smart black uniform, and later when two members of the Grossdeutschland Regiment arrived. They told us they were the Lifeguards of the German People, and they showed us their guns and even allowed us to sit in their car, a camouflaged Mercedes 170 with the roof folded down.

Many weeks were spent away from home, including long hot summers at the holiday resort of Ahlbeck on the Baltic coast, provided free of charge by the State. We built a huge altar with an enormous wooden sword in the middle, surrounded by flags, taking turns guarding it while learning new songs, reciting the motto, 'We are born to die for Germany'.

I didn't see anything sinister in this, being a child with my friends, and we all took part.

Clear goals were set for us, and even clearer enemies; we were frequently shown pictures of scruffy communists wearing huge flat caps trying to destroy our flags, fought off by our brave comrades, and photographs of ugly men with big noses and the slogan 'Jews are our misfortune!'. Unsure what this meant at first, I wondered why having a big nose made a person untrustworthy.

We sang songs such as 'I am a Jew, do you know my nose' and 'Ikey Moses has all the money'. The message was relentless and so when I came home I became suspicious of anyone with a big nose, even our local pastor.

When I realised what it really meant I could see why certain things were happening, and yet again nobody complained. No-one dared. We were told it had to be, to save Germany, and besides, we were all riding the same wave in a powerful tide and to swim against it would be unthinkable, and impossible.

Two boys I knew well in my class no longer came to school because they were Jews: surprising because neither had a big nose.

Young people like me were promised a bright future, provided we swore total obedience to the Fuhrer. But what does this mean to a child? No more or less than obedience to a parent, teacher, or any other responsible adult. It became natural to begin and end every public encounter with the Hitler greeting; our teachers used it all the time, every stranger used it, even the postman delivering a letter, and in shops when buying anything they would first say 'Heil Hitler' before 'Can I help you?' or 'Good morning' until it became automatic. I don't remember anyone asking why; we just did.

Even my father had stopped commenting. One day while reading the newspaper, he dropped it onto his lap and looked across at my mother. "They've banned all trade unions with immediate effect." He shrugged.

She made some brief comment such as, "Well then," or similar, and that was it.

Our brilliant science teacher Mr Klein stopped coming to school, having been replaced by a man half his age and nowhere near as good. Another great teacher who made us laugh with hilarious impersonations of government leaders was also replaced. They couldn't teach us anymore, and where they went, nobody knew; we didn't ask, but I never forgot. Why did we not ask where they had gone? I don't really know the answer to that. They just weren't there anymore, and life carried on.

When I was very young my father spent long periods out of work, and times were hard, but after the Nazis took over in 1933 things improved. Soon my father and everyone we knew had jobs and were happy; flags flew everywhere, with lots of singing, and cheerful music playing all the time.

We didn't question why no-one criticised the government, or why we didn't listen to foreign radio broadcasts. Apparently, they were spreading vile lies about Germany and that's why we couldn't listen, so our own government broadcasts and newspapers were all we knew of the world. When everything went well, why would anyone want to listen to critical foreigners or moan about the government?

*

"Do you think for a moment Keller and the others don't know what's going on?" Erich said, staring at me. "He didn't just come here to speak to Trautloft and other air force officers, as Galland did. I would guess he also had to report back about the progress of the Actions. You heard what Horst said: he saw plenty of air force personnel, so there's no way he and the rest of Command doesn't know. Where do they think everyone disappears to for days at a time with the SS? They are obviously trying to make people think it's not happening, officially, hence the bonfires of paperwork, so there's no documentary proof."

I nodded, a little confused. "But no-one is told not to talk about it, even those who witnessed it, like Horst."

"I know, but they don't say anything," Erich said.

"Then why not? If it's part of their duty, why don't those involved openly brag about it, as we do with shooting down enemy aeroplanes? I never hear anyone even admitting it happens, let alone taking part."

"It's obvious," Erich said, with a shrug. "They know it's utterly wrong."

"Exactly, and there's nothing we can do, if ordered to take part. We won't always have a Colonel Lutzow to keep them away, will we?"

Erich looked at the door while moving closer to me. "Did you hear about Marseille?"

I had to think for a moment. "Hans-Joachim Marseille, of course. 150 victories in his 109. Awarded Diamonds to his

Knight's Cross. Killed in Egypt last year. I never met him, but I heard he was a good man, obviously a great pilot."

"That's him. What you don't know is the Gestapo caught him trying to cross the frontier into Switzerland last summer, in disguise, with false papers."

"What? Why would he do that?" I probably looked as surprised as I did confused.

"Because he found out about the mass killings all across the East, and wanted no part of it. The Gestapo gave him an ultimatum: arrest and an ignominious end for him and his family, probably in a concentration camp, or return to Egypt and carry on. What would you do? He obviously chose the latter. A few weeks after returning to the desert he got into trouble in his 109, bailed out, and his parachute didn't open. He didn't even try to open it, apparently."

"Good grief," I said. I didn't know what else to say.

Erich nodded. "This is no ordinary war, Paul. We are not just killing Ivan as an enemy combatant; we're exterminating him along with his entire family, everywhere. You know what they told us about the Bolshevik hordes, the communists, and the Jews. It's happening all across the East, from what's left of Poland, all the way to Moscow, and probably has been ever since we arrived. How long have we been here now? This isn't France, where we tangle with the RAF's boys in blue on a warm sunny afternoon, finish at 1700 hours, and then home for a quick bath and a bottle of champagne. We are engaged in extermination, and we are part of it, whether you like it or not."

Almost dark now, rain droplets ran down the window like racing tears.

"One thing's for sure," he said, stubbing out his cigarette on the floor, "Horst is right. We can't afford to lose this war, because God help Germany if they ever do to us what we've done to them."

40

In the second week of April, as soon as the weather cleared, Ivan flew over and damaged an Fw190 A4 from No. 2 Group, before our flak crews frightened him away.

On 17th I flew down to Siverskaya in a Storch, early in the morning. Gazing down at the countryside, the trees coming into leaf, the conversation with Horst and Erich had been on endless repeat in my head until I realised I'd shamelessly killed it and buried it in a pit at the back of my mind, as though I'd never heard it. I didn't know what else to do.

The ground crew at Siverskaya made several A4s airworthy after initially believing they were only fit for spares. It's amazing what can be achieved in adversity. Happily reunited with my friends Helmut Missner, Reinhold Hoffmann, and Fritz Tegtmeier, that same afternoon I took off in one of the reconditioned A4s, flying alongside all three.

In two pairs, as Fritz's wingman, we searched the skies around Lake Ilmen, soon engaging a dozen La-5s. Though obviously inferior to any Fw190, the La-5 was not a bad aeroplane, and we could tell these pilots knew their machines well.

They immediately broke formation and turned on us instead of heading east and running, like so many others. We had a fight on our hands and so for the next twenty minutes we watched each other's backs, in between catching an occasional shot.

Two La-5s went down before we had to break off. I claimed a partial kill in exchange for a few holes in my airframe.

Just after landing, Helmut shut down his engine and came over as I climbed out. He put an arm around my shoulders, speaking directly into my right ear as though passing a secret. "I made you a promise, if you remember," he said. "It's time I fulfilled it." He drew back, looking me in the eye with a cheeky grin, and must have seen how puzzled I looked, but he smiled. "We'll get cleaned up and changed, and go this afternoon, in a couple of hours, alright?"

"Go where?" I asked, admitting defeat immediately.

"Into the woods," he replied, smirking, drawing me along with a hand on my shoulder towards our barrack. "You'll enjoy it, believe me, but keep it to yourself," he whispered, right index finger vertical over his lips, "because not everyone knows."

He and I were not due to fly again that day, and the spring sunshine warmed my back as it broke through the trees while showering in the open. We couldn't enjoy this kind of easy luxury in winter, but life was so much easier when no longer deep frozen.

As I dressed, Helmut appeared, freshly scrubbed and shaved, wearing what I knew to be one of his best uniforms. He had a bottle of some sort in his left hand wrapped in a copy of *The Eagle*, and I still had no idea what we were doing, until I saw a huge bunch of daffodils in his right hand. He'd obviously pulled them up from around the trees, but they nonetheless made a magnificent display and would be a pleasing gift to anyone, particularly a female. Then I remembered.

Rattling a bunch of keys, winking with a boyish smile, a few minutes later we climbed into an air force *kubelwagen*, usually reserved for officers. I looked around, suspiciously, as though in the process of stealing it, and he noticed, shaking his head.

"Relax, don't worry, we won't be long," implying we had at least some consent. We drove around the airfield perimeter and turned right onto a track towards the woods.

I'd seen the old man lead his Panje pony this way, hauling the cart, and I wondered if we were going to spend a thrilling afternoon chopping wood. If we were leaving the airfield we'd probably go via the main gate, but we weren't. With the track in a dreadful state, we bounced around in our seats over hard ruts of dried mud and I had to hold on, to stop myself from being thrown over the side.

After five uncomfortable minutes, we pulled up outside a log cabin with a square brick chimney coming out the roof. I could see a similar cabin a few hundred metres into the wood, and then another beyond that, and wondered if they were all occupied, and by whom.

Helmut had already leapt up the four wooden steps to the door with the flowers behind his back before I'd climbed out the car. He knocked loudly, looking back, smiling. No answer. He knocked again and the door opened, so I ran over and followed him inside.

In the one room, maybe ten metres by five, a large white-painted brick stove, two metres high and almost as wide, dominated the middle of the floor, with bundles of dried herbs hanging around the outside.

It had an opening on one side, a huge oven big enough for a man to climb in, with a chimney going up through the roof. An iron pot simmered inside, filling the cabin with warm home-cooking smells. Straw and blankets covered the flat top of the oven, like a bed, and against the opposite wall stood a rough, dark wood table and four chairs, which all looked home-made, as indeed did everything. Several of our air force blankets lay on the floor next to the stove, on top of what looked like one of our army mattresses in the blue and white check pattern.

Helmut hugged a woman as tall as him, despite her bare feet; her black dress, clearly meant to be worn with heels, trailed on the floor. She gave out a brief squeal of protest as he continued embracing her. Masses of thick brown hair covered her shoulders, partially obscuring her face. Well-built without being overweight, her dress clung to her body, exaggerating her curves. As homely as the place she lived in, when I saw her face I guessed she must have been at least ten years older than us, if not more.

The daffodils in her right hand, she pulled herself away from Helmut, laying them on the table before reaching into a cupboard, lifting out a tall white vase. She filled it with water from a jug in a tin bowl, arranging the flowers before placing the vase on the table. Then she saw me.

"Who is this?" she said in German, turning to Helmut, who had placed the bottle and the magazine in the middle of the table.

"Anna, this is Paul," he replied, proudly, retrieving three small shot glasses from the cupboard, slamming them down on the table. "Paul, meet Anna."

For a moment I thought I was going to be hugged, but she wrung her hands together again before pulling up a chair and sitting down. She smiled with a brief nod as Helmut dropped the magazine on the floor and opened the bottle.

"Pleased to meet you, Paul," she said, as Helmut filled the glasses with vodka.

"*Nazdrovie*," he said, as they clinked, before we swilled them down in one. He poured another, but her hand fixed over hers. The hot spirit burned all the way down my throat, chasing the first, and within seconds my head announced its arrival.

Anna's round face lit up with a wide smile of beautiful white teeth, and I was immediately captivated by her eyes every time she turned towards me. A second look confirmed they were as unnaturally blue as I first thought.

Suddenly she stood and, looking at Helmut, said, "*Vy gotova*," as he finished another glass.

I recognised the word 'ready' as she moved towards the stove.

Helmut stood up, steadying himself on the table with his right hand as he winked at me. Anna stepped around the stove out of view as my friend followed. I fumbled in my tunic for my cigarettes. Guessing what might be happening, I was shocked, excited, and curious, all at the same time.

They talked for a few moments with brief laughter before it went quiet. I lit a cigarette, picked up the *Eagle* magazine from the wood floor, and flicked through it, as though waiting to see a doctor.

The old man and his Panje pony strolled past the window, staring at our *kubelwagen* and then briefly in my direction before disappearing into the wood. I found a ladle, dipped it into the pot, and took out huge chunks of potato and tender pieces of meat. It tasted fantastic and I wanted to help myself to a huge portion but only took three mouthfuls. I pulled a chunk of bread from a loaf under a cloth, pushing it deep into the stew.

Sitting at the table, I lit another cigarette, resisting the temptation to lean forward and investigate the groaning sounds from the other side of the huge stove.

The sun forced its way through the dense covering of pine branches and I realised this place was probably invisible from the air at all times of the year.

After ten minutes Helmut reappeared, standing at the far corner of the stove, adjusting his trousers. He moved over to the table and dropped himself down heavily onto a chair like a sack of potatoes, before issuing a terrific sigh. He took out his cigarettes and lit one, inhaling deeply.

"Your turn," he said, smiling.

41

Anna sat on a home-made chair with her back to the wall, smoking. Her legs were crossed, her feet resting on the end of a blanket-layered army mattress. She stood up, ushering me into the chair. Still with a cigarette in her right hand she knelt between my legs.

Like any new experience, I had no idea what to expect, certainly not this. My first intimate contact with a woman over in just a few minutes, I buttoned up my trousers, spent and finished, still in the chair. It had been so quick that Anna had not finished her cigarette when she moved to join Helmut at the table. I neither fully appreciated nor understood why it had been done.

They were talking, but I couldn't make it out, other than some brief mumblings and laughter from Helmut. Stunned at what had just happened, I couldn't quite believe it. It had been fantastic, of course, but all too brief, immediately leaving me wanting more.

When I joined them at the table Helmut gave me the broadest grin, offering a shot of vodka, which I took.

"Everyone should have their turn in the woods, don't you think, Paul?" he said, laughing. "So remember, if she opens the door for you, you're in business, otherwise she's busy, or not in, isn't that right, Anna?"

She nodded and smiled dutifully.

"Come on," he added, standing up. Leaning over the table, he gave Anna a gentle kiss on the cheek. "We have to take the car back." He stepped out the door.

Anna rose to her feet, leaning into the stove, stirring the contents of the pot, and I tried catching her eye to say goodbye, but she didn't even look.

Five minutes later we were back on the airfield, pulling up in the car. A wisp of smoke rose from somewhere in the woods behind us and I wondered if it could be Anna's place. What would she be doing now? I thought of her eyes, her mouth, her hair, and her long slender fingers. Perhaps cooking, or making tea? It didn't take me long to realise she had stolen every thought in my head.

Helmut didn't tell anyone where we'd been. I, however, wanted to climb onto the nearest roof and shout about it, but I didn't say a word.

I found Reinhold and Fritz in the barrack, and I thought I heard one of them mention the woods, but I couldn't be sure.

We were back on ops early the next day so we had a few games of cards after dinner before we all turned in for the night.

*

Eight of us took off, climbing to three thousand metres, escorting Heinkel 111s from KG53 as they attacked railway lines and depots at the other side of the Volkhov River. Surprisingly, we only saw twenty bombers; a year ago there would have been a hundred or more.

Even before we crossed the river the bombers were attacked by a huge mix of around forty La-5s, Airacobras, and P40s. We had a difficult job keeping them away, and two bombers were shot down despite our best efforts, but seven or eight of the enemy were sent earthward in blazing fireballs.

Another group of Sturmoviks broke through our defences on 18th April, dropping bombs on the Palace Airfield, damaging an Fw190 A4, this time belonging to No. 1 Group. I heard it had been repaired in a few hours, which did nothing to reduce the CO's anger.

To make things worse, they did it again the next day, this time causing only minor damage to a visiting Me110. Sent up to find this roving band of cement bombers, we shot at some but didn't bring any down.

Three days after my first trip I returned to the woods, alone. This time I walked through the trees along a direct footpath I'd seen the old man use with his pony. I reached Anna's cabin in less than fifteen minutes.

With no signs of life and no vehicles outside, I considered turning around, abandoning the idea, until the front door opened and she stood there, creating a cloud of dust in the doorway with long sweeps of a broom.

I felt awkward, staring at her just as she saw me.

If she'd shouted, "Go away," in Russian, or even in German, I would have, and I'd probably apologise. But she didn't. She leaned the broom against the outside wall and stood at the door, holding it open. She then looked inside and then at me. I was in business, as Helmut would say. She didn't say anything but just smiled. Considering this as confirmation, I climbed the four wooden steps and walked in.

The flowers Helmut had given her were still in the white vase on the table. The afternoon sun and the stove warmed the cabin, and when I entered she glanced outside, closing the door behind me.

Wearing a lacy white blouse and knee-length blue skirt, her long brown hair hung about her shoulders, thick and curly, her eyes bluer than ever. She looked absolutely fabulous. I merely stood there, staring, watching her every move when she sat down on the floor near the chair where I'd had my first encounter.

She ushered me over to some blankets spread across the mattress. As I turned to join her I noticed a loaded MP40 machine pistol hanging on a nail behind the door.

"What's that doing here?" I said, in my best authoritative German.

Anna now lay full length on the floor, busy removing her skirt. She looked up. "Oh, somebody left it yesterday," she replied, in broken German, which I barely understood, but the shrug of her shoulders indicated her unconcern. It never crossed my mind she might be connected to local partisans. I thought of going to take hold of the gun but decided to leave it, and when I turned back she lay naked across the blankets.

Joining her, I realised my hands were shaking wildly, as though I was about to engage an enemy in combat for the first time. In a way, of course, I was.

She obviously noticed because she shook her head, taking total charge for the next twenty minutes until we finished.

Without looking at me or speaking, she dressed and stepped outside, leaving me prostrate on the bed, naked from the waist down. A few moments later, ignoring me, she returned, picked up her broom, and resumed sweeping around the table.

Feeling incredibly vulnerable, I put on my trousers and, leaning with my back against the stove, lit a cigarette.

When I exhaled, the smoke was intercepted by wide bars of sunlight from the window in the front wall of the cabin like a film projection in a cinema. I became almost overcome with fatigue, suddenly incredibly relaxed, more than I ever thought possible.

My back warming from contact with the stove, I heard Anna singing.

"What is that?" I shouted in Russian.

It stopped as she appeared at the corner, broom in hand, smiling. "You speak Russian?"

"Just a little."

She nodded. "It's a folk song, 'The Long Road'. Do you know it?" she said, in Russian.

"No," I replied, also in Russian, before drawing on my cigarette, as she resumed sweeping and singing.

Yellow dust mixed with my cigarette smoke, giving the blue-grey film projection a brownish hue.

At that moment I didn't know what to do. I knew I had to return to the airfield, but I didn't want to. The most beautiful thing I had ever seen, Anna, was mine, so I didn't want to leave her. Odd thoughts filled my head, all connected to her, thoughts I had difficulty in dismissing.

I heard liquid poured into a tin bowl, followed by intermittent splashing. My mother made similar noises when she washed clothes.

Standing up, I fastened my buttons and leaned on the stove.

She looked at me briefly, her arms immersed in soapy water, part of the wet clothing hanging over the edge of the bowl. After drying her hands she reached down into a cupboard, removing a hugely elaborate metal urn on a stand with a tall ornate lid and a small tap on one side. "Tea?" she said, with a flick of her hair and broad smile.

I nodded as she opened a packet of German army tea, liberally scattering the contents inside, adding water from the jug and gently sloshing it around. She then opened the bottom of the huge stove and, with a tiny shovel, removed some of the hot coals, dropping them down a wide pipe in the centre of the urn. She loaded more coal until the pipe was full and within a few minutes steam emerged from the top. It was the first time I'd seen a traditional *samovar* in action.

We drank the tea with army sugar and when finished she looked at me warmly. "Are you going now?" she said in perfect German, with a slight tilt of the head, looking cheeky, and extraordinarily beautiful.

I shrugged, and before I could form a reply she added, "Or do you want some more?"

At first I thought she meant tea, but she wiped her hands, grabbed my arm tightly, and hauled me to the floor, pausing to remove her skirt again, which she hastily abandoned in a half-rolled heap.

This time we were on more even terms as I dared to take charge, and thirty minutes later I dressed again, this time to leave.

She permitted a kiss on the lips before I left, jumping the front steps in one, whistling a bright tune, the Horst Wessel, as I walked back through the woods. I tried remembering the song she had been singing, but it had gone. The afternoon sun spilt through the trees into thousands of flickering columns of yellow, made almost tangible by drifting smoke from a nearby fire.

My lungs filled with a heady mix of wood smoke and pine as I flashed through the trees at a brisk walk. An aeroplane passed overhead, the engine idling ready for landing, and I followed it with my gaze, trying to catch a glimpse, as though ten years old again.

When could I revisit Anna? It would only take a few minutes and no-one need know. I smiled and turned to look back. The cabin had already disappeared, but I remained on the path that led to it, Anna's path, so I still felt close to her.

Suddenly I realised I should have brought the MP40 with me. Russians were not permitted to own firearms, unless they were cooperating with us. I laughed out loud. Anna was very definitely cooperating with me, for certain.

42

Throughout May and into June, too busy to return to the woods, on every flight I tried in vain to see the cabin, sometimes flying far too low in an effort to see her perhaps standing outside, waving. Anna would have to wait a while longer as the war became more intense by the day.

We were shooting down huge numbers of the enemy, and the CO of No. 1 Group, Walter Nowotny, reached his hundredth kill, which soon afterwards rose to 124. His notoriety had reached Berlin, and one morning a tall man in a grey raincoat burst into our barrack demanding to see him, notepad and pen ready with two cameras slung around his neck. He introduced himself as Joachim Fischer, a photographer from the Special Purpose Luftwaffe War Reporter Operational Company.

Walter Nowotny broke off a free hunt early in order to return and see him.

Mr Fischer photographed the hero in front of his aeroplane, sitting on the wing, standing beside it, and vaulting athletically from the cockpit in dramatic poses.

As usual, our star aces were removed from front-line duties and sent on leave, which really meant publicity tours and more photographs. In the next few weeks we saw him in *The Eagle* a few times, following him on the radio and in the press.

By the middle of June No. 2 Group, led by Captain Jung, had finally parted company with their tired 109 G3s and G4s, now flying the new Fw190. Together we flew with Heinkel 111 bombers of KG53 and Stukas from StG5 helping to destroy railway bridges across the Volkhov, some almost fifty kilometres behind the lines.

We returned to the same targets several times, but always via different routes, when reconnaissance photos showed the bombers had missed. Either that or the bridges were being repaired in record time. We bombed a new Russian airfield that had appeared to the south-east of Schlusselberg, only to discover the whole thing a fake, with canvas aeroplanes and dummy buildings. Good reconnaissance photos proved we had expended a lot of precious fuel and munitions on a devious Russian trick.

They brought forward more anti-aircraft guns and by July we could not believe the flak around these bridges. I heard numerous contacts on my airframe and, flying through the clouds of bursting iron, my cockpit filled with the characteristic smell of near misses. As the main arteries supplying Leningrad, and the front around Volkhov, they made us work hard as we threw everything at them.

With a handful of other pilots I had one day's rest on 2nd July but, only wanting to sleep, I had something else on my mind, having not been for nearly two weeks.

After pulling up a handful of red flowers, I marched at a decent pace along Anna's path to her cabin, without telling anyone. On arrival I saw a Mercedes 170VK car with a partially torn canvas roof parked outside. It had army number plates but an SS police badge on the back. I wondered whether to continue, or return to the airfield, so I leaned on the back and lit a cigarette, trying to decide.

With her door being closed, I wondered if she had been arrested and her cabin searched. A few minutes later male laughter came from inside and, when the door opened, three SS police exited, adjusting their uniforms, laughing. One held an MP40 by the pistol grip as though he'd just used it.

Oddly self-conscious, I threw my flowers under their vehicle. They saw me but made no effort to acknowledge me until they reached it.

One of them, a corporal, said, "You know the old saying, don't you, Sarge?" he said to me, staring straight into my eyes from barely a metre away. I didn't reply, but he continued anyway. "*Rein muss er, und wenn wir beide weinen.*"

Blind drunk, his face utterly expressionless, a sarcastic smile emerged from the right side of his mouth as one of the others slapped him on the back, saying, "Come on, we have to go."

The driver, a lieutenant, said, "Good hunting, young man. She might still be awake, if you're lucky," as he started the car.

Before they set off he shouted, "She used to have lice, you know, so be careful," and he laughed, driving away.

Anna's dead, I thought, *the bastards have shot her.*

I leapt up the steps in one and ran into the cabin. Curled up on the mattress, her knees up to her chest, she lay naked and crying. The MP40 had gone from the door; an empty bottle of schnapps lay on the table across a copy of *Untermensch*, the periodical promoting race theories about Russians as criminals and cretins.

The cabin reeked of tobacco and sweat, with no sunshine through the windows. It seemed entirely different.

I must have known what had happened, but I didn't want to think about it, or even acknowledge it. I filled the *samovar* with water, tea, and hot coals from the bowels of the stove, as Anna had done.

With two cups of tea and Dr Oetker biscuits, I sat beside her on the mattress.

She turned towards me, taking the tea with, "Thank you," in Russian. Pulling up a blanket, she covered herself, wiping her eyes and nose with a corner, sipping in silence.

We sat like this for several minutes until we had finished the tea. Someone came to the front steps. I wondered if the SS had returned but could hear no vehicle.

A male Russian shouted for Anna. He must have seen the Mercedes drive away and thought she'd be alone.

She dressed in a panic, the same long black dress I'd first seen her in, and was quickly at the door.

She called the man *papochka*, 'Daddy'; I heard *nemetsky*, 'German' and some movement. I stood up as he appeared, his face flushed, and both fists clenched. Anna pushed him back, shouting so much and so fast I only recognised the occasional word.

The old man left, hauling his pony and cart, shaking his head, cursing loudly. Anna watched him from the window and reached into my tunic for my cigarettes. She lit one and dropped the packet on the table, trembling.

In a flash she picked up a jug and ran outside. I followed but stopped at the door, wondering what she was doing. At the foot of the steps she removed the dress and tipped the water over her nakedness. She re-filled it from a barrel, rubbing her body all over, repeating the process several times, until thoroughly soaked and gasping for breath.

Watching it all, I had no idea what to do.

She slid the dress over her head onto her wet body and came back inside, now calm. The cotton stuck to her wonderful curves and my thoughts at that moment were utterly inappropriate. Sitting at the table, she lit another of my cigarettes. From a wooden box by the stove she took out a bottle of vodka and two glasses.

We drank in silence, filling the glasses in quick succession.

Taking my hand, she led me to the mattress where we lay side by side. Holding me so tightly I thought she'd bruise my arms, eventually she moved her head onto my chest. As she relaxed her grip, her breathing slowed and I realised she'd fallen asleep. Her hair covered my face and I couldn't move. It smelled of her, and the cabin, and wood smoke. Odd thoughts returned: of staying here forever, just like this.

An aeroplane roared overhead, stirring us awake. She kissed me, smiling as she rose to her feet. I had to leave. I didn't want to. I would have given anything not to. She kissed me again.

"*Blagodaryu vas*," she whispered. Thank you.

When I stepped outside I saw the flowers I'd intended on giving her had been crushed flat into the hard earth.

Then I knew the old man she called Daddy was the same man I had shot at with my pistol.

As I walked back to the airfield I remembered what the SS corporal had said. I'd heard it before, a well-known air force saying, but I never really understood the significance until now.

In the woods on Anna's path I said it out loud.

"It's going in, even if both of us are crying."

43

On 4th July 1943 we gathered at the Palace for a special briefing. It had been a long time since I'd seen so many pilots in one place, or senior officers in their best uniforms. Golden pheasants, as we called party officials, rarely seen anywhere near the front, were also there. Pilots I didn't know well, such as Heinrich Jung, Hugo Broch, Max Stotz, and Hans-Joachim Krochinski, but also those I knew: Otto Kittel, Erich Rudorffer, Ulrich Wernitz, Gerhard Proske, Sergeant Pilot Georg Fureder, and a new man I was beginning to like a lot, Sergeant Pilot Richard Raupach. We'd already flown together a few times as a pair on free hunts and I rated him a good flyer, not out to take unnecessary risks: trustworthy, in other words.

Holding a bundle of papers, the CO began, after briefly checking faces.

"No. 1 Group is migrating south, like wild geese, to Orel, in support of our ground forces for Operation Citadel, which begins tomorrow. There are more German forces gathered near Kursk than we used in the entire western offensive. We are going to smash Ivan once and for all, ending this charade he has created. We will not spend another winter fighting in Russia, gentlemen."

Cheers erupted with spontaneous applause. At last we were taking the offensive to them. This time they would be defeated, we were absolutely sure of it.

As the noise died down the CO continued.

"There are some changes, so check the duty lists. Some ground crews have already arrived in the Central Sector. Most of No. 2 Group will remain here, but the main effort is south. Squadron Commanders have already been briefed, and let me tell you, gentlemen, we have never been better prepared."

He paused.

A familiar face appeared as Major Hubertus von Bonin stood next to him. In a gesture that was more than merely symbolic, Captain Trautloft handed all the papers to Captain von Bonin, who promptly saluted and nodded.

"Gentlemen," Captain Trautloft said, "tomorrow is my last day as your commanding officer. I have been instructed to fly a pen for a while as an air force inspector."

Everyone groaned a little, followed by good-natured booing and laughter.

He smiled. "You will still see me around because I'm remaining here in the Northern Sector, so behave yourselves," he added, to more laughter.

We'd miss his flying and his leadership. He'd been instrumental in the successful relief of the Demyansk pocket when he shot down a Yak-1 and Pe-2 near Kholm, adding to his four victories in March.

But it was great to see Captain von Bonin again after our time in France.

When I saw the duty sheets on the board I gasped to see my name amongst pilots of No. 2 Group, and not No. 1 Group, whom I'd been with since my arrival in Russia. I would not be heading south but remaining at Gatchina and Siverskaya. I didn't mind; Kursk and Orel were a long way across Russia, and I thought of Anna, whom I'd not seen for a while, wondering when I'd see her again.

I'd be busier than ever after No. 1 Group had gone, even though they now only numbered around twenty fully serviceable aeroplanes.

No. 3 Group had moved west, flying their new 109 G4s, and No. 4 Group flew in Belgium, so the Green Hearts were thinly spread in Russia.

*

Grisha Bogdanov learned fast and worked hard, earning favours, if you can call having enough food to survive as a favour. He quickly realised survival as a prisoner of war takes tenacity and determination. First in the queue meant at least warm soup, and the ten loaves of bread supplied once a day to all the POWs in the building came past him first, enabling him to tear a huge chunk for himself before passing it on. Such behaviour is selfish, of course, but essential.

Further up the line the others would get very little and the last nothing at all. That's how it goes. He'd been there when he first arrived.

Now handling engines, straight out the crates from the factory in Bremen, Germany, he hauled them along on the chains and pulleys towards the airframes.

It's straightforward enough, installing a radial engine into the fuselage of a Focke-Wulf 190, when that's all you do for sixteen hours a day, seven days a week with no more than a five-minute break. You become good at it.

His mind wandered to better things, particularly after the bread and soup when at least some of the hunger pains were gone. He thought about his home in Dubna, a village a hundred kilometres north of Moscow, overlooking the wide, timeless Volga. He heard the Germans had been, dreadful rumours of what they'd done, but could find no up-to-date news.

Cigarette smoke drifted around and he indicated to the owner with two fingers to his lips, so the tiny smouldering clump of tobacco was passed over for a few moments, enough to get the nicotine hit before handing back the remains.

Four of them worked on each aeroplane, with two Germans supposedly supervising at all times. Other than to communicate for work they couldn't talk to one another. But these men were trusted, to a point, and the Germans not always present.

Suddenly he heard a gruff Russian voice deep in his right ear, startling him. He backed off, turning his head immediately. Alexander, one of the team, moved away, angry, checking the Germans hadn't seen him. It probably looked like he'd kissed Grisha on the side of his head.

He left it an hour, resuming work on the underside of the aeroplane before he did it again. This time Grisha heard him clearly as something was pushed into his right hand.

"You have access to the oil and fuel lines. Put these inside, in every engine. It will run, but after a few minutes it will stop, and then ha! They will never know who did it!"

Alexander's breath stank of his rotten tobacco-stained teeth, and as he moved away he drew his right hand across his throat in the classic fashion.

Grisha looked around, then into his hand: a tight ball of brown mud the size of a pea and a tiny piece of blue cloth.

An engine swung gently above Grisha's head, so he reached up, drawing it close. After identifying the fuel and oil lines, he shoved the illicit substances one into each with the kind of practised sleight-of-hand rapidity impressive to any magician. If the engine didn't stop through lack of fuel, it would overheat and fail after being starved of oil. He knew the risks of this sabotage; he also knew that Alexander was right: it wouldn't be detected for many days, all being well.

As he matched the engine to the airframe a sudden commotion began at the other end of the line: dogs barking and Germans shouting, the type which could only mean danger for people like him. Two SS police with snarling Alsatian dogs straining at the leash marched down the line towards him, with an anxious-looking man in a dark suit he'd only seen once before.

The production manager pointed directly at Grisha. Alexander had moved away behind the aeroplane, glancing at the closed doors nearest to them, and then at Grisha. There was no escape.

Informants were everywhere. A prisoner could easily betray another for a loaf of bread or the promise of better treatment. Grisha had survived so much, only to now face an ignominious end. He searched the faces of those closest. Which one had betrayed him?

Instinctively looking down in the usual subservient manner, Alexander and the others raised their hands.

"You!" one of the SS police shouted at Grisha. A sergeant, thick-set, with a ruddy complexion, typical of the sort. "Stop what you are doing!" he yelled.

Grisha took a step back as the engine swung in a gentle arc on the end of the chains. Is this it? His filthy dead body would soon be lying on the cold concrete floor, the tattered rags of his uniform soaked in blood.

The one without the dogs had his MP40 in both hands ready to fire, pointing at Grisha's chest. "This one," the manager said, "and the two behind as well," he added, writing on a scrap of paper, leaning his head to one side close to the engine, staring at it.

He wanted the serial numbers, uninterested in Grisha, or anyone else.

"Bring that over here, quickly," the SS sergeant yelled, waving his right arm as though directing traffic.

The huge doors were drawn open and Grisha, Alexander, and the others in his team hauled the engine along the overhead runners. An Opel Blitz lorry reversed inside, stopping abruptly, close to Grisha.

He wondered if it would be examined before being packed. They couldn't possibly find anything, even if they did, surely?

Alexander looked on as a group of prisoners brought wooden crates, one for each engine. With no delay, they lowered them into the back of the lorry, amid a great deal of German shouting.

The vehicle started up and drove away. The doors closed and work resumed.

44

The next day, 6th July, Richard Raupach and I were ordered to ensure the safe arrival of an unusual visitor to Siverskaya airfield, in my first op as a member of No. 2 Group. Descending from the west at two thousand metres, a Heinkel 111 emerged through wide gaps in fair-weather cumulus, with another aeroplane following closely behind. From fifty kilometres away we provided close escort, and as our airfield drew near, the Heinkel broke away and the aeroplane behind lined up for a landing.

What an odd-looking aeroplane, and a type I'd only seen once before at Siverskaya, though there were quite a few at Heiligenbeil.

The Heinkel circled above the field and we all watched with interest as the huge Gotha 242 transport glider made a perfect approach and landing. With exceptional skill the pilot guided it across the grass to within fifty metres of our servicing hangars, exactly where he'd been told to put it.

We landed without engaging the enemy, shut down our engines, and made our way over to the glider. The rear doors had already opened and we were immediately enrolled with half a dozen others into removing the contents.

A huge amount of food and ammunition came out, as well as sacks of precious mail from home, and the main cargo, three open wooden crates containing new BMW801 engines, complete with full cowlings. We dragged the first one out on rollers amid a lot of cursing and shouting.

The Gotha pilot, a young white-haired lieutenant, stood at the front, marshalling the rest of us, dragging it towards him as we pushed from behind, sweating profusely in our shirt sleeves. Still wearing his cap, the lieutenant cursed like an angry sergeant major in a string of expletives with a pronounced Austrian accent. On such a hot day we all found it exhausting.

An Opel Blitz lorry arrived, using a crane to carry away the first engine. All three looked fresh from the factory. A member of Siverskaya's admin staff removed the mail in a *kubelwagen*, and two army lorries took away the ammunition and food, heading towards the main gate.

That same afternoon eight of us took off for a free hunt on our side of the river, engaging a variety of enemy aircraft and ground forces in a quick sweep, discharging all our ammunition on anything we could. Small arms fire and flak struck our aeroplanes, but we all returned uninjured.

That night, over a glass or two of schnapps, we gathered for an informal meeting. Tactics, enemy strength, and various targets were discussed, before Gunter Scheel indicated for me to follow him towards one of the larger hangars.

"I have a wonderful surprise for you, Paul," he said, offering a cigarette. "Come with me."

I saw Karl busy at an Fw190 with other black men, the new engines I'd seen earlier hanging above three aeroplanes.

"These A5s are being fitting with the new 801Ds, and yours is one of them. Karl will tell you more about it, but in essence you can get a power boost when you need it most. I'll be trying one too, but yours will be ready first, Paul."

Gunter looked on, beaming with pride as though they'd been hand-made by himself. "They arrived today from Heiligenbeil."

I smiled. "I know; I helped unload them."

"It's going to have a shiny new Green Heart on the side, and it will be your aeroplane, with the code letter 'A' in white," he said.

Tins of yellow paint were dotted around, with black men busy daubing it under the wingtips and the nose. I couldn't wait to take it up.

The significance of Heiligenbeil had completely slipped my mind.

I should have been due for an op in the morning, but Karl informed me my A4 had indeed sustained damage from the previous day and was unserviceable. There were no other aeroplanes available and with the A5 not being ready, I found myself grounded.

The woods beckoned.

My pockets bulging with cigarettes and coffee, I made my way along the track, on a wonderful July morning, to find Anna's cabin looking like a cottage from a children's nursery rhyme, with wildflowers growing all around and a thin finger of smoke rising from the chimney.

I knocked and waited. It occurred to me that I could walk straight in, not because I was German but because I considered her to be my girlfriend, and as such I should be entitled to do so, but I didn't; I waited for the signal.

The door opened and there she stood, smiling: business as usual.

But something seemed different. She threw her arms around my shoulders and hugged me, kissing my lips, long and slow, pressing her body against mine, just the greeting I had hoped for.

The next wonderful thirty minutes passed quicker than any in my life. We paused briefly for coffee and cigarettes before resuming. Afterwards it seemed the whole world had stopped and I almost fell asleep. I had to be back at the airfield for midday and by now it must be getting pretty close.

Along with cigarettes and coffee, I gave her money. She put it all in a cupboard, except for the money, which she folded and pushed somewhere into her clothing. I meant them as gifts, not payment. A man doesn't pay his girlfriend for her affections, but he does bring gifts when he can.

We made love one more time before I dressed. She sat next to me and we shared a cigarette, passing it back and forth, blowing the smoke high into the roof space of the cabin. I blew a series of perfect smoke rings that hung in the still air, causing her to giggle like a child.

"When the war is over, what will you do?" she asked, in Russian, turning to face me, the blue in her eyes deeper than the summer sky.

"We'll get a bigger house," I said, laughing. "One with a decent toilet and not a bucket surrounded by nettles; I've had enough of being stung on my arse."

She laughed. "*Krapiva*," she said.

"*Brennesselstch*," I replied. Nettle sting.

We both laughed again.

I hadn't realised what I'd said about us, though I remember saying it now. It didn't seem significant at the time.

Anna lit a cigarette and sat up, holding it between her lips. She wrapped a long wide bandage around her naked right foot, pulling it up over her toes first and then lifting the sides over the top, working back towards the heel, taking great care to ensure there were no prominent folds. Then she repeated the process with her left foot. Why would she do this, when she had no injuries? Then I remembered; these were not bandages but footcloths as once used by Prussian soldiers instead of socks, still widely used in Russia.

Anna put on some boots that looked suspiciously like German army issue. Rising to her feet and standing rigidly to attention, proudly naked but for the boots and looking totally gorgeous, she saluted smartly before marching around the room, singing, her hair cascading around her shoulders. Teasing ruthlessly, she knew exactly what the effect would be.

How could I resist?

I'd be late, so we kissed, a long, lingering embrace at the end of which she whispered something I couldn't quite hear. It didn't matter; I knew I'd be back very soon. I ran through the woods as fast as I could.

*

That same afternoon we engaged in ground strafing near the Volkhov River and similar ops daily as part of Operation Citadel. We flew exhausting ops like this until 15th July when we were suddenly told to stand down, as our pilots returned from the Central Sector. Operation Citadel was over.

No formal victory communication followed, even though we knew it had been a success. The Red Army had been stopped, so why no celebration? The explanation for what had happened in Operation Citadel had a familiar ring, reminding us of Stalingrad. Obviously, the unthinkable may have happened.

We drank far too much that night, suspecting what it meant.

In the morning we took off once more, eight of us splitting into pairs, heading east as usual, blasting away at anything Russian we came across, either on the ground or in the air. Nothing had changed, as it no doubt wouldn't for a while, even though unknown to us, the Red Army had begun chasing our ground forces west across central Russia.

When I returned to Siverskaya, the word *Vermisst* on the duty board jumped out at me. I noticed it instinctively, without looking directly at it, the rotten word springing from the wall as if lit by a ten thousand-watt bulb, striking the reader in the face like a hammer. I already knew the name from the location on the board, but just to confirm I read it aloud: Gunter Scheel.

Reinhold had been his wingman that morning. I found him still outside at his aeroplane talking to Karl.

"Where?" I said, and he knew exactly what I meant. I never heard him go down and nothing over the R/T, and I felt incredibly guilty.

"It's too far, Paul, he's gone."

"Where?" I repeated, taking a map from his right hand and opening it, laying it on the tailplane. "Show me."

Reinhold stabbed his right index finger onto the paper between our lines and Volkhov town.

"What about local landmarks, anything nearby? What's Ivan doing?"

"It's too far, Paul, you know it's over a hundred kilometres from here." Reinhold held my arm, gripping it so tightly I thought he'd break it.

"Show me, exactly," I said, forcing him to look closer at the map.

"That's where Gunter went down," he said, drawing a small circle on the paper. "There are two forested areas with a strip of flat land in between. That's where I last saw him."

Grabbing his map I jogged over to our only remaining Storch. Even though I saw a parachute in the back, I didn't bother. When I switched on the electrics I noticed the fuel tanks were full. A tremendous surge of adrenalin came over me as I started the engine. Reinhold shouted something, but I turned the aeroplane around, lined up, and took off.

45

Heading north-east, I settled the aeroplane at 350 metres. In a headwind of around 20kph I made slow progress, but it meant the flight back would be quicker, hopefully with Gunter on board. I thrashed the little Argus engine at eighty per cent power, watching the temperatures and pressures closely, and making Mga airfield in forty minutes. My fuel still good, I flew straight over.

The enemy had moved closer to the airfield and ten minutes later I heard small arms fire contact my airframe.

Welcome to Russian territory, I thought.

Compared to a 109 I seemed like an autumn leaf drifting helplessly on the breeze, unable to use my power and speed in evasive manoeuvres. Instinctively lowering the nose and applying full power, I still pushed the little aeroplane to every limit in the book, weaving around in the process. Safe for a moment, up ahead I saw woods to my left and right, a bonfire in a field, and lots of figures gathered around.

Throttling back, I dropped to a hundred metres for a closer look. I saw a vehicle at the bonfire and bright flashes, followed by more contacts on my aeroplane as rifle bullets struck the wings. I turned, as close as I dared. The black crosses on the wings were all that was recognisable. The entire fuselage had burned away.

A bullet smashed through my cockpit, missing my head by a few centimetres. I turned the Storch around, unable to make out anything else down there and unable to land. Although wrecked, from the description Reinhold had given me, this must undoubtedly be Gunter's aeroplane.

Hovering briefly overhead, as slow as I dared, willing things to be different, I hoped in vain that I could still land and pick him up, even though I knew I couldn't. I'd never felt such frustration in all my life.

The small arms fire intensified, so I banked away, heading west.

After another anxious few minutes crossing the lines, I landed at Mga, needing fuel and a strong drink. I shut down the engine and jumped out as machine-gun fire rattled somewhere nearby, with pilots running around and aeroplane engines being started.

"What the hell are you doing here?" one of them asked me, parachute in hand. Although his face looked familiar, I couldn't remember his name.

"I came to see if I could pick up one of our pilots; he went down east of here," I said, aware I sounded miserable.

"Scheel?"

"Yes," I replied, picking up.

"Didn't anyone tell you?"

"What?" I said.

Did he have good news? Maybe Gunter would suddenly appear from the dispersal with a bottle and sarcastic comments. I looked around but saw no-one.

"He deliberately rammed a Yak-9 after a lengthy dogfight with the bastard." He shook his head. "You know how it is, sometimes you get like that. He went down with a hell of a thump, and I didn't see him get out."

He forced a smile, drawing closer, patting me on the back twice. "Sorry," he added, before walking away.

I wanted to scream, or punch someone, or sit down with a drink and wallow in my own misery, but I just stood there.

Vehicles were being loaded with men and materials, amidst a lot of shouting and revving of engines. Then I remembered Hans and the dugout, and despite knowing I should return the Storch to Siverskaya without delay, I made my way over there.

The front door stood open, the inner one missing. The generator still hummed, but if it had been an aeroplane engine it would have worried me because of the rough running, coughing like a consumptive old man.

Part of the main room had collapsed and most of the furniture had gone. The corridor was the same but still passable, with occasional flashes of daylight through holes in the ceiling. I heard sounds of life, so I stepped over a mound of earth and proceeded down the corridor. The bookcase stood at the end, but I could barely see it due to half the bulbs no longer working. Most of the contents had gone.

At the entrance to the radio room I heard crackling Russian through one of the speakers, and music. *That* music again, at a particular part, the third movement, slow and beautiful. As I edged forward into the doorway, I saw Hans, crying like a mourner on the front row of a funeral.

With no idea what to do I stood there. A few seconds later I decided to leave, unnoticed, but then I couldn't, it wouldn't be right, so I took some heavy steps and coughed twice, which was easy to do with my new smoker's cough.

He turned. "I'm not leaving yet," he said, handkerchief in his right hand. The music was barely audible, calm and quiet, the opposite to events around us. "Have you come to get me out?"

I looked at him, shaking my head. "Hans, I don't understand."

"The airfield is being evacuated, we're all going, retreating, but not retreating, as they say, regrouping, so have you come to pick me up?"

I hadn't, but now he said it the empty Storch would be ideal.

"I can take you to the palace. I have a Storch here, but I have to leave right now," I said, moving away from the door, stepping aside as though allowing him to pass by if he wanted, which he clearly didn't, remaining seated at his radios.

"I have to stay behind to destroy these," he said, looking up admiringly at his equipment. Along with the music, a regular burst of static from another speaker sounded like a heartbeat, becoming fainter all the time, as though the equipment itself was dying.

The bulb above us dimmed, going out for a moment before flickering back on. The generator struggled.

"Honestly. Paul, I'll jump on a lorry. The SS will be the last to leave, so I'll go with them."

Why did I not believe him?

He leaned forward, holding some papers. "I've written more language notes for you, and there are some fresh intelligence reports that must reach the palace. Can you take them?"

"Bring them yourself," I said, testing.

"You'll be quicker, in your aeroplane," he replied, with a half-convincing smile and a wink. "Go on, I'll be alright. If anything happens, remember, I speak better Russian than they do themselves."

Just then a shell exploded only a few metres from the entrance. The entire bunker shook and the lights went out as more of the roof fell in.
    "Quick, get out!" Hans ordered. "I'll be right behind you."
    Outside there were chaotic scenes: the sharp rattle of an MG38 somewhere down the airfield, and an MG42 close behind me in the woods. I turned to look as a line of men fell to the ground while standing rigid, like manikins pushed over in a shop window: Russian POWs.
    To my right an air force lieutenant I'd never seen before shouted me over.
    "Is that your Storch?" he demanded, pointing.
    Another shell exploded near the runway and everyone instinctively ducked.
    "Yes, sir," I replied, trying to see whether Hans had emerged yet.
    "Then you will take me and this man, right now," he said, as a sergeant with his entire head bandaged stood leaning on him, clearly badly wounded.
    I hesitated; no-one had put any more fuel in it.
    "Right now, Sergeant," the lieutenant repeated, pointing a P08 pistol at my head.

46

The wounded man had to be carried to the aeroplane, where we bundled him into the back seat, slumped in a heap. The lieutenant took the middle seat behind me and strapped himself in as I slammed the door.

An angry SS sergeant banged on my window with the barrel of an MP40, shouting something unintelligible. As I strapped myself in, the lieutenant shouted, "Let's go!"

When the engine started, the wash from the prop almost blew the SS sergeant off his feet. To my astonishment he raised the machine pistol, aimed it directly at me, and cocked it, ready to fire. Pressing hard on the brake, I turned the aeroplane sharply to the right as he took a fatal step back. The prop caught his head first, throwing it back in an instant, severing it at the throat. A spasm in his right hand pulled the trigger, discharging the magazine harmlessly behind us. The head lay face up on the grass, still in the helmet, staring in disbelief.

The rest of him splattered over the nose of the aeroplane. The engine coughed in protest, dumping the heavier bits in chunks of shredded uniform, his legs up to the knees still standing in the boots.

With no engine checks I taxied at high speed to the threshold area, lowered ten degrees of flap, and applied full power.

A few seconds later as we lifted off, a line of tanks broke through the trees on my left and for one wonderful moment I thought they were ours. A dozen raced across the airfield, bounding along so fast it looked like they were on rails. We didn't have any tanks as fast as that or in such numbers, so I knew full well what they were; they'd been my target so many times.

In less than five minutes the Red Army had taken the airfield in their T-34s.

At a hundred metres up I heard a bang from the Argus engine and all power ceased. Still over the airfield, the propeller stopped. Instinctively I set the aeroplane into a glide to buy time.

We had about twenty seconds before we touched the ground, so I wondered how far we could get from the Russians, if at all. Directly below us the airfield was alive with T34s like fleas on a dog and at this rate I'd have to ask them to move so I could land safely.

For a moment I thought of my parents, and Anna sitting at the table in her cabin.

With nothing to lose, I tried the start-up procedure again: switched off and on again, fuel on, mags on, throttle set, engine primed once, and starter engaged, not simply desperation but the correct emergency procedure, though praying was not part of it.

The prop turned several times and each rotation brought us ten metres closer to the ground. At fifty metres the Argus burst into life, giving us full power immediately.

The faces below turned and rifles were raised to their shoulders. I pushed the nose down to get us as much speed as possible and we cleared the airfield perimeter at ten metres, as the first bullets struck the aeroplane. If we'd had full tanks, with three heavy people on board we'd never have made it.

Staying low, we remained at this height, hedge-hopping all the way. By a miracle, the fuel lasted and we made it home.

The wounded sergeant died. The lieutenant, a man by the name of Rolf Dolze, thanked me profusely, apologising and shaking my hand as though he never wanted to let go. The dead man had been his brother-in-law.

Dolze told me he was a senior administrative advisor, not a pilot, had never fired a shot at anyone in his life, and would recommend me for a medal, promising to make sure my CO knew what had happened. I wondered if this included the accident with the prop.

The Storch looked a mess, and I couldn't believe it got us back. The airframe was pitted with holes and streaked with remnants of the SS sergeant, the back seat a pool of dark congealed blood. I had to report my unauthorised use of it, and also take the papers to the CO that Hans had given me. Fully aware that my attempt to find Gunter had been foolhardy and may have brought serious trouble on myself, I prepared to defend my actions.

But then I experienced the bitter taste of failure: I had left two people behind, Gunter Scheel and Hans Weber.

The Palace Airfield was busy but serenely quiet by comparison to Mga.

I knocked on the CO's door and waited.

"Come in," he shouted.

I walked in and handed over the papers, which he began reading immediately.

"My God," he said, scanning the first page, shaking his

head. "Right," he added, reaching for a Juno, a Finnish cigarette.

An open bottle of schnapps stood on his desk and he poured himself one, emptying the glass in two gulps. His hands shook, and I noticed a small area on the right side of his chin he'd missed when shaving, the way my grandfather sometimes did.

Although considered to be a reasonable man, I didn't know Major Reinhard Seiler well, so I therefore hoped my inevitable punishment would be fair and proportionate. At thirty-four years of age, the oldest pilot amongst us. The Knight's Cross of the Iron Cross with Oak Leaves hung around his neck, and the Spanish Cross in Gold with Swords and Diamonds glinted on his tunic. He looked me in the eyes as he began speaking.

"What you did was an obscenity, Goetz, a flying obscenity. Taking that Storch and almost getting yourself killed in the process. You are not listed as a rescue pilot, are you? Not only this, you took a 109 G5 for a joyride recently, which I overlooked at the time, but this is too much. Do you understand?"

I had no idea he knew about the G5. Without realising, I stood rigid to attention at the front of his desk, staring past him at the wall, nodding and agreeing to everything.

"I should confine you to barracks for a week at least, or perhaps strip you of your rank and send you to a flak unit. How would that be?"

Oddly enough, despite feeling wretched, I thought about what my parents would say, my father in particular, remembering when he'd asked if I had to pay for the aeroplanes I'd damaged. I admonished myself; I'd abandoned two friends and should be punished. But could I use anything as mitigation?

"I wanted to bring Gunter back, sir," I said, still to attention, my eyes fixed on the wall.

The CO took a long pull on his cigarette, exhaling with an equally long sigh. "I know you did, Goetz. I know that." He shook his head. "Sit down," he muttered, almost inaudibly, nodding at the chair beside his desk.

He saw me looking at the bottle, took a glass from a drawer, and pushed them both towards me.

I poured a full one and knocked it back.

"You've been through it, I realise that. Scheel was a good man and my friend too. What you did was wrong but commendable, so I won't take any action against you, this time."

He filled both glasses and we raised them together.

"To absent friends," he said, as we drank them down.

He smiled and briefly shook his head. "Don't do it again, right? That's the end of the matter. Now, go to the palace, clean yourself up, and get some sleep. We have a celebration in the great hall tomorrow."

Standing to attention, I saluted before I left, as he continued reading the intelligence reports. No mention of accidents with propellers.

*

As wonderful as always, most of the palace seemed occupied by wounded troops and the delousing facilities were busy. Vehicles of all sizes packed the front yard, and the sound of shouting and stamping of feet filled the corridors. My old roommates had left, our beds now occupied by army officers.

Luckily, I found my champagne crate in one corner of the room amid a pile of uniforms and, inside, a bottle of schnapps, some cigarettes, my letters from home, and my book: everything as I had left it.

That night, the casino was packed, mainly with army and SS, with a curiously hedonistic atmosphere, the like of which I'd never seen before: packets of Pervitin everywhere and most people drinking heavily. I knew a few, but after a while I left, still exhausted.

With nowhere else to go I found a mattress and slept in my old room near a window. My new roommates spoke to me briefly, unconcerned as to my identity. All three appeared exhausted and slept long hours.

With no ops in the morning, we were due to meet in the great hall at 1600 hours, so in the meantime, I hitched a lift to the airfield to see Karl.

"She's all yours tomorrow!" he shouted. "We've been working flat out to get it ready."

My Fw190 A-5 'White A' stood proudly in the hangar with a tarpaulin over the nose.

"It has that new engine I told you about, straight from the factory at Heiligenbeil. It hasn't been flight tested yet, of course, because of the fuel restrictions, but you can do that tomorrow when you take her up on the first op. There shouldn't be any problem."

How thrilling! I couldn't wait.

He showed me the minor differences inside the cockpit and I was so excited I wanted to jump in right away.

"And, of course, you'll have one of these," he said, pointing to a trolley laden with bombs.

My heart sank. We'd been warned we would be flying more fighter-bomber ground attack duties than ever before. I'd seen similar bombs carried by Stukas, and I didn't relish the prospect of 250kg of high explosives under my seat. I decided I'd find the target quickly and be rid of it.

*

The CO entered the great hall at precisely 1600 hours to a rapturous welcome. With Army and SS officers also there, it must have been for a good reason. The cooks brought food and schnapps, serving everyone where they stood, as though at a party.

Suddenly I felt a thump in the back and turned to see Reinhold, Helmut, and Fritz, my roommates from Siverskaya, and then Horst and Erich.

"We're still here, but at the other side, with the army," Horst said. "So you'll have to come over and join us." He gripped my right forearm and looked me in the eyes. "I heard what you tried to do, for Gunter. I'm sorry it didn't work out. But I knew you'd be back."

It was wonderful to be together again, like old times.

The CO tapped his glass with a pen and everyone hushed.

"Where is Sergeant Helmut Missner?" he demanded, searching the room.

"Here, sir!" Helmut shouted, winking at me as he nudged his way through the crowd. When he reached the CO he threw up a very smart salute, reciprocated immediately. For a moment we had absolute silence as the two men stared at one another. Cheers and laughter followed, before the CO nodded, indicating with his hands for silence again.

"Gentlemen, we have been blessed by God with the ability to fly our wonderful aeroplanes in this just cause," he said, pausing. "But it's bloody sad that he cursed us with having to do it here," he added, to a huge roar of laughter. When it died down he continued. "It is my proud honour to announce that Sergeant Missner shot down his nineteenth Ruski yesterday."

More uproar, loud cheering, and cries of, "So what!" filled the room.

"So what indeed, gentlemen?" the CO replied. "I agree, it's not unusual, and even expected. But this latest victory takes the Green Hearts' total to five thousand enemy aircraft destroyed in combat."

There were gasps all round, and yet more applause, with cheering so loud Stalin must have heard us in the Kremlin.

47

How clever of the CO, turning recent bleak events into a fantastic celebration.

No-one mentioned Operation Citadel, or the fact that JG54 had lost nine pilots while taking part, with two more badly wounded.

With take-off not due until 1100 hours in the morning, Monday 19th July 1943, I woke up at 0600 hours to write letters, one to my parents and one to Inge, despite still not hearing from her for several months.

At 0800 hours I walked into the woods along Anna's path, pockets bulging with Reemtsma cigarettes as usual. I could have an hour with her, maybe a little more, but even a minute would be better than nothing. The closer I came the faster I walked.

The door stood open, but I could see no sign of her. Inside, everything seemed in order, as always, but where was she? Maybe collecting supplies, or visiting someone?

Small tank tracks passed the cabin, possibly from a half-track, so I sat down on the steps and lit a cigarette.

Half an hour passed, but the woods remained quiet. I wanted to see her more than anything, but she didn't return.

Eventually I walked away, turning to look back every minute, as the cabin disappeared into the trees.

*

The briefing was short and routine. Sergeant Richard Raupach and I were to fly a free hunt together, each carrying a single 250kg bomb, our target being any trains we could find, or a bridge, ideally both at the same time. With troop concentrations between Mga and Volkhov near Voybokalo, thirty kilometres east of Mga, much of the flight would be over hostile territory. We tried to ignore this fact.

The cockpit of the A5 was hot even with the canopy open. Given only enough fuel to get us there and back directly, the days of flying with full tanks for long, lingering patrols were gone.

Karl helped me strap in as usual, and I started the aeroplane myself. It ran smoothly, with all the temperatures and pressures reading normal.

My ammunition counters full, I thanked Karl when he reminded me about the bomb. I could hardly forget, and we both laughed, but he had a serious point. The take-off run would be longer, and the aeroplane much slower, until I dropped it.

"There was no clock," he shouted, "so I fitted a new Kienzle this morning, so look after it." He smiled before walking back towards the hangar.

Easing the throttle forward, I joined Richard at the threshold area. As soon as we lined up side by side we took off.

The rate of climb seemed noticeably poorer, but we remained at four hundred metres heading east, passing over our lines a few kilometres south-west of Mga. As we prepared our approach to the target area, the engine of my A5 coughed and, to my horror, the needle on the oil temperature gauge spun into the red.

My engine was rapidly overheating and I had no idea why. Instinctively I wanted to throttle back but, with little height, I carried on. We'd only been in the air fifteen minutes and had already crossed over the Russian lines.

Richard was two hundred metres to my left, both just four hundred metres above the ground when my engine failed.

The prop came to a sudden stop and my aeroplane went quiet. At this height I'd only have around ninety seconds before I hit the ground. I pulled the bomb release and it dropped, immediately giving me a lift, slowing my descent.

I shouted over the R/T, "Engine failure. I'll have to put down."

Too low to bail out, I'd already lost a hundred metres and the instruments told me a restart would be fruitless. I urgently needed a long flat field with a nice firm grass surface.

Turning towards a northerly wind, I tried buying as much time as possible.

The map told me I was gliding over peat bogs, making a wheels-down landing impossible. Selecting an area of higher ground surrounded by trees, at one hundred metres, I lowered some flap and raised the nose a little to slow down. There were no vehicles or troops visible, so I turned off all the switches, tightened my straps, and held on.

The headwind helped as my aeroplane touched down, gently at first, skimming the surface, but then a lot of silver birch saplings I hadn't noticed before struck the leading edges of my wings, causing a rapid halt.

My first thought was that I'd made another perfect forced landing – my fourth – and no-one had witnessed it.

As yet I detected no fire, but just in case, I opened the canopy and climbed onto the wing immediately.

Oddly enough, with Karl foremost in my mind, I reached back inside and pulled the new clock from the instrument panel. It wouldn't fit in my pockets because they were still bulging with the cigarettes meant for Anna. My first few minutes in enemy territory were therefore spent rearranging myself to find space for the damned clock.

I noticed my right hand bleeding, so I removed the first aid kit from the fuselage hatch and sat against a tree to dress it. With birds singing all around, I listened out for vehicles and voices but could hear nothing, so I lit a cigarette.

What should I do? I placed the map on my knee, looking towards Siverskaya, over one hundred kilometres to the west, meaning I must be at least fifty kilometres behind the lines. The southern edge of Lake Ladoga, about twenty kilometres to the north, now lay in enemy hands. It seemed my only option would be to head west, keeping my head down, but perhaps I should sleep now and wait until evening? Nights were brief at this time of year and drowning in a Russian marsh seemed as bleak a prospect as captivity.

Too impatient to wait, I set off, after firstly dropping my leather flying helmet onto the seat and closing the canopy. The hot, impractical helmet muffled my hearing. Closing the canopy had become a habit, like shutting the door when you leave the house. Abandoning my aeroplane meant parting company with my only connection to home.

Walking west, always west, with a ridiculous stoop causing backache, I stood upright. For about a kilometre I pushed through woodland and dense summer undergrowth, until the trees stopped. Open marshland lay ahead as far as I could see.

It could be like this all the way to Siverskaya. According to my map, minor roads occasionally passed through, but they would be busy with the enemy, so must be avoided. Trudging over thick tufts of marsh grass, I came to a lake with taller grasses around one side. I could wade or swim across, or walk around on the higher ground; I chose the latter.

After another kilometre I sat down, exhausted and thirsty. Surrounded on three sides by water, I wondered if it would be safe to drink. Parts of it looked clear, but it gave out the classic swamp smell when disturbed. I knew I'd have to drink soon, but for now I resisted.

The ground becoming firmer, I slid into a natural trench, a *Rachel*, more than two metres deep, taking me in a northerly direction, before turning west again. As I picked up the pace the *Rachel* deepened further; I knew if this continued my chances were good. What a fantastic stroke of luck.

I'm not sure how far I'd walked in those meandering ditches, reminiscent of the trenches in the 1914–18 war, perhaps several kilometres, when I made a decision that would haunt me forever. Standing at a T-junction, without thinking, I took the right fork. I'd become too confident and careless.

There were shouts of "*Nemetsky!*" as I appeared in full view, ten metres in front of them. I couldn't turn and run; they would have shot me immediately as all six were pointing their rifles at me. Instinctively raising my hands, shutting my eyes with final thoughts of my parents and Anna, I wondered if I'd hear the bang from the gun that killed me.

Part 3

1

Prisoner of War Camp 7270/16
19th April 1947

"He's watching you again, Paul," Hermann groaned.

"The man's a prick," I replied, angrily.

The cart had sunk even deeper into the mud.

"We've overloaded it," I said with a long sigh.

"Maybe the prick will come over to help us?" Gerhard laughed.

"Who, the Siberian?" Hugo said. "Not a chance."

Hermann dropped his spade, adding another shoulder to the cart, and gradually the four of us hauled it free.

"It's getting dark, and we can't possibly get any more peat in here. You'd think he'd call it a day," Gerhard complained, leaning on it, utterly exhausted. "Why don't you tell him, Paul?"

"Let's get it onto the track and I will," I replied, pushing again.

Finally it moved onto firm ground and the others looked at me, expectantly.

"It's full!" I shouted at our guard.

He looked around, and then at his stolen Luftwaffe pilot's watch. "Right, we go, now," he ordered, waving.

His Eastern accent was difficult to follow, but he understood every word I said. After nearly four years my Russian was better than his.

Hauling an ancient wooden cart packed with 800kg of wet peat through ten kilometres of mud is almost damn near impossible. The track disappeared every few metres, and adding to our problems it had started raining again, making the peat heavier and the mud even thicker. After working since first light it was now late afternoon and we were finally on our way back to camp.

Dragging the load we made no conversation; we were too exhausted. By the time we arrived darkness had descended.

Vitaly opened the gates as usual. A fair man, for a Russian, he often turned a blind eye when he caught us stealing extra bread and milk. I'd almost grown to like him.

"How are you this evening, Vitaly?" I asked.

He frowned, shaking his head. "I miss my wife," he said, giving the cart a peremptory shove to get it inside the gate.

He always said this, and I always gave him the same reply. "Then I'm glad I never married," I said, just as he shouted at our escort to speed up.

It seemed we had something in common: we both disliked the Siberian.

Our group of four had missed the regular mealtime at 1800 hours, but we were given a pot of cold soup and bread as hard as wood. We scraped the pot between us in turn, obtaining just enough to rid ourselves of the worst hunger pains. It's amazing how much better the world feels when hunger is not your main problem.

My prison clothing had been wet for most of the day in

a cool breeze and so I needed to dry it out, because the night would be cold. I had a spare shirt and trousers, but the last time I checked they had become infested with lice again. Someone had taken them, intending to keep them, no doubt, but discarded them when they realised. I hope they'd put them on first and had taken some of my little horrors with them. The shirt could virtually walk across the floor on its own, it was so alive. *Do I catch pneumonia or do I become a host to these again?* Not much of a choice. I had to get dry and warm up; I'd been ill twice the year before and so I didn't want to risk it again.

They'd stopped giving us wood for our stove, so I stripped, wrapped myself in a filthy blanket, and hung my clothes from a roof beam to dry, as did everyone else. My own stink used to make me nauseous; now it reminded me I was still alive.

We wandered around, wrapped up tightly like ghostly survivors of a sunken ship, and when I came to put my clothes back on, my lovely thick shirt had disappeared. I don't blame the thief. Everyone has to survive. I'd taken my eyes off it for too long, becoming careless. I found another, in worse condition than mine, and put it on, regretting it immediately.

Hundreds of lice lined the armpits, as I soon discovered. Not even my own. It seemed others had the same problem as I heard angry shouts throughout the night. The first time I heard, "Damned malinki partisans!" I thought we were being attacked by men with guns, not Russian lice.

"Did you hear the latest, Paul?" Gerhard said as he lay down on the floor next to me.

"No. What rumour is it this time? Did we win the war but nobody told the Russians?"

He laughed. "No, sadly not," he replied, with a wry smile, forcing more filthy straw underneath his skeletal frame. "I heard from a Hungarian there are some interrogations coming up, next week. You haven't had the pleasure yet, have you?"

"No. That's because I'm not an officer like you. I'm... I *was* just an ordinary bloody pilot," I said. "I filled in the form when I arrived but have heard nothing since."

"A German officer interrogated me the first time, back in '44, a man called Raier. He said he was from the National Committee of Free Germany."

"They were only interested in officers," I said, "not people like me."

"Bloody traitors, the lot of them," Gerhard said. "Antifascist scum."

"So what do they ask, the Russians, if I am to be interrogated?" I said, lying down, my head propped up painfully on a bony elbow, facing him.

"The usual stuff; what you did in Russia, where you were posted, that sort of thing. It all seems pointless now, though, doesn't it?"

I nodded, my head moving slowly in my hand.

"It doesn't last long, there are so many of us to get through. But don't admit any wrongdoing, obviously, not that you ever did, in the air force. Remember Seidel? When they rolled up his sleeve and found out he was SS they went mad and beat him half to death."

"I was out digging at the time, but yes, I remember you telling me."

"They were livid he'd got this far without being discovered. They dragged him away to God knows where, poor bastard, to another camp, probably. Then there were the other three, last year."

"They were making a point."

"We were all made to watch, remember?"

"Yes, of course."

"All three shouted, 'I die for Germany and the Fuhrer!' as the chairs were kicked away."

"I know, Gerhard, I saw it."

"But they also ask whether you knew any Russians, so if you did, don't tell them." Gerhard laughed. "I suspect that's what they are really interested in, the collaborators. You know how paranoid Stalin is." He groaned before turning over, drawing a blanket up to his neck.

I thought of Anna. She hadn't been on my mind for months, not as much as in May 1945. The war was over; we'd lost, so we could all go home and I could see Anna on the way. I'd stay for a while, perhaps live with her in the cabin. I could chop wood and sleep with her every night, feeling her body close to mine, the smell of her. It would have been wonderful. But I didn't because I was still here, working myself to death as a slave.

"By the way, Paul, do you know what day it is tomorrow?" Gerhard said from under his blanket.

"Sunday, I think, why?"

"It is, but the date. What date is it?"

"Now you've got me. I've no idea." I thought for a moment. "I know it's 1947, and it's April."

"It is, you're right. But it's the 20th tomorrow," he said, before laughing so much I thought he'd choke.

Then I remembered: Hitler's birthday.

2

Because they called us alphabetically, I was one of the first. The badly lit interrogation room in Block 8 stank of stale sweat and suspicion, but I could see no blood on the walls or even the floor, which I considered a good sign.

I sat on an uncomfortable chair, with no padding for my bony arse, behind a plain desk with the only window on my right. The filthy glass barely let in any light.

Two male officers, one much older than the other, sat opposite, with a female also wearing an army uniform. A single sheet of paper lay on the desk, the questionnaire I'd filled in on arrival: full name, date of birth, home address, education, civilian occupation, with date and place of capture, but now with a number stamped on it: 140493.

"Olga, get his name, his rank, and his station," the younger officer said, adding, "and tell him to roll up his left sleeve."

She looked worried, but I detected a faint smile.

"Give me to see your left arm," she said.

I rolled up my sleeve. She nodded.

The two men took a close look.

"Your name is being?" she said, in poor German.

Should I say something in Russian? I didn't know what to do. These three had only arrived that morning in a group of about thirty interrogators, none of whom I'd seen before. If one of our guards had been in here, they would have known I could speak Russian.

"Paul Goetz."

"What soldier were you?"

"Fighter pilot," I replied, in exaggerated German.

"What rank is you was in war being?" she said, in German so poor I could barely understand.

"Sergeant."

"Where?"

"Siverskaya."

Shit. I said it with a thick Russian accent. I was so used to it.

They looked at one another but said nothing. I'd got away with it.

"What regiment?" her left hand ready with a pencil on a notepad.

I wondered about telling them. The war had been over for almost two years, so there were no longer issues over operational secrecy. I now had to be careful in case I implicated myself in anything. Remembering what Horst said about the Krasnogvardeisk Action, I decided I couldn't even admit knowing about it.

Nothing I had done had been outside the constraints of acceptable warfare. My conscience was clear.

"I flew Fw190 fighters in Jadgeschwader 54."

The two men immediately began arguing.

The youngest said, "He's not SS; he's only a fucking air force sergeant; why are we wasting our time on him?"

While the other said, "So what, he's a fascist, isn't he? I want to find out more about him."

The older one then handed the female a sheet of paper, a list of pre-prepared questions.

"When was capture, what is happening?" she said, looking into my eyes.

Her accent sounded the same as Anna's, but she was nowhere near as pretty, even though she had masses of thick hair, like Anna. The dismal uniform didn't help. But she was definitely female, and only the fourth one I'd seen since 1943. Her tunic strained against the pressure of an ample chest and, for a moment, I wondered what her breasts looked like. I thought of leaning forward and unfastening the buttons as I had with Anna's blouse so many lifetimes ago. *God that would have been nice*, I thought, *just for a few moments*.

We had a female dentist and a female nurse, and I had once seen a woman walking past the peat fields two summers before. She just appeared from nowhere carrying a small dog, wearing a dress made of curtains from a wartime German train, the letters DR perfectly positioned over her thin backside.

"I crashed on 19th July '43," I said, "near Voybokalo."

"What was mission?"

"A free hunt, from Siverskaya."

"How long you at Siverskaya?"

"Two years."

"How you warm in winter?" she said, which was odd, and I didn't understand at first. Another argument started between them, all about me, which seemed to go on forever.

I gazed out the window. Fair-weather cumulus drifted overhead at about 1500 metres, in a gentle breeze from the north-east: not bad flying conditions, though dark skies followed. It might rain later.

They shouted at me. Spittle flew from the mouth of the older man every time he spoke, some of it catching on his huge bushy moustache, gathering in droplets like morning dew. He looked like Stalin, obviously deliberate.

She asked the same question again, and this time I realised what she wanted.

"We burned wood, whatever we could get." Not entirely sure where this was going, I saw no reason to be dishonest. "We cut down trees at the airfield."

Remembering what Gerhard had said, I avoided telling them about the old man and his Panje pony. Not for his sake but for Anna's.

"You take wood from Russian houses?"

"No." I could see now. They were trying to find out if I'd been looting, or worse.

"Food from Russian people?"

"No."

"You kill civilians?"

"No."

"You rape women?"

"No."

"You burn houses?"

"No."

"You starve people of Leningrad," she said, as all three stared. I'd been involved, of course. The ice road had been a constant target. I took part in enforcing the siege in which we were now told almost a million civilians had died of starvation. What could I say?

"I flew my aeroplane, that's all I did."

After a momentary silence all three began discussing my fate again, at length. Astonishingly, I heard the words 'theft' and 'looter' repeated several times. I had been involved in neither.

Stalin placed a brown leather bag on the table, taking out a sheet of paper bearing the grand title 'People of the Soviet Union' in huge red letters. He filled in some gaps in the text with my name and a few dates.

The female pushed her notepad across the desk, saying, "Sign it. This is transcript."

It was entirely in Russian. Stalin then read from his grand paper, also in Russian, with no German translation. Had I not understood some of it, I doubt I'd have known what they intended.

"You are charged with looting from the people of the Soviet Union, in that between 1941 and 1943 you wantonly destroyed trees at Siverskaya airfield and stole timber. You are therefore sentenced to ten years' hard labour."

I stood up, seething with anger. "You can't do this! This isn't right! That wasn't looting," I shouted, in perfect Russian.

Stalin slapped me across the face, almost knocking me to the floor. "You speak Russian, fascist?"

The other one drew his Tokarev pistol, aiming it at my face from less than a metre away. I raised my hands above my head. Liquid ran from my nose onto my top lip and when I gathered it up with my tongue, it tasted warm and sweet.

"You are a fascist invader, a looter, a thief!" Stalin shouted. "You will never leave Russia!"

He drew his papers together and pushed the pen at me. "Sign it or we will shoot you right now."

The female stood near the door, a look of horror on her face, the younger man still pointing his pistol at my head. I picked up the pen and signed my admission of guilt, just as a drop of blood splashed onto the paper.

3

"Don't worry," Gerhard said, trying to light the shortest cigarette butt in Russia. He managed one puff before it burned his fingers and he dropped it. "That's nothing. Our unit lived in a *kolkhoz*, a communal farm, for a month, and I made the mistake of telling them. They charged me with theft of a pig and ten chickens. How the hell did they know?" He looked at me, smiling, his eyes more grey than blue. "Do you know what sentence they gave me?"

"Was it as bad as mine?" I said, shaking my head.

"Twenty fucking years' hard labour," he said, laughing. "That was last year. If I survive this shithole they won't release me until 1966."

He laughed again, but I didn't find it funny, at all, as a dark sense of foreboding descended over me.

In the morning, before we set off with our cart, I told Vitaly about the lice. He shrugged and seemed disinterested, but I knew he took it seriously. He gave me a Papirossa cigarette, not a butt but a full one straight from the packet, which I later shared with my friends.

Given no bread with the warm green water they call soup, even before the working day began, hunger pains were severe. All conversation inevitably turned to food.

"So, Paul, stollen or sausage?" Gerhard asked.

Before I could make my usual reply, Hugo jumped in. "Not this again, Strattman," he said with a deep sigh.

Gerhard always asked the same question and we all gave him the same answer. It was one of our games: what would be better, a kilo of stollen or a kilo of sausage?

"Would it be warm or cold?" Hermann asked, playing along.

"Either," Gerhard replied.

"Cake would be better because we need the calories, digging this shit all day long. There are no calories in meat," Hugo said.

"There's fuck all in cake, idiot, you need protein, the body needs meat," Hermann said, almost in a whisper.

"So you say," Gerhard added.

"I'd want some of my mother's one-pot stew," I said, breaking the rules. They all scowled before smiling. "I can smell it now."

"Stew is not stollen," Gerhard laughed.

"Sausage stew then," Hermann retorted.

"If that's the case," Hugo began, "I'll have a fried pancake with grated potatoes, eggs, and flour, followed by some beautifully tenderised beef in the biggest fucking schnitzel you've ever seen. I can taste it. You know when the meat is so tender…"

My stomach had long since given up expecting decent food, now probably no bigger than a thimble.

"You'd be ill," I suggested. "If we were given anything like that now, it would kill us."

Gerhard nodded, as we all did. We decided it would be better if we stuck to existing on our coloured water.

At least the weather gave us a pleasant south-westerly breeze and brilliant white fair-weather cumulus drifting over, with no rain likely.

The walk to the fields was tolerable with a cart containing only four peat-cutting spades; sometimes the idiot Siberian would ride along when feeling spiteful or lazy, but today he walked, gazing into space as usual.

"Did you ever speak to those in Block 4?" Gerhard asked, marching side by side.

"No," I replied. I suspect he knew I hadn't, because we weren't allowed to mix freely outside our own block.

"I spoke to one last night on burial duty," he said. "You wouldn't believe what he told me."

"Try me," I said, because very little surprised me anymore.

"He was a Stalingrader. He told me the rumours are true. Close to a hundred thousand of them were captured alive, including Paulus."

I stopped, causing him to do the same as the cart nudged us in the back. "How do you know it's true?"

"Because the man told me, and why should he lie? He said he was a captain and saw Paulus the day he gave up, 2nd February 1943. They found him in the basement of a department store, happy to surrender, so he said."

"Then where are they now? Have they been repatriated?"

Gerhard laughed. "Now you're dreaming, Paul," he said. "They are all dead, most of them anyway."

"What? How?"

"Starved to death, disease, shot, everything, so he said. Do you know they marched them all the way here from Stalingrad immediately after the surrender? There were huge columns of them, ten kilometres long. They weren't given any food or water, and if you fell behind, they'd shoot you and leave you in the road. If you needed a shit or even a piss you had to do it while moving or run ahead and do it, because if you dropped behind with your arse out of your trousers, your prick would be the last thing you ever saw."

I thought of the Russian POWs at Heiligenbeil, and of the ice road column.

Just then the Siberian shouted, "Get moving!" so we pulled at the cart again.

"It was February, so you know how cold it gets, Paul. They didn't even provide shelter, so of course most of them died. They were exterminated."

"I want to speak to him myself. What's this captain's name?"

"You'll never manage it." Gerhard said, shaking his head.

"Just give me his name and I'll find a way."

"It was Haider, I think, but it won't do you any good."

"Why?"

"Because he's dead. He told me this just before he died. It was him we were burying."

*

Prisoner of War Camp 7270/16 lay isolated from the world in a huge area of mixed woodland, hence the name, Forest Camp. We believed the rumours that it was about four hundred kilometres north-west of Moscow and about thirty kilometres south-east of a town called Borovichi. None of us knew for sure, but some rumours became accepted truth over time. If so, then from our perspective we were over 150 kilometres east of Lake Ilmen, so I doubt any of us had ever flown over it.

We weren't treated like prisoners of war, more like slaves in a labour camp. Today would be no different to any other. We cut peat for ten hours before dragging the load back to camp.

The Siberian was obviously feeling generous, or hungry, because we arrived at 1730 hours, in plenty of time for the meal. Our group of four called ourselves the Strattman team, after Gerhard's surname, and as a lieutenant, he held the highest rank. We stuck together whenever we could and looked after one another. You couldn't survive alone; you'd die without at least one other person looking out for your welfare.

When I'd been sick the previous year, I'd collapsed unconscious in the fields. My own fault; I'd been drinking bog water and contracted dysentery again. We had to shit and piss out in the fields when working and remembering where we did it was almost impossible, the landscape was so uniform.

Hugo told me the Siberian wanted to leave me there and he'd even chambered a bullet in his rifle to finish me off, but the others convinced him to bring me back, lying prostrate on top of the cart. They told him that if he shot me they'd tell his officers that I'd escaped. The cart would have been incredibly heavy for the three of them, but they did it.

They took me to the infirmary, an undeserving euphemism for Block 1, where the sick are taken to die. Everyone knows what it means to be sent there. They pretend it's an infirmary because the last time the Red Cross visited they criticised our captors for not having one. Apparently too many deaths were now an embarrassment to those in the Kremlin.

So I lay for days with a fever and a thirst I'd never known before, but at least in a bed, of sorts, and not on the bare floor. Someone said I had typhus, but I had no idea. I thought it was dysentery. They gave me no medication, as far as I know, and, too ill to get up, I pissed and shit in my clothes all the time.

Nobody was allowed to visit and the woman known as a nurse came every day with a bowl of soup and the occasional mug of water. If asleep, I got nothing.

After four or maybe five days I gained enough strength to stand, horrified at my condition. My own stink upset the nurse because she ordered me to strip and go outside.

Staggering out the door, I found two buckets of water and she shouted, "You must wash," as she left me there.

The buckets were heavy and I only managed to tip the first one over my head. I gasped at the cold. If it had been winter I would have remained filthy. I sat in the other bucket and washed my stinking arse.

I used the first one to shit in, but only a few splashes of foul-smelling yellow liquid come out, then I found a cloth and washed myself. She reappeared with clean clothing as I watched her burning my old rags. Although wretched, I had signs of improvement, and when I returned to my bed most of the shit had been wiped off onto the floor. After getting dressed I lay down and passed out.

The next morning I was woken up by a crunching noise like someone stepping on broken glass. This weird sound came closer, occasionally accompanied by screams of pain, like someone being tortured. I thought I was hallucinating when suddenly I felt a filthy gloved hand being forced into my mouth, along with something metal bashing against my teeth.

Another hand on my forehead held me down and I just managed to lift my arms and push away whoever it was.

The female dentist had a pair of plyers in her right hand and shouted, "I thought you were dead," with no apology or remorse.

She moved over to the man in the next bed, who hadn't moved for two days, and repeated the process, this time pulling out two gold teeth, dropping them into her coat. There was no blood and he didn't protest. He couldn't; the dead don't complain.

She roamed the infirmary with her plyers all morning, singing, crunching her way to a pocket full of gold.

4

On Sundays they usually gave us the day off. This particular day would have been an ideal opportunity to attend the delousing hut, which thanks to Vitaly was operational again. Not a moment too soon; I was enduring fresh misery as the lice in my clothes had multiplied. While working, they weren't so much of a problem, but as soon as I settled down at night under the blankets they made life hell and quality sleep impossible.

When Vitaly informed his colleagues some of us were infested again, our captors fell into general panic, always fearful of typhus, not for us but for themselves.

Our barrack resounded with loud Russian shouting, "All prisoners must go through the process immediately!"

Firstly we had to shave everywhere until no hair remained on our bodies. This took time and, to our continual surprise, the female nurse had the job of making sure we'd done it properly.

In the delousing hut we all stood in lines as she closely inspected every crevice. Gerlach, a Berliner, farted in her face so she slapped him hard across the backside. We all laughed, and she didn't find it amusing when he asked her to do it again.

A huge coal stove made it hot and steamy, like a sauna. We rubbed our head, groin, and armpits with a foul-smelling paste before washing with bars of rough soap that felt like grit. With plenty of hot water and steam, we almost enjoyed it, in winter, the only time we were comfortably warm.

Clothes that were not falling apart were saved, the others burned. I sent everything to be incinerated. The salvaged stuff hung up over the steam and when we got it back the lice were burnt and their eggs had turned brown. That's how you can tell when a malinki partisan is dead.

We all wandered around with shaven heads, like inhuman beasts. For some men the hair never returned and they looked twenty years older. We went through the delousing a few times; if they provided better living conditions then perhaps it wouldn't keep happening.

Prison clothing re-issued, some looking new, we dressed the same as the Russian criminals we saw near the camp, but they were treated better. Very few of us had any wartime uniform left.

*

Back in the fields we discussed the latest rumours. They told us two years ago that we would be allowed to write home, but so far it hadn't happened. This rumour had begun again and we dared to hope it was true.

We didn't even know for sure if our families knew we were alive. The Red Cross may have informed them via the lists the

Russians kept, but until we received letters from home we had no confirmation.

And what of Germany? None of us knew anything other than a few major political events the Russians wanted us to know; otherwise they enjoyed keeping us ignorant. The camp commander, a colonel, gathered all four hundred of us outside on 9th May 1945 to inform us of Hitler's death and the end of war in Europe. Of course we didn't believe it, after all the rumours and so much propaganda flying around. But then sometime in the autumn, we were shown Russian newspapers with dreadful photographs of Berlin. The Americans had also dropped atomic bombs on Japan, so the whole thing really was over.

German officers from the League of Free Germany visited in 1945, showing us newsreels of Berlin in ruins, entirely occupied by the Russians. We wondered what the British and Americans could be doing, and heard yet more rumours they were about to fight the Russians using their atomic bombs, but of course this didn't happen.

Whenever we discussed these issues we always told one another how we came to be captured. We re-lived it again and again, wondering if things had only been different, we could have made it safely back to Germany. Gerhard and Hugo knew my story; I'd told them a dozen times how unlucky I'd been. Simple decisions made in haste without thinking can have catastrophic results.

Hermann was the same. "When my 109 was hit I should have turned around 180 degrees immediately, instead of making ridiculous assumptions," he said, looking down at his feet.

"It wasn't your fault," Hugo said. "You weren't to know they'd advanced that far, not in a single day."

"I shouldn't have been so bloody stupid."

"You weren't; it was just one of those things, an easy mistake," Hugo said.

We did this all the time: reassuring one another that our capture had been unavoidable. It made our existence a little more bearable.

My spade cut a beautiful slice of dry peat, filling me with pride. I tried my best to produce perfectly shaped blocks ready for burning in the winter, not because I loved the Russians and wanted to keep them warm, but it gave me a sense of satisfaction that I could produce something decent. Not only this, but the regular shapes were easier to stack in the cart.

"Yes, I remember you telling me," Hermann said, turning a huge fold of peat with one cut.

I stopped and leaned on my spade like an old man, the way I'd seen my father do so many times. "You ran, didn't you?" I asked, but Gerhard jumped in.

"He ran like a fucking hare, but they still caught him," he said, laughing.

I shrugged. "There's nowhere to run if you're thirty or forty kilometres behind the lines; you're bound to bump into a Russian, like I did. You could hide, I suppose, live off the land for a while."

"Not in the middle of fucking winter," Gerhard said. "I was captured near Wesenburg, trying to get to the coast, February '44, remember?"

Pausing briefly, he seemed about to resume a lengthy discussion but, after a deep intake of breath, he just said one word: "Bastards."

He swung his spade high into the air before hitting the peat, splitting a thick tranche that fell perfectly to one side.

"It shouldn't have happened," he added.

"Of course not," I said, bemused. "Not to any of us."

With accuracy borne of much experience I cut a huge slab into ten perfect sections, all identical. Nodding, with a tremendous surge of satisfaction, I took a step back to fully appreciate my achievement.

5

As we hauled the cart past the gate that afternoon I asked Vitaly about the latest rumours and he gave us the most wonderful news.

"It's true," he said. "You each have one postcard to send home." He winked, and I smiled back.

After unloading the cart in record time, we found our hut to be as studious as a college library, with everyone reverently holding their blank cards, thinking about what to write, many with pencils in hand. Some wept, wiping the tears from the precious paper.

My postcard lay on my bed space and I waited twenty minutes for a pencil. I wrote down my parents' address first, so I knew how much room I had left.

What could I say?

"Dear Mama and Papa, I am alive and well and missing you very much. I hope you are both well. Tell me everything about home and what you are doing."

I didn't know what else to say, adding, in surprisingly good handwriting, being the first time I'd written anything in four years, "Please write back as soon as possible," and I wrote the Forest Camp address in full.

"Do you think they'll actually send them?" I asked Hermann.

"They wouldn't give them to us if they weren't going to," he said as he walked around the hut, gathering them up. When they were all in he said to me, "Here, take them to your mate, Vitaly."

Excited chatter accompanied our turnip soup that afternoon, with morale higher than ever.

We counted the days to receive a reply. Four weeks or so for the postcards to reach Germany, and another four weeks for a reply, if they wrote back immediately, which we assumed they would. We therefore had eight weeks to wait. How exciting.

In the morning, drifting in and out of sleep as the first dawn light filled the hut, I dreamed of home: sitting in my father's favourite chair, smoking and laughing while telling him how awful Russian cigarettes were, as my mother busied herself in the kitchen. It had been years since I had felt so positive, and with new rumours of repatriation, hopefully our nightmare would soon be over.

"This is the last one. Get him. There he is, Goetz!" a familiar voice shouted in Russian. The doors to the hut had been thrown open and someone grabbed me by the shoulders and hauled me onto my feet, dragging me across the floor and out of the hut.

"What are you doing, who are you?" I protested.

There were three or four of them, maybe more, and I recognised the closest immediately. Vitaly.

In heavy rain they threw me into the mud, where they kicked me about the face and body.

As I pulled my arms over my head, Vitaly shouted, "Fascist pig!" as another added, "Looter, thief!"

Hauled to my feet again they carried me to a vehicle and threw me inside, where I landed on something cold and bony. The door was slammed shut and the engine started. The vehicle bounced around as I tried in vain to sit up.

"Give me your hand," someone said, in very well-spoken German.

I took it, pulling myself up onto the bench seat, to lean against the side, and looked around. With just two small windows in the doors I could barely see maybe a dozen figures crammed into the back of the van, one on the floor.

"What the hell is going on?" I said, realising my bottom lip had split, sending blood all over my face. My ribs ached and my right leg had caught the door on the way in and hurt like hell.

Someone laughed.

The well-spoken man spoke again. "Have you been interrogated recently?"

"I have, why?"

"And what was the sentence?"

"Ten years' hard labour."

"Same for me, so this is it. We are being transported to another camp."

I wept. I don't mind admitting it. Suddenly all hope had gone. I leaned on the wall of the van next to someone warm, and passed out.

It was almost dark when the van finally stopped; I'd fallen, my head resting on something hard. The man on the floor next to me was naked, cold, and dead, so I climbed back up onto the bench. He'd obviously been stripped of all his clothes by others in the van.

An entire day had passed. Someone had shit themselves and the vile smell dominated everything. Dysenteric shit smells far worse than any other. Perhaps it had been the dead man, now merely referred to as the corpse.

My stomach rumbled, but worse than this my mouth felt like sandpaper.

The doors finally opened and we were ordered out to stand in line. Two of them couldn't stay on their feet and were taken away with the corpse. Then we were dispersed. Someone grabbed me by the collar and hauled me fifty metres before throwing me onto a wooden floor. In the darkness, I tried to get up but passed out again.

A light flashed in my eyes. Could I be dreaming again? Faces appeared in a flickering light, like that from a candle. Perhaps I was dying? I heard voices, and then someone saying my name.

"It's Goetz, Paul Goetz; I'm sure it is."

Someone held the back of my head and I sensed liquid on my lips. So incredibly thirsty, I dreamed of someone giving me water. I drank as much as I could, and even though I knew it to be only a dream it tasted so very real.

The voice seemed closer, right next to my head.

"I know him from Schuren."

Another voice, vaguely familiar added, "If it is, I know him too."

After a pause another face filled my vision.

"Yes, it's him alright."

6

Prisoner of War Camp 7270/3

When I woke up daylight streamed through a filthy window. Above me the ceiling looked the same as the hut at Forest Camp, with huge rough-cut pine beams running all the way across. Had it not been for the pain in my ribs and left leg, I'd have assumed the last twenty-four hours had been a nightmare; that is, running parallel to the actual one. Even my nightmares were real.

"He's awake," someone said.

Footsteps and then vaguely familiar faces gathered around.

"Are you sure it's him?"

"Absolutely."

My eyes opened and yet, in my dream, I saw my first instructor on 109s, Sergeant Armin Scholl sitting in front of me, now old, with a bald head, staring. Beside him sat Klaus Hager, the glider instructor from Schuren, also an old man. I closed my eyes to dive back into the dream, but I was lifted by the shoulders and forced awake.

"Welcome to City Camp, Paul," Klaus said. "Hungry?"

I could only nod. My neck hurt.

A piece of bread with some sort of animal fat on it, and a tin mug of warm liquid gave me the impetus to sit up further, leaning against the wooden wall.

When I finished eating I stared in disbelief at Klaus and Armin. Klaus shook my hand. He was real, after all, though entirely different. Still as solid as a tree and possessed of a roguish masculinity, his once-thick arboreal arms were now more like brittle twigs. How they had recognised me, I had no idea, still being practically bald from the recent delousing.

"Christ, I'm glad to see you," I said, finishing the contents of my mug. "Where the hell am I?"

Armin shook my hand before standing up. No longer the athletic man I knew, like all of us, his clothes hung on his frame as though outfitted by an overly generous tailor. His fresh complexion had gone, replaced by the standard jaundiced yellow.

"I'd guess you were at Forest Camp, is that right?" he said, looking at me and then briefly out the window.

"Yes. I've just spent all of yesterday in a van. I can't remember anything," I groaned, taking a sip from the mug. What wonderful coffee, and so sweet.

"This is Camp 7270/3, City Camp, as it's more commonly known. It's the sister camp to the one you've just left. They bring all the bad boys here for interrogation," he said, "amongst other things."

"It's nearer to Borovichi; that's why they call it City Camp," Klaus said.

"I've heard of it," I said, struggling for breath in between coughing. "But I've never met anyone who's been here."

"No, you won't," Klaus said. "They don't ever move anyone

back to a camp they were at before, it's deliberate policy. They want to keep us isolated from the rest of the world."

"I've just been interrogated at Forest Camp," I said, coughing again, "sentenced to ten more years."

Klaus laughed as a whistle blew outside, followed by loud Russian shouting.

"It's time for work. Come on, we'll have to help you because you don't want to know what would happen if you can't work," Armin said. "Can you stand up?"

I had no idea, but I tried, and after a supreme effort I gained my feet.

"Right, we'll carry you as best we can, and if possible we'll put you in the cart, but you must walk for a while first, alright?"

I nodded. It all sounded familiar. We were peat-cutting. Someone put a coat on me and I walked with two others on each side, tightly wedged in the middle. Dragging a cart with a rope along with a crowd of others, we passed a gate. My legs had almost given out when we stopped and they lifted me into the cart, where I passed out.

When I came to, I saw they had built a wall around me in the huge cart on a wooden floor, with open sky above. I had to move every now and again to make way for more bricks until they had filled it, and I occupied a tiny space at the end while we trundled back to camp.

It seemed much further than ten kilometres, and I had to get out and walk the last part with the other twenty men. After a head count in Russian while passing through the gate, we had the usual soup and stale bread. I waited for Armin to finish before I could get my share; there were no spare eating utensils and my own were at Forest Camp.

The same thing happened the next day, but by the third day I felt strong enough to contribute. We weren't collecting peat, but bricks, from a factory, and we hauled them in an enormous cart more than twenty kilometres.

I asked why Klaus and Armin were there, being both instructors, not front-line pilots.

"I was at Siverskaya when it was finally overrun, in January '44," Klaus said. "We had barely half a dozen serviceable aeroplanes and I should have got out in one of them." He stopped, staring at the ground. "It didn't happen."

Discussions about the circumstances of capture were always like this: introspection, anger, regret, and then silence. Even after so much time.

"But I don't understand. Why were you there?" I asked.

Klaus shook his head. "When were you captured, Paul?"

"July '43," I replied.

"By the end of '43 front-line squadrons were running out of pilots. They cut the training programme as much as possible but then they decided we should be sent to the front, replaced with injured pilots. It didn't work very well, but what could they do?"

"I was captured near that shithole, Staraya Russa, in January '44," Armin added. "I took on a massive swarm of the bastards, mainly La-7s, on my own, which was not unusual actually. There must have been fifty of them. I got two before I had to bail out or burn."

One of the wheels of the cart squeaked badly, overheating, so there could be a problem on the return journey when we'd loaded it, unless we found some grease from one of the other wheels. We could usually find some hiding behind the hub flange that escaped the wind and rain. Sure enough, I found a smear and rammed it as best I could into the bearings. It would help, though not ideal. Like everyone, I'd become an expert on early twentieth-century Russian agricultural vehicles.

Once full, we dragged it back, and luckily the wheel stayed on, still squeaking but with more of a bass tone, the continuous noise being the nearest thing to music I'd heard in years, rising in a series of rapid crescendos then fading away as quickly, as though the composer was mad, or Russian.

Too exhausted to talk, we ate our turnip soup and wooden bread in silence.

With food in our stomachs the world returned to relative normality and conversation resumed. I told them about Anna. I wanted to talk about her because I wanted to see her, more than anything else in the world. They were unimpressed.

"I was married. I still am, I suppose. We have two children," Klaus said.

"So have I." Armin nodded. "I had a house two kilometres from fighter school. I often used to walk home to see them."

"We haven't heard anything since before the war ended. So please forgive us for not having much sympathy for your Russian tart," Klaus said, making me angry and offended.

"She was good, though, wasn't she?" Armin added, smiling.

"Are you saying you knew her?" I said, stunned.

"Anna, the tall woman in the woods? Of course," he said. "Come on, Paul. She serviced everyone at Siverskaya. Surely you knew that?"

His tone of voice, at first laden with sarcasm, changed to something more fatherly. "It wasn't supposed to happen and so obviously nobody talked about her."

"I'm surprised she wasn't constantly pregnant, with you lot on her all the time, poor woman," Klaus said, shaking his head.

"She nearly died when giving birth to her idiot son, and from then on…" Armin said.

"Who told you that?" I asked, interrupting.

Armin shrugged. "I'm sorry, I thought you knew," he said, with a vaguely sympathetic smile.

"When did you last see her?" I said, failing to disguise my concern.

"Christmas '43, and then a few days before we were overrun. A group of us went to see her for one last time, with some brandy, and…" He stopped. "She disappeared after that. I called at her little hovel just before I was captured, but it looked deserted. I mean, empty, unoccupied. All the clothes and things had gone."

"She wasn't there the last time I visited, in July '43," I said.

Armin shrugged. "Remember the old man? He was her father and the boy was her son," he said. "Her son always seemed to be in trouble, and her father had a temper too. The old man and that idiot son of hers would often get themselves arrested for one thing or another, usually because they were late for work or had been caught stealing. Typical Russians. She'd find out and come along to bail them out. I found it hilarious. Everyone at the airfield knew and trusted her, but nobody could actually admit it, if you know what I mean. Of course we did as she asked; we all needed her. She was gorgeous, wasn't she?"

He stopped for a moment. "We missed our wives."

I shook my head, and even after hearing all this I still missed her and wanted her. My opinion hadn't changed. I didn't care what Armin said.

"I met them a couple of times," I said, "the old man with the Panje pony and the boy. I almost shot them."

Armin laughed. "Yes, that's them. She was married too, did you know?"

"No, I didn't, but I suppose she must have been."

"Her husband was trapped in Leningrad before the siege. He knew we were advancing and likely to reach the city, but he still went there to visit his mother, apparently."

He paused, looking me in the eyes. "Would you leave a woman like Anna if you didn't have to? What a fucking idiot."

7

"There's going to be a hanging," someone shouted, bursting in the door.

"What, where?" the man opposite said.

"Barrack six has found their spy."

"How do you know?" Armin said.

"A Hungarian in a burial party told me, from that block," the man said, rushing over to the window.

"Anyone we know?" someone asked.

"It's the Russian. They've finally proved it."

Klaus grabbed my arm. "Come on, we're on shit parade."

He ran outside around the back to our latrines and prodded inside the pit with the clean end of a broom handle. He shouted for me to help so I joined him. The stirring of the shit had to be done regularly so it settled and to find out if we needed a new pit. The same thing happened at Forest Camp, and in winter it wasn't so bad, but we were almost in May.

The flies were as thick as bonfire smoke. Klaus frequently volunteered for latrine duty; he enjoyed wandering around camp with impunity, picking up news and meeting other prisoners.

We took our sticks to the rear of barrack six, watched by two Russians who couldn't have been less interested. They knew we were stirring the shit. As they turned away we climbed onto the wooden frame of the latrine, high enough to see in the window of the barrack. A hole in the glass had been stuffed with a cloth, so I pulled it out.

The Russian stood on a chair, hooded, with a rope around his neck, the other end lashed to the middle ceiling beam. I'd heard rumours they had a Russian amongst them, denying he was a spy, but now it seemed his luck had run out.

An officious man, wearing the usual prison clothing, but with the tattered remains of a German army officer's cap set at a perfect angle, stood next to him, reading from a scrap of paper.

Why should this man be treated like this? Unlikely to be a genuine Russian, perhaps he was an informer? It was common in the early days for someone to inform on others for extra bread or better treatment, but not now. Old scores had long since been settled.

"You are an enemy agent and a Bolshevik. Sentence is to be carried out immediately," the officer shouted.

"For God's sake, the war's been over for two years," I said. "If he really is a Russian and they kill him, you know what will happen to us, don't you?" I whispered.

"My thoughts exactly," Klaus replied. "They must be mad."

"So we have to stop them," I said.

Klaus said nothing, but I could see in his face that he was thinking deeply, like the time when we first met, walking towards the aeroplane, without saying a word, before subjecting me to thirty minutes of high-stress aerobatics.

Suddenly he jumped down and started running, and I followed. He kicked open the doors to the barrack, shouting. By the time I followed him inside, two Russian guards were behind me in the doorway. The chair had been kicked away and Klaus grabbed the man, as one of the guards fired a shot into the roof.

Pandemonium broke out as more Russians burst in, hastily fixing bayonets to their rifles, thinking they had a riot on their hands. Another shot rang out, and one grabbed me from behind, hauling me towards the door. Another struck Klaus with a rifle butt and also the man, still with the rope around his neck, and the last thing I saw was him being carried out the barrack.

*

I woke up, with others I couldn't see, in near total darkness, probably one of the punishment rooms, 'the dungeons', as we called them. I'd known Forest Camp had half a dozen, but so far I'd never had the pleasure. They obviously had the same at City Camp.

With no idea how long I'd already been there, my head hurt and I was extremely thirsty. Assuming I'd also been hit with a rifle, I fell back to sleep on the bare wooden floor.

Suddenly a door opened and daylight exposed the faces of my fellow inmates, about a dozen, crammed into a wood-panelled room with no windows, partially underground, that stank of body odour and faeces. Damp seeped in through the walls between the planks but at least we weren't cold.

A Russian came down the steps with a pot of soup and some bread in exchange for a full bucket of shit and piss. Some of it slopped over the rim onto his coat as he climbed the steps and he cursed loudly. I heard it being swilled away outside and he then threw it back into the dungeon, narrowly missing my head. Not completely empty, some of the contents splashed across my face.

I looked up and shouted, "Watch it!" in Russian.

Two of them stood in the doorway looking down.

"You make trouble in barrack six," one said.

I shook my head, shielding my eyes from the light. "No, I tried to stop a lynching," I protested, in my best Russian.

"You are a troublemaker. You will stay down there for one month."

The door slammed shut with a rattling of chains. Darkness returned.

So that was it, my punishment for saving a man's life.

Ironically I soon discovered we were better fed in the dungeon than in the general barrack. If there were five or six such dungeons they'd probably lost count how many of us there were, so they unwittingly gave us more.

We sang songs, told stories, talked of food, and I learned quickly that you could shit more easily in an empty bucket; a full one meant your arse and balls would sink into the mess because you couldn't see to judge it correctly.

Surprisingly, after protesting several times, they gave me my own bowl and metal spoon, which I kept.

One night, while we ate the soup, I asked the guards for another blanket and, to my surprise, they threw half a dozen down the steps. They were filthy and full of lice, but warm.

As the days and nights passed – we couldn't tell one from the other – I occupied my time by listening out for the daily routine outside: footsteps, shouting, vehicle movements, mostly the same every day. The whistles were blown at regular times: 0600 hours and again at 1800 hours, when work details left and returned, so at least I could keep track of the time, and I didn't have to work, always a bonus.

We had no washing facilities in the dungeon, and couldn't shave. It was too dark anyway. Living like a bat in a cave became claustrophobic, but at least we were warm and dry.

The smell must have been horrendous, though other people's were masked by my own stench.

I'd counted fourteen or fifteen days when we were all ordered out. Sucking in lungfuls of fresh night air, we were escorted back to our barracks and thrown inside the doorway, my bowl and spoon under my shirt.

"Welcome home," Armin said. I didn't know whether to laugh or cry.

*

In the morning I ate potato soup with my own bowl and spoon: such luxury. They never asked for them back. I considered it almost worth the fourteen or so days to get these.

No sign of Klaus.

Two weeks later, he returned fit and well, but caked in filth, as I no doubt had been.

A week after this a man appeared at our barrack room door as we were preparing for work. I didn't recognise him, but he knew me immediately. Like all of us he looked painfully thin and had clearly just been released from a dungeon.

"Goetz," he said, embracing me. It wasn't until he said, "Thank you," I realised I knew him, but still not his name.

"A moment later and you'd have been dead," Armin said.

"Yes, thank you," the man said.

He took a step back and nodded. When he peered over the top of his round glasses I was immediately taken back to Mga airfield, watching the butterflies caught in the camouflage netting while listening to Shostakovich.

"My God," I said out loud. "Hans Weber."

He nodded.

Tears ran down my cheeks as I wept like a child.

8

"Yes, I'm the Russian," Hans said, shaking his head as we hauled the empty cart across the endless plain.

Under the deep blue cloudless sky, the temperature already twenty degrees, we only had half a barrel of drinking water between us. It would be a long, hot, thirsty day.

Hans volunteered information, mitigation, perhaps, for why his accusers had turned on him.

"I knew one of the guards quite well before the war, a musician," he said. "He gave me a few things and we spoke frequently about music and Leningrad. I think some people were jealous. When the Russians raided our barrack and confiscated money and a bottle of vodka, they chose me as their scapegoat. Then when the Russians threw some colleagues into the dungeon, accusing them of plotting an escape, my own friends 'arrested' me. I've been here in this camp since '43; they know me. It's absurd."

I shook my head.

"But some of them are still fanatics, Paul; you know the sort, full of Nazi ideas even now. They'll never give up, will they? Besides, the Russians will take every opportunity to brutalise us; they don't need an excuse."

"Yes, I know." Too out of breath, I couldn't say much more.

The rope tightened, cutting into my shoulder, causing me to wince. We had no cushioning flesh on our bones, so dragging the cart was agony if done incorrectly.

But how wonderful to be with Hans again. I had so many questions.

"I last saw you in the dugout. You were about to leave."

He shrugged, allowing the rope to slacken, making it easier to talk.

"I was captured the same day you left in the Storch. A shell hit the dugout, most of it collapsing on top of me. I crawled out and the Russians thought I was a ghost. 'Miracle man,' they shouted. They were about to finish me off, until I told them in my best Russian, 'I am a good radio operator, I could be useful,' so they ordered me to interpret for them."

"Then what?"

"Our forces recaptured the airfield a few days later, so they moved me around, eventually sending me here. But I did work with them for a few weeks, operating their radios, and one of ours they'd captured. They gave me a Russian uniform because, dressed as a German someone shot at me twice, and a Russian even tried to slit my throat. So I arrived here dressed as one of them. That's when they started with the nickname, and it stuck. They used me as an interpreter for months after my arrival, until they drafted in those females."

"You were lucky, but unlucky too," I said, "same as me."

"So, Paul, tell me how they got you," Hans said, beginning work by turning over a huge fold of peat with one cut.

I stopped, leaning on my spade. "I was in a *Rachel*, you know, one of those enormous ditches, doing really well—"

Hans interrupted. "Why did you crash? Were you shot down?"

I shrugged. "No. My engine stopped."

He laughed, shaking his head. "What?"

"Yes, it started overheating and stopped."

Hans nodded. "I've heard of this so many times," he said, hitting the peat with a clean blow. "It happened to other things too, not just our aeroplanes but tanks as well."

"What did?" I said, bemused.

"Sabotage," he replied. "Think about it. We were using slave labourers, for Christ's sake. What did we expect?"

It had crossed my mind at Heiligenbeil, but I'd dismissed it. Now it made sense.

"So you turned right instead of left in that ditch of yours. Then what?" he said, chopping the peat into blocks.

"They were just standing there, six of them."

"So why didn't they shoot you?"

"They were going to, because, thanks to you I understood them, but then one said, 'Don't shoot him yet, we must get some information first.'"

Hans smiled.

"Another said, 'He's a fascist, I want to kill him and piss on him,' or something similar, the filthy bastard. The oldest had red piping and a brass star in his epaulettes, an officer. He looked at me and said, 'What you from?' in poor German. Just then another stepped forward and said, 'Get him to dig a hole and we'll put him in it,' but the officer stopped him.

"He then asked me the same question again, so very slowly, I pointed to my pilot's badge with my left hand. '*Pilot*,' I said, and then, '*Letchik-istrabitel*,' fighter pilot. The effect was astonishing. They all looked at one another.

"The officer spoke first. 'You speak Russian?' he said.

"'A little,' I answered. 'I crashed a few kilometres from here, before my mission, my engine stopped.'

"Still using my left hand, I slowly reached into my pocket and took out a pack of Reemtsma cigarettes and gave it to the officer. I then handed them a pack each, delighting them all. One lit up straight away.

"The officer ordered them to lower their guns. He took my P08 from my holster and we sat down together in the *Rachel*, smoking and talking like old friends. We spoke about our families and the one who had wanted to kill me and piss on me actually thanked me for the cigarettes. He asked for my pilot's badge, so I gave it to him. I found it odd; if they'd shot me straight away they would have had everything anyway."

"You were very lucky," Hans said. "Those cigarettes obviously saved your life."

"Maybe."

"And because you could speak Russian. It's not so easy to kill in cold blood if you get to know someone, even a little."

Hans resumed his work but paused, looking back. "Why the hell did you have so many cigarettes?"

With a long sigh I glanced westward for a moment before answering. "They were meant for someone very special, but I never got the chance to hand them over."

He thought my capture amusing, and at first I felt insulted, but then for some inexplicable reason I found it funny too, laughing more than I'd ever done in years.

*

For the next two months right through August we cut peat, filling the bigger carts in the same group as we'd carried the bricks, about twenty of us.

When I'd been at City Camp for over four months the first mail arrived for POWs. Nothing for me, but I hoped my parents had received my letter and there'd soon be a reply. I remembered I'd given my address as Forest Camp, but surely the Russians kept records and would send any mail on?

Of the hundred or so in our barrack only nine received anything, and they entertained us all with their tales from home, wherever that might be. Those who didn't mind sharing their letters read them aloud in a communal story time-cum-news bulletin.

The most shocking fact we learned was that people back home had known all along that we were here; thanks to the Red Cross we hadn't been forgotten.

"Germany has been divided into two, with the Russians controlling the east, and the Americans, British, and French in the west," a sergeant from Dusseldorf read, as we all listened, spellbound. "The West German capital is Bonn, not Berlin," he said. "Berlin has been divided up between the Allied powers."

This news received groans and general shaking of heads.

"At least Germany still exists," someone said.

"What a mess," Klaus added.

"The British and French never intended to invade Germany in 1940, neither did the Poles or the Russians, or anyone else. The Nazis lied to us," the Dusseldorfer said.

"Who told you that?" Klaus asked, more than a little angry.

"It's in my letter. It's what everyone is told."

"And you believe it?"

"Why would I not?"

"The victors always write history," someone added.

"So who do we believe?" I asked, to blank faces.

"What is the truth anyway?" The Dusseldorfer shrugged.

After a few moments' contemplative silence someone behind us dared to ask the obvious question.

"What has it all been for?"

We turned to see a diminutive man sitting cross-legged, shaking his head. He slept at the back of our barrack, but I didn't know him well.

"We came here in '41 to destroy Bolshevism, and now they occupy half of Germany."

9

"There's some international concern about us," a Berliner said, breaking the despondency, with ten men leaning over his shoulder trying to catch a glimpse of his letter.

"I know about it. It's the Moscow Agreement," a major said, his letter in both hands. "Signed earlier this year, so my sister says."

We sat around, hanging on every word as though God himself was speaking.

"The governments of West Germany, Italy, Hungary, and Spain have been campaigning for our release. Even the British and Americans have been asking," the major said, raising a few eyebrows, with mutterings of astonishment. "My wife says the agreement compels Russia to release us all by the end of 1949."

Unable to continue, the major's eyes filled up.

The man next to me, a big fellow, who no doubt would have been well-built if he'd been fed properly, began sobbing.

The toll of captivity was self-evident as the hardship lines in his face filled with tears from blackened eyes.

This set me off too, and almost everyone present. Could it really be true?

We dared to believe it for a few days but heard nothing more. Our captors said nothing either. With no good news or confirmation, gradually the hope dwindled, snuffed out yet again.

In early September we dug up the last potatoes. Endless fields filled with row after row that my friends had planted months before. Some ate them raw, paying the price with violent stomachache and sickness. Always tempting, because the food hadn't improved, frustrated to see it all going elsewhere, but I resisted.

The long working days in the summer often matched the daylight hours, exhausting us, but now the light faded earlier.

One afternoon in October, as we hauled the last of the potatoes into camp, a huge crowd of new arrivals stood at the gate. There must have been a hundred or more, all on foot, looking half-dead.

"Siberian convicts," Armin said. "Look how they treat their own people, it's disgraceful."

"They are not Siberian," someone said. "I've seen men like this before, at my last camp in the south."

"Who are they then?" Armin demanded.

"Japanese."

The newcomers were pushed and beaten towards a barrack that had been empty for a while, but we were shocked at how they conducted themselves; when a Russian shouted at them to move faster, the Japanese themselves beat their own men. Their officers enforced brutal discipline, much to the amusement of the Russians and to our bewilderment. It was the first time I'd seen any of our former allies at close hand. Some members of our air force had visited Japan during the war, but I didn't know anyone who had met them personally.

As the autumn winds began biting, the usual inexplicable sickness ran through us as it frequently had at Forest Camp; we each took it in turns to spend a few days in the infirmary. Our condition had no treatment, not being a disease of any sort; sheer exhaustion caused it, the cure simply a few days' rest. Every morning we would be assessed, and if deemed fit for work, the Russian would shout, "Okay," or, "Not okay."

In the first week of November as the bitter cold returned, we had six deaths in camp, one in our barrack. This was a lower number than usual, but we'd just had a long hot summer, and the worst was yet to come. Dozens usually perished every month in winter.

Rudolf Strackhof, a Konigsberger infantryman, in his mid-forties and captured when the city fell, had constant dysentery, continually losing weight, until one morning he didn't get up.

Four of us from our barrack were on burial duty, and because all six had died within a few days, we put them in one hole, with Strackhof on top. Being minus ten and the ground as hard as concrete, we couldn't dig very deep. As we covered the grave, one of the party, a religious man, said a few words and we stopped shovelling for a moment. He nodded, picked up his spade, and we finished the job.

Such graves were all around the camp and, as at Forest Camp, the piles of disturbed earth became harder to avoid. We couldn't match up the names with the plots, there were so many.

One afternoon, someone spotted a dog gnawing at Strackhof's arm, eventually ripping it off and running away with it. From then on, the burial parties stopped and the Russians took the dead away in a horse-drawn cart.

We always found a positive, though; we usually divided up a man's possessions before the Russians got a chance, and I nabbed Strackhof's boots. Only thin canvas, they were still better than the ones I had, because Strackhof had spent so much time in the infirmary. In all, ten of us benefitted from his death.

10

The first heavy snow would always be the worst, despite knowing it would soon be coming. Even in minus twenty, we had to work as usual.

Wearing all the extra clothing we slept on as bedding during the summer, we now wore all of it, but of course, it was never enough.

The intense cold made peat-cutting impossible, so we hauled bricks from the factory.

In December they replaced the cart with a huge sledge, which we dragged like a herd of pack animals, draining every bit of energy we had and further accelerating our weight loss.

We worked harder than in the summer; you couldn't stand still even for a few minutes because the wind would take a hold of your entire being and freeze you to the bone. We covered our faces with cloth, otherwise the snot in our noses froze solid and even the moisture in our eyes would freeze our eyelids shut.

Dark most of the time, we worked in a twilight world seen through gaps in thin slits of filthy material. We hauled bricks from the dimly lit factory all the way to camp, feeling our way like a procession of the half-dead blind. We'd pick up any item of clothing from anywhere, in whatever condition, just to be a little less cold, and so the inevitable always happened: lice multiplied.

Christmas 1947 was close to minus fifty degrees. Even the Russians understood the futility of trying to work, so they allowed us to stay in the barracks for a few days. What sheer luxury, because they even gave us wood for our fire. I suspect they didn't relish standing out there in the blizzards either.

On Christmas Day we lit candles, carefully saved for months, placing them alongside photographs of our families. We gathered around to sing carols, the flickering light making us look like pasty grey spectres.

Early in January 1948 I contracted dysentery again and spent a few days in the infirmary. I recovered well and just before I left, a nurse visited us in our beds early one morning shouting, "*Vactsina!*", telling us to roll up one sleeve. I knew what she meant, but not the reason, guessing it could have been a vaccine against typhus or cholera. This was all a bit late considering so many of our colleagues had already died of these things, and of dysentery, and starvation, and cold. I wondered if they were trying to prove something, perhaps telling the Red Cross, and therefore the rest of the world, they really were looking after us. The fact they used the same needle on probably six hundred men didn't seem important to them.

"They are going to interrogate everyone again," Klaus said on my return to the barrack.

"How do you know?" I asked, consumed by a new despondency.

"Look," he said, pointing out the window.

Two black ZIS-110 limousines, the usual means of transport for Red Army officials, had pulled up. Several army officers, each carrying the ubiquitous brown leather bag, stepped out and walked towards the garrison barrack. The smooth glossy sheen of the vehicle's paintwork contrasted sharply with the roughly piled snow beside them.

"They might not do all of us, and probably not here," Klaus said. "Sand Camp's not far away, so be prepared for another move."

This thought almost broke my heart.

Two more days passed without work but then we woke to a calm morning and the blowing of whistles. More than a metre of snow had fallen and we were ordered to clear it from the limousines and pathways throughout the camp. After that, as we prepared the sledge, Klaus and twenty others received orders to remain behind.

The rest of us left for work, heading out across the virgin snow, a few men short, as the first signs of dawn stabbed at the milky-white horizon. Probably minus twenty degrees, with no wind, a dry atmosphere pervaded, with the promise of sunshine, so provided we kept moving we'd be alright. Days like these were survivable. Strong winds would cut through our rags and bite the nose off the face. We could always tell a Stalingrader because most were missing the end of their nose, and when the hut creaked in the wind like an old ship in a rough sea before leaving for work, we knew the burial parties would be busy.

When we found our drinking water barrel frozen solid, I reached down and gathered a handful of snow. I was about to eat it when a Stalingrader pushed my hand, knocking it away.

"Don't," he said.

"I've done it before, last winter, and the one before that," I said indignantly.

He stopped, staring deep into my eyes. His were a dull grey, partially closed to keep out the cold, as though peering into the distance.

"And did you get sick?"

I'd been inexplicably ill the last time, so I nodded.

"I watched so many die from that. They gave us nothing to drink, so we ate snow. We all did at first. Then they died. But many continued. They knew it would kill them, but they did it anyway. Thirst does that."

He shrugged, sounding breathless with a terrible rasping cough like a very old man, even though he probably wasn't even thirty. "They died quicker. Maybe that's what they wanted; who knows?"

My gloves were wearing thin due to the edges of the bricks catching on the material, and I made a mental note to look out for another pair. Looking around I wondered if anyone near me might die soon. Perhaps it could be the Stalingrader? It sounds heartless, but that's how it was.

Without prompting, the coughing man continued.

"They force-marched us for weeks throughout February '43, backwards and forwards, going nowhere. We stood in the open every night, sleeping whenever we could, standing in a huddle, hundreds of us, like sheep. We woke one another up every hour, because if you were left alone you'd die. If you sat down you'd die. Some wanted to, of course. If you had nothing on your head, or if you ate snow, or if you were always standing in the wind, you'd die. In the morning the dead lay all around us. We sheltered behind them and took their clothing. So you don't eat snow, okay?"

He looked at me with complete emotional detachment as though he'd been explaining the rules of a card game.

"I don't understand," I said, genuinely intrigued. "We are a labour force; why did they not keep everyone alive to work, and why don't they look after us properly now?"

Facing me again, after loading two bricks into the sledge, his face covering slipped, flapping around on the side of his head like an unravelled bandage, stained and filthy. In amongst the patchy grey stubble, the skin on his face hung like distressed leather on the elbows of an old flying jacket, the end of his nose black, and his eyes sunk deep inside jaundiced sockets.

"Atonement," he murmured, before moving away.

We all got like that sometimes, with bad days when we just didn't want to talk about anything.

Stacking bricks, our minds wandered. One brick is much like another, but occasionally there'd be a particularly nice one that stood out above the rest: naturally smooth and shiny, perfectly formed. When I found one of these I wanted to smash it, and sometimes I did, overcome with rage. Why should one of them look better than all the others? How dare it? Too nice, too prosperous, too different, so it had to be destroyed.

*

Klaus and the others were interrogated, returning to us immediately afterwards as another twenty were called.

"They found out I'd been in Russia before the war, learning to fly at Lipetsk," Klaus said. "They wouldn't let it go. They were different this time, though, shouting, hitting me across the face more than usual."

When they called my name I followed, relieved. At least they weren't dragging me away somewhere else in the middle of the night.

In the dismal interrogation room, one male officer and a female interpreter sat opposite.

11

As soon as I sat down I volunteered my knowledge of Russian, thinking it might speed things up. Silence followed, and then a staring competition, during which no-one said a word for several minutes.

I broke the spell by turning my head towards the door.

"You are Paul Goetz, air force sergeant?" he asked, in Russian.

I nodded, facing him.

He looked about thirty, a lieutenant, with short black hair and a neatly trimmed moustache. To me he had an athletic build, maybe because everyone else looked so thin. Smart and business-like in his Red Army uniform, he spoke in an articulate manner, addressing the woman formally as 'comrade interpreter'. She was lovely: slim and blonde, German-looking, with a wonderful smile.

"You were at Krasnogvardeisk?" he said.

"Yes."
"When did you arrive?"
"December '41."
"September '41," he said.
"No, *December*."

He paused, writing something down. "You know the village, at Krasnogvardeisk?"

"Of course."
"You were there."
"No. I've seen it. I know where it is."
"You've been there."
"No."
"You took people from the village?"
"No."
"You had colleagues who took people from the village?"

I knew where this was going. I shook my head.

"You were an accomplice."
"To what?"
"The killing of villagers."
"No."
"You were stationed there."
"I didn't arrive until December."
"You know about the killings?"
"I didn't arrive until December."
"You killed Jews?"
"No."
"Women and children?"
"No."
"You killed partisans?"
"No."
"You are guilty."
"No."
"You are German, so you are guilty."

I hesitated. He noticed. This man seemed different. I could see him looking for signs, searching my face. He didn't write anything down but stared intently at me across the table. He watched my hands too, because unknown to me I'd started wringing them together, and had started fidgeting.

For what it was worth I replied, "No."

"You were an accomplice."

"To what?"

"You were an accomplice in the Krasnogvardeisk massacre, October 1941."

"No."

"You can prove you were not there?"

I hesitated again. He knew I couldn't. How could I?

"If I had my pay book I could prove when I arrived in Russia."

Some of my countrymen still had theirs, but mine had long since disappeared.

"You destroyed Gatchina Palace?"

What did he mean? It was fine when I left it.

"What? No. I was captured in '43, what happened after that—"

"You are arsonist?"

"No."

"You were stationed there and you cannot prove you didn't take part in killings or burning the palace. You are an accomplice to war crimes. You are a war criminal."

He nodded to the woman. She had been writing in a notepad the whole time.

"Sign it," she said.

"I won't sign this," I said, bracing myself.

"You are refusing to cooperate?" he said, with a scowl.

I folded my arms indignantly, saying nothing. To my surprise he didn't seem particularly bothered. He signed the notebook, told her to countersign it, and then placed his brown leather bag on the table, unfastened the buckles, and carefully put the notepad inside. He stood up and banged his first on the door. One of our guards appeared.

"Take him back; we have finished with this one."

I stood up, perhaps looking somewhat bemused, and he paused in the doorway and looked at me, speaking in perfect German.

"You will never be released."

12

The Japanese left in March 1948. We had no idea where they went. They shuffled away one night into the fog like a herd of lost sheep with their officers barking in their ears, beating them with sticks. Still awaiting sentencing for war crimes I hadn't committed, I didn't care what happened to them. Despite reassurances from my friends, once again I found myself descending into a dark pit of despair.

"The palace at Gatchina was destroyed by our forces when they left in January '44," Klaus said. "I thought you knew? 'Scorched earth', Hitler called it. Deny the enemy shelter, so they destroyed it all in the retreat, everything."

I understood the reasons. In war, you don't give anything back to the enemy that he can use; the Russians did the same to us. But I thought of the grandeur of the palace, and then of Anna and her cabin.

"To them we are all guilty by association," Klaus explained

as we shared a two-centimetre Russian Papirossa cigarette butt casually dropped by one of the guards. "It's as though it was you who pulled the trigger every time, as though it was all of us, irrespective of where we were."

We hauled the cart again, and I noticed it had a new wheel, because the dreadful music had stopped. This time it had been filled before we left, and would be empty on the way back; we were planting seed potatoes.

Even though they knew the risks, some men still ate them and were ill almost immediately. These men were a great incentive to refrain from this stupidity.

The soil had thawed and we used the same peat-cutting spades to dig the potato furrows.

"I knew about the Krasnogvardeisk Action," I said to Klaus.

"They probably knew that; they just wanted you to know."

"You mean they wanted me to know that they knew that I knew, but they didn't want to tell me they knew that I knew?"

Klaus laughed.

I laughed also. "I didn't take any part in it; I was told about it."

"Who told you? Stalin?"

We laughed again, but then Klaus became serious.

"Of course, so what?" he said, dragging a sack of potatoes behind him. He was now an expert farmer, having done this four years running. "They don't care, really, do they? Revenge has nothing to do with justice. Besides, hundreds, perhaps thousands of those Actions were performed, all across Russia, and in Ukraine. The SS were proud of them and quite a few ordinary soldiers too."

The look I gave him demanded further explanation, so he continued.

"You shouldn't worry about the politics of it, Paul. Even if you were involved, and you say you weren't, we were professional soldiers doing our jobs, my friend. We have nothing to reproach ourselves for. You certainly don't."

*

More rumours of mass repatriations circulated, but as usual nothing happened. If sentenced again to many more years I really would never leave, and it worried me. I thought of the graffiti on the palace wall.

In April we were back to peat-cutting, returning to an old familiar job, and the fact I was good at it didn't make it any more enjoyable. As I laboured with my spade, I wondered about my friends, not just at Forest Camp but the ones I'd known in JG54. I constantly asked for news about my old squadron and sometimes bumped into late prisoners, as we called them, like Oskar Weiss, captured at the end of the war, or just after. We didn't get many because most had flown west, but I was desperate for news.

Oskar had been a fighter pilot, captured early in 1945, flying the Fw190 D, the Dora, as it was known.

"We were shooting down hundreds," he told me, "thousands." He looked up as the clouds rolled by.

"So were we, here in Russia."

"The American heavy bombers were a nightmare, Paul, you should have seen them. We fired everything at them by the end, including rockets, and even dropped bombs on the bastards. I spoke to an American B17 pilot once. Do you know they had a limited tour of duty? Fifty missions or something like that."

"Don't tell me they'd then go home?" I asked, sarcastically.

"Pretty much, yes. Astonishing, isn't it? The British had similar, two hundred combat hours, so I heard."

"Different to us," I said, "we'd carry on fighting until dead or captured, or both."

He grinned. "Yes, quite," he said, pausing for a moment as he helped lift a huge slab of peat. "Did you hear about Nowotny?"

"No," I replied. "Is he coming here?"

"He would have wished he could," he said with a smile. "He was killed in his 262, in '44."

I'd only heard about the Messerschmitt 262, and never seen one, like the Dora, but this was a revolutionary jet-engined fighter.

"He'd been leading a new squadron of these fantastic aeroplanes at the time."

"What happened? Was he shot down?"

"No. They think he had a catastrophic engine failure when landing."

I immediately thought of what Hans had said about sabotage. It seemed he'd been right; another rumour come true.

"You knew von Bonin too, didn't you?" Oskar said, pausing for breath.

"Yes, he was my CO in France—" I said as he shook his head, interrupting.

"He was killed in action, in late '43, in Belarus."

I wanted to ask if he knew the circumstances, but I stopped. I'd have liked to hear about some others, but suddenly I didn't want to know. Happier in my ignorance, I imagined all my friends had survived the war, perhaps now married, raising a family in a prosperous new Germany. Of course I knew this would be unlikely, but I needed it, so I held on to it tightly, like a man clinging to a life raft in a choppy sea.

The black ZIS-110 limousines returned in June. We heard rumours that no further interrogations would take place, but we were each to be spoken to in turn and given our fate.

A smart, highly decorated Red Army colonel, conducting himself in a very calm manner, ordered me into the interrogation room, confirming my identity before reading a page of red Russian type.

"Under Paragraph 17 of the Russian Penal Code it has been proven that in 1941 at Krasnogvardeisk in Leningrad Oblast you were an accomplice to, or had knowledge of, or had been in the area of a war crime. You are therefore sentenced from this date to twenty-five years' hard labour."

I spotted my original questionnaire amongst the papers, now looking tatty around the edges, and everything relating to me had 140493 stamped on it: my prison number. He looked at his watch and wrote something down. To my surprise, he asked me to sign it, which I did, handing me a copy before being ordered back to my barrack. I couldn't be bothered to protest anymore; the malaise had taken over.

The ludicrous charge seemed so broad; it could have caught anyone alive in the entire war that happened to have passed near Gatchina. At least it had already started, and had not been added on to my other ten years for looting, which seemed to have been mysteriously forgotten.

The sentence came as no great surprise, and for this reason, I wasn't as upset as I thought I'd be. If still alive, I would be released in 1973. What a different world it would be.

13

THE BARRACK ONCE OCCUPIED BY THE JAPANESE remained empty until one night in July 1948, when a column of ghosts arrived amid odd shouting and crashing about. It must have been around 0300 hours and the sun, already climbing above the trees, cast long red shadows as the crowd trudged around outside kicking up the dust.

Those of us who could be bothered stood at the windows to watch, close enough to hear them speaking and, yet again, surprised, but only in a kind of apathetic, disinterested way.

"Spaniards," Klaus said. "Poor bastards," he added, before returning to his bed. At least that's what we suspected, mainly because we knew the shouting wasn't Rumanian or Italian, and certainly not Japanese.

In the morning this was confirmed when some of them were put to work with us. Hardly any could speak decent German and little Russian, but luckily, some of our group spoke good Spanish from their time in the Condor Legion, so we extracted every bit of news we could of the outside world.

To our astonishment they told us Franco was still in power. He'd allowed thousands of Spaniards to fight with us in their Blue Division, but so far, he had escaped a similar fate to Hitler. Never short of questions, we found them interesting.

They knew things we didn't, and vice-versa, but most interestingly, dates had been set for repatriations to begin: 31st December 1948, for a twelve-month period until 31st December 1949, when all POWs should have been released, with the all-important caveat: unless the prisoner had been found guilty of war crimes. I couldn't understand this because everyone I spoke to had been sentenced in a similar way to me, meaning no-one would be released. For this reason none of us believed these new rumours.

Autumn passed and winter returned like a recurring nightmare, plunging us into everlasting freezing darkness once more.

Peter Semder, a tall, really nice Bavarian, dropped a brick on his hand and it soon became discoloured and septic. All of us had cuts, bruises, and grazes, but this was particularly bad. We asked for medication and they gave him some powder to mix in his soup, but a few days before Christmas he died. He had bequeathed his spare shirt to me. I drank a toast to him with my soup the first time I wore it.

Peter's closest friend in the camp was a man by the name of Kohler, from the Rhineland. Despite living in our barrack, I didn't know his rank or his first name, or even which branch of the armed forces he'd served in; we no longer cared. Everyone noticed him withdrawing into himself and he stopped talking. We knew what this meant; we'd seen it so many times. One evening, after the soup, we found him in his bed space, curled up like a baby. He'd missed the meal and someone said he'd stopped eating altogether. He looked dead.

Without warning, Klaus ran over and, with what must have been an enormous effort, hauled him to his feet, pushing him hard against the wall. Kohler screamed something in Russian, perhaps fearful of being arrested or destined for a beating until he saw his assailant.

"What are you doing?" he shouted.

Klaus slapped his face, not hard but enough to gain his total attention. "You won't!" he shouted. "You fucking won't, not now, you just fucking won't, you bastard, do you hear me?"

"What?" Kohler protested, genuinely confused.

Klaus hit him again and when I tried to intervene, Armin grabbed my shirt, pulling me back, shaking his head. Pinned firmly against the barrack wall with both of Klaus's hands gathering up his shirt at the neck, their faces were just a few centimetres apart, as though about to kiss.

"You won't fucking give up now, do you understand? Semder wouldn't want you to die, would he? You've come this far, you won't give up now! I'm fucking telling you, I'm ordering you, is that clear?"

Kohler nodded wildly. "Yes, yes, of course, sorry, yes, sorry," he cried.

"Stand up!" Klaus shouted, letting him go.

Kohler stood rigidly to attention, arms by his side, shaking violently, tears pouring down his face. "I'm sorry," he murmured, sobbing.

"Get hold of yourself. You'll be released soon; you don't want to be buried out here in this shit, do you?"

"No, I'm sorry, you're right, sorry."

Kohler wiped his face with a sleeve and shook his head, taking deep breaths as though waking from a dream, or a nightmare.

He looked down at the floor and across at me. I didn't know him at all, but he smiled and nodded, as though acknowledging a truth, accepting the admonishment. From that moment he was back with us, alongside the living. I'd never seen anything like it.

*

Early one morning Klaus left the barrack in a hurry. He did this a lot at that time every day, and I wondered why, so I followed.

He disappeared inside the latrine shed at the rear of barrack three and, ten minutes later, emerged with the same man I'd seen him with before from that same barrack. No longer naïve but curious, I slipped away without either of them seeing me.

Later on I found him alone near the cart.

"I saw you, earlier," I said.

He knew.

"I'm not judging you, Klaus."

"What are they going to do, Paul, court-martial me, throw me out the air force?"

"As I said, I'm not judging."

"We're all going to die in this hell-hole. I need some pleasure. I want at least something before I go. You know I'm not alone, don't you? What else do we have?"

"I know."

"It's not just the sex. It's the contact with another human being. You miss your Russian tart, don't you?"

I nodded. "How they can expect us to live without women."

"Paul, for God's sake, I never cared for them anyway, not really."

"But you said you have a wife, and children?"

He smiled. "Paul, you're such a lovely man. How you can be so deep into hell and remain like this, I've no idea, but don't you dare change. If you want my advice, get whatever you can, from whoever you can, whenever you can."

Taking hold of my head firmly with both hands he kissed my filthy, sweaty forehead, before walking away.

My first kiss in five years.

14

We trudged through the darkness of January 1949, wishing at every moment our pitiful lives would accelerate towards spring, as the intense cold never stopped biting chunks from us. February brought the same misery, but with the welcome signs of lengthening days, even though the cold persisted, claiming too many comrades. Our captors still took away the dead in the back of a cart, perhaps because of the Red Cross, who seemed to be visiting more frequently, and not only because the camp had run out of burial space.

No-one discussed repatriation anymore, since the December deadline passed when it should have begun. We merely existed in our darkness, working and sleeping, with absolutely nothing in between.

When spring finally arrived, we rejoiced and, as usual, the death rate began to slow. June was unusually wet, but the land dried quickly when the rain stopped.

In the summer of 1949 we saw more aeroplanes than usual. Most flew far overhead, but we always watched, with wistful glimpses into our aviator past. Aeroplanes crossed the sky faster than ever as more jets appeared, and in July we had an unforgettable close encounter with the new Red Air Force.

The first sign came when I heard Klaus shouting, "What the hell is that?"

It skimmed the horizon, getting closer, heading our way, as we all watched. Leaning on our spades, the small silver jet circled around as the engine coughed and black smoke belched from the rear. None of us had any idea what we were looking at, but we knew it was in trouble. Sure enough, the undercarriage lowered and the pilot lined up his astonishing machine on our cart track, probably thinking it was a decent road. He did well for the first hundred metres, but then the main wheels caught a rut and broke away, causing it to slide along in what some of us knew would be a terrifying experience. The engine screamed, then a loud bang.

He came to rest fifty metres from us, remarkably intact, and we ran over to investigate. The canopy opened and a young boy stared at us from the pilot's seat, obviously in a state of shock.

Geibel, a former SS officer, hauled him from the cockpit, fixing his huge bony hands around the pilot's throat, choking him.

"What the fuck are you doing?" I shouted.

"Killing the commie bastard," Geibel replied.

Klaus thumped Geibel in the face, knocking him away. "You fucking lunatic! The war's been over for nearly five years. He's nothing more than a child! Are you totally fucking insane?"

The boy struggled to his feet, terrified.

"It's alright, don't worry, you'll be okay," I shouted in Russian.

Trembling with fear, he moved over to me, one of his protectors.

"Where are you from?" I asked, glancing at his machine.

The gaping air intake forming the entire nose of the swept-wing single-seat aeroplane had taken some knocks after the front wheel collapsed, and various chunks of mud and stone had obviously been ingested into the engine.

"53rd Fighter Aviation Regiment, comrade," he replied, probably believing me to be Russian.

"Where is that?" I asked.

"Siverskaya."

I couldn't resist the next question. "And what is this fantastic aeroplane?"

"They will kill me. It's new, only this week, and I crashed it."

I smiled. "Don't worry, if it's an engine failure it's not your fault."

He shook his head. Looking ten years of age he must have been at least seventeen.

I repeated my question. "What is it?"

"It's a Mig-15."

Luckily we saw no fire, and as I moved for a closer look our guards arrived.

"Get back!" they shouted at me, and then, "Move away from them, comrade," at the bemused pilot. "They are Nazi prisoners!"

The boy took several steps backwards, a look of horror on his young face.

"Back to work, all of you!" they shouted.

The boy stood with our guards until a lorry arrived an hour later. Two men examined the Mig before taking the boy away.

The aeroplane remained for two days, as a brief,

tenuous glimpse at the outside world, before being partially disassembled, loaded onto a lorry, and removed.

*

"They are going to pay us," Armin said, settling on the bench with his breakfast soup. The early morning sun filled the dining hut, already pleasantly warm. It would be another hot July day in the fields.

I laughed. "What with, potatoes?"

"No, seriously."

I ignored him.

"I heard it too," Hans said, "in roubles, actual money."

"Roubles aren't real money," Klaus said, laughing.

"I heard we are each going to be paid five roubles a month," Hans added, taking care to eat his soup with slow deliberation, because it would be twelve hours until we had more. "Not only that, but they will allow us to buy things too."

"Like what?" Klaus said. "A train ticket to Germany?"

Everyone in earshot laughed. It seemed unlikely, and if it sounded too good to be true it usually was. We dismissed this rumour quicker than most others, even though secretly, of course, we hoped it to be true.

We'd finished off our drinking water by midday as the temperature must have reached forty degrees. A few pools of bog water remained in the deeper areas, but despite my thirst, I resisted. I'd rather live with a pounding headache from dehydration than spend a week with dysentery again. We had the problem that, as the months and years rolled by, we began overtaking the areas in which we'd once used to relieve ourselves. So we ventured a little further in order to preserve our dignity, those of us who had any left, and to find water clean enough to drink.

A few days later, our water barrel empty and thirsty as hell, with the tacit approval of our guards, I clambered over the next rise into another *Rachel*, similar to the one in which I'd been captured all those years before. Jumping in without really looking, I lost my balance, rolling down the dusty black earth, coming to rest in a heap of wretchedness.

The number of my comrades who had died during the last winter now became immediately evident.

The vile nature of our captors was plain to see as the skeletal remains of Peter Semder and so many others lay in the open air. Stripped of their boots and outer clothing, rags still clung to their bones in places.

Instinctively scrambling out, I stood at the top, looking around. My friends were cutting peat a hundred metres away near the cart, oblivious. Tears ran down my face, not for Peter, a man I hardly knew, or for any of the others, but much more selfishly than that. Release from this hell would never happen, so I too would end my days here, stripped naked and dumped like trash in a Russian peat bog.

15

The tears dried quickly in the warm breeze. Returning to work, I covered my head from the sun as best I could with strips of rag so it wouldn't become like the skin on Klaus's head: cracked and burned like brown bread in an oven. I hadn't seen a mirror in years, so it could already be close.

We worked noticeably slower, but it didn't seem to bother our two Ukrainian guards whom we'd nicknamed Hermann and Josef, after Goering and Goebbels. One was easily as fat as Goering, while the other, a little man, ran around after Hermann as though his servant. They left us alone while they sat together in the sun, alternately smoking and sleeping. We could easily have crept up and beaten them to death. But then where would we go?

Mini-tornadoes erupted across the vast plain hurling great clouds of choking dust high into the air. We stacked more dry peat into the cart a metre higher than normal, for much less weight. If we'd been on piecework we'd have made a fortune. They promised us extra bread for a bigger load, and we always hoped they'd keep their word, when very often they didn't.

In the summer we washed our clothes and bodies easily and more often from barrels of water around the camp and sometimes with the greatest rarity, soap. In winter we rarely shaved, barely washed our hands and faces, and never anything else, for weeks at a time.

To our surprise, more delousing vans appeared and we queued patiently, standing naked in the sun, after shaving totally yet again. Our pale, emaciated bodies soaked up the sunshine, instinctively turning towards it like houseplants.

A month after the first rumour about pay began circulating, to our utter astonishment, it came true. Five roubles for each man and, to huge excitement, a list circulated containing things we could buy. It all seemed so unbelievable. I ordered an item I'd not seen since my capture, and something no-one had. When they saw my purchase at the end of September, during the potato harvest, I had to guard it with my life. I would need another two months of saving to buy toothpaste, but even without it, the first time I brushed my teeth in over five years seemed surreal, and I felt cleaner and more civilised immediately. I'd been dogged by toothache most of the time so it could be too late for some of my teeth, but this crude Russian toothbrush was another step towards a return to civilisation.

Fifty roubles bought a bottle of vodka, not a rare clandestine supply after bribing the guards with watches or wedding rings, but openly and legitimately. We all decided we would club together and save for Christmas.

More soap appeared, and we no longer had to shave using blunt razors left over from delousing. We had mirrors too, and I didn't recognise myself, astonished at how anyone else had recognised me.

In November two more delousing vans appeared on a particularly cold day, so we welcomed the hot water and steam. We wondered why they'd put us through it again until, to our amazement, we were issued new prison clothing, including warm hats and new footcloths.

"Better than socks," Klaus said, expertly unrolling one across his right foot. No-one had any socks left and I remembered the first time I saw them when Anna had wrapped them so beautifully.

My own footcloths were nothing more than a few thin strips of tatty cotton, so the new ones were absolute luxury.

Christmas 1949 was my best in years. We saved bread and extra soup, made sure there would be wood for the fire, lit candles, and sang songs. We had legitimate cigarettes and alcohol, without fear of confiscation. They even gave us the day off.

Due to the appalling weather in January 1950, we spent a few days indoors, many more than usual. I began putting on weight. How did I know this? For the first time during my captivity I had to use a different notch in my belt, but in the other direction.

Halfway through the month, a huge amount of mail arrived. Much of it had obviously been stored for years because the one letter addressed to me was dated September 1943, postmarked 'Elmshorn', though I didn't recognise the handwriting. It had been in the German forces postal system and redirected several times, a miracle it reached me at all.

Someone had opened and re-sealed it, probably more than once, but I took out the remaining contents: a single page of handwriting and a faded newspaper cutting. My heart rate tripled, as though in combat, as I sat down to read.

Dear Paul,

We had a lovely service by Pastor Hellmich, well attended, despite the rain. You can be certain that I made sure your parents were placed next to one another. By the way, we saved a chair, a bed, and some cutlery from the house, which I will keep for you. When do you think you will be getting leave? It was a shame the air force couldn't release you in time for the funeral.

Best regards,
Frau Helen Berger

A grainy photograph showed a mass funeral, with dozens of coffins draped with flowers, as brown-shirted Nazis stood around at one side. Dozens of civilians were standing on the opposite side under black umbrellas. The text on the cutting read: "The funeral for the victims of 3rd August 1943 British terror bombing which killed sixty-one people, of which thirty were men, twenty-nine women, and two children, in Elmshorn."

I recognised the name: Heinrich's mother. I read it several times before staring at the paper cutting again. All these years I'd been in captivity, in every dreadful moment I'd been thinking of my father in his favourite chair and my mother waiting patiently for news of my return.

16

For a week Klaus never left my side. He dragged me out of bed every morning, watching me eat every meal. Walking with me to work, he remained close all the time, even when I went for a shit. I knew his intention, because I'd seen it so many times, and I admit for those first few days I stumbled around in the darkest void of despair. When it gradually lifted I realised, as odd as it sounds, that finding out so late had probably saved my life.

In the first week of February 1950 we were deloused again. I had a few in my armpits and crotch but not as many as before, and everyone had to go through the process, whether they needed it or not. Although still as strict, our captors didn't shout as much. They weren't polite, but something had changed. We had so much bread our stomachs actually began protruding, to great amusement, and I was forced to let my belt out another notch.

I remember the date so well. Who could forget? 15th February 1950. The day we were each issued identical brown leather suitcases and told to pack our belongings for a long journey.

"We can't trust them," Armin said, standing in line near the door, suitcase at his feet.

"What do we have to lose?" Klaus said with a pronounced shrug. "Would you rather stay here forever?"

"I agree, Klaus," I said, "Let's get going."

We stood outside as it began snowing. The late morning sun tried but failed to show a presence. A whistle blew and we were waved on, past the empty carts and an untidy stack of peat-cutting spades already rusting.

We walked for an hour, hundreds of us in our new top coats and hats, carrying our suitcases like a shabby army of travelling salesmen. At a railway line we were herded north, walking along the track for another hour to a small unmanned provincial station. The snow stopped falling and the sun came out. Daffodils peeked through the frozen earth in a neat border around the building.

Sitting on our cases, we lit Papirossa cigarettes.

"Where will you go?" Klaus said to Armin. "You can only go to the West if you have family or some other important connection, work, maybe. If not, they are making us stay in the East, under this lot." He nodded at one of the guards.

"Weidemann's from Leipzig, it's in the East now. He's already been told he can never go to the West, poor sod," Armin added.

Klaus looked at me. "What about you, Paul? Do you have any other connections in the West?"

I shook my head. Then I remembered Inge. "I had a girlfriend, well, more of a pen pal, near Berlin."

"Does she live in the city?" Armin said.

"I don't know her address, I always wrote to her at the factory."

"Which was what?" he said.

"She worked at the BMW plant."

"When did you last hear from her?"

"Her letters stopped early in '43."

Armin shook his head, and I saw the look he gave Klaus.

"The Americans flattened the whole area in '43, several times over. Sorry, Paul."

Nothing surprised me anymore. I had wondered about Inge, and I suppose I already knew. So I had no connections to the West, other than the town of my birth.

The train heaved to a stop in a cloud of steam and we boarded. The seats were filthy but comfortable.

As the whistle blew and we started moving, Klaus shouted as though we were under attack. "Look, look! Just look at that!"

"What?" I said, following his gaze out the window.

"Look at the fucking guards. They've left us!"

We all stared as though witnessing a miracle.

"There are some on the train, I saw one standing with the driver," Armin said.

"One?" Klaus said. "One?" he repeated. "There are none in here and none in the next carriage."

"So what? Are you going to jump off and run away?" Armin laughed, leaning back in the seat. "This is the middle of fucking nowhere and we are going home, so why walk when you can sit here?"

Although tempting, after so many years, we agreed with Armin.

The train rattled on for hours after dark and then slowed in a mass of steam and screeching wheels.

"Out! Out!" shouted someone from the platform, in Russian and then German. I'd been asleep, as had many others. On a gate topped with barbed wire fencing, lit by spot lights, a sign read 'Camp 7270/5'.

Some refused but, after shouts of 'hot soup' and 'bread' they were persuaded. Not only this, but the few guards I could see had no rifles or machine guns, only pistols in their belts.

Our numbers had depleted to about four hundred, but we each found a comfortable bunk in what appeared to be army barracks. Iron stoves burned fiercely and we had hot coffee and even biscuits. The lights were turned out soon after the meal and, conditioned as we were to prison life, we all slept.

In the morning, amazingly, we wandered around freely, discovering another six barracks, all full. Similar to those at the previous camps, each held about a hundred.

From curiosity, and the fact we were allowed, I visited each one.

Amidst the throng inside the third barrack someone slapped me on the back. "*Vermisst* but not dead yet then, Goetz?"

I swivelled round on the heels of my new Russian boots.

Gerhard, Hugo, and Hermann stood with the biggest grins of their faces; the Strattman team reunited.

17

"Here," Gerhard said, pulling my arm, "have a drink with us, we have real vodka."

We hugged. They looked fat with shiny red faces like farmers. I should have known there could be a possibility of meeting them, but no-one thinks such wild hopes would come true. We sat on the floor, passing around a small bottle.

"You look well, Paul," Hermann said, as Hugo nodded.

"So, where have you been?" Gerhard asked. "Let me guess, they smuggled you out so you could live in a five-star hotel with room service and regular visits from nymphomaniac chambermaids."

"Not far off actually," I said with a shrug. "Peat-cutting at City Camp," to which we all laughed.

How odd to see them again. Fantastic, of course, but with a dark edge: a reminder of so many years struggling together as slaves. We'd survived.

Gerhard threw me a serious look for a moment, fumbling around in his pocket, leaning forward with an outstretched hand.

"Here, I think you must have dropped this," he said, as an object fell into my hand. I knew immediately. I'd carried it for years, surviving so many searches by our captors, who never kept it, always throwing it with disdain into the snow or mud, only for me to rescue it each time. A link to flying aeroplanes in the good days, before this nightmare, and Gerhard knew how much it meant.

The Kienzle clock had stopped at 1125 hours, 11th June 1943, when I removed it from my cockpit, the same moment my life had been paused for almost seven years. I thanked him, and he knew. I thought I'd never see it again.

Perhaps there were other things I might see again too, I wondered.

The soup contained meat, with chunks of vegetables so huge they were identifiable: carrots, peas, onion; unbelievable. The floorboard bread had gone, replaced by something soft and probably only a few days old. It could even have been fresh; they had a bakery on the camp, the smells from which drove us mad.

More mail arrived and those lucky enough read excerpts to the rest of us. The day after our arrival, newspapers were handed out; this sounds fantastic, but they were all Russian, mostly the latest *Pravda*. Those who could, like Hans, translated for us. I could read some items, but a small crowd gathered around Hans as he read it several times.

"The Western allies continue being unreasonable," Hans read. "Their aggressive posturing towards the people of the Soviet Union and German Democratic Republic is reminiscent of the fifteen-month Berlin debacle that ended in September."

"German Democratic Republic?" Gerhard said, puzzled.

"It's what the Soviets call East Germany," Hans interjected, to laughter and shaking of heads.

"So what's upset them now?" I asked.

Hans showed me a photograph of a sleek four-engined piston aeroplane with no guns, bearing American markings.

"Hang on," Hans said. "There's something about currency in West Berlin. They are referring to the time the Russians blockaded the western side of the city for fifteen months, so the Allies supplied it by air."

"A city? For fifteen months? You're joking?" I said in disbelief.

"I heard it too," Hugo added. "In the West they called it the Berlin Airlift. Eventually the Ruskis gave in."

I could see what Gerhard was thinking.

"If only we'd had such aeroplanes in '42. We wouldn't have lost Stalingrad. Imagine that? We'd never have been trapped in this shithole for seven fucking years."

*

A fortnight passed and the weather improved. We were deloused yet again but in return given more new clothes and bedding. It seemed they would keep on doing it until every single malinki partisan had either died or fled.

By mid-March the lists appeared. 'Home Lists', as we called them: names with places at the side. 'Paul Goetz – Elmshorn, West Germany'. There were travel instructions with strict warnings not to deviate from the approved route. Transit papers were to be issued with a small amount of cash.

Nothing happened for another two weeks. Every day we greeted one another with, "Good morning, we're going home tomorrow, did you know?" Some seriously considered escape. If only we knew where we were.

Groups would gather in the evening, drawing maps on newspaper, assuming we were somewhere west of Borovichi, perhaps near the Volkhov River; no-one remembered passing over it.

We discussed what we were going to do if and when we made it home. The teachers, medical personnel, and civil servants hoped they would return to their old jobs. Some wanted to stay in the air force.

Photos showed Germany as a ruin but with building work progressing rapidly.

"Perhaps we'll become brick-layers," Hugo said, and we all laughed.

Many had no family alive; I was not alone.

"I'm going to run an orchestra again," Hans said, beaming. "I may even come back here one day, on tour," he joked with a sardonic smile. "You could lease one of those fabulous American aeroplanes, Paul, and fly us around Europe, and even America."

For a moment it seemed a great idea. Why not? We had to wake up from our institutionalised coma, the one telling us such things were impossible.

"When did you last hear music, I mean, decent music?" I asked him.

"Yesterday," he said, surprising me. "There's a radio in the main guardroom. I asked them to let me listen for a while. They've stopped playing Shostakovich regularly, but I did hear Tchaikovsky."

"I've missed it."

"Not as much as I have," Hans said.

He began humming a tune, the one we both knew so well.

"I saw you with Vlasov," I said, almost absent-mindedly,

suddenly remembering, as I lit a Papirossa. "In February '43, just before I went to Heiligenbeil."

Hans smiled. "Really? He was a clever man, Paul. What a shame his efforts were wasted; it could have worked."

"I heard about it," I said, nodding.

"They asked for Russian speakers. Vlasov was touring Army Group North, testing opinion. He told us about a strip of coastline in the Gulf of Finland between Oranienbaum and Peterhof, opposite the fortress at Kronstadt that we never occupied. Vlasov proposed taking this over as the headquarters for his Russian Liberation Army."

He could tell he'd impressed me. "So what happened?"

Hans shrugged. "We had Vlasov, also Generals Malyshkin, Zhilenkov, and Trukhin, all on board, and thousands of 'line-crossers' every day joining us. We could have had millions, Paul. *Operation Silberstreif*, we called it. Stalin could have been overthrown in six months. What a different world it might have been, eh?"

I looked at him, puzzled.

"Keitel blocked the whole idea. That's all I know. I was with them three weeks before they sent me back to my radios at Mga. I never saw Vlasov again. I've no idea what happened to him. I told our Russian friends in the guardroom all about it, the first time I've ever mentioned it to anyone, but they'd never heard of him. They are too young."

He shook his head, before continuing. "That is, except one, much older than the others, the sergeant with all the medals. He denounced Vlasov as a traitor, shouting at me, really angry, telling me I shouldn't have got involved in Russian affairs, calling me a Nazi; obviously a lunatic. There are still fanatics on both sides, Paul, even now."

18

On Monday 3ʳᵈ April 1950 a Russian stood in the doorway of our barrack, his uniform soaked from heavy rain. Probably only nineteen or twenty, around the age I had been when I first arrived in Russia, he'd never seen the horrors any of us had.

"You go tomorrow," he said. "All this barrack, the train is at 0900 hours. Be ready."

That night we drank whatever we had, singing and laughing.

In the morning nothing happened.

We were ready with our meagre belongings and freshly shaved heads, but no-one came, so once more we returned to our bunks.

At 1200 hours, hearing shouting and whistles blowing, I thought we were under attack.

"Train is ready, come on, train is ready now!"

Hermann, Hugo, and Gerhard wished me luck as I joined Hans, Klaus, and Armin in the crowd heading for the station.

We waited an hour before it arrived and climbed aboard

in an untidy scrum. I could barely cope with the excitement.

In a throng of bodies and suitcases pushing to get on the train, Hans shouted, "Paul," as he rolled over in a crumpled heap onto the platform. Others pushed and shoved, stepping around him, cursing. He dropped his case and shouted again. The train whistle blew and the wheels turned. Hans lay flat on his back staring up at the sky. *What on earth?*

"Hold this," I said to Klaus, thrusting my case at him before jumping off.

Hans was gripping his stomach, obviously in great pain. I couldn't see anything wrong, but now, on his side, he pulled his legs up to his chest.

Unfolding him, I saw a small rip in the front of his coat. I unbuttoned it to find his clothes soaked in blood. I lifted the pullover and shirt to see a wound in his stomach pumping rhythmically in full flow like an upturned bottle of red wine. I pushed my hand onto it, but the blood forced its way between my fingers. Blank faces looked down from the train. The angry Russian sergeant from the guardroom walked briskly away, a knife in his right hand, turning back briefly, smiling.

With an arm around Hans I lifted him up, watching the life drain from his face, his eyes fixed in a blank stare. His head loose and heavy, it fell forwards onto his chest. The concrete around us flooded with thick, dark red blood.

"Paul, come on!" Klaus shouted as the train gathered speed.

I lay Hans gently on his back. Looking down from the train with resigned indifference, no-one came to my aid, so I climbed aboard.

*

When I woke up the train had stopped. The sign at the station read 'Gatchina'. I shut my eyes and when I opened them again the sign was still there. It wouldn't go away, teasing me with false promises. Anna looked the same, like seven years ago, standing on the platform, waving. Hans lay on the bloodied concrete and I heard that music again, the gentle part, his favourite. Two coffins were also there: my mother and father, next to one another for all eternity. How nice. Thank you, Frau Berger, you were very helpful.

A whistle blew and I woke up from my dream. The train moved. The sign passed the window: 'Gatchina'.

I grabbed my case and jumped onto the empty platform.

Walking out the station, I made my way to the main road heading south just as it started raining. Tears added to the rainwater on my face so I wiped it with my sleeve. I washed my bloodied hands in a puddle. No-one spoke to me as I walked through the town and out the other side.

Then a vehicle stopped and I heard a shout. "Hey, you, do you want a lift?"

A middle-aged man leaned from the window of a Ford lorry, smiling. Without thinking, I climbed in.

"I know who you are," he said, nodding, "and I know exactly where you're going."

How could he, possibly?

"You're a flyer, aren't you, a pilot?"

I nodded. "Yes, I am," I replied, in Russian apparently accented to somewhere east of the Volkhov.

"I knew it," he said. "I bet you're with that lot at Siverskaya flying the new jets, am I right?"

I nodded. "Yes, that's right."

"I won't ask you anything else, comrade; I know it's all very secret."

In his warm cab a trickle of water ran down the back of my neck, so I leaned into the seat to kill it.

My driver changed the subject but never stopped talking.

"I was a prisoner of the fascists," he groaned, "for years."

I forced a smile.

"Building enemy aeroplanes in East Prussia, and then in Germany."

I suspect he thought I'd look incredulous, but I merely smiled again.

"We fixed them, though," he continued, "we sabotaged their engines, all the time."

He laughed, but then scowled, shaking his head. "We did a great job, but when it ended my own people interrogated me, comrade, and beat me, can you believe that?"

I could, but I didn't say so.

"Of course I went home eventually, to my village north of Moscow, on the Volga, to find it deserted. The fascists had killed everyone."

Suddenly it seemed like the war had ended only yesterday.

"So I came back here. There's plenty of work, rebuilding the palace. Have you seen it, comrade?"

I nodded. "Gatchina? Yes, I know it."

Thankfully he didn't ask how.

"They say it will be a museum, open to the public, even foreign tourists. Wouldn't that be something?"

I nodded, not really listening but looking for cabins in the trees.

The twenty-minute journey was oddly unreal: the daydream I'd had a thousand times while cutting peat.

The entrance to the airfield appeared as my dream predicted, but now different. The Luftwaffe sign had gone, replaced by '53rd Fighter Aviation Regiment' in huge red Cyrillic script. The gates stood open and unguarded, with a track nearby leading into the wood.

"I'll get out here, *tovarisch*," I said.

He pulled over. "I can take you into the base, I have security—"

"No, thank you, I'd like to walk," I insisted.

After shaking his hand, I jumped out. The rain had stopped. I waited for him to drive off before walking into the track.

My boots were soon muddy. Passing a cabin I didn't recognise, I continued, amongst the remains of daffodils and tulips.

A cabin appeared in dappled sunlight, surrounded by flowers, the same one but with even more flowers around it. It couldn't be. I heard singing, the folk song 'On the Long Road'.

I stopped at the bottom of the steps as the door opened and she saw me.

Anna propped it open with her broom, looked inside and then at me. We both grinned.

I was in business.